HE HAD
MORE THAN HIS LIFE
AT STAKE . . .

And he was angry. Bitterly angry. He pressed the Turk back toward the hangings, slashing and hacking at him, the blood singing in his ears with the cool joy of good swordplay. The Crow felt the wall against his back, and smiled, parrying Gurney's stroke. But Gurney feinted, and the blade came whizzing from the left when it should have been met by the Crow's steel at the right. Too late, the Turk tried a clumsy parry: the blade sliced into the muscle of his left shoulder, and as Gurney drew it back he felt it grate on bone . . .

Bantam Books by Sam Llewellyn

DEVIL'S REWARD
SEA DEVIL

DEVIL'S REWARD

Sam Llewellyn

DEVIL'S REWARD

A Bantam Book / July 1979

PRINTING HISTORY

*Originally published in England in 1978 by Arlington Books,
Publishers, Ltd., as GURNEY'S REWARD*

Bantam Books are published by Bantam Books, Inc. Its trademark, consisting of the words "Bantam Books" and the por-
trayal of a bantam, is Registered in U.S. Patent and Trademark
Office and in other countries. Marca Registrada. Bantam
Books, Inc., 666 Fifth Avenue, New York, New York 10019.

PRINTED IN THE UNITED STATES OF AMERICA

Prologue

Ioannis Kallikratides the Klepht lay on the warm ledge as still as a snake. His black eyes gazed unwinking at the cove three hundred feet below, at the horse-shoe of glittering sand flanked by bastions of limestone. The waggon road, a thread of dust in the brown August grass of the foreshore, lay empty, whipped by the north wind that raised little sparkling waves on the sapphire Aegean under a sky scoured of cloud.

Ioannis shifted, very slightly. The pleats of the full skirt of his uniform rustled on the lichen-covered rock, and the six rows of silver buttons on his waistcoat made a little tinkling sound. Bees droned in the wiry thyme of the slope that soared up the base of his crag. A crow drifted upwards past his face on a current of air; but Ioannis' eyes stayed fixed on the gently rising land to the northwest.

In the sun which slanted over the mountains inland, something flashed. A window seemed to open behind the black eyes, and the Klepht crawled backwards into the shadow of the rock buttress. He unwound the scarf of dirty white silk from his neck and waved it three times, at the full arc of his arm, towards the lowering massif to the southeast, into which the road disappeared in a narrow defile. Then he squinted his eyes into the deepening gloom. From a pinnacle commanding the mouth of the defile, something white flashed an answer.

The Klepht slid from his perch, slung his long musket, and began to pick his way downwards through the boulders and scrub.

In the blue darkness of the ravine, twenty Klephts

1

—brigands—clad in caps of tasselled velvet, black waistcoats studded with silver, full-sleeved shirts and wide skirts of linen, silver knee plates and curly shoes, faded like moths into the cracked and fissured cliffs. For a moment the hard stone reverberated to the metallic click of musket-locks and the thin, hard hiss of sharp steel drawn from brass-bound scabbards. Then there was only the wind blustering among the rocks and the distant hum of the insects.

The band of Mordrutsos numbered fifty men, and they marched in a proud double file. At the head of the column rode two horsemen on sleek black mares, and behind, weapons clanking as they marched, came the men on foot, clad in motley rags that had once been Albanian costume, and a lumbering waggon drawn by four scrawny oxen. Snatches of song came down the wind into the mouth of the defile. The elder of the two horsemen took a long pull from a wineskin, wiped his thick black mustachios, and passed it to the younger man riding at his right knee. This companion shook his head, gesturing at the road where it sloped upwards into the yawning chasm ahead, and turned in his saddle. At his sharp bark, the rabble fell quiet and fingered their weapons apprehensively; the waggon wheels groaned as the incline steepened and the oxen leaned deep into the yoke.

Ioannis crouched at the levers with his brothers, waiting until the last straggler had entered the defile. Then he put his weight on the timber and heaved. With a rattling crunch, the great boulder left its earthen socket and began to roll, end over end, bounding from the rocky face, down into the rearguard.

The last man in the file was the first to see the landslide leaping down upon him, but his warning shout died as a boulder the size of a hogshead smashed him to pulp. His companions stopped, turned, and were themselves struck down; as the survivors stood gaping, the musket-barrels poking from the heights bloomed smoke and noise, and a sheet of lead blew them down like corn before the sickle.

Ioannis and his brothers were coming down the cliff in grasshopper vaults even before the rocks had ceased to roll. Most of the travellers were down, but the two horsemen and the fifteen or so men who had preceded the waggon were running for the cover of a garden of boulders on the seaward side of the ravine, and already lead was spitting from their cover.

A huge rock had rammed into the waggon's nearside wheel, and the path was strewn with boxes and chests. Ioannis took cover behind one of the larger chests, and ran his fingers over the iron traceries that covered its lid and sides. Above the lock was an ornate calligraphic inscription. The hasp flew back, and he wrenched the lid open. His eyes widened for a second; then he smiled a fierce smile.

The elder of the two horsemen lay gasping out his life, blood pumping from a ragged hole in his neck. His companion levelled his pistol at a barely-visible head behind a rock twenty-five yards away. Tears were streaming down the furrows in his cheeks as he loosed his ball and groped at his cummerbund for his next pistol. His fingers found none, and he sighed. His companion half-raised himself, eyes starting from his head with the effort. Beneath the olive tan, he was ashy grey.

"Theodore."

The younger man stopped, put his ear close to the old man's mouth. "Yes, father? They shall suffer for this, you can be sure, the jackals of Ioannis Kallikratides."

The old man nodded, and seemed to breathe easier for a moment. Then a spasm racked him, and he coughed red phlegm. "It is right so. But that is the way. We are undone by the cursed letters of the infidel. Would that I had never seen that hog of a pasha

—would that I had never heard his damnations—"
The head fell back and the eyes glazed, staring sightlessly at the narrow strip of darkening sky.

His son kissed him roughly on the cheek, then got
to his feet with a hoarse yell that rang round the crags
like an eagle's scream. Drawing his sword, he began
to run for the waggon, jerking and weaving. Ioannis
sighted coolly on the centre of the black waistcoat
gleaming with dull silver, and gently, with the touch of
a poacher tickling a trout, squeezed. The young man
flopped head over heels to the ground and lay twitching.

To the lone watcher crouched in his robe on the steeps
of the headland, the struggle in the ravine came as a
rattle of musketfire and a drift of powder-smoke.

As the firing died he shook his turbaned head. His
hand strayed to the octagonal brass buckle of his belt,
and the eyes, wide-set beneath bushy brows, closed for
a moment as if in prayer. Then he drew a dulled brass
telescope from the scrip which hung at his side beneath his dun surcoat and focussed it on the patch of
deepening shadow where the road wound into the defile.

Behind the inland peaks the sun sank, casting the
cove and its flanking masses of rock into half-light.
Haji Basreddin, whom men called the Eagle Owl, adjusted the focus of his glass as the first ant-like figures
moved slowly onto the brown sward behind the beach.
The powerful magnification of the Swiss lenses revealed a knot of brigands struggling with a chest
covered with intricate arabesques of iron. As the last
of the figures debouched onto the grass, one of them
waved and pointed seaward. Basreddin re-aimed his
glass, sand and sea blurring, but the object of the
pointer's attention was hidden by a buttress of limestone thrusting into the dark water.

The men on the shore struggled with their burden
to the beach and stood waving, expectant. Round the

buttress came a small lugger, sail unsheeted and flapping in the breeze, held off the cliffs by four men with long poles. The lugger grounded on sand with a shock that Basreddin thought he heard, its crew staggering a little as it struck; the watchers waded into the water, bowed down under the weight of the chests, and were dragged aboard with their burden. With a rattling boom of canvas the lugger put her stern to the shore and headed off on the port tack, driven by the steady breeze at her quarter.

No sound came off the land now; the bees, struck dumb in the shadow, had gone to their hives, and when Basreddin ran swiftly to the ragged cleft of the ravine the silence welled up thick from its depths. He looked carefully over the lip of the rock. Below, a pile of white objects, strewn like rag dolls, surrounded the wreck of the cart. Nothing moved.

When the rumble of gunfire rolled down the wind from the sea, Basreddin thought at first it was thunder. But the air was clean and dry, so he ran from the brink of the ravine to the crest of the small hill that crowned the headland.

About three-quarters of a mile out from the land, a cluster of rocky islets rose from the waves. As Basreddin watched, a three-masted ship with a double row of gunports disappeared behind them, heading to the northwest. Among the cluster of jagged spines thrust from a turmoil of white water, the lugger, her half-deck awash, heaved sluggishly up on the humped back of a wave. Through his glass Basreddin saw the hull come down on its beam ends across a black smear of reef, tiny figures flung this way and that into the tossing waters. For a brief moment, bow and stern heaved up, sundered amidships: then they rolled and slid from view. Basreddin kept his glass on the rocks for perhaps five minutes more, but there was nothing to see except the short waves boiling among the limestone fangs.

As he closed his telescope and started to walk southwards, he paused and looked out to sea. A last ray of sun, funnelling through a saddle of mountain inland, caught the scarlet flag at the frigate's spanker peak. Its silver crescent glittered for a moment in the light. Then the sea fell dark, and Basreddin resumed his course towards the looming wall of mountains to the south.

1

High in the West Tower of Sea Dalling church, Charlie Jarvis was cleaning the light. Whistling between his teeth, he scrubbed at the greasy film of soot on the caloptric reflector, burnishing the polished tin with his frayed cuff. Then he trimmed the wick with his knife, struck flint and steel, lit the flame until it burned to his satisfaction, extinguished it, and crossed the stone-flagged floor to the north window.

Below his vantage point, the delicate Gothic pilasters and traceries swept vertically down to the rough grass and neat stones of the graveyard. Beyond the vicarage, with its paddock and copse, the cottages of Sea Dalling sprawled down the gentle hill to the Cut and Captain Gurney's shipyard, set behind the sea wall. And beyond the sea wall, the grey-green marshes sprawled out, shot with tidal creeks, towards the slate of the February sea, threatening under a dark bowl of sky.

Charlie shook his head. She were fair to blow again tonight, by the looks of it. How they nor'easterlies did mess up that reflector. Still, Sea Dalling Tower was the brightest light on the North Norfolk coast these days, and the fishing lads had Captain Gurney to thank for that. Used to be there was nowt but a little fire of coals up here; the bones of the smacks and wherries out on the sandbars off the Point had their own story to tell about that. He were none too bad a boy, that Captain, even if his idea of a boat looked like something you'd whittle a stick with. Charlie shook his head again. If he'd had the light in afore brother Tom put his smack on the Hood in a gale, Tom might still be here. He sighed, and turned his gaze inland, down the long straight mile of the Sheringham road.

A horseman was driving his mount towards the village. Even from where Charlie stood he could see the gouts of mud on the rider's black cloak and the lather of sweat at his horse's withers. Rush, rush, rush, thought Charlie, fingering his cutty pipe. Bloody impatient. He turned, clumping in his heavy boots across the floor to the low door which gave onto the one hundred and five steps down to the west end of the church. As he let himself out of the door in the nave, he looked quickly round, then genuflected to the altar and slipped into the churchyard. Bit of a bloody Dissenter, that parson. And a hell of a tongue. Catch a man at his proper devotions and hold him up as an example to the parish come Sunday, more'n likely.

He was under the slate roof of the lych gate when the church clock boomed the first stroke of noon, and his step quickened. As he started to walk towards the village, he heard hoof beats and a voice halted him.

"Hey! You!"

He turned. The rider was approaching at a trot. Charlie was not sure he liked being addressed in this way, but he was an accommodating man, and the rider, from his boots and his flat-crowned hat of muddy beaver, was obviously Quality. He removed his pipe from his mouth.

"Aye, Sir?"

The voice was imperious. "Where will I find Captain George Gurney, my man? Come, don't stand there with your mouth open, speak!"

Charlie, scenting largesse, swallowed his pride. "Mostly this time of day he'll be down the yard there. Down Staithe Street."

"Good. Look here, take my horse, would you? I'm cursed sore and I'll walk. Put her in a stable—there is an inn here, I suppose? Of course. And take this."

Before he knew what was happening, Charlie found

himself with a shilling in his right hand and the reins of the horse in his left, watching the stranger's back receding down the hill towards the Cut.

The stranger was in an extremely poor humour. As he stumped down the rutted and potholed track that was Sea Dalling's main thoroughfare, he cursed roundly at the abominable Norfolk roads, the burnt beef and sour ale that had been his breakfast some six hours earlier at the Bell in Norwich, and that pot-bellied under-secretary at the Horse Guards who had seen fit to uproot him from London in mid-winter and send him on this zany's errand.

He rounded the corner of the netshed at the bottom of Staithe Street, and found himself on a broad, sloping yard, covered with small craft. To his right, inside the sea wall which blocked his view of the open sea, the yard was fenced off. Inside the fence, the ribs of a large ship in the early stages of building sprang from their spine of timber, and beyond, two low, black hulls, one of them showing signs of near-completion, lay in the slips. In and on the ships swarmed more men than the stranger would have thought possible in a village the size of Sea Dalling.

He passed through the gate, walking stiffly, and picked his way through the casks and the piles of timber towards a weather-beaten shack which leaned wearily against the sea wall. A stout man of some forty years looked up at him from a table covered in rolls of paper, and fixed him with his single eye.

The stranger cleared his throat. "Captain Gurney?"

"Nay, lad, the name's McIver. The Captain's out wi' the caulking gang on the *Vampire*." The beetling brows lowered. "But may I ask your business?"

"My errand is with Captain Gurney and with him alone."

McIver shrugged. "Aye, well, have it your own way. Though there's nae much that's the Captain's business he doesn't share with us. Come, I'll take you to him."

The Scotsman set a cracking pace over the slips,

and by the time he came to a halt under the knife-edged bow of the furthest of the hulls, the stranger's mood had, if anything, deteriorated. McIver cupped his hands round his mouth and bellowed "Captain! Company! Could be a bailiff, could not be. Very persistent."

The knock of the caulking hammers stopped, and Captain Gurney dropped down the side of the schooner as if the eighteen feet were four, and looked the stranger up and down. His manner, the stranger felt, was insolent in the extreme.

He was a tall man of about twenty-five, strongly built, with a spiky mop of fair hair much clotted with pitch from the caulking. The eyes he turned on the stranger were pale blue and faintly quizzical.

"Good day to you, Sir." The eyes flicked up and down once. To the stranger's mind came the conviction that he was being weighed on an extremely sensitive scale. "I have not the pleasure of your acquaintance, I believe."

"Perhaps the letters that I bring will remedy that."

"Perhaps. Come with me, if you would be so good." The young man turned to McIver. "Get the lads back to it, and make sure that they pound those seams well. Keep 'em warm."

McIver grinned and nodded, and swarmed up the frowning bulwark with an agility surprising in one of his solid construction. Captain Gurney and the stranger set off across the yard.

"Letters, you say," observed Gurney. "They must bring urgent news indeed, judging by the state of your clothes. You rode from Holt?"

"From Norwich."

Gurney looked at his visitor with a new respect. "Norwich, eh? Twenty miles if it's an inch. Good travelling. Come in here out of the wind." He pushed open the door of the shed, swept rolls of paper from the desk and the two crude beechwood chairs, and sat down, waving a hand at the other. "A glass of cognac against the weather, perhaps? You must be chilled to the bone." He poured. "Your health. Throw a billet on the fire, would you? And now, perhaps you will tell me what brings you out in the east wind in this most inclement weather. Cuts like a knife, that wind."

The stranger handed over a packet, thinking as he did so that this somewhat work-stained gentleman obviously, was not as sensitive to the rigours of the climate as he pretended. His top-boots of brown calf had seen better days, and seemed rather more ventilated than their maker had originally intended. The tar-stained trousers tucked into the boots were little better than canvas, and as for the shirt—well, perhaps a ruffled silk shirt without collar or cravat was customary morning wear in North Norfolk in February, but in London it would be thought rather chilly than otherwise. As Gurney cracked the large red seal and perused the contents of the packet, the scar that ran across his right temple from eyebrow to hairline pulsed and a red flush spread from his collar—or where his collar would have been had he been wearing one—to cover his face. He sprang to his feet.

"So you are Morpurgo? It seems that I owe you an apology. My dear Mr. Morpurgo, how can I ask your forgiveness? Jervy Hutchinson must be my dearest friend and patron. How is the old windbag? And what is this that he says you must tell me?" The stranger was shivering now, his muscles stiffening. As he opened his mouth to speak, his teeth clacked like castanets. "But it can surely wait. Come, before you take an ague. Mrs. Cox at the Dun Cow will have dumplings a-boiling, and they will warm you."

Morpurgo liked to think that he was a man who would rather harbour a grudge than otherwise, but he found himself disarmed by the Captain's confusion. So he gracefully allowed himself to be steered up Staithe Street, through a herd of cows milling aimlessly by a milking shed, into the snug of the Dun Cow, where he was confronted with a quart tankard of very dark ale and a heaped plate of dumplings with the flavour of ambrosia and the consistency of stiff glue.

The Captain left him to struggle with this repast and dived into the taproom, whence soon came raucous shouts of mirth and a clattering of stout boots. As he was swallowing the last of the ale, his host returned.

"Finished? Good. We'll away to the Hall now. That old thief, Charlie Jarvis, has just learned that he'll get no second shilling for walking your mare to the stables. Ready?"

Gurney set off inland at a cracking pace, turning to the right on the rutted coast road. "I must apologise for the state of the roads. We've been here only a couple of years, and they say it takes a time to make the acquaintance of the magistrates." He grinned ruefully. "I fear the magistrates are none too taken with me and mine. The yard, you know. They seem to have some notion that I'm in trade. Well, damn them, if I'm in trade, so is old Jervy. How is the old boy, anyway?"

Morpurgo pursed his lips and looked tactful. "The Admiral is in passably good health and spirits, Captain, though somewhat troubled by the gout."

"Somewhat troubled, eh? I'll wager that isn't the half of it. I remember once when we were off Kingston in 1812 I rolled a two-pound shot against his foot." He shuddered at the memory. "Double watches for a week. He's a tartar, that one."

"Indeed." Morpurgo reflected that had he not stumbled against the Admiral's stool three days ago he would in all probability be comfortably ensconced in St. James' at this very moment instead of tramping the rural wilds with this cheerful ruffian. "Yes, he is indeed a hard taskmaster. He seems to think highly of you, however."

"Aye, well, that's his hardship. You wouldn't think it from the uproar he made when I suggested he commission two new schooners from my yard here!

Deuced Yankee privateer's hookers, he called them.
But he'll learn. He'll learn."

Morpurgo hid a saturnine smile in the collar of his
cloak. It was as the Admiral had said. A fireater, this
one, and well primed for what the Navy had in mind
for him. But that would keep.

The two men had for some time been walking along
a lane, open on the one side to rolling plough dotted
with stands of oak, beech and elm, and bordered on
the other by a high flint wall. As they rounded a curve
in the wall, a tall wrought-iron gate guarded by a lodge
came into view, and Gurney opened the wicket to let
his visitor pass. An elderly man digging over the patch
of garden behind the lodge doffed his hat, and Gurney
waved to him cheerfully.

"Afternoon, Arthur." He turned to his guest. "Welcome to Sea Dalling High House, Mr. Morpurgo. I
trust that we shall be able to make your tiresome
journey worthwhile."

Three hundred yards later, the beechwoods that
arched over the drive gave way to an open expanse
of parkland, set here and there with oaks, leafless under the grey sky. Directly ahead of the walkers, a
pile of grey masonry lay across a slight rise in the
ground. Morpurgo blinked. Much of the house was
entirely ruined. The central mass—Morpurgo, who
knew his architecture, having been on the Grand Tour
not ten years ago, immediately thought of it as the
bailey—was festooned with ivy. The west wing appeared still to have a roof, though it sagged badly at
the ridge, and on closer inspection proved even to
be glazed as to its windows; but the east wing was
little more than a pile of rubble; its windows gaping
sockets, the tall tower at its easternmost tip a truncated tube of masonry, like a maimed fang. Extraor-
dinary. Morpurgo stole a glance at his host, striding
at his side whistling, hands in pockets.

"A . . . unusual residence, Captain Gurney."

"Unusual? Oh, you mean the east wing. I suppose you're right. Still, it's home. And there's Arabella."

A horsewoman was approaching, her habit flowing out behind the snow-white rump of her mount as she thundered across the green grass of the park towards them.

She reined in, slid from the saddle with a lithe grace, and flung herself into Gurney's arms. Morpurgo turned hastily away and became improbably interested in her horse. By the time he had fully appraised himself of the fact that it was an Arab, about fifteen hands, and really a stunning lady's steed, and was feeling guilty about the lack of apples in his pockets, his host and the lady had disentangled themselves. Morpurgo tore his gaze away from the horse's reproachful velvet eye and found himself face to face with one of the most beautiful women he had ever seen. He was dimly conscious of Gurney's voice, a long way away.

"Mr. Morpurgo, may I present my wife? The Lady Arabella, Mr. Morpurgo. Friend of Jervy Hutchinson's. Come all the way from London to see us. Charlie's got his horse."

The Lady Arabella smiled, and Morpurgo rocked a little on his heels. He was by no means a man for the petticoats, he liked to think, but those eyes! Great pools of violet where a man could drown and die happy. That mouth! A red bow framing teeth of white jade, set in a face with skin like thick cream and bones chiselled by angelic sculptors . . . He realised that his own mouth was hanging open, and shut it with a click, bending hastily to kiss the proffered hand.

"How delightful that you should have come to see us. I fear you may find us a little barbarous after London, but you must tell me all that is going on there. I so seldom pass time there since George pressed me into service at Dalling." But the dazzling smile she turned on her husband said that she would never consent to be anywhere else. Morpurgo was surprised to find himself overwhelmed with jealousy. "Well, Mr. Morpurgo, I shall see you later. I must away and see to the baby pheasants. Perhaps I could show you them?"

Gurney had Morpurgo by the arm. "No, my dear, we'll go up to the house. Poor fellow's half dead."

"Very well." Gurney assisted her into the saddle and she cantered towards the lodge, her golden hair streaming out beneath her little hat.

By this time Morpurgo was near exhaustion, and he almost had to trot to keep up with Gurney. Like a man in a dream he allowed himself to be ushered through the oaken door of the bailey into a great stone-flagged hall where a log fire blazed in a gigantic hearth and two greyhounds leaped at his face, licking enthusiastically at his nose and mouth. He dimly remembered being shown a surprisingly comfortable bedroom where a tub of hot water stood steaming before a roaring fire, washing the mud of the road away, and sitting in a tall wing chair attempting to review the papers whose contents he must use later. Then he slept.

Round the long mahogany table in the Great Hall at Sea Dalling High House a buzz of conversation mingled with the candlelight, and died in echoes in the darkness that lay in the corners and vaults of the high ceiling. There were six people at dinner. Gurney, at the head of the table, was engaged in animated conversation with his right-hand neighbour, a stringy lady of about thirty-five, clad in an extremely unsuitable gown of white silk, who was explaining with many gestures what sounded like the plot of a novel. Gurney was enjoying himself. Euthymia Henry's novels were a byword at Dalling, as their complexity of plot was equalled only by their ferocity of language; she spent most of her waking hours attempting to find a bookseller who would publish them for her, but the letters of rejection she received were invariably so shocked that Gurney could never see why she did not give up the battle. But as Euthymia's genteel voice continued to rattle in his right ear, he hardly heard her anguished account of her latest reverse at the hands of Mr. Murray. He was watching the other end of the table.

Arabella was looking happy, though Mr. Morpurgo was proving rather difficult. A very stiff one, that. God knew how Jervy stood that long face glooming at him over the morning mail. Truth to tell, that probably had a lot to do with his presence here. But at Arabella's other elbow sat the inimitable Sir Patrick Fitzcozens. Paddy claimed to have broken every bone in his body at least once, mostly due to sudden and violent partings of company with a long succession of horses, and on each fracture hung a lengthy and amusing tale. Even Morpurgo appeared to be taking an interest, damn him. He should be making himself pleasant to Isabel, George's reforming Quaker cousin, sitting at his left, sipping water from her wine glass.

"Don't you think so, George?"

He turned to Euthymia with a start. Cursed absent-minded, he was getting these days. Old age. Second childhood at twenty-six. "Ah, yes, indeed, Euthymia. Do you not agree, Cousin Isabel?"

Cousin Isabel tucked her chin firmly into her square white cambric collar and pursed her lips. "No, George, I do not, and I am surprised at you for asking. If Euthymia wishes her heroine to be violated by a pack of Spanish brigands, that is her business. For myself, I wish no part of it."

Gurney sighed mentally. The fading Euthymia, with her Byronic visions of odalisque-hood, and the blooming Isabel, who, however hard she tried to hide her beauty behind the plainest of Quaker clothes, was magnetically attractive to the opposite sex. And they always ended at each other's throats.

Euthymia drew herself up. "I merely mean, my dear Isabel, that we women, like a free people, must be *mastered* if we are to bloom to the full. Poor weak creatures that we are without the gentlemen."

"Oh, pooh, Euthymia! Really, I declare that I think you are touched in the head to babble so. If a farmwife can work with her husband in the fields—yes, if Arabella can ride and look after the house while George is in the yard, whence then comes this cult of enslavement and idleness that you propose?"

"Enslavement and idleness never! Call it rather the means to enjoy to the full the arts and letters of our civilisation! The leisure to divert ourselves with the fruits of men's minds. To build Temples to Beauty and worship there!"

Isabel looked grave. "Precious little beauty have I seen in the Fleet and the Marshalsea, Euthymia. While you and your like are drinking tea and reading silly novels in your Temples of Beauty at Bath, the world ignores you and life goes on, raw and dark."

Euthymia, surprisingly, smiled. "Raw and dark! Oh, Isabel, in your prison visiting and your praying there is a great poetess struggling for expression! What a loss you are to the Palaces of Culture!"

"Heavens, woman, enough of your silly vapourings." Isabel's cheeks were colouring, and her pleasantly-rounded breasts heaved beneath her drab dress. Gurney was beginning to feel a little desperate. It looked as though he would have a full-scale battle on his hands if he did not act, and act quickly; but he was by no means at his best when it came to stepping between such redoubtable females as these.

He looked imploringly down the table and caught Arabella's eye. It was sparkling with mischief. Gurney saw her signal unobtrusively to the footman, and then she broke the silence. "Perhaps, Euthymia and Isabel, we should leave the gentlemen to their port?"

And may God have mercy on their souls, thought Gurney, as the ladies left for the drawing room. Still, Arabella could keep those two apart without difficulty. As the door closed behind them and the footman drew the cloth, the three men pulled their chairs together. Gurney extinguished all the candelabra but one and passed the port.

Fitzcozens was visibly shaken by his vision of Isabel.

"By cracky, George, she's a game one. I'm not sure I don't mean to have her."

"She's too much of a handful for you, Paddy. And besides, she'd never have a smashed-up pagan like you."

"We'll see." Paddy, presumably to steady his nerves, tossed off his glass and leaned back in his chair. "We'll see. Meanwhile, give the decanter a fair wind, sharpish now." He drank again. "That's better. Ye know, I might join the ladies. You two will want to be talkin' about London, no doubt. Cursed boring place. Rotten Row, forsooth! Call that riding?" And so saying, he got to his feet and limped from the hall.

Gurney turned to Morpurgo. "Well, now, Mr. Morpurgo. I doubt very much that old Jervy sent you here for the sake of your health, bracing though the air may be."

Morpurgo touched his hands one to the other, steepling his fingers. The candlelight threw his hollow cheek into dark shadow as he cast his head forward and cleared his throat, looking down at the table in front of him.

"You should know, Captain Gurney, that we at the Admiralty have been following your progress with some interest since your return from the East and your ah, *resignation* from His Majesty's Navy."

"But not with enough interest to commission the ships that I build."

Morpurgo spread his hands. "Unfortunately, this is beyond my sphere of influence and competence." Pompous ass, thought Gurney, sipping his port. "My field is rather more political, and it is for this reason that Admiral Hutchinson asked me to visit you here."

"I heard a whisper that Jervy was tied up with a lot

of devilish dark stuff. Didn't sound like him, but with you lawyer sailors it's always damned hard to tell."

Morpurgo's face was blank, uncommunicative. "Really? How idle gossip does travel, to be sure. Be that as it may, the Admiral sent me to ask a favour of you on behalf of His Majesty's Government."

Gurney slumped back in his chair, eyelids half-lowered. Morpurgo thought he might be drowsing, but when the pale blue eyes opened again they were keen and bright. "All right, enough beating about the bush. What does he want?"

His visitor made a gesture expressive of distaste at his bluntness. "Very well. You are aware of the current situation in Greece and the Aegean?"

"Only that the Greeks are struggling to cast off the shackles of Turkish rule, and seem to be making quite a good job of it. Isn't Byron there?"

"He is. But this does not bear on my errand. As to the Greeks making a good job of freeing themselves from subjection to the Turk, they are doing quite the reverse. The story you see in *The Times* is that promulgated by certain gentlemen in whose, ah, pecuniary interest it is that the news from Greece should be encouraging to those with money to invest in the cause of Liberty."

Gurney's eyes were wide open now. "You interest me strangely," he said. "Proceed."

"Yes. The facts of the Greek situation are as follows. The government, which at present is in possession of neither funds nor power, is in the hands of Prince Alexander Mavrocordato, as you probably know. What you probably do not know is that the noble Greek Klephts—brigands—whom Byron finds so romantic are a greedy rabble, perpetually at odds and just as ready to fight among themselves as with the Turkish oppressor. You may also remember—my sources imply that you are by no means an innocent on the Stock Exchange—that a loan has just been opened in support of the Greeks. Frankly, given the nature of the gentlemen who are promoting this loan, I should consider it a most unwise investment; but that is neither here not there. What concerns us at the Admiralty is the almost limitless possibilities for further dissension in the Greek ranks that this huge sum of money opens. It will be a veritable Apple of Paris to the factions, and might result in a fatal division at a most inopportune moment."

Gurney was perplexed. "Why should this moment be more inopportune than any other? They seem to have rubbed along all right for the past couple of years."

Morpurgo drummed his fingers impatiently on the table. "My dear Captain, please do not be so naïve. Do you seriously imagine that a European country could be in a state of complete topsy-turveydom without some Great Power or other seeking to benefit from the situation at the expense of its neighbours? And in Greece, everyone wants a finger in the pie, if only to keep Russia out. You will probably be aware that Russia is hanging a mighty weight of troops at Turkey's northern borders. Well, it has come to our attention that Mehemet Ali of Egypt may be heading for a landing on the Peloponnese with a large Fleet; and this Fleet is led by men who fought under Old Boney himself." He leaned forward in his chair, his face earnest. "Captain Gurney, the situation in this troubled land may shortly become desperate."

"Come come, Morpurgo, enough of this 'troubled land' stuff," Gurney shook his head. "You don't really expect me to believe that you've come all this way just to give me a lesson in politics? Where do I fit into all this?"

"I am coming to that. A few days ago, one of our agents returned from Greece with disquieting news. Certain papers of critical importance, whose contents I cannot at the moment divulge, even in the strictest confidence, disappeared. We know how and where, and our agent was confident that they could be retrieved, but their retrieval is a mission which demands rather special skills as well as the complete trustworthiness of whoever carries it out. I believe that you are acquainted with the problems of sailing such waters as the Aegean, Captain Gurney, and that your ship the *Vandal* is ideally suited for the task. Furthermore, it has been suggested to me that you speak the necessary languages. To this I would add that you would have the satisfaction of aiding the new Hellas, a project which must be close to your heart, for I know of your love of the arts and sciences."

Gurney laughed, shortly, "Quite a change of tune. Squabbling brigands in one breath, and the new Hellas in the next. Well, Mr. Morpurgo, I fear your errand has been in vain. My commitments here are heavy. I must deliver the two schooners you saw to Aberdeen by May. What is to stop you sending a frigate of His Majesty's Navy to collect these documents, and have done with it?"

"What stops us is the need for discretion."

"Very well then, why can't your agent pick them up and deliver them to the Navy in the Ionian Islands? They belong to the Crown, do they not?"

A curious smugness spread over Morpurgo's face. He looked like a card-sharp who has just succeeded in manoeuvring the ace out of his sleeve and into his hand. "We cannot send our agent because he is not a free man at this moment. In fact, he is the captive of the Mainiot Klephts in the Peloponnese, and is, I hear, in daily peril of his life. It seems that only the fact that he knows that in the same place as these documents there is a considerable quantity of treasure keeps him alive." He looked sharply at Gurney, who was finishing his glass and appeared to be on the point of rising. "I should have thought the prospect of a treasure would be rather appealing than otherwise to one in your position, Captain. It is an expensive business, running a shipyard and managing an estate of this size."

Gurney decided that he definitely did not like this smooth and insinuating individual, but there was certainly something in what he said. Those two ships on the slip were financed by a series of heavy loans, secured by the estate and the yard itself. The one thing he could not afford to do was go off on one of Jervy Hutchinson's wild goose chases. Not only was there the delivery of the two Aberdeen ships; he needed a constant stream of orders to keep his credit good, and even working full out it would take him two years to get out of debt. "No," he said. "My commitments here will not permit me even to consider going."

Morpurgo sighed. "Dear me," he said mildly. "This is a great disappointment. I shall be forced, then, to tell certain people in London that you are no longer taking your responsibilities seriously."

"My responsibilities? Let me remind you that I am no longer a naval officer, at your beck and call."

Morpurgo smiled his irritating smile. "I was not referring to your, ah, *patriotic* responsibilities, Captain. No, it was your *financial* responsibilities I was meaning. Those loans which, I believe, finance your shipyard at present. If you persist in your refusal to perform this service, I regret that I shall be forced to apply pressure to your bankers; pressure which will give them no choice but to foreclose."

There was a silence. Gurney stared at Morpurgo in astonishment. "Did I hear you correctly?" His voice was cold and dangerous. "You threaten an English gentleman in his own home? You, an assistant to Jervy Hutchinson? Good God, man, Jervy would never hear of such a thing."

"Yes." Morpurgo's smile was smooth and hard. "Admiral Hutchinson is indeed a gentleman of sentimental and outdated ideas. But he is now more concerned with matters of policy than of execution. I put it to you that you are faced with a simple alternative. Either you undertake this mission and thereby earn

not only a considerable treasure but the goodwill of
His Majesty's Government; or you fall into financial
ruin. And your debts, if they are foreclosed, are now
sufficient to put you and your wife into the Fleet."

Gurney's hands clenched convulsively on the arms
of his chair. "Am I to believe that you are sitting there,
having eaten my dinner, telling me that you will put
the people of my village in the poorhouse and my
wife in jail if I do not do your dirty work? I have
killed men for less, Morpurgo. For much less."

"But you will not kill me. Be reasonable, Mr. Gurney. Oh, and another thing. This spy you are to rescue
is well-known to you. A Mohammedan fellow, who
goes under the name of the Haji Basreddin."

"Basreddin?"

"One and the same."

Gurney leaned back in his chair. "Mr. Morpurgo,
you have, I perceive, been playing with me. The mere
mention of Basreddin's name would have sufficed. I
do not share your opinion that friendship is secondary
to consideration of property and finance."

"How rare, how very rare." Sarcastic. "Well, then,
you can pretend to yourself that it is friendship alone
that animates you." The eyes narrowed. "But bear in
mind that if you fail, your money and your hands are
forfeit. There are still those in the Admiralty who
would love to see you fail."

"I shall not fail."

"Let us hope not, for your sake and that of your
dependents. Now, a toast to a successful enterprise!"

Gurney stood up.

"I think you have drunk enough of my wine, Mr.
Morpurgo." He picked up a handbell from the table
at his side and rang. The butler appeared. "Mr. Morpurgo is leaving us now," said Gurney. "Please have
his horse brought round to the door and his bags
packed."

"Very well, Mr. Gurney." The butler withdrew.

"We sail," said Gurney, "in three days, on the morning tide. Tell that to your masters, you dog. Now, get out of my house. And if you speak so much as a word to a living soul, I will kill you." And taking Morpurgo by the elbow, he led him to the front door and put him outside into the cold Saturday rain.

* * *

Matins at St. Saviour's Church, Sea Dalling, was not usually a well-attended service. Particularly when, as today, there was a morning tide. But the congregation this cold February Sunday numbered one hundred and eighty souls, many of them, in Parson Leggatt's experience, beyond any hope of redemption. Which meant that only forty-three of the village's inhabitants were absent. As he ran his eyes over the faces, his mystification deepened. Even the Chapel lot were here, and amazement on amazement, the fourteen Catholics who lived in a tight huddle of cottages, halfway to Morehouse. There was Henry Priest and his father, Jed, both of them doomed for the goat side at the Last Judgement. And young George Jarvis, whose expressed wish it was to spend every moment that he was not down at the shipyard in the taproom at the Dun Cow. And Volnikov, McIver and O'Shea, the Godless lot Captain Gurney had brought back with him from his travels. Really, it was all most peculiar. But Parson Leggatt was not the man to let such an opportunity slip through his fingers. As he intoned the collect for the day in his fruity baritone, he mentally tore up the sermon he had planned, an interesting disquisition on the need for purity of body and soul during Lent. In its place, he decided he would put in a good hour on the Return of the Prodigal, treading lightly over the elements of forgiveness in the parable and dwelling a good deal on the Wrath to Come.

Parson Leggatt's mane of snowy hair fairly bristled with satisfaction as he trumpeted the last verse of the day's psalm. Out of the corner of his eye he saw

George Gurney stride to the lectern to read the lesson, as he did every Sunday. The Parson settled back in his stall and allowed his mind to toy a little with his sermon. Then he stiffened and sat up, listening.

Gurney looked up from the great Bible and swept the faces before him with his eyes. Arabella, at the front, demure in a little hat and a dark cloak; then the village worthies and the half-gentry; and behind them, the mass of small farmers and yardmen, with their wives and children. And behind them again, *Vandal's* warrant officers and skilled tradesmen—Volnikov the Russian, towering bearlike over his neighbours; one-eyed McIver, uneasy in his Sunday blues; Mather the American sealer, staring open-mouthed at the stained glass of the windows; and O'Shea, the gunner, with his perpetually harried expression, glancing nervously about him, as if looking for avenging Jesuits behind the pillars.

He cleared his throat. "Before I read the lesson," he said, "there is something I must talk to you about. I apologise to Parson Leggatt for using the Lord's house for this purpose, but this is a matter which reflects on the village as a whole. Chiefly, it is a matter of the Government. For reasons I can't go into, they want to close the yard down." He paused; the silence in the church was brittle with shock. "I don't have to remind you that life is easier at Dalling since the yard."

A general murmur of assent passed from man to man. Four years ago, existence had been a continual battle with poverty, starvation, and exploiting landowners. But since Captain Gurney and Lady Arabella had come to the house there was a living to be made. And, until now, security. Gurney's voice rang again round the fan-vaulting.

"Unless I sail on Tuesday's tide, for the Mediterranean, in my ship yonder, the Dalling yards will close. What I ask of you is this: to come with me on *Vandal*, sixty of you, and be my crew. It will be no easy passage. Those are wild parts, and some may die.

But I put it to you like this; it is war, war against the fine London gentlemen who would take the very bread from your mouths. And is that not a fit cause for which to risk your lives?" He paused, and when he spoke again his voice was quiet. "Think on it. A return to the bad old days, or danger in strange lands. A hard choice, particularly for those of you with families. But one we must make, and soon. I am in your hands. Give me your answers after the service, at the church door. Now. Here beginneth the first lesson."

When he had finished he walked back and sat beside Arabella. She squeezed his hand, and later, as they sat through the longest sermon he had ever heard the Parson drone, she held it still. At length, the congregation rose for the final hymn. Parson Leggatt knew that he should have felt a satisfaction at the power and breadth of his sermon; but as he looked down the nave at the nine-score faces, he saw only worried expressions. And he was worried himself. It was unthinkable that the yard should close now. He greatly enjoyed his talks with George Gurney, and the young Captain's cellar was better than passable; but above all, he had plucked Dalling from its Dark Age. And that into the Dark Age it should fall again was— well, it was unthinkable.

The Parson realised that the last verse of the hymn was upon him, and walked slowly from his stall to the altar, singing lustily the while, and the "Amen" that followed his Blessing was strong and firm. Sea Dalling knew it needed all the assistance it could get, both temporal and spiritual.

Gurney and the Lady Arabella were the first to leave the church. On his way out Gurney had beckoned to McIver, and now they stood in the porch, out of the drizzle, beside Parson Leggatt as the congregation filed out. As each man passed he touched his forelock and said "aye" or "nay." McIver then recorded his name in the book he carried. The "ayes" far outweighed the "nays."

"How did it go?" asked Arabella, as the carriage bounded along the rutted road towards the High House.

"Excellently," said Gurney. "More than a hundred volunteers for *Vandal*. The ones who couldn't come all had good reasons—not that they needed them, God knows. And about thirty of the women said they'd go to work in the yard. I'll leave Jedediah as Foreman."

"They are a charming lot. But can you imagine Jed trying to keep his nieces in order? It'll be a shambles, poor fellow."

Gurney grinned. "I think you'll find he can keep his end up. And anyway, you'll be keeping an eye on things, won't you?"

"Of course." Her smile was white in the gloomy interior of the carriage. "For as long as I'm here. But who knows, I may take it into my head to follow you."

"Damn it all, Ara, you will not!" Then, sheepishly, "Hell take you. If you will, you will. But don't expect any help from me."

"Certainly not," said Arabella. "At any rate, if we are to be poor now it would be a terrible extravagance."

"We are not," said Gurney, "going to be poor. Not if we come back alive."

Arabella's face grew serious. "Oh, George, I don't mind if we have no money. Just bring yourself back in one piece, please." She was stroking his face with long fingers, her eyes bright with tears.

"Don't worry. I will. And the men," said Gurney.

The carriage stopped on the gravel sweep before the High House, and the tiger jumped down to open the door. As the Captain and Lady Arabella went in, both tall and fair in their sombre Sunday clothes, the butler saw that they walked close together, that Lady Arabella dabbed at a tear with her handkerchief and that the Captain's jaw was set, grim and firm. But when they had been upstairs in Her Ladyship's bou-

doir for a while, the butler was reassured to hear
laughter begin to tumble down the great stairs.

2

It was blowing half a gale out of a clear sky from the
northeast as the twelve-gun topsail schooner, *Vandal*,
all sail set, butted the first of the steep Lead seas beyond the Point. Gurney was sweating, despite the cold;
taking a one hundred and fifty-foot schooner out of
the twisting, sandbar-treacherous channel was no pic-
nic even under ideal conditions, and today it was
not far short of hellish. He handed the wheel to Dutch
Pieter, his coxswain, and mopped his brow with a
silk handkerchief. Astern, the loom of the low Norfolk coastline was already little more than a dark
stroke across the horizon, the two towers of Sea
Dalling church mere pencil scratches against the
patchwork of heath and plough. As Gurney watched,
something flashed from the west tower. Charlie Jarvis,
he thought, up there again, polishing his caloptric reflector. Poor old Charlie. Nothing would bring his
brother back from that skeletal ruin on the Hood.

Gurney felt sad, suddenly. During the past seventy-two hours he had worked hard and slept little,
and now the realisation of what he was doing hit him
like a cold slap of water. He knew that he loved the
High House, the yard, and most of all Arabella, and
leaving them was painful. But more painful in the abstract than actually. And he was not much in the habit
of dwelling on the abstract when the actual demanded
his attention. Time enough for maunderings of that
kind later. Now there was work to do. Three days in
mid-winter was little enough time in all conscience to

provision for three months and sixty men—*Vandal* was sailing with a war crew.

"McIver!" The Scotsman, shipwright, bo'sun and first mate all at once, presented himself. "Aye, McIver, it's good to be away to sea again. Take her for me; I'm for checking the stores." The most easily visible part of the ship's supplies were tied up or caged on the deck. Six fat pigs squealed at the fo'c'sle, five dozen hens huddled miserably in their coops, and below, in a specially-built stall on the gun-deck, Mrs. Siddons, the Jersey cow, braced her legs against the bucking deck and cast anxious glances at the unfamiliar world with her great liquid eyes.

Gurney passed on to the magazine. *Vandal's* battery had changed a good deal since he had the leisure to experiment a little; now she mounted five twelve pounders a side, with one huge sixty-eight pounder long tom to port and starboard at the widest point in her beam, firing ball or shells packed with powder and fused. O'Shea, the little Irish gunner, mutineer and fugitive from justice after the horrible slaughter on *Hermione*, stood at his side shifting from foot to foot and fidgeting with his forelock. When Gurney nodded and passed on he looked relieved, as well he might. O'Shea was in charge of *Vandal's* armament, responsible only to Gurney, and he spent his life in alternate fits of delight at the latitude allowed him by his Captain and terror that somehow, somewhere, something had been forgotten.

Vandal's water party had spent much of the past three days by the River Stiven pumping fresh water into casks, rowing them on to *Vandal's* mooring in the Pit, and filling, gallon by muscle-wrenching gallon, the great water-tank below the gundeck amidships. Gurney checked the gauges, then passed on to the lower forepeak. There were not as many barrels of salt junk there as there should have been. Three days was too short a time to travel the country in search of suitable animals. For the third time Gurney made a men-

tal note to put in at London and purchase more. Then
he ran up the companionway, settled his fisherman's
cap of navy wool well over his ears, and stood once
again at the taffrail, where he had courted Arabella,
staring back over the heaving grey of the muddy sea
to the wind-whipped shores of his home.

Arabella, by the pillared windows of the West Tower of the church, was watching too. With her telescope
she could just make out the tall figure, bulky in a suit
of heavy blue serge, balancing against the pitch of
the schooner's stern. As the yards of the square topsails came round and the ship set her forefoot to the
east, parallel with the shore, the figure dwindled, a
mere speck beneath the tall cloud of canvas at the
schooner's spars. Her eyes clouded, grew remote. She
stood there for perhaps five minutes. Then she smiled,
a long, lazy, sly smile, and hurried down the hundred
and five steps to where Charlie Jarvis was holding her
Arab mare.

The northeasterlies carried *Vandal* down-Channel,
across the Bay of Biscay, past Portugal, and through
the Straits of Gibraltar. Then their luck deserted them.

Gurney, seated at the oak table in *Vandal's* after-
cabin composing a letter to Arabella, flung down his
quill pen in disgust. *Vandal* was pitching like a cork
in the lumping sea that had come up with the east
wind, which had been freshening steadily since nightfall three hours ago; the lantern was swinging crazily
despite its gimbals, and every now and then the wood
stove belched acrid smoke into the cabin. And Gurney
could not concentrate on the ordering of new timber
for seasoning in the Dalling yard or the final schedules
for the Aberdeen schooners on his slips. There was an
unease in his mind that he could not pin down—something that was not explainable by the foul wind
against which *Vandal* was battering, close-hauled on
the starboard tack, heeled until her lee gunports were
awash and the cold March sea squeezed through her

creaking seams. He shut the lid of the inkwell, shoved the half-finished letter under the blotter, and went on deck.

The wind was raw and wet, and he winced, blinking the water from his eyes and huddling into his thick pea-jacket against the blast. *Vandal*'s decks were darkened, the only light the dim glow from the binnacle reflected from the helmsman's glistening oilskins. Even under double-reefed fore- and mainsails and a single topsail, *Vandal* was making a good ten knots; as Gurney peered up at the drum-taut canvas of the main, she knifed her bow into a wave and a sheet of spray hissed down her flush decks, flooding the lee scuppers with foam as she slid into the trough.

The lookout's hail was thin and ragged, scattered by the wind. "Sail ho!"

Gurney walked quickly forward, bracing himself against the swooping, bucking deck. "What'd you see?" He found that he had to bellow in the man's ear, and even then the wind whipped the words away almost before he spoke them.

The lookout pointed about ten degrees on the starboard bow.

"A light, Cap'in. Leastways, I'm sure I saw 'un. But she int there no more." Gurney strained his eyes into the darkness. The night was black as pitch, the sky dense with low cloud. Nothing.

"Well, whatever it was it's gone. Still, let's have a man up the foretop. God help us if we run afoul of some Dago on a night like this." He turned up his collar and stumped aft again, worried. Bloody Froggie trick, running blind before this gale without a light to his name.

He turned to the helmsman, who stood rocklike on the grating beside the wheel, passing the brassbound spokes through his fingers with the delicacy of a master fiddler. The compass card hung on north-north-east and a half east.

"There's some bloody Dago up ahead, showing no

lights and likely going downwind like the hammers of
Hell. Keep your eyes and ears peeled, Pieter."

"Right you are, Captain." Pieter turned his eyes to
the foretop, where the extra lookout was presumably
straining his eyes into the murk. Gurney noted with approval that even when the man was paying no mind
to the compass, the ship deviated not a hair from
her course. *Vandal* ploughed forward into the black
seas, her decks bare but for the five men of the storm
watch and her lookouts. Below, men and animals slept
or stared uneasily at the deckhead above their ham-
mocks, damp and miserable, surrounded by the creaks,
groans and rattles that made the music of one hundred
and fifty fine-honed feet of precision sailing machine.

Henry Priest, poised in the foretopsail yard sixty
feet above the deck, shifted his grip on the spar and
spat a stream of tobacco juice to leeward. Frankly
the Mediterranean was a disappointment to him.
When he had signed on with the Captain he had told
his missis that he reckoned the South Seas, wherever
they might be, would be a right nice little lay for a
few months. Better than the bloody North Sea, any
road. But when you got down to it, this little blow
was not much better than a lot he had seen on his
timber runs in the Baltic. Only difference was there
weren't any bloody wogs racketing round the Baltic
without lights. He resumed his patient quartering of
where he reckoned the horizon would have been. If
you could have seen anything, that was. Blacker 'n
the inside of a bloody cow.

Henry and the bow lookout saw the light at the same
time, a couple of chains off the port bow. Both of
them yelled and Gurney leaped to the wheel, spinning
the spokes towards him, dragging *Vandal* up head to
wind. She responded like the thoroughbred she was,
canvas rattling and booming. The captain of the
strange ship, however, seemed never to have heard of
the rule of the road, and turned hard-a-starboard.
Henry tightened his grip and watched, fascinated, as

the yellow lamp, now visibly reflecting on a grubby lateen-mizzen, drove under *Vandal*'s bowsprit like a moonstruck rabbit under a ploughshare.

Gurney saw it too, and joined with the helmsman, flinging the spokes away from him, bellowing at hands on deck to slack off the topsail braces. But the gale was firmly in the squaresail, driving *Vandal*'s nose across the wind, and her stern, backed by the three hundred tons of wood, iron and flesh travelling at the same speed as a cantering Suffolk Punch, knifed into the fishing boat amidships like an axe into a cheese. Gurney lost his footing on the deck as *Vandal* staggered with the shock, writhing forward into the legs of three men scrambling out of the waist cabin companionway, knocking them into a sprawling heap. Then he was on his feet, roaring at the men on the deck to ease sheets and braces as the fishing boat's weight dragged *Vandal* broadside on to the wind, and she went down onto her beam ends.

Fore and main gave with a rattle and a roar, leaving her broached broadside to the ugly waves, foam-crested now, plugging in out of the eye of the wind. *Vandal* was still moving through the water, but sluggish, dragged back by the wreck that hung under her bowsprit, a mass of jagged timber pounding and thrashing at the flare of her bow. In the pitch blackness, men were running in all directions. Many of them had been awakened by the impact, and were now like sleepwalkers, dazed and leaderless on *Vandal*'s rolling deck, where the sheets from the great fore-and-aft sails whisked like a pit of serpents. Gurney cannoned into a burly figure, and by the gleam of the single eye in the dark mass of the face recognised McIver.

"Thunder and teeth, what a bloody mess. Get her head to wind while I see if there's anything still alive on the bloody Dago."

McIver grunted. McIver grunted a lot, but it was a tribute to his triple-tanned leather lungs that you could hear his grunts over a force eight easterly. He turned, roaring orders in a profane Highland monotone. Gurney sent two men aft to the sail locker for a boarding net, snatched a lantern, and ran forward to the bow.

The scene on *Vandal*'s deck was one of chaos resolving itself, under McIver's curses, into some kind of order; what he saw in the dim yellow light of the lantern was chaos unadulterated. Under *Vandal*'s forefoot was a mash of wreckage, boiling in a seething cauldron of white water. As he looked for signs of life her stem pounded again into the tangle of timber and cordage that had once, by the look of it, been a Balearic fishing-smack. Now only the part of her forward of the waist remained, canted steeply away from *Vandal*'s bow; everything aft of her mainmast—including her cabin, Gurney realised with a sinking of his stomach—was chopped to flinders. He held the lantern above his head. It was impossible to see anything in the madly flickering shadows of the wind-dashed glim. But was that a face, down there in the midst of the grinding hull of timber? An arm lifted feebly towards the lantern. The net was hanging over *Vandal*'s side now, into the lee of her bow, but the arm could not reach it, seemingly trapped in the welter of the wreck. Gurney stripped off his coat and seaboots and turned to the man at his side.

"Give me a line; I'm going in after him." The man stood, open-mouthed. "I said give me a line! Are you deaf, damn you?" Shivering, Gurney made a bowline round his waist, grasped the netting where it hung over the cathead, and climbed down the side. As soon as his feet touched the water he let himself fall back, swimming towards the loom of the fishing boat's hull. Something smashed into his ribs, winding him, but he kept swimming until a chance shaft of light from the lantern, high, unattainably high above him at *Vandal*'s rail, illuminated the whites of the eyes of the arm's owner. With a desperate lunge he grabbed the man by

his collar, waving his free hand at the light above him.
He felt the bight of rope tug under his armpits, and
he and his quarry were being dragged the fifteen feet
back towards the ship's side; from somewhere there
came a harsh, animal screaming, but he paid no attention. Then the netting was under his hand and he
was shouting in the fisherman's ear to tell him that he
should climb; but the face was a blank mass of darkness in the roar of the sea, and when he tried to clamp
the hands to the netting they twined in and stayed,
rock-steady, without moving. He cursed and worked
at the bowline, hanging on to the refuge of the netting with his free hand, binding it round the fisherman's thick chest. The waves had sucked him under
the hollow flare of *Vandal*'s bow, out of sight of the
men on deck, and when the man on the line began to
heave, the fisherman, limp but for the hands clamped
to the netting, went upwards like a rocket. And the
netting went with him. Gurney, now with neither netting nor bowline linking him with his ship, lay like a
feather in a whirlwind, under the smooth black overhang of *Vandal*'s bow as McIver brought her head to
wind.

Gurney waited for the net, but it did not come. And
then he realised that the ship was moving away from
him faster than he could swim. He shouted, but in the
roar of the gale it came out as a thin keening. And still
no net came down. He was under *Vandal*'s bowsprit
now. Twenty seconds would leave him alone, adrift in
this whitecapped sea filled with wooden teeth. Like a
great axe *Vandal*'s stem fell from the top of a wave
and sliced deep into the trough. As the bowsprit swept
stiffly down above him, Gurney grabbed for where he
knew the bobstay should be. The middle fingers of his
right hand caught in one of the links of the chain, and
he crooked them round the slimy iron as *Vandal*'s bow
went up again, up, far too fast. With a sort of de-
tached curiosity he felt the fingers slip from their
hold, felt the nail of his ring finger tear away as the

chain soared to the crest of the next wave, and the salt water bite into the exposed quick. He was very tired, his breath coming in great sobs, choking and sputtering as wind-driven sheets of water wrapped themselves round his bobbing head, filling his mouth and nostrils. He knew he had but one more chance. As he felt himself sink into the trough, he let himself slide down: then, as the rise of the next swell began, he kicked upwards and hurled himself with all his strength out of the water, his arms raised above his head, fingers spread. When his face broke surface the bowsprit was directly above him, stooped low across the water, and he locked his hands in the attitude of a prizefighter acknowledging the crowd. For a moment he was falling back; then the stay took him in the palms of the hands and he was yanked upwards with a jerk that nearly took his arms from their sockets and he was dangling, feet out of the water, over the trough of the next wave. The bows came down again and he manoeuvred his foot round the chain, consolidating his grip fraction by tiny fraction, clinging to the iron as if it were a woman.

It was two or three minutes before he found the strength to move very slowly up the bucking stay to the bowsprit; and by the time he crawled off the spar onto *Vandal*'s deck his muscles were like paper and all he could do was lie gasping by the fo'c'sle rails until McIver and another man came and leaned solicitously over him. He struggled to his feet, shaking his head against the waves of dizziness, and went aft, McIver trotting anxiously at his side. Gurney took the wheel from the helmsman, his damaged hand throbbing. *Vandal* was heavier in the water than he remembered, sluggish to respond; her roll was somehow soggy, too. He turned to McIver.

"What's the damage?"

"Lot of planks stove forward, Captain. Making water fast. We'd best get a sail under there."

"Very well. See to it, would you?" As McIver turned

away Gurney remembered. "Where's that man we pulled out of the drink?" McIver shook his head.

"Dead, Captain. Ribs all to flinders. Had to cut his hands off the netting, though, couldn't shift the bugger."

"Any other survivors?"

Again the shake of the head. Gurney dismissed him to muster a damage party and double up the men on the pumps. Poor devils. Dago or no, that was a stupid way to go, running downwind with your eyes tight shut. And there was no way even of knowing the name of the ship. Somewhere, tomorrow or the next day, or next week, a handful of women and a few children in some red-tiled huddle of shacks would realise that the men were not coming home. Another disappearance at sea. It was all so bloody anonymous. No war, no blood, no rage: just ten seconds of horror, the crash of the shock, and you could be spiralling through the black, water flowing in sluggish whirls and eddies through mouth, nostrils, lungs. But that man in the water had not wanted to go like that. Better for him if he had, really.

Gurney shook his head. Waste. Damn silly waste. Plain carelessness. And now he was going to have to put in at some yard and patch up *Vandal*. Do more than patch her up, actually; she would have to be as good as new for him to be easy in his mind during the cruise ahead. He summoned up a map of the Western Mediterranean in his head. Precious little in Spain, Gibraltar too far. Looked like Marseilles or Toulon. He made a face. Not Toulon. The French Navy had come off the slips there, and although that was over and done with, it was still too recent for comfort. No, it looked like Marseilles. Good yards there, and the people hadn't liked Boney messing with the Mediterranean trade. Pro-Bourbon anti-Bonapartists to a man. And by dead reckoning from his last sight, *Vandal* could reach port on this tack if the wind held. Four days at least, then a week in the yards. With

Basreddin captive in some bandit stronghold in the Peloponnese. God damn all crazy Dago skippers. He looked guiltily round, as if the dead could overhear him, and apologised silently to the departed crew; then he handed the wheel back to Pieter and went below.

The third day in Marseilles was drawing to its close. Gurney, McIver, and Mottin, the shipwright and chandler on whose slip *Vandal* now lay hove down, were walking up the Canebière, away from the Vieux Port, in search of dinner. Mottin, a smallish, sourish Marseillais with eyebrows that met across his low forehead and hands that danced perpetually in the air, was talking. Indeed, it sometimes seemed to Gurney, whose French was at best broken, that Mottin never stopped talking. Since they had taken *Vandal* out of the Vieux Port and round to Mottin's slips, Gurney had been subjected to a barrage of information on topics ranging from Mottin's natural genius as a shipbuilder to the absolute perfection of Marseilles as a place to raise a family, via politics, art and the price of carrots. It had been the latest topic, whose fascinations were wearing thin for Gurney and his mate, which had reminded him of dinner; and now, on the Canebiére. Mottin was planning to give them the best bouillabaisse of their lives and talking about himself with his usual refined modesty.

"We go, my sirs, to an establishment which call himself *Chez Pierre*, who is a friend of mine, one of the ones—and though I am a modest man I admit there are many—who know that without me Marseilles would still be a leetle fishing village. For when they are thinking of make improvement, they come to me and say, 'Gaston, we need your advice.' And I am not proud. What is it to me that I would have been mayor of this city had not certain ill-disposed people spread among the good burghers the rumour that I was owning bordellos? Rubbish! I am merely a part-

ner, and not an active one at that. Except in sampling
the wares, and that, as Descartes may have said,
whoever he was, and why should I care, that, *mon
capitaine,* is not action, eet is passion." He slapped his
leg, roaring with laughter at his own wit, then stepped
in a pile of filth lying in the gutter at the side of the
road and cursed blackly. Gurney had to suppress a
smile. Mottin's emotions careered across his face like
squalls across the sea, following each other in such
quick succession that it was impossible to keep up.
Still, he seemed a good shipwright, and that was what
mattered. Gurney composed himself, made sure he
was looking interested, and winked at McIver, sat-
urated with dour Scots gloom in the middle of all
these foreigners. Mottin was away again. This time, in
deference to the political susceptibilities of these towering *rosbifs,* he chose the monarchy as his talking
point.

"'Ow well I remember the years of the Terror, the
revolutionary scums parading down and up our
Canebière with their caps and their scythes. La Mar-
seillaise, pah! In a year we were starving, those bastids
make sure of that. Nothing to trade in the sea, because as soon as out the sheeps are, English or Français
or Espanish boom! and down she go away. Me, in that
time I have special drawer make for the *chaise percée*
with picture of the King, so every day I can go to
think loyal thought. But my stomach, she always empty, for no trade, no ships, no money. Now all have
change. You saw zose big docks."

Gurney was puzzled. "Dogs?"

"Yes. Docks for sheeps."

"Sheepdogs! I don't understand."

It was at that point that Mottin stopped in the middle of the pavement and, in front of a growing crowd
of passers-by, commenced to give a very fair imita-
tion of a seventy-four gun ship of the line in dry
dock, being built, caulked, payed, and sheathed. It
was a fascinating performance, not least, as a cou-

ple of tough-looking bystanders did not hesitate to
point out, because of the ambiguity of many of the
gestures involved. Indeed, one of the bystanders
aforesaid seemed to be under the impression that Mottin was touting a new brothel, and harsh words were
exchanged when he tried to get the address from the
Frenchman. By the time Gurney realised what Mottin was driving at, he was near-helpless with laughter,
and the shipwright was fuming. Even McIver's gravity seemed shaken.

"Dry-docks? For ships."

"Uffcoss! What you theenk? The best the newest
docks at Marseilles. You see them yourselfs."

Gurney nodded. He had wondered why such
enormous docks and slips should have been necessary
in a yard like Mottin's which, though bristling with
work, seemed to confine itself largely to the building
of smallish merchantmen. Had they been at Toulon,
he would have assumed that their function was to pro-
duce warships; but at Marseilles, surely not. Mottin
resumed his lecture.

"Ah, yes. They pay me good to build zem beeg
sheeps, those Egypts. Three seventy-four-gun sheep,
very modern, all refinements, very fast. Deliver last
month. Much, much money; all gold, no notes." He
smiled with self-satisfaction. "Me, I peety whoever it
is who receive crac boum from they sheeps. Good
sheeps."

Gurney was eyeing him narrowly. So it was true.
An invasion of Greece would not be a matter of any
Army supported by a few rotting feluccas armed with
antique field-pieces; by the sound of things there was
a strong modern Navy, and a Navy to be reckoned
with. If the men were up to the ships. No reason
why they should be; the Egyptians were not notori-
ous for their discipline, and discipline was an important commodity on a 74. Still, this bore thinking about.

It was at that moment that the noise began. Noise
there already was in plenty; the Canebière was a

heavily-trafficked street. Nor were the Marseillais themselves noted for their taciturnity. Indeed, it seemed impossible for a Marseillais to pass the time of day with an acquaintance without the conversation developing into something which, had it emanated from a darkened room, would have given the impression that a singularly noisy *crime passionel* was being committed within. This noise, however, consisted of a good deal of shouting, punctuated—Gurney pricked up his ears—with the clash of steel on steel. And the raised voices were not speaking the nasal Marseillais French, but a guttural roar of German.

The noise grew louder, and from the dark doorway of a wineshop burst a brawling knot of figures. As Gurney watched, he realised that there were only two actual combatants. A tall, fleshy man in a brilliant yellow uniform that Gurney could not place was hacking at a smaller individual, also uniformed, with a long cavalry sabre. The smaller man was getting the worst of it, pressed back against the trunk of one of the tall plane trees that lined the boulevard, but such was his agility that his opponent could not make contact. The wild swings he was making with his sabre gouged great chunks of bark from the tree; and then a particularly violent swing cast him off balance and he staggered, cannoning into Gurney and breathing stale wine all over him. He turned, scowling.

"*Raus, dumkopf!*" The voice was a throaty bark; in combination with the red, sweat-dabbled face with the duelling scars on the left cheek, Gurney found it extremely irritating. He felt his temper, never the most passive of his emotions, come to the boil. Before he rightly knew what he was doing, he reached out and grabbed the Prussian by his orange cravat.

"It strikes me, Sir, that you are in need of a lesson in manners."

The Prussian's flat, bloodshot eyes widened a little, as if he could not believe what he saw. Then the lipless mouth opened in a snarl, betraying an un-

fortunate absence of front teeth, and he swung his
sword at Gurney's head in a flat arc. Gurney ducked,
and felt the wind of the blow on his cheek. He caught
a glimpse of McIver, fists clenched like hammers,
moving in at his shoulder, and Mottin edging away
towards the shelter of a fruit-stall; then he moved inside the Prussian's sword-arm, took his head in chan-
cery, smashed his free fist into the yelling face, and
threw him with a cross-buttock into the filthy gutter.

He looked about him. The other brawlers had fallen
silent, and the way they were looking at him was not
reassuring. One or two of them had drawn their
swords, and despite their laughable yellow uniforms
they had a menacing air. Even the gentleman whose
life Gurney had presumably come near to saving was
looking somewhat aggressive. Once Gurney had intervened, with the best of intentions, in a lovers' tiff
between Ivo Dauncey and Fenella Bassett. The attitude of these comic-opera captains now reminded him
strongly of the torrent of abuse to which he had been
subjected by the immediately reconciled lovers. Not
for the first time in his life, he cursed his temper.
There was work to do in Greece, and the delays were
serious enough without further complication.

He addressed himself to the Prussian's opponent, a
fair, wiry youth of about twenty. "Permit me to introduce myself. I am Captain Gurney, of the *Vandal*."

The youth looked bored, "*Ach, Gott*. Can you not
see, you fool, that you have pushed your English nose
into an affair of honour between gentlemen and soldiers?"

Gurney shifted disconcertingly. "You will forgive me
ah, Kolonel is it? for intervening. If you will pardon
the remark, your recent ... military engagement ...
seemed to be more pothouse brawl than affair of honour." The Kolonel drew in his breath sharply and
reached for his sword. "But at least accept my apologies." Discretion the better part of valour in this
case. No sense in putting an untimely end to *Vandal's*

errand. Let alone his life. "It seems that the rigours of campaigning in barbarous France must somewhat alter the rules of honour."

The Kolonel nodded curtly, and sheathed his sword. "*Ja*. Well, it is not impossible that this is the case. You will perhaps join us in a glass of wine?" His face relaxed, the mouth stretched into a grimace that seemed meant for a smile, and he pointed to the tree. "Herr General von Kratzstein has in bad humour been today; it seems he is the forest confusing with the Turks." He tittered, a peculiarly girlish giggle, and his overdressed companions ho-hoed with him. Their eyes did not share the joke with the rest of their faces, Gurney noticed. "You haf yourself introduced. I wish to do the same." He walked down the file of his companions. "Kolonel Stahlkeber, Kolonel Albertus." Six heels clicked together like a spaced broadside. "I myself an Kolonel Ziehendorf, and he in the gutter—" more dutiful ho-hoing—"is, as I haf already said, Herr General von Kratzstein, Officer Commanding the Heidelberg University Brothers for the Liberation of the Heroes of Hellas from the Shackles of the Mussulman. Herren Kolonels Stahlkeber, Albertus?" More heel-clicking. "You will be so good as to assist the Herr General within, and we will take wine with the brave Kapitan Zur Zee and his men. After you, Herr Kapitan."

As they entered the *estaminet*, the noise and smoke were like a wall. If the proprietor, wiping his hands on his dirty apron, was put out by the return of the brawlers, he showed no sign, and he ushered them with much respectful bowing to a round table at the rear of his establishment. Von Ziehendorf called for wine and, at Mottin's rather timid insistence, a *marmite* of bouillabaisse, though he frowned at the latter and spoke disparagingly of it in comparison with bratwurst. While they waited for the food to arrive, Gurney asked the Kolonel how he and his companions came to be in Marseilles.

"As the name of our unit implies," he said, fixing Gurney with a steely eye, "we are bound for Hellas. It is our mission, under the leadership of General von Kratzstein, to see in the oppressed land of Plato and Homer, the Golden Age Reborn. *Hoch!*" He stood and raised his glass. "The Golden Age!" His associates, including von Kratzstein, supported by his men, rose and drank.

McIver whispered across to Gurney, "I don't know how he gets it down him, Sir. Must have a head like a rock."

Gurney smiled and flexed his bruised fingers. "Yes. Look at that eye, too. A right shiner he'll have. Interesting bunch, this."

Their hosts reseated themselves, wiping their lips and recharging glasses. Ziehendorf was conferring with Kratzstein in an undertone. The General scowled, then inclined his head. He faced across to Gurney, and bellowed. "So, Englander! That was a neat trick you showed me there. I shan't forget that in a hurry. The throw, I mean." His empty gums bared. "By God, we are in need of excitement. Six months we have been in Marseilles trying for a ship to Greece, but these degenerate Latin pigs will not let us embark." A chorus of growls from the Kolonels. "But we shall show them, and then the sodomite Ottoman will cringe in his harem before our steel." Another toast. "Tell me, Kapitan, what brings you to Marseilles?"

Gurney was wondering how to change the subject—these Prussian lunatics appealed to him not at all, and he had no intention of revealing to them their shared destination—when Mottin broke in.

"*Le Capitaine, mon Général et mes Colonels,* is on the same errand as yourselves: to liberate the Greeks from their shackles." The little man had been silent for some time, and the words poured out like water from a burst dam. " 'E 'as come through appalling tribulations in his fast ship to prowl in vengeance, a wolf among the Turk Jackals. *Ma parole* but I would go with you in a flash if I did not have my wife, seven children, and my shipyard. It makes to run hot the blood to see such a force of dedication. I am sure this is the same force that threw the accursed Bonaparte from the soil of Europe, and it makes me, Gaston Mottin, shipwright of Marseilles, the Jewel of the Midi, proud, yes proud, to be here eating the bouillabaisse, drinking the good wine of the south with men of such mettle. Ouf!" His last word emerged as a strangled yelp, the consequence of McIver's nailed seaboot taking him smartly six inches below the left knee.

Gurney kept his face impassive, but he was furious. Von Kratzstein was regarding him with gluey Teutonic affection.

"So. You will please give passage to Greece to me and my men?"

"I am afraid that is not possible," said Gurney. "The port authorities, I am told, are less than friendly towards ships offering passage to those with errands such as yours."

Von Kratzstein snorted. "But you are on the same errand—"

"No. Not exactly. But I am sorry. There is nothing further to discuss. My ship has a full complement; we have a mission to fulfil and no room for passengers." And particularly this brawling comic-opera rabble, he thought.

The Prussian's face darkened. "Passengers? Pah! Fellows in the struggle for a Free Greece, and you call us passengers?"

"The situation is beyond my control. My regrets."

Von Kratzstein slumped back in his chair. "Very well, then. If that is your final word, I must bow to your judgement." The look he gave to Gurney said he was by no means as sure of the correctness of his judgement as his speech implied.

Gurney rose. "Well, gentlemen, I wish you luck. I am sorry not to be able to oblige you. We must away." And with that he, McIver and Mottin left the tavern.

After they had left, von Kratzstein summoned the landlord to their table; when the man returned to his kitchen he carried a purse that clinked. Ten minutes later a ragged street-Arab slipped out into the crowds that thronged the Canebière and disappeared in the direction of the port.

"Impossible! You are bloody impossible! Explain yourself." The enormous Russian with his head bowed under the deckhead of *Vandal's* after-cabin winced. Every time the ship rolled, his shoulders struck a beam, and every time his shoulders struck, a jagged splinter of pain lanced through his temples.

"Well? What do you say?" Gurney, palms flat on the chart table, was having trouble maintaining his semblance of righteous wrath. Volnikov, his carpenter, suffering from what looked like a truly fearsome hangover, did not trust himself to speak. The remorse was too strong. He stood mute, miserable. "Oh, Volnikov. What can I do with you! Look here, I don't mind if you get beastly drunk, but I do draw the line at your going for Mr. McIver with a chisel when the *maquereaux* bring you back aboard. You're going to have to keep your tools to yourself if you're to stay on this ship."

A new agony came into the carpenter's eyes. "No. You vouldn't please, Captain, don't send me ashore. No more booze, I give up."

"You've given up before."

"Yes, but this time I dint know. In this house a voman gif me yellow drink, Absan."

"Absinthe. God almighty, man, how have you stayed alive till now? Next thing someone will give you a tumbler of aqua regia and then where will you be?" Probably passing his glass up for another noggin, thought Gurney with some gloom. Volnikov had the constitution of an ox. No, a rhinoceros.

"Well, this time I'll be easy on you. Two weeks' pay, and I'll tell Lady Arabella about you in my next letter."

Volnikov grinned. "Aye, aye, Captain Gurney. You sen' her my respects too, though." Arabella had pressed Volnikov into service for the refurbishing of the High House, and with her customary blend of guile and genius had persuaded those barrel-like fists to carve designs in walnut that would have been the envy of a Grinling Gibbons. Ever since, he had been devoted to her. Damn the man. You'd have to go a long way to find a carpenter like him. Gurney would no more put him ashore than cut off the fingers of his left hand. And he was left-handed.

"All right. Get out, and don't let me see your face for a couple of days." The Russian, bear-like, turned and lumbered up the companionway. Gurney went back to the charts he was studying of the Aegean. The Isles of Greece, forsooth! Where burning Sappho loved and sung. Sunk, more like. A romantic spot for a tour in some rich dilettante's pretty yacht, to be sure; but for a ship which would have to sail, and sail hard, day and night, it was a different story. A tangle of unlit rocks, distinguished only by a few day marks, when you could see them, which was rarely enough, particularly in the spring. The only predictable thing about the weather was that there would be a lot of it, and you wouldn't see it coming. In addition, the indigenous population of those paradisiacal islets was more likely than not to slit your throat without the formality of an introduction. Or so he had heard from men who knew the waters; his own experience was limited to a trans-Aegean cruise during which he had lain unconscious in the hold of a Turkish despot's slaver, and he doubted whether that would serve him any too well. Still, he had good charts, and his experience against the American privateers in the West Indies had taught him to visualise difficult waters better than most. He had five days of study before his landfall at Cape Matapan. What he needed now was some air.

As his head came out of the companionway, shouting broke out forward. In the general run of things *Vandal* was a quiet and orderly ship, run with easy but precise discipline, and fo'c'sle fights were rare. Gurney walked forward, casting a critical eye upwards as he went. McIver had her well trimmed to the brisk sou'wester blowing over her starboard rail. The shouting started again with renewed intensity, and Gurney quickened his pace.

Immediately aft of the fo'c'sle companionway was the fore-hatch. The cover was off, and it was from here that the noise was coming. Gurney stood at its edge and looked down. A seaman glanced up as his shadow fell on the deck below.

"What's this all about, Pringle?"

"Stowaways, Sir."

"I see. My compliments to Mr. McIver—I believe I heard his voice—and would he see me?"

"Mr. McIver's laid out, Sir. Stowaway smacked him one with a keg, Sir." Pringle's tone was lacking in regret, Gurney felt. McIver was not averse to backing his sharp tongue with a rope's end when the need arose, and Pringle was not the most hard-working man on the ship.

"I see. Stand clear below." He dropped through the hatch to the gun-deck and looked about him.

In the fore bulkhead were the stores lockers. One of the locker doors now stood open, and McIver lay on the deck before it, a red trickle of blood seeping across the snowy planking by his head. The cluster of men at the door fell silent at Gurney's approach.

"Where are they?" Even as he said it he knew it was a stupid question. The sight of McIver on the deck was having an unsettling effect on his temper, and he fought for control. At least the bo'sun was breathing. "How many?"

"Couldn't rightly say, Sir." Henry Priest. Good man, Henry. "More'n two, that's for sure. Been talking foreign in there. Jarman, sounds like. Can't get in, though." He gestured to the deck. "Playing hell with the stores in there. Bust Black Jimmy's arm, too." Black Jimmy grinned and held up his right arm, which had developed an extra elbow nine inches from the hairy wrist.

"Very well. Get that seen to, Jimmy." He cupped his hands round his mouth. "You in there. This is the Captain. If you are not out of there by the count of ten I'll smoke you out and shoot you down like dogs as you come. Pistols all round, Henry. Now, one!"

On the count of four a figure stumbled out, followed by three others, and stood blinking on the deck. Gurney's jaw dropped. The canary-coloured uniforms were filthy, the beards had sprouted, and someone—more than one person by the quantity—had been sick. Very sick indeed. But there was no doubt about it.

"The Heidelberg Grand Army!"

Von Kratzstein clicked his heels and drew himself to his full height, bringing his head into violent contact with the deckhead.

"And what the bloody hell do you mean by coming aboard my ship when I specifically refused you a passage? Not to mention laying out my bo'sun and smashing up a good man?" Gurney was seething. "Give me one good reason—just one—why I shouldn't heave you overboard."

"Herr Kapitan." Von Kratzstein's head was obviously still paining him, and he looked at Gurney with watery eyes. "It is for Greece that we have done this. You as a gentleman and a scholar must appreciate—"

"I appreciate nothing, you arrogant buffoon. How did you get on my ship?"

"Ve had you followed from the tavern and discovered your whereabouts. The night you sailed, during a commotion caused by a drunken Slav peasant, we climbed up the side and hid in there. Now, could I trouble you for a drink of water? I have been very ill."

"All in good time. I must decide what to do with you." He fell silent for a moment. "You have put two good men out of commission. The four of you, if you apply yourselves diligently, should in time become a reasonable substitute for one of them. McIver has a hard head. Yes, get yourself cleaned up," he wrinkled his nose, "and report to Henry Priest here. He will find you some employment." He turned to Henry. "There is some oakum to be picked for spare caulking. Also, the men's heads stand in need of a thorough cleaning; I can smell them from my cabin. And the ship's laundry. Keep 'em busy and when we decide they've worked their passage, we'll put 'em ashore. Clear?"

"Aye, aye, Captain Gurney."

Von Kratzstein was yammering, his English breaking down under strong emotional pressure. "Kapitan. Zis iss not gut. My honour will not permit me—"

"You may find it surprising how honour takes second place to necessity, Herr General. Should you still consider yourself wronged at the end of your, ah, engagement, you shall have what satisfaction you require. Now, *auf Wiedersehen*, Herr General, Herren Kolonels."

Four pairs of heels clicked and four landsmen's heads cracked painfully against the deckhead. Gurney managed to hold his laughter back until he got on deck; but then he doubled up and stood, roaring helplessly at the white water creaming at *Vandal's* lee rail.

3

It was at six bells in the morning watch of the fifth day that *Vandal*'s lookout raised Cape Matapan broad on the larboard bow. That southernmost Cape of the Mani, middle finger of the Peloponnese and a tombstone for countless ships, today lay calm and serene under a clear sky. The wind raised only the lightest of ripples on a sea of deepest indigo as *Vandal* eased sheets and turned north, parallel with the rocky steeps of the western shore of the Gulf of Lakonia. Evening was heightening the richness of sea and sky when *Vandal* picked her way towards a horseshoe cove in the tall cliffs of bone-grey limestone.

Gurney had the chart spread over the after-cabin skylight. McIver was at the wheel, ghosting the schooner in between the reefs as his Captain called out the marks ashore, lining rocky peaks with other rocky peaks, reefs with notches in the ragged mountain ramparts inland. He was sweating. Even with two leadsmen forward, making alternate casts and calling back the depths once every thirty seconds, it was horribly tricky work, nosing blindly into the tangled mass of reefs which lay beneath the innocent surface of the smiling sea. And life was not made any easier by the fact that Gurney had to map the depths cried by the leadsmen;. he had an uneasy feeling that he might have to get out of here, one day, with a lot more haste than he was entering now.

As the ship came closer to the shore, Gurney levelled his glass at the cove. At its northern extremity, protected by the headland, lay a little crescent of shingle; its southern and western sides were a sheer curtain of grey rock falling perhaps two hundred feet vertically into the limpid blue, diagonally split by a great shadowed crack. No sign of life. Appearances could be deceptive, however; Gurney had considerable respect for anyone who could hold captive his old friend Basreddin, who, besides the formidable repertoire of illusionist's tricks that went with his calling as an itinerant dervish, was as bonny a fighter as you'd find in a long day's walk. If such people wished to remain invisible, then invisible they would bloody well remain. He called down the deck. "My compliments to Mr. O'Shea, and he is to proceed. Wads only, no shot."

Two guns of *Vandal's* larboard broadside boomed; after a thirty-second interval, another. For a moment the billowing white smoke obscured the shore; then it cleared, and the beach was alive with running figures, and a longboat was pulling out of the cove. McIver, at Gurney's elbow, grunted.

"Look at that. Not two oars in the water at the same time. Useless bunch of wogs."

Gurney grinned. True blue McIver. "Don't judge them too harshly, now. They may look a slovenly mob, but I've no doubt they know what they're doing. Away now, and let's have the best bower out. And just in case, we'll have springs on it. I can't see anything to shoot at just now, but you never know."

The longboat came alongside with a neatness that belied its crew's inelegant oarsmanship, and two men ran up the Jacob's ladder into *Vandal's* waist. Many of the schooner's crew had suddenly found an excuse to be on deck, and not surprisingly; the visitors were unlike anything that even Gurney had seen before.

One was very short, and apparently in poor physical condition, panting by the entry port; the other was six inches taller than Gurney, haggard of face, and composed, it seemed, of the bare minimum of skin and bone. Both were dressed in the uniform of the Klephts—curly-toed shoes, silver knee-guards, full knee-length pleated skirts of white linen, and black velvet waistcoats closely sewn with rows of silver buttons, the whole topped off with a tasselled cap of black velvet. Someone in the foremast shrouds whistled, and the small man's hand leaped to one of the six pistols at his belt. Gurney frowned, hissed "get that man's name" to McIver, and walked forward to greet his guests.

The small man seemed to be the spokesman. "Welcome, Captain," he said in near perfect English, his teeth showing beneath heavy black mustachios. "You are somewhat late, but we are nonetheless happy to see you. Permit me to introduce myself. I am Pausanias Metaxas, and this"—he waved upwards, in the general direction of his companion's chin—"is Diplas."

Gurney bowed, somewhere between amusement and astonishment. "Honoured to make your acquaintance, Sirs. I am George le Fanu Gurney; of my errand I believe you already know."

Metaxas nodded. "Yes, indeed. There is one ashore to whom your arrival means much." He shrugged. "Myself, I don't know how saving one infidel Turk will help us drive the rest of the cursed brood from our shores. But you Franks, in your wisdom, doubtless have the answer." In the small black eyes there lurked a little demon of irony. "Now, to business. The infidel dog says he would have speech with you, so you had better come ashore."

Gurney decided that he would as soon put his head into a running noose as trust this pudgy little man. "Very well. But forgive me if I ask you for a guarantee of safe conduct. I would not like to become hostage myself, and I am sure you know that I would fetch a goodly ransom."

Metaxas found this extremely amusing. He bent double, puffing and wheezing like a small stream-engine in the extremity of his mirth. But when he straightened up, though his sides still heaved his little eyes were chips of obsidian. "You jest, Captain! No? Well then, what do you suggest?"

"It seems reasonable that since you will have me hostage, someone should be left behind here as an earnest of your good intentions. Mr. Diplas and your boat's crew, for instance."

"Certainly! With all my heart! Though I assure you that the precaution is entirely unnecessary. Diplas will stay, will you not, Diplas?" Diplas opened his mouth and gargled. "Ah, I forget to tell you. Diplas had the misfortune to fall in with the Turk, and feeling timid and not wishing to talk, he . . . took measures. Open wide, Diplas!" The lanky Klepht opened his mouth and bent towards Gurney, lips pulled back from stained horse's teeth. There was no tongue, merely a scarred stump wagging obscenely between the molars. "With his own teeth."

Gurney felt sick, but he kept his face composed. "Fascinating. He must have been hungry indeed. Now, if you will call your men aboard, shall we go?"

Metaxas nodded. "With the greatest of pleasure. But before we come to know each other better, I would like to show you some points of local interest. In case you have . . . ideas." He waved towards the rocky cairn which crowned the headland to the north. Smoke bloomed from a pile of rocks, followed by an explosion; a tree of water grew from the sea twenty feet ahead of *Vandal*'s bowsprit and collapsed in on itself. "Twenty-four pounders. Ten of them. So good behaviours, yes?"

"Even if my intentions were aggressive—and I can assure you they are not—I would, it seems, have no option. Now, your men."

Defiance was written large on the swarthy faces of the oarsmen as they came over *Vandal*'s side, and Metaxas spoke sharply to them in Greek. They were a weird-looking rabble, the splendour of their uniforms being matched only by their filthiness. While Gurney would not for one moment have held *Vandal's* crew up as models of politeness or decorum—indeed, they had been chosen for precisely the opposite qualities —models of politeness and decorum they were in comparison with the Klephts. But curiously enough, when one of them spat juicily on the planking between McIver's feet and the mate leaped forward to dispense summary discipline, it was not Gurney who intervened. From the neighbourhood of the fo'c'sle hatch a brilliantly dressed figure rushed aft and grabbed the Scotsman by the arm.

"Not zo vill you treat the Freedom Fighters of Hellas! Leaf alone!"

McIver whirled on him, fist upraised. "Prussian scum!" he roared. "Who d'ye think you are?"

"Stop!" Gurney's voice was sharp. "Let him go, McIver. General von Kratzstein, control yourself. Get a bucket of water and sluice that filth off the deck."

"Herr Kapitan! I demand to be ashore put with my men. Here."

"That will depend on Mr. Metaxas' views when we return. In the meantime you are part of my ship's company, and I'll thank you to speak when spoken to. Mr. Metaxas, if you are ready, we shall go ashore."

McIver stood shaking his head, as if to say that matters had come to a pretty pass when heathen Greeks could hawk all over his clean decks without let or hindrance, while von Kratzstein hauled a bucket of sea water and sluiced the offending stain from the planking. Gurney kept his face stiff and hard as he gave the bo'sun his instructions; in the flurry as a boat's crew was told off from among the watch on deck he managed to get a few words with him out of earshot of the Greeks.

"Listen. I don't much like this, but if there's any hint of trouble you get the hostages on deck as a shield, make sail and get the hell out of here. Don't wait around. Understand?"

McIver didn't like it, that was plain to see. "Lord, Captain, I thought these men were our allies. Bloody rabble."

"That's as may be. Now for God's sake keep your opinions to yourself and your eyes peeled. If we're not back by two hours after dawn tomorrow, get ready for trouble. Clear?"

"Clear."

As eight stalwart Norfolkmen pulled the longboat towards the beach, Gurney and Metaxas fell into an edgy silence. It was plain that the Greek was not pleased at leaving hostages on *Vandal*, though he tried to cover his uneasiness. Gurney searched the beach and the rocks ahead of him with a wary eye. As they drew closer, he saw that the rock-face was pitted with holes, some of them large enough for a man to stand up in. What had appeared to be a crack in the grey stone of the cliff-face could now be seen to be a huge sheet of rock, like a flat of scenery, which blocked the mouth of a cathedral-tall cave from inquisitive eyes at sea.

"Yes," said Metaxas. "With the aid of a little gun-powder, we enlarged what was already there. The Mani is famous, you know, for possessing the entrance to Hades; that is, so to speak, the servants' entrance, the main portal being round the Cape."

"Well, well," said Gurney. "How interesting."

Metaxas bared his teeth in his transparently false smile.

Gurney found the man puzzling. He had heard much about the hospitality and straightforwardness of the noble bandits of the Greek mountains, and Metaxas jibed with what he had heard in terms of neither manners nor appearance.

The longboat nosed in alongside a quay that appeared to have been hacked out of the solid lime-stone, and its two passengers climbed ashore. Metaxas pointed to a flight of steps which disappeared up-wards into the gloom of Hell's Gate. "Here. Follow me, and watch your step. The exhalations of the land of shadows make the stone treacherous."

They began to climb. After about a hundred steps Metaxas called—panted, rather—a halt, and collapsed onto a damp stair to catch his breath. Gurney went to the outside of the little landing on which they had paused and looked down. A glimmer of light from the mouth of the cave reflected on a long pool of water, a perfect natural dock basin. Below in the dock lay two ships, and on their decks Gurney caught the gleam of cannon. Truly an excellent base against the Turk, an impeccable deepwater anchorage, and a raiding party moving inland would have either to scale the cliffs—difficult, if they were not flies—or come up this bottleneck flight of stairs.

Metaxas began to climb again. After five minutes the path branched out into a tunnel of its own, which debouched halfway down a hillside of broken grey stones, among which a few tufts of grass and delicate star-like flowers struggled for a rooting. From the tunnel mouth a path, little more than a goat track, wound through the boulders towards a hilltop formation of huge rectangular rocks set on end, which, to Gurney, looked almost man-made. It was towards this formation that his guide was pointing.

"Behold. The towers of the Kapetanos Nicholas Mavromichaelis." Gurney looked harded. Sure enough, scarring the soaring flat planes of the sides of the towers were black embrasures. As they drew closer, other paths converged with the one on which they were walking, swelling it until it was a river of stones and trodden dust disappearing into the dense shadow between the feet of those weird limestone obelisks. At the door of the highest they came to a halt. As Metaxas hammered on the iron-bound wood, Gurney noticed with a shock that the pillars supporting the huge lintel were of delicately-fluted marble, pillaged no doubt from some classical ruin. So this was Greece; not, as he had been led to expect by Euthymia Henry

and her ilk, a sort of mountainous croquet lawn
covered with pure white columns, but a pile of tor-
tured, ravine-split mountains, set with bizarre forti-
fications, populated by murderous brigands. In that at
least Morpurgo had been right.

The door swung open, and Metaxas stood aside,
motioning him in. The portly brigand's face had been
losing its self-important smirk with every foot above
sea level, and here, at the highest point yet, there was
a cringing in his mien very different from the bombastic assurance with which he had boarded *Vandal*.
They walked through store-rooms filled with boxes,
bales and casks to a flight of stairs which disappeared, much after the manner of a Norfolk windmill,
Gurney thought, through a hole cut in the rough plank
ceiling. Gurney ran up, found himself in what was
obviously the kitchen, a room thick with smells and
noise as perhaps five buxom women bustled round
the charcoal stoves, weaving their way in and out of
clusters—mobs, rather—of angel-faced children who
fell suddenly silent as Gurney entered, then, as one,
said something which was obviously a polite greeting.
The cooks also suspended operations, smiled, and
spoke welcomes; then one of the children saw Metaxas
and shouted something which even across the languages was far from polite. The black-shawled old
lady cutting cucumbers at the little table in the corner
batted the impudent one on the ear with a knobby
hand, but the women were hiding smiles now, casting
luminous glances at Gurney from great dark, sympathetic eyes. Beside the charm of this welcome, Metaxas' self-importance seemed churlish indeed. And
it was evident that he was not over-popular in the
Mavromichaelis household. When Gurney turned to
him, he waved a fat hand in deprecation. "Only wom-
ens and childrenses. Come." The man was put out, his
pride punctured, his English showed the strain.
"Come, come." He went to the next flight of stairs,
missed his footing in his anger, and would have fallen

had not Gurney taken him by the elbow and steadied him. A titter ran round the room, and Gurney hid a smile. Poor Metaxas.

The fat man's next attempt at the stairs meeting with more success, they passed up through the next floor, where perhaps a dozen long-haired, mustachioed Klephts stared blankly at Metaxas and murmured their salutations to Gurney as they lounged, pistols and curved steel yataghans at hand, round the cannon which crouched against the embrasures in the walls. Again, Gurney had the feeling that it was Metaxas, not himself, who was the stranger here; and that Metaxas felt the same was evident from the fine beads of perspiration beginning to stand out on his sallow brow. He passed hurriedly to the next flight of stairs, dragging Gurney after him; as he mounted the steps his pace slowed, and when he turned to shush a question Gurney started to ask, his expression was that of a priest taking a favoured initiate to visit an entire timber of the True Cross. Gurney found himself straightening his cravat and wishing he had had the forethought to bring a pair of gloves.

The first thing that struck him as he arrived in this third storey apartment was its size. Through the blue wreaths of tobacco smoke the ceiling was half as high again as that of the room below, the beams carved, painted and gilded with a crude half-Byzantine, half-Arab splendour. The walls were hung with thick rugs, silk by their sheen, and trophies of long muskets and beautifully worked and damascened yataghans.

Lounging on a divan under the window at the west end of the room were two men. The evening sun, now casting its rays almost horizontally across the earth, took Gurney in the eyes and he looked away, dazed. Metaxas was talking, a thin edge of fear in his voice.

"Eentroduce Kapetan Gurney, here, Kapetanos Nicholas Mavromichaelis, there. All together now." He spoke a short sentence in Greek. One of the figures under the window groaned as if in pain, but Gurney

paid no attention. As his eyes became accustomed to
the light they fixed as if riveted on the other man. For
beneath the soft black velvet hat, above the embroidered jacket and the blue silk breeches tucked
into gold-worked gaiters, was a familiar, eagle's face,
matted with beard and eyebrows, from whose thickets
glittered two cool, sardonic eyes. Basreddin! Gurney
made as if to rush forward in greeting; but a dark lid
fell over one of those cunning eyes and a very faint
shake of the head stopped him in his tracks.

Metaxas was looking at the second man, the groan-
er, a glutinous false pity welling up to cover his slimy
face, making small crooning noises in Greek. When the
recumbent one spoke, his voice was a little less accommodating than the snarl of a dog; but Gurney had a
feeling that the hostility was directed more at the
fawning Metaxas than himself. The fat man seemed
to agree; his master's question put him in such a state
that he could barely translate.

"The Kapetanos ask, 'Are you English come for
rescue Mussulman spy?'"

"Tell him I am."

More Greek. "Kapetanos say this is Mussulman spy.
He wonder why you want him. Is only Turk."

Gurney grinned inwardly. "Mere Turk that he is,
and admittedly worth only a very small ransom, it is
possible that he has some insignificant bagatelle of information that might be of passing interest."

"Kapetanos say this man valuable, very. Good doctor." And the Kapetanos would appear to need a
doctor. His left leg was in bandages below the silk
pantaloons, his face pale, and every now and then as
he changed position he gritted his teeth and rolled his
eyes above the eight-inch mustachios that split his
face in two.

Gurney made a gesture signifying, he hoped, his
entire indifference to Basreddin's continuing captivity,
freedom, life or death. "Before I can make you an
offer for his freedom, I must have speech with him,

to know what he is worth to His Majesty's Government."

Mavromichaelis nodded, then stopped as if struck by a sudden doubt and rapped out a stream of Romaic. Metaxas looked puzzled.

"Kapetan say how does he know you are from English, not Turks? He say you tell him who win last year Dar Bi."

"What?"

"Race for horse. Dar Bi."

Gurney laughed, then felt profoundly uncomfortable. The Klephtic captain was eyeing him from between slitted lids, and he suddenly realised that he had no idea what horse had been first past the post in the classic. Arabella would have known, damn it, and Paddy could have told him—wait! Paddy! That day last year when Paddy had arrived with a new coach-and-four, thanks to his winnings on—"Mr. Udney's Emilius."

The severe lines of the Kapetanos' face fractured into a broad grin, showing an unlikely number of very white teeth. He tried to leap to his feet, arms outstretched, then fell back on his divan, groaning and cursing the pain in his leg. He spat a series of instructions at Metaxas, who bowed repeatedly and backed down the stairs. They sat in beaming silence, Gurney trying to maintain the pretence that he had never seen Basreddin before in his life, until Metaxas and two servants bearing trays came rattling and puffing through the door. Over spoonfuls of rose-leaf jam, thimbles of thick black coffee and sips of icy spring water they struck up a stilted conversation, which consisted in the main of Mavromichaelis reciting the names of every Derby winner since the dawn of Man and Gurney nodding frantically and trying to remember appropriate lines from the Homer of his childhood. Eventually, he found he could communicate in a sort of *lingua franca* composed of classical Greek, Italian and snippets of Arabic.

If the wounded Klepht was somewhat mystified, his bottomless reserves of courtesy prevented him from showing it; and this rather stilted form of small talk continued until the sweating Metaxas waddled back into the room.

As the servants brought the four-foot cherry-wood pipes known as chibouks and helped light them with chips of charcoal, the conversation turned to the conduct of the war against the Turks.

Mavromichaelis seemed concerned not so much with the Turks as with rival Klephts; Gurney got the impression that the war was more a pretext for jockeying for position among various petty tyrants than a fight for freedom. Perhaps Morpurgo had been right. And Mavromichaelis was in a bad humour.

"Damn this leg," he said. "Had it not been smashed by a bullet, I should even now be collecting gold and Turks for my men. But as it is they are leaderless, and they begin to yap and snarl at each other like hounds too long in the kennel."

"How did you come by it?"

"A lucky shot from a Turk in the mountains. At least, they say it was a Turk." He glared at Metaxas. "I am surrounded by traitors, I think. The only one who has my interests at heart is this Mussulman quack who binds up my wounds." Mavromichaelis rambled away again into his tales of strife between brigand and brigand.

Gurney found it difficult to concentrate, anxious as he was to speak with Basreddin. Eventually it was Basreddin who leaned over and whispered in the Kapetanos' ear. The Kapetanos scowled and said something.

Metaxas looked horrified. "The presumptuous pagan orders the Kapetanos to take his rest for cause of the wound. The Kapetanos begs your forgiveness and asks that you will join him later in conviviality. Meanwhile, he says, perhaps you should interview the spy." He assisted Mavromichaelis to his one good foot. The

Kapetanos draped an arm over his shoulder, and the two of them, the fat interpreter and the lanky, six-foot Klepht, staggered to the stairs leading up to the next storey of the tower.

Gurney and Basreddin were on their feet, hands clasped, laughing like maniacs. Basreddin's face was alight, his devious eyes now expressing an emotion that was curiously like relief. "George! At last! Well, it is truly good to see you."

"The feeling is mutual." Gurney stepped back. "The complete brigand, to be sure! Your gift for blending with the scenery is quite uncanny."

"After what your loyal villagers did to me in Norfolk, it is barely surprising. Allah knows it was cold enough in that blighted country even without those peasants persecuting me as a wizard and locking up their children each time I stepped out."

"Yes. Still, one can see their point. It was Ramadan that did it, you know. Sleeping all day, then carousing all night in the Dun Cow! And smoking hashish in the taproom! They talk of you still."

"As they should. It is not for the sake of anonymity that one performs the Indian Rope Trick at your village Harvest Home. Truly, the rose in the garden of oaks profits little if it hides its perfume. But enough of this, old friend, it is good that you have come. Even I, Haji Basreddin, was feeling like a caged linnet that watches a cat all day."

"A life for a life. If it wasn't for you I should be dead, or a bound slave in Dyarbakir; as always I am at your disposal."

Basreddin bowed deeply. "All debts are paid as Allah wills, friend. Now, I must tell you how I came to be here, for there is little time to waste."

As Basreddin's face darkened under its accustomed mask of gravity, Gurney realised that there were hollows and lines under the thick beard where there had been none before. "Very well," he said. "I am all ears."

"Know first," Basreddin began, "that I have been in

the hands of these wild men three months now. In-
cautiously, I wandered into a storm in the mountains,
not itself a thing of great consequence, but as I slept
in a cave of snow a band of them came upon me. In-
sufficiently vigilant was I, and when I awoke I
was bound and brought hither. Truly is it said that in
the summer, the jackal fears the lion; but in the winter the jackal may prevail." Same old oracular Basreddin, thought Gurney, but he hid his impatience;
well he knew the Sufi's pace now, like that of a great
river marching slow but relentless to the sea. "When
they found I was one of the Faith they would have
killed me straightaway—superstitious men they are,
and much bruised by the heel of the Ottoman—but I,
ah, persuaded them otherwise. For they are but crudely versed in the healing arts, and many of them were
sick. I did what I could, and Allah willed it that he
whom you met, the Mavromichaelis, came to hold me
in friendship. He is a wise enough man, for a brigand.
But even that might not have sufficed, for his warriors are the sons of moonstruck hyaenas, and when
crazed with blood, love to kill, and kill very slowly.
I therefore made it clear to them that I had certain
knowledge which, in the right quarter, would be worth
great treasure; for if there is a thing they love more
than blood of True Believers it is English gold. And
they took a message to a certain Englishman of whom
I know, a lover of the Ancients, and he took that message on. It is a goodly time now that I have been the
eyes and ears of His Majesty, here and elsewhere."

Gurney nodded, his thoughts for a moment far
away. So that was why those horsemen—coaches,
sometimes—would pull up in the dead of night at the
isolated flint cottage near Morehouse which he had
lent Basreddin. And why once, when Jervy Hutchinson
was visiting the High House and Basreddin had come
up to discuss the acquisition of a new stallion, the
two of them, the gouty Admiral and the dark-robed
Dervish, had withdrawn into a corner and spent the

better part of a day in hushed conversation. "Yes," he said. "Now I see. Deep as ever, Haji. So when you protested that the east wind was too much for your warm bones and left for a, ah, salubrious peregrination, it was not entirely for your health's sake?"

"Indeed not. Though your English Levanter would freeze Hell itself. Tell me, are you all well! The Lady Arabella? Are the icy halls of the High House ringing yet with the laughter of sons? But I forget. This question English does not ask to English. And English Basreddin is, in the service of His Majesty, may Allah shower blessings upon him and may his shadow never grow less."

"Little chance of that. His appetite, for women as well as victuals, seemed undiminished when last I met him. Tell me now, though, what is this treasure of which you speak? I was led to believe that what concerns their Lordships of the Admiralty is more a few scraps of paper." Gurney eyed Basreddin narrowly. The Sufi's ability to weave a tiny thread of truth into an enticing tapestry of myth had, before now, earned him an excellent living as an itinerant tale-teller; God knew what wool he had pulled over the eyes of these ferocious but unwary Klephts.

"Wait a little, and all will become clear. As I was saying. In order to preserve my life at the hands of these brigands, I spoke—in a roundabout manner, to be sure—of the loan that has been raised in the medinas of London. Simple souls that they are, they somehow got the impression that on your ship would be the first portion of this hoard—one hundred thousand gold pieces, to be precise. One hundredth of this, they came to believe, Allah only knows how, His Majesty will give them in ransom for his loyal servant, the Haji Basreddin. Wait!"

Gurney was on his feet. "What? All I have on *Vandal* is two hundred guineas and a lot of rotting salt horse! And here we sit while my ship lies under the guns of a pack of bandits who think she's a floating

Mint? Hell's teeth, man, what are you thinking of?"

"Calm yourself." Basreddin's eyes were deep and luminous. Gurney knew he was being hypnotised, and had seen others fall under the spell of those glowing orbs; but he fell silent despite himself. "Do not be concerned. My captors are under the impression that the gold is stowed with such cunning that the ship must be riven asunder to get it; and they will not rend her asunder where she now lies. The water is deep. And besides, the English are their allies in the war against the Turk, and Mavromichaelis is too honourable a man to fire on any ally. Though his men would each slit their grandmother's throat for a week-old loaf." He grinned. "No. Hard by an anchorage two days' sailing from here, in shallow water, lies the treasure of Osman Bey. And with that treasure lies the letters you seek. This treasure is worth almost all of the entire loan; one thousand gold pieces beside this hoard is as a lamp beside the Moon."

"And how, if I may venture to inquire, do you know of its whereabouts? And that no one has already taken it?"

The Sufi shook his head. "I watched from the mountains as the jackals of Ioannis Kallikratides massacred the hyaenas of Mordrutsos in the defile by the shore, stole the chest, and met their doom among the rocks. This treasure carries the malediction of Osman Bey, which he uttered as he lay living but dismembered by the citadel of Praxos and Mordrutsos' men laughed and played like children with the coins; it is written that none may covet it and live."

"I see. You wish to incur this malediction yourself?"

The Sufi spread his hands. "In my ponderings, I have realised that there are others who covet the hoard more than I; perhaps the curse will fall on them. But no matter. A man who is falling from a high branch may clutch for support even at a serpent."

Gurney grunted. Personally, he had little belief in maledictions, having survived a goodly number himself. There, were, however, some practical considerations that the Sufi seemed to have overlooked.

"How exactly am I meant to recover this treasure under the noses of the escort which the good Mavromichaelis will undoubtedly send?"

"Allah will undoubtedly send inspiration. Meanwhile, I propose that you establish some pretext for proceeding to the harbour where the treasure lies; I shall persuade the Kapetanos to allow me to join you, to care for those five men of your crew who are at present afflicted with the trembling fever."

"What five men?" Gurney was puzzled.

"You will remember them, and soon; for those, I believe, are the footsteps of the Kapetanos and his interpreter on the stairs. One thing. Do not trust the interpreter."

Mavromichaelis hobbled down the stairs and sank, groaning, onto the divan, fixing Gurney with his hawk's gaze. Gurney smiled, trying to display a breezy confidence he did not feel. "The Haji Basreddin seems to be well-enough informed," he said. "The ransom you demand is high, though. Very high. Still, if you insist"—Metaxas, providing a running translation for the Klepht, signified that he did, and strongly—"then I must, with certain conditions, agree." He studied the high-boned face for signs of gullibility, and saw none.

"Conditions," said Metaxas, "will be discussed in the morning. Now it is time for wine. The Kapetanos is happy that you are here, though he is less happy about conditions. Conditions, he says, are for later. Now you will make celebration with him."

As the first bottles of wine arrived, followed by trays of food and more wine, Gurney felt himself become more and more favorably disposed towards the Klephtic Kapetanos. Soon the room, filled with good fellowship and the fumes of retsina and tobacco, was spinning gently round his head, and he felt himself among friends. Metaxas drank little and sat apart, his eyes darting from one man to another like little black marbles, while the windows darkened and night, pricked with little golden stabs of lamplight, fell across the jagged mountains of the Mani.

Somewhere a bell was tolling. Gurney opened his eyes and closed them again hurriedly; it was still dark, and he had slept too little. He had a pounding headache. He pulled the sheepskins over his head and waited for the bell to stop. But it rang on, and the extra sense that had warned him before of approaching danger was nudging him. He rolled from under the skins and shrugged into his coat, struck flint and steel and checked the priming of the Manton pistols he carried in its pockets. His bedchamber was on the fifth storey of the tower of Mavromichaelis, directly beneath the roof.

From below came the sound of shouting. Buckling on his sword and snatching up the lantern, he ran for the stairs and cannoned into Metaxas as the interpreter came through the trapdoor in the floor. They crashed down the stairs to the storey below; Gurney landed on top of Metaxas and picked himself up. Metaxas, winded, was gasping incoherently. "Ixos! The Turk has ravaged Ixos and stays in the harbour! We sail now, to save whom we can! Kapetanos say, you bring your ship, help fight!"

Ixos. A little island in the Cyclades, Gurney recalled from the study of his charts. But to fight with these brigands against the Turk, he, an Englishman, technically if not actually neutral? Dimly, Gurney realised that here was a situation that could be turned to his advantage; but his head hurt and he was half-asleep. He fought for lucidity. If they were willing to risk *Vandal's* supposed treasure in an engagement with the Turk, then they must be desperate for firepower; and if they were desperate, now was a chance to try another ploy. "Tell the Kapetanos that I would be delighted to fight the Turk if I can take the spy Basreddin as my surgeon."

Metaxas was half-mad with impatience. "Yes, yes, I will tell the Kapetanos. With surety, of course. I myself will come with twenty men, to see that no eventualities arise.

Gurney stiffened. "You imply that I could be false to my word?" Bloody right—he would be false to his word.

The little Greek puffed out his cheeks and smiled an oily smile. "Better safe than sorry, my mother, God bless her soul, would tell me, Captain." Metaxas always seemed happiest with the smell of treachery under his nose. "Well?"

"Lead the way, Mr. Metaxas."

The interpreter broke into a run. As they joined the throng of men streaming from the village down the track towards the cove, Gurney found Basreddin at his side and was reassured. The Sufi seemed to sense this. "I have been in that tower too long," he said. "It will be good, should we be fortunate, to spill a little Turkish blood."

Gurney nodded. His head was clearing, and he was not sure he was entirely delighted that this Greek jaunt promised more violent entertainment than a pleasure-cruise in the Aegean. He sighed. Impossible to achieve anything without making a damned circumbendibus about it. At least he would have Basreddin aboard. Possession, after all, was nine points in the law; and if the tenth was a thousand pounds easy to hand, it was no great hardship.

4

By the time Gurney climbed through the entry-port into *Vandal's* waist, the dawn was coming up. In the half-light land and sea were drained of colour; the stars were flickering out, and the pale glow of the eastern horizon foretold fair weather. Gurney made a swift inspection of the ship. McIver had taken his warning of the previous night to heart, as was only right. Hands stood by the capstan and halyards, and the gun-decks were in a state of readiness which must have caused considerable alarm to the mute Klepht Diplas, particularly as the mate had sprung the ship round so her broadside covered the harbour entrance. Gurney sent him to see to the accommodation for the twenty Klephts, bristling with weapons, who formed Basreddin's escort, and then trained his spyglass on the entrance to the cave. As he watched, the bow-sprit of a ship inched from behind the buttress of rock that masked Mavromichaelis' haven from the open sea. The first ship was followed by three others; Gurney guessed that there would be an outhaul line anchored to the rock on the far side of the cove, so that the pirates—privateers, since the establishment of the Greek Republic—could warp out in anything short of a hurricane.

He turned his glass to the cliffs. Some late arrivals among the Klephts, scorning the stairway through the cave, had doubled ropes over boulders at the top of the precipice and were coming down the sheer face in great bounds. As he watched, one figure leaped a full fifteen feet out, released his rope, caught the foretop-sail yard brace of one of the feluccas, and slid to the deck. A faint patter of laughter and applause came across the water, and Gurney grinned. They were a spirited lot, these Greeks, and they mixed their ruth-lessness with a carefree sense of fun which had made a large contribution to the ache that still throbbed be-hind Gurney's eyes. He shouted down the galley com-panionway for coffee. Warming his hands on the mug —the air was chill, and unlike his crew he had not yet breakfasted—he gave his instructions to McIver. *Vandal* came up to her anchor, and her main and foresails inched up the masts as her topsails fell on their clew-lines.

The land breeze struck firm, and the helmsman put the wheel hard down. As she paid off towards the gap in the reef and the rim of the sun crept over the horizon, Gurney passed the word for Metaxas.

The fat man was munching on a piece of flat bread, and there was a flask in his hand. He was sweating despite the chill, and when Gurney caught a whiff of his breath it became apparent that he was making an early start at acquiring a little Dutch courage. A very early start; even with a fair wind, Ixos lay fourteen hours away. Gurney hoped that the interpreter would not be dead to the world by the time he was needed.

As it turned out, the wind stayed fair and the high-prowed Greek ships were faster than they looked, so that the sun was still well up in the sky when Metaxas, reeling a little but still his own man, pointed to something on the starboard bow. "Ixos," he said.

Gurney turned his glass towards the low pall of smoke that hung over the horizon like a mourning plume; but there was nothing to see—no sail, no island; just a sullen drift of tar-black fumes marring the blue Aegean sky. McIver came up and saluted.

"Signal from yon Greek, Sir. Heave to for council of war, accordin' to one of them savages." He jerked a thumb at the knot of fustanellaed Klephts lounging, smoking, in the sun by *Vandal*'s rail.

"Very well then, McIver. Heave to it is."

The mate saluted again—the prospect of battle always seemed to fill him with an exaggerated sense of proprieties—and started to bellow orders. Gurney told one of the ship's boys to acknowledge the signal and went below to *Vandal*'s stern-cabin.

When the Klephtic leaders clattered down the companionway, they found the young Frankish sea captain and the Ottoman spy bent over Metaxas' chart of

Ixos and its approaches, deep in conversation. What they did not realise was that the conversation had nothing to do with the chart; their loud protests at the idiocy of letting a Mussulman in on the plans for an exterminatory counter-attack on his brothers in religion bid fair to turn to violence. Indeed Metaxas, who had remained on deck to welcome his fellow warriors in the cause of freedom (though, Gurney suspected, he was more interested in keeping an eye on McIver and the movements of the gun-crews), went for his yataghan. Basreddin watched the three-foot hook of shining steel at his throat with amused contempt, then looked the interpreter in the eye. The hand holding the sword began to tremble convulsively; then the weapon leaped from his grasp and clattered into a corner. Metaxas staggered back, white and shaking, and the other four Klephtic leaders made the *cornu* with their fingers against the evil eye; but all kept their hands away from the pommels of swords and pistols as if they were red-hot.

Metaxas refreshed himself from his flask and seemed to recover a little of his poise. He moved behind the chart-table, taking upon himself the chairmanship of the meeting. The other Klephts seemed to defer to him—after all, was he not the confidant of Nicholas Mavromichaelis?—and Gurney, though he did not trust the man, saw no option.

"Know first of all," began Metaxas, "that the harbour at Ixos faces south. It is guarded on the west by a battery built by the Venetians in olden times, and on the east by a high cliff which is unscaleable and crowned with a fort of massy stone. The village lies between the two; it is a perilous harbour to enter. However, our messengers tell us that the fort, being impregnable, is occupied still by our brothers of the Islands, and that when he made his escape they were putting up a stout resistance. What I propose, therefore, is that the most heavily-armed of us make a frontal attack on the harbour of Ixos, while the others, joining the Fleet—"

"What Fleet?" Gurney interrupted.

"The loyal ships of the Islands, who have been warned also; we have a system, you know, of messengers and heliographs. But come, now to business." Gurney suppressed the thought that he would believe in this Greek Navy when he saw it and not before, and turned his attention to Metaxas' podgy finger where it stabbed the chart.

"You see here, on the north side of the island, the beach is steep but sandy and the approaches quite easy?" They looked nightmarish to Gurney, and the tiny seed of respect planted by the Greeks' superb shiphandling germinated into something like admiration. "Here we run the ships up the beach and land the men for an attack on the battery and the town from behind. Simple."

"One moment," said Gurney. "Who will make the frontal attack on the harbour?"

"You will." Metaxas' chubby cheeks were crinkling with merriment. "You, my bold Frank, with your big guns and your fast ship, will flatten the Turk and be gone before he knows what happens."

Gurney demurred. "But there is that within the ship which means she should not be exposed to unnecessary peril . . ." The idea of risking his ship and his crew in a well-defended harbour he had never seen before appealed little to him.

"No, my friend. You are the best armed of us, and about that other matter, your valuable ballast, I leave you with these thoughts; not only will the . . . ballast . . . be easy to recover from the harbour of Ixos, which is, after all, a mere forty feet in depth, but I shall also take the spy, Basreddin, with me into one of the other ships; his life will be surety for your cooperation."

Gurney shrugged. It was no more than he had expected. "But how, with one ship, am I to take on a

battery of Turks, who will likely have a furnace for
their shot?"

The smile on Metaxas' face did not waver. "That,
Captain, is your own affair. It is true to say that your
real task is to distract the attention of the Turks, until
we can come up on their rear; we should be, ah, *grateful*"—he cast a meaning glance at Basreddin—"if you
were to do all in your power to achieve this end. Now,
Philodorakis here will chart you a course to the harbour approaches, and then we will leave you." A wiz-
ened old salt with very few teeth and six pistols at his
belt grinned at Gurney, marked a position on the
chart, and pencilled a course, demonstrating in dumb
show the marks and sight-lines. Then Metaxas waved
Basreddin on deck and followed with the other captains. Gurney was uneasily conscious that he was leaving his fate in the hands of one who was at best less
than trustworthy, and as he shook Basreddin by the
hand he knew that the Sufi felt the same. But Basreddin nodded, and made a curious little sign with his
right hand and muttered an Arabic phrase that Gurney understood was a spell of protection. Then he and
his captors went over the side and the longboat pulled
away towards the caiques.

As *Vandal* heeled again to the westerly wind and
started towards the first of her marks, Gurney clattered down the companionway to the gun-deck. Mc-
Iver had knocked the bulkheads out last night, and
now the entire length of the schooner was one dark
gallery, lit only by the shafts of light that streamed in
from the open hatches and scuttles. The bronze of her
twelve guns, ranged blunt-snouted against the blank
covers of their ports, gleamed back in the gloom.
O'Shea was fussing anxiously over a man replacing
part of the tackles that would stop the larboard midships sixty-eight pounder blasting itself through the
other side of the ship with its recoil. Gurney tapped
him on the shoulder and drew him aside.

"Well, O'Shea, it looks like your children will have work to do before they're much older. How is it?"

"Not so bad, Sor, not so bad. Course with this bunch of farm boys there's no telling what might happen had she come to push and shove, but all in all it could be worse."

Gurney grinned, aware as he did so that his face was tight. "Let's hope so. If you haven't managed to din a bit of sense into them by now, God knows you never will."

"Born in the blood, it is, Sor, though it's true to say that the trainin' counts for much. There's an old Navy man for each gun, and I've no doubt that the other ploughboys know how to use a fowling piece."

"Aye, my poor pheasants could tell me a thing or two about that, I'll be bound." Gurney looked hard at O'Shea, and the Irishman looked uneasy. More than once he had come to the Sea Dalling yard with pheasant feathers sticking to his jersey. "But that's by the by. We'll be in a Turk harbour in a couple of hours, and there'll be ships there, and a battery. Frankly, we're sticking our necks out, so I want every shot to count. Any gun captain who fires before his orders is to be logged and will be docked two weeks' pay. As to the sixty-eights; fused shell against the ships, then empty shell cases into the embrasures of the battery. I want splinters and a lot of them." He unrolled his chart and showed the gunner his field of fire. "Anything that moves, give it a whiff of grape. It'll be Turkish, sure enough. Clear?"

The Irishman was holding back his excitement, but only just. "By Gor, Captain Gurney, clear. Aye, aye, Sor. Permission to clear for action, Sor?"

"By all means."

As Gurney climbed back onto the sunlit deck the light hurt his eyes. A good two-and-a-half hours to sunset. As he swept the horizon with his glass, he wondered for a moment how many of his crew would see that sunset. The gun-deck would soon be a roaring shambles, wood-splinters shredding flesh like wet paper, the sand on the deck muddy with blood . . .

During the next hour the hills of Ixos grew high ahead and to port. The western end of the island sloped gently down to a shore of rocky white beaches. To the east, where the harbour lay, outcrops of limestone sprawled at the crests of a series of ridges that ended with a sugar-loaf shaped eminence, its summit crowned with grey walls and a squat block of masonry. The Venetian fort. Smoke was rising from several places on the western end, and with his glass Gurney could see a point of flame that must be a burning barn; but the greater part of the pall lay over the eastern end of the island, borne by the breeze and rising from behind the headland sheltering the harbour and the town. *Vandal*'s escort had disappeared behind the headland which now lay on her larboard quarter, and Gurney anxiously scanned the rest of the sea about him for ships; but he saw none.

A reef which lay about a quarter of a mile offshore came into line with a white daymark on a hillside inland, and Gurney ordered the helmsman to port his helm until he had the fort over the tip of the point that hid the harbour; then he summoned the boarding party. The men stood in the waist. George Jarvis, sixteen years old last birthday, stood beside Henry Priest, nervously fingering the stock of a musket almost as tall as himself. There was a mutter of nervous conversation. Henry made a wisecrack to George, who smiled, not hearing, his eyes fixed on the Captain. At the back of the little crowd stood von Kratzstein and his men, each attempting an appearance of noble defiance and succeeding only in looking as if carved from wood by cuckoo-clock makers.

"Right, you men. We're going into the harbour yonder. You know your places. Topmen, I want to see the blisters on your hands when we come out of this. Anything that moves, kill it. Watch on deck, there'll be no boarding until I pass the word. If something happens

to me, take your orders from Mr. McIver, that goes
without saying. That's all. Except that the odds in
there will be five to one, and if we want to get out we
shall have to cut ourselves out. We will. Good luck!"

The men dispersed to their positions in grim silence,
except for von Kratzstein and his henchmen, who
were arguing fiercely among themselves in guttural
German. Von Kratzstein made a silencing gesture and
stepped forward.

"Herr Kapitan Zur Zee?"

"What is it?"

"My men and I are not sailors. It is therefore not so
good to us to fight in the battles of seamen." He
smacked his sabre. "We are cavalry men, used to the
battling mit horses."

Gurney shook his head wearily, trying to control
his temper. "Herr von Kratzstein, although you were
not invited onto this ship in the first place, you persist
in trying to advise me as to its command. You and
your henchmen will either obey my orders or go below, into the bilge, and keep the magazine company."
The Prussian paled. "Not a desirable alternative, I
perceive. Now. To your stations, and if we find any
horses in the harbour I promise that we will let you
battle with them. Satisfied?"

The duelling scars stood out livid in von Kratzstein's
face, but he stumped forward to the hammock-
padded bulwarks where the sharp-shooters lay ready.

Vandal was close to the point now, on the tack
which would bring her round the headland and into
full sight of the harbour. There was deep water right
up to the rock, but Gurney kept off lest he lose his
wind. The limestone slipped away about a musket-
shot to larboard, and slowly, inch by inch, the village,
a cluster of little white houses straggling up the throat
of a saddle between the fort and a neighbouring hill,
came into view. Gurney barked an order at the helmsman, and *Vandal* bore up until her bowsprit was
pointed at the south window of the little basilica above

the quay that lined the waterfront. Or where the window would have been, had it not been concealed behind the maintop of one of the three Turkish frigates moored, gunports leering sickeningly to seaward, to the quay.

Gurney's stomach turned to lead. "Teeth of Hell!" he roared. "Guns! Those ships, aftermost first, fire as you bear, go!" And seizing the wheel from the slack-jawed helmsman, he yawed Vandal violently to starboard. She came with a rattle, steadied up as the wind came out of her sails on the jibe.

As the ship came round and onto an even keel, he heard O'Shea's voice, high in the uncanny quiet, sing out "sixty-eight!" Then every timber of Vandal's frame shuddered as the great gun roared, followed by the lesser booming of the rest of her larboard battery. Smoke hung in a thick white cloud between the quay and the Vandal, and Gurney wrenched the spokes of the wheel towards him, dragging her bow up to the wind to present her other broadside to the enemy.

Vandal's second broadside roared through the thinning smoke. As she came out of the white cloud, the man beside Gurney made a sound in his throat and disappeared. Gurney looked round. The helmsman's top half lay on the deck, but where the rest of him was, only God and the twelve-pound ball that had taken him in the small of the back knew. The smell of raw meat mingled with the gunpowder. Someone was being sick in the waist.

Muskets were banging from the tops now, and as he watched the foremost of the frigates at the quay loosed her broadside. Holes appeared as if by magic in Vandal's sails, and something whirred past Gurney's ear like a partridge. The Turks seemed to be firing high, but once they had the range, Vandal would be a sitting duck. Time for a run to seaward before they had the chance.

Gurney shouted to McIver and put the wheel over. As her stern came across the wind and her booms crashed over, the popgun bang of the sternchasers was echoed by a heavier roar. Gurney felt his ship shudder like a wounded animal, and the wheel bucked in his hands. The battery! They must have been asleep till now, but they seemed to have woken up at last, bad luck to them. McIver was bellowing for the fire parties, and a chain of buckets was passing below. Gurney found himself praying under his breath as *Vandal* slid slowly, far too slowly, to seaward, her broadsides pounding as he twisted her. He looked back as the sixty-eight pounder boomed for the last time. The aftermost of the ships at the quay was a mastless hulk, and wisps of smoke were issuing from her hatchways; as he watched, the high poop windows of the second frigate were lit from within by a red glare, bulged like a bladder, and fell into ruin. Then the headland was between them and the harbour, and they were headed for the open sea.

Gurney profited by the respite to inspect his ship. Apart from a few loose ends and several holes in the sails—high, he noticed, blessing the incompetence of the Turkish gunners—things did not look too grave. No major damage, at any rate. He turned his eyes to the deck, and the ghastly smear at his side where the bisected helmsman lay. Time enough to count bodies later; what mattered now was to see if *Vandal* was in any condition for her next diversionary swoop into the harbour. With any luck, the Turks would be under the impression that this was an isolated reprisal and would not be ready for Act Two of Gurney's little play. That Act Two depended for its success on the correct timing of Act Three, the arrival of the Greek troops from the rear, was something Gurney did not like to think about; there was little point anyway, since their nonarrival would certainly be fatal.

McIver was in front of him, knuckling the peak of his cap. "Bit of a mess below, sir. The frigates didn't do much harm, but that battery's pretty much smashed up the after-cabin and put a ball or two down the middle of the gun-deck." Gurney noticed he was sweating. "We have them cooled now, sir, but there was a near thing with the magazine. Hot shot lodged near the hoist, sir. But it's out now."

"Anything below the waterline?"

"No, sir, that last salvo was the one as got us, and the most of it went over. It's a mess, but it's no' too dangerous.

"How many hurt?"

McIver looked down at the helmsman, his face impassive. "Apart from this one, two men crushed by the larboard sternchaser when she were blown off her trunnions and one taken in the chest by a splinter. Few burns and cuts, otherwise. Not bad, considering." Not good either though, Gurney reflected miserably. It was not as if it was wartime, or that any concrete objective lay behind this waste of life. Just the squabble of a group of bloody Greeks with a group of Turks, and you could not truthfully say that one was much better than the other. He sighed. "All right, Mr. McIver, we'd better go back in again before they send that frigate after us. Clean up what you can now, then get the men back to their positions. Now then. Ready about!"

Vandal came round and began once more to make for the headland that closed off the harbour. The light was fading now, and the red glow from the burning frigate danced and flickered on the underside of the smoke which hung in the air above the town and lapped at the darkling walls of the Venetian fort. Gurney frowned. Something was not right. He had looked at that fort, supposedly held by Greek patriots, but there had been no firing directed at the harbour, no flag. Strange. There was a flag now, a speck at the end of its pole, but as he focussed his glass on it another drift of smoke hid it from view. Then the headland fell away to larboard and they were in the harbour again, the embrasures of the battery gaping black a short musket-shot away. The men at the mainsheet fell still and silent for a moment, watching death staring impassive from those skull-like sockets of masonry; Gurney could even see the Turkish gunners' slow-matches like red fireflies in the gloom within. *Vandal's* broadside and the battery spoke simultaneously. Several of the men on *Vandal's* deck threw themselves flat —as if that would have done any good—as the battery's quarter-ton of metal sleeted through the air above their heads; but as Gurney had hoped, by coming in fast and close he had caught the Turkish gunners over-elevated, so the bulk of their shot had again gone hopelessly high. *Vandal's* broadside, however, seemed to have been singularly effective. Even after the smoke from the firing had cleared, dense vapours rolled from the enemy embrasures. Gurney put the helm over, to present as small a target as possible to the shaken battery and his reloaded broadside to the remaining frigate; the men at the mainsheet picked themselves shamefacedly up from the planking.

It was as O'Shea was lining the larboard sixty-eight pounder on the midships gunport of the frigate's lower tier that the guns in the fort spoke. Gurney, confused for a moment by the huge concussion of the sixty-eight pounder, assumed that the Greeks had at last found the initiative to man their pieces. It was not until something sighed down through the air like a diving gannet and disappeared with a frightful crash through *Vandal's* deck-planking that he realised what was going on. Wisps of smoke and screams came up through the hole, and a runner bolted from the hatchway like a rabbit.

"Mr. O'Shea compliments, Sir, an' there's a bloody great hole 'twixt wind and water, and the after twelve pounder starboard side is halfway out of the bloody port, Sir." The boy looked calm, but Gurney could see that the eyes were glazed and snapping with panic.

"Very well. Tell Mr. O'Shea that we'll pull out of here and see what can be done." Where were those bloody Greeks? They should have been here long ago

now. God damn them. Beset on three sides. Gurney
cursed himself for a madman that he had allowed himself to be drawn into this, spun the wheel, and turned
Vandal's nose to the open sea. McIver was chasing
men to the rocker of the pumps in an attempt to
stem the water rising in *Vandal's* well from the hole
made by the huge projectile from the castle. *Vandal*
was too close below the guns now for them to do her
any harm, but the battery across the bay seemed to
have recovered itself and was making good practice,
the shot kicking great flakes of rock from the cliff and
skipping unpleasantly close to *Vandal's* side.

Then, as *Vandal* came round towards the harbour
entrance, disaster struck. A twenty-four pound ball
from the battery, hitting the water forty feet from her
transom, bounced like a flat pebble and blasted
through the double planking of her counter, spraying
jagged splinters of wood and iron in the small space
where the blocks and cordage of her steering-gear re-
layed the commands of the wheel on the deck above
to her tiller. Gurney felt the wheel jump violently
and fell back, nursing his hand. The spare helmsman
grabbed the wheel, but the spokes spun uselessly
through his hands; the ship, undirected, began to come
up into the wind and hung in irons under the bristling
guns of Ixos.

Gurney, cool as ice, beckoned to McIver. "Tops'l
braces and bring her head off the wind. Look sharp."
McIver, a dark figure against the fires ashore, ran
forward, collecting men as he went; musketry still
rattling from the tops, and a ripple of flashes from the
waist showed that von Kratzstein and his men were
doing their pathetic best to sell their lives dearly.
Gurney shouted to Dutch Pieter the coxswain and
ran below, into the wreck of broken glass and smashed
timber that had been his cabin, and pulled up the
hatchway in the deck that led to the steering-gear
housing. As he lit a lantern, he was surprised to note
that his hands were not even shaking; but time seemed

to be moving terribly slowly. He let the lantern down in the darkness and groaned. The tiller socketed to the great rudder-post was scarred but sound, but the tackles which moved the tiller, gearing down the helmsman's effort so he could comfortably move the rudder through the water, were in ruins. He turned to Pieter. "Get some men and rig relieving tackles, fast. We'll have to try to blow her out of here on the topsails. Five minutes, or we're dead."

The dusk seemed bright after the darkness below, and for a moment he was cheered by it. Then the battery roared again from the distant shore, and *Vandal*'s foretopmast with its two square sales seemed to bow, came upright on its shrouds, swayed, and collapsed with a rattle and a roar onto her foredeck. Rudderless, unmanageable, the schooner drifted down the wind sideways, towards the quay with its two burning hulks and the frowning ramparts of the Venetian castle. Gurney paced the deck in an agony of impatience. If the Greek attack did not come within the next thirty seconds, he would be forced to strike his colours—his colours in name only; for it was the blue cross of Alexander Mavrocordato's Greece that fluttered at the main peak.

The battery ashore bloomed smoke again, and *Vandal* staggered. They were getting the range now, those gunners, and they could sink her with half a dozen more like that. But whether to sink her or take the risk of being murdered ashore if Metaxas failed to arrive? Gurney made his decision, and roared, "Cease firing! Down anchor!" He moved slowly, shoulders slumped in dejection, to the cleat by the main boom gooseneck, and brought the blue and white ensign to the deck. Then he lined up the men, and waited helplessly as the boats pulled out from the quay and started towards his ship.

Stained with smoke and blood, they were an ugly lot. But it was not their physical appearance that depressed Gurney, shamed him so he could hardly look a man of them in the eye. It was the dejection of them.

As the Turkish boats came alongside, McIver broke in on his thoughts.

"Beggin' your pardon, Captain, but it's a bastard, this. Every one of these men thinks it's his fault. They're that good a crew."

Gurney shook his head. "There's only one person at fault, and that's me. I should have known better."

A flush covered McIver's features. "That's not correct, Captain." It was the nearest thing to a flat contradiction that McIver had ever offered him, and it surprised Gurney beyond measure. "It's they bloody Greeks," said McIver.

"All right, then." Gurney grinned ruefully. "It's the bloody Greeks." But he felt a little better—at least, until a supercilious Turkish officer came up the Jacob's ladder with his men. *Vandal's* crew were herded into the boats like so many cattle, Gurney last, as befitted a Captain. As the boat took him ashore he looked back. In the gathering dark his ship's outline was somehow ragged and unbalanced without the topmast. All she needed was relieving tackles, though, and she would then be easily sailable. But he would not be the one to find out, unless the Greeks found some courage somewhere. And Gurney had few illusions on that score.

As they stepped ashore, Gurney cast a despairing glance into the deepening shadows of the hills. But no explosion, no point of fire, not a movement signalled the presence of Metaxas and his men. Surrounded by jeering Turkish guards, the weary procession shambled between burned and gutted houses up the steep cobbles of the village street, until the portcullis in the gatehouse of the Venetian fort fell behind them like the crack of doom.

The officer in charge of the guard barked a command, and they came to a halt. Gurney looked about him. In the gathering dusk the ramparts were lined with turbaned soldiers in baggy trousers. Something moved in a corner of the courtyard, and a harsh voice screamed *"Prodosia!"* Treachery! But who was the betrayer, Gurney wondered? He watched in fascination as one of his crew's escort walked over to the screamer, bearing a guttering pine-knot torch. *"Prodosia!"* the man screamed again. In the torchlight Gurney saw that the shapeless mass, surmounted by a head, lay in a pool of blood. Beside him were stacked four bloody objects. As the guard brought the torch down into the man's face and his cries stopped, Gurney saw that the objects were two legs and two arms, stiff with *rigor mortis,* and that the screamer had been raw stumps at shoulders and thighs. Gurney turned his face away, feeling sick, and put his arm round young George Jarvis. The boy was retching helplessly. "Pay no mind to him, George. Poor devil's out of his misery now, at any rate."

"But what are they going to do with us, Mr. Gurney, Sir?"

Gurney smiled at him. "They're in no position to do anything. We're subjects of His Majesty, and if they touch a hair of our heads they'll have a Fleet to reckon with." He could feel his smile cracking, though. *Vandal* and her crew were well beyond the reach of the King's retribution now, and in this grim bastion the best they could hope for was slavery. And the worst . . . Gurney looked again at the mutilated corpse in the corner. The worst did not bear thinking about.

The officer was shouting now, haranguing the prisoners in what Gurney realised was some sort of broken English. "Kapetanos and officers step forward. I count three. If not by three, men will kill all with gun and sword. One." Gurney looked up. Two cannon were trained into the courtyard, and by each of their touchholes stood a turbaned gunner with a glowing slowmatch. He took a step forward.

"Two."

"Everyone stay where they are," shouted Gurney. "You, Turk! I am in sole command of these men. They are under my orders, and mine alone. I demand that they be treated with the respect due to prisoners of war."

The officer walked slowly across to Gurney. In the wavering light of the torches the smoke-blackened faces of *Vandal's* crew were shiny with sweat, despite the chill of the night air. The Turk came to a stop nose to nose with him, his high-cheekboned Tartar's face flat and expressionless under the turban. "As prisoners of war. Yes." He turned and spat a few words at the guards. "I will show you what we do with prisoners of war." The soldier left the courtyard, returning in two minutes with a Greek. They dragged him across to an oaken door set in the rough masonry of the courtyard wall. The door was pitted and streaked with ominous stains. One of the soldiers held him captive up against the door, while the other climbed a mounting-block at its side, grasped the man's head, and forcing it against the rough oak, nailed a bayonet through the cartilage of each ear and into the wood. The man supporting him let him fall and the Greek's face was wrenched into a tight grin as the flesh pulled back from his teeth. Not a sound did he utter. Gurney could hear George Jarvis whimpering behind him.

"It is so that we treat the more fortunate of our captives," said the officer. "Reflect on this until the morn, when you will all make the acquaintance of the impaler's stake. Even you, Captain. But come. First, our Bey would have speech with you."

As they were hustled out of the courtyard, the Greek's tormentors were winding a lighted slow-match between his toes. *Vandal's* crew were taken through an iron-grilled door and down some stairs, while Gurney was dragged towards a more splendid portal which presumably gave onto the living-quarters of the Bey. The Greek's first scream rang for a moment in the stone-flagged hall within; then the sounds became muffled as the thick door was closed and bolted.

The man who swung out of the shadows on the far side of the great stone fireplace reminded Gurney irresistibly of a pike. Flat, predatory head with a broad jaw and long canine teeth, eyes that would have been surprised in their roundness had they not been set close in the sides of his head, like a fish's, and seemingly covered with a slippery mucus. And when he spoke, he spoke in the kind of voice a pike would have used if suddenly given the power of speech. "Captain."

Gurney felt like a small fish swimming past a dark hole beneath a tree on a river bank. The voice was deep and velvety, but there was a curious emptiness to it. It was not a voice that could have spoken poetry or words of love; it was the kind of voice that must since earliest infancy have spoken only to gratify its owner's predatory desires. With those glaucous eyes on him, Gurney felt almost kindly disposed to the officer of the guard.

The Bey moved towards him, little legs, twinkling rapidly in curly-toed slippers under his heavy cylindrical body. When he stopped his face was inches from Gurney's. Gurney had to restrain himself from turning away; under the musky perfume that covered the Turk like a cloud was a stench of decay.

"Two of my frigates. Two." A puff of foul breath enveloped Gurney and his gorge rose. "Very silly, silly man. You fool. For what were you looking? To restore the Athens of Plato and Aristotle, no doubt? And what have you achieved? I will tell you. You have lost your ship—a fine ship, which will be a great ornament to my little Fleet, though not"—an additional film of mucus fell over the fishy eyes—"a fit substitute for my frigates.

"That will teach you to mix with those little Greeks who play like monkeys on a dunghill. The arrogance of you Milords, with your culture! It is we of the Ottoman Empire who are cultured, Milord. When your ancestors grovelled with the dogs in the filthy rushes

of your draughty castles, we were building wonders
for the world to marvel at. Barbarians, destructive
barbarians. And you dare challenge our ships?"

Gurney was incensed. "Had your gunners been
worth their weight in dog's muck, Sir, you would have
your frigates yet. If you are to indulge in war against
your vassals you could at least train your men."

The rims of the Turk's mouth—they could not properly be called lips—pulled downwards and outwards.
"We do not expect, Captain, piratical attacks from
our subjects. Which brings me to the point at issue.
The point! Very good, no? But I digress. You and
your piratical rabble are not, as I am told you claim,
prisoners of war. You are rebels against the will of
the Sublime Porte. I have neither the desire nor the
power to sell you into slavery, though some of you
are pretty. No. Tomorrow at the second hour after
dawn, you will each suffer the discomfort of a greased
stake in the fundament. That," he chuckled, "is the
point. Take him away." And he swirled back into the
maw of shadow behind the mantel.

As Gurney was led in dumb misery down wet stone
stairs, head bowed, he was angry—not with his captors, not with the chance shot which had wrecked his
ship's steering-gear at the vital moment, but with himself. McIver was wrong. It had been his folly, and his
alone, to have trusted the Greek Metaxas with not
only his own life but that of the men in his charge.
That it should come to this, a desolate ruin of a hope
he had shared with Arabella, and the hopes of the men
of Sea Dalling; a disgusting death in agony, in
furtherance of a non-existent cause. The excitement of
battle had left him, and in its place was an emptiness.
Futility. But as rough hands flung him into the slime-
floored dungeon which held the Vandal's crew,
packed like smelts in a barrel, he straightened his
shoulders. A roar of greeting told him that his men
were still behind him; and in the hours before dawn,
there was time for miracles. He looked round the cell,

a low, vaulted chamber about fifty feet square, ventilated by two little barred windows. A miracle was indeed going to be necessary.

5

Basreddin dragged the little skiff up onto the low ledge of rock, turned it upside down, and set about hiding it with stones. At his back the cliffs of the citadel at Ixos reared their three hundred feet of riven rock towards the invisible scud of clouds above; beneath his feet, a narrow ledge gave onto a fissure standing diagonally upwards above him. The Sufi breathed deeply several times, his eyes closed; it had been only just after sunset when he had dropped astern of the caique in his skiff, and then there had been four hours of hard rowing. But fortunately the breeze had been under his stern, for otherwise he might still be out there, struggling with the black waves of the recalcitrant Aegean. Muscles relaxed, mind hanging in his body by a thread, he stood like a man of string and rags, in meditation. Twenty breaths later, when he opened his eyes, the freshness he felt was that which in a normal man would have come from a four-hour slumber. He turned on his ledge, adjusted the great coil of rope he had purloined from the caique over one shoulder, and set off up the fissure.

As the Ixiot refugee had told him on the caique, the crack sloped up for perhaps sixty feet; Basreddin could walk upright in it at first, but then the two lips of stone came closer together and the angle steepened, and he had to make his way laboriously up by jamming his back against one side and his feet against the other. The crack became almost a chimney, and the sweat began to trickle down his forehead and into his eyes. He looked out and down. Seventy-five feet below, the little waves dashed themselves to foam on the rock. And he was not even a third of the way up the cliff.

The chimney narrowed still further. A thought floated disturbingly across his mind. What if that damned Ixiot had told him wrong? But no. No man could resist the suggestion of the Second Order with a lie, save another adept. Basreddin relaxed totally for a moment, wedged in his crack in the rock, and concentrated on stilling the tremor that was beginning to develop in his left knee. Then he wriggled his back to the right, out into space, bracing the leathery soles of his feet against the far side of the fissure. For a moment he was falling; then his weight hit the palms of his hands and he hung, in the attitude of a man trying to prise open a door. With tiny movements of his hands and feet he inched upwards, until the crack was so narrow that he could jam in a hand, make a fist, and hang suspended until his scrabbling toes found a purchase.

When the face began to slope away from him he felt a distinct sensation of relief. For a few moments he sat on the slope, feeling the softness of the tussocks of spring grass and sea-pinks that clung somehow to this narrow belt of crumbling earth, little more than rotten rock, that striped across the cliff above the sheer precipice below. Above him a dark overhang frowned out like the brow of an intellectual giant.

By the time he was up he was breathing easier, picking his way up the crumbling and treacherous surface, and faced at every step with an agony of loose earth and stones. His path was marked by a continuous shower of soil and pebbles bounding out over the sheer of the cliffs and pattering into the sea one hundred and fifty feet below. When he reached the foot of the overhang he did not pause. Working his way sideways to the left, keeping his weight as far as possible on solid rock rather than soft earth, he strained his eyes upwards into the murk, looking for the boulder which the Ixiot's hypnosis-sharpened memory had told him rested on the very brow of the overhang. Then he had it; fifteen feet above his head and a little to the right. He made his way gingerly down the slope until the jut of the boulder was directly above him, slipped the coil of rope from his shoulder, and swung the grapnel at its end, as a hammer-thrower swings his hammer. Then he let fly. The rope snaked into the darkness above him, then fell back. He threw again, then twice more: but it was not until his sixth attempt that the grapnel caught behind the boulder. He tested it, his heart thudding. He could not put his full weight on it for fear of losing his balance if it gave way; so it was with a prayer and a curse that he grasped the one-inch manila firmly and swung his feet off the ground.

Halfway up the rope he paused and looked out. Below him the crumbling slope swooped down at a terrifying angle, and his eyes, following it, were drawn out into the void beyond the clifftop, where the sea gleamed from time to time a ghastly distance below. He began to climb again. His hands felt a grating from the taut rope, a grating which grew into a continuous movement and the grapnel gave and he was falling, biting back a yell; then it caught again and he climbed like a man possessed, wrenching his mind away from the sickening gulf below.

When he arrived at the boulder he clung to it, panting. The life of a wanderer on land and sea had left him with a great distaste for steep places. Although with George Gurney he had been up more masts than he could remember, that was an entirely different business from his desperate scramble in defiance of gravity up this crumbling knob of treacherous rock.

He looked up. Above the light bulge of the summit the square lines of the fort stood out against the sky, lamplight burning dim in a couple of the topmost embrasures. There were no human figures visible on the battlements, even to the Sufi's keen night vision—for who would expect intruders to come up that perilous sheet of rock with barely enough footing for a seagull? Basreddin anchored his rope firmly to the boulder and set off up the last of the cliff, a relatively simple matter after what had gone before, moving like a spider from toe-hold to toe-hold, finger-grip to finger-grip, working entirely by touch. The cloud had thickened, extinguishing the last remnants of starlight, and he moved now in a world that was precisely the size of the radius of his limbs and the next foot of rock in his upwards path. Once his hand crept over a ledge and came down on a pile of feathers and twigs, crushing eggs; the tenant of the nest leaped screaming into the night, and the shock nearly tore him from the cliff-face; but he climbed on, until his uppermost hand touched mortar and smooth masonry. To the left here, the Ixiot had said, were the windows of the cells, little eyes set deep in the living rock below the curtain wall.

*   *   *

Gurney was close to the window, lost in thought. The rushlight the gaolers had given them, the better to stir up the infection of horror in their condemned captives, danced in the greasy sheen of sweat on his face. He had passed from his mood of bitter self-recrimination into a dull apathy, in which grief at the fate of his crew chased the tail of fear that he would be overcome with terror the next day, faced with the impaler's stake. He had half-decided that the best course of action would be to rush the gaolers when they came to take him away on the morrow. If they were to die, better to die fighting than suffer the indignity of being led like lambs to the slaughter. Then he thought of those cannon trained down into the courtyard, of the blizzard of iron balls that would roar and bounce on the flags and walls, tearing through flesh and bone, and he sighed. Death was death, however it came; but there was bitterness there for Arabella and Basreddin, both relying on him, believing that he was destined for greater things than off-hand butchery at the hands of a Turkish lordling with whom his country was not even at war. He shoved his hands deeper in his pockets. Outside the rusty grillework of the window, a seabird screamed, and he envied it its freedom. It screamed again, and he remembered a ride on the endless yellow beaches of Sea Dalling, ornithologising with Arabella, watching a pair of Arctic skuas wheeling, screaming that same scream against the pale northern sky.

Arctic skuas? In the Aegean?

He grabbed the rushlight from its filthy ledge and thrust it into the window alcove. Outside, suspended in the darkness beyond the bars, the feeble light glinted in the black pupils of two eyes and shone from a broad grin of regular white teeth.

"Greetings, Giorgiou. Now, if you will kindly cease to stand there gaping and get to work, I can stop this ridiculous impersonation of an apple-stealer and stand again on flat ground."

A broad file poked through the grillework and clattered on to the ledge.

Gurney's mind clicked smoothly into gear, his morbid introspections swept away like mist before a gale. He turned to the man next to him.

"Sing a hymn."

The man—it was Henry Priest from the foretop, a blood-stained bandage at his forehead, stared at him dully, uncomprehending. "What?"

"Sing a hymn. Any hymn. *Rock of Ages.* And pass the word for Volnikov."

Malik the guard woke from his alcoholic slumber in the filthy straw of the cell corridor as the deep voices of the infidels passed into the second verse. He groaned, clutching his brow. But they were to die, and Malik, a reasonable man in his own estimation saw no reason why they should not die solaced by their stinking religion. He had found that a little religion made an infidel writhe better as the stake took him in the guts. He would give them a few minutes before he shut them up. Lying back in his straw, he fell again into an uneasy slumber—he had a nervous stomach, and rape and retsina, while he enjoyed them both thoroughly, had an unsettling effect on his delicate constitution. By the time he was snoring again, Volnikov's mighty arms had taken him through the vertical bars, weakened by the salt air, and he was starting on the horizontals. The raucous devotions of *Vandal*'s crew took on a new jauntiness, and in the din even the Russian carpenter could barely hear the file biting into the rusty iron under his nose.

Malik was not the only Turkish raider having an uneasy night. High in the bailey, the Bey was lying troubled beneath his furs. Those frigates burned to the waterline in the harbour were but recently arrived from the Marseilles yards, and they had not been cheap. Their loss, combined with the ill-will of certain powerful men at the court of the Sultan, could cost him the skin from the soles of his feet, if not his head. But before then, those Christian dogs would die, and die unpleasantly; that was a consolation, at least.

A thin sound, between a groan and a whine, was finding its way through the cross-shaped embrasures of his chamber. He dabbed his temples with a silk handkerchief soaked in eau-de-Cologne, but to no avail; he knew his neuralgia had hold of him, and that there would be no further sleep. And all because of those Christians, who now, it seemed, were keeping their spirits up with song. Such consolations were inappropriate, the Bey decided. He tugged the bell rope at his side and lay back among his cushions.

Ten minutes later, Malik awoke again, and lay for a moment trying to unscramble his thoughts. Then as the dreams faded, he realised what had woken him; the tramp of boots on the stone stairway now mingled with the lusty bellowings of the Christians within. He stumbled to his feet, wiping the sleep from his eyes, and assumed an attitude of what he hoped was careful vigilance which cunningly disguised his inability to stand on his feet unsupported by the shaft of his lance.

Volnikov had one bar to go and the *Vandal*'s crew were on the third verse of *Soldiers of Christ Arise*, having worked their way through the liturgical calendar while the carpenter's temper worsened as his file grew blunter. Gurney was, on the whole, pleased; not only did there now appear to be a way out of this seeming death-trap, but the basses and tenors trained by Parson Leggatt and Arabella at St. Saviour's, Sea Dalling were putting up a brave show. Good lads one and all. Gurney opened his mouth, filled his lungs, and began to conduct his men into verse four.

Basreddin, anchored to the bars of a nearby window, hanging like a money-spider against the naked rock outside the cell, heard the singing stop suddenly in mid-verse, and Volnikov's curse. He also saw the Russian's fingers unclasp from the file, watched the blade of metal slip casually through the bars and bound, clinging, down the cliff-face and away into the night.

Inside the cell, the air was thick with tension and moisture, mainly because the carpenter's vast bulk had been blocking the free circulation of air for the past two hours. But there was also the matter of the ten armoured Turks who had burst in through the door. Gurney's heart was in his mouth. Had they heard the rasp of the file? Were *Vandal*'s crew to meet their death now, rather than in the morning?

The officer of the guard was striding towards the window, eyes invisible under his turban, shouting as he came. "Enough! Dogs of Franks, you have little to sing about and few hours remaining. Pray if you like,

but do not disturb the sleep of our Bey. Otherwise—"
The long lash in his right hand snaked out. A man
twenty feet away screamed and clapped his hand to
his eye and fell back, blood welling up and running
between his fingers.

In the silence the quiet moaning of the blinded
man rang like a knell. Turning on his heel, the Turk
wrenched open the cell door, called his men, and
stalked out. After he had gone, there was no rustle of
relief, no murmur of conversation.

Gurney turned to Volnikov. "Well?"

"File's gone, Captain. No other."

Gurney felt the blood begin to pound in his temples. "O, you bloody fool, what did you do that for?"
The Russian shook his head, his knuckles hanging
nearly to his knees.

Gurney relented, as always. "Ah, God. You dropped
it, you suggest something."

Volnikov put his great arm into the embrasure as if
absentmindedly, and, still looking at Gurney, locked
his fingers on to the grillework. Then the muscles of
his arm stood out in sharp relief in the flickering candlelight, and sweat started to run down his forehead.
Clouds of dust were coming from the embrasure, and
a dragging, grinding sound; then the Russian's face
relaxed, and he held something large and rusty under his Captain's nose. The grille. Basreddin swarmed
in after it, and stood for a moment, pumping Gurney's
hand in silence.

"Good to see you again, my dear fellow." Gurney's
voice was close to breaking. Then he collected himself
and began to give orders in a low undertone. Five
minutes later, the men started down the rope, one
every minute by Gurney's watch. At a hundred feet a
minute, that would mean three men on the rope at
once. Still a deuced dicy business, with the rock rubbing and fraying at the manila, but the best that
could be expected in the circumstances. McIver, first

down, had commandeered a dozen shirts to pad the worst places, but still . . .

Gurney began to recite the Anglican Litany in a low voice. Its muted drone and soothing response sounded convincingly like prayer for the benefit of the Turks, and its panicky invocation of the Lord's assistance against fire, flood and crop failure served to put *Vandal*'s present troubles into perspective. Even von Kratzstein seemed to find some kind of solace in it, though Gurney reckoned that by the scared glances the Prussian threw towards the window he would cheerfully have gone down on his knees to the first idol that presented itself to hand.

After twenty men had gone, Gurney said "Amen" loudly and firmly and stepped in front of the window. Von Kratzstein, next out, had nerved himself for the descent, and was evidently none too pleased.

"Vy are we not goink more?"

"Because, Herr General," Gurney had to make a huge effort to keep the irony out of his voice; this was neither the time nor the place, "to get off this devil's wart we must have boats. Mr. McIver and those twenty have gone to borrow a few from the Turks. Does this meet with your approval?"

The Prussian gulped and began a prayer-meeting of his own as Gurney struck up a long-winded extempore rendition of some of the Captivity Psalms, his hands clasped behind his back, holding a bight of the escape rope as it looped from a sinister-looking ringbolt in the cell wall out into the darkness. He was on the fourth verse of Psalm 137, getting more worried by the minute and blessing the ecclesiastical upbringing that had given him fuel for such occasions as this, when the double tug came from below. Without missing a beat, he waved von Kratzstein towards him and onto the rope, speeding him on his way with a swift kick. Gobbling sounds of pure terror came from the Prussian's throat and he vanished into the night.

During the next forty minutes, Gurney's congregation grew steadily smaller. Finally he was the only inmate of the cell. He grasped the rope, muttering, as he swung out of the window, "as it was in the beginning, is now and ever shall be, world without end, Amen," planted his feet against the rock and began to walk down. As he passed the first three places where McIver had padded the rope, he felt bristling manila fibres. Nearly through. He quickened his pace, trying to put weight on the rock rather than the rope. The overhang forced him to come down with his full weight on the rope, and he held his breath until he landed on the crumbling stripe below, where eighty pairs of feet had worn a deep trench to the head of the vertical waterfall of rock that dropped to the sea one hundred feet below. Gurney took a deep breath and launched himself into space. As he bounded down, he could feel little twangings in the rope as strand parted from strand, and there was a stretch to it which was not as resilient as he would have liked. But with each step the consequences of a fall became less serious. Eventually he allowed himself to look down at the dark shapes of the three boats that McIver had somehow spirited out of the harbour. The rest of the climb passed in heart-pumping little steps down the face. When he finally arrived on the ledge at the bottom of the cliff, he was bathed in sweat and panting.

Basreddin was standing there to greet him. "Felicitations on your safe arrival, O Giorgiou. Truly, the Greeks make stout rope."

Gurney nodded. "Aye. Though I don't know if it's the Greeks who made that rope. With their gift for treachery, I'd not be surprised if they stole it off their allies. Having first hanged them with it out of hand." He looked up. "Still, whatever its origins it's served us well. Pity to leave it behind really." He gave it an affectionate tug. Somewhere high on the citadel mound, fibre parted from fibre, and coil after coil came

pouring down on top of him. Basreddin stepped
hastily aside. When the rope had finished falling, he
looked for Gurney. His Captain was bent over the edge
of the rock platform, being very sick.

The weather had changed since nightfall. The wind
had backed round to the north, and now blew directly
over the land and swooped down, eddying over the
harbour. In the short, steep waves it kicked up, the
overloaded boat, its usual crew of five now supple-
mented by fifteen, lay low in the water. Gurney,
standing at the tiller as the six oars dragged the hulk
leadenly across the harbour, shivered as a gout of
spray slid down between his collar and his neck. He
was starting to become short-tempered. To go without
dinner was bad enough; but to undertake an entire
day's fighting, followed by a betrayal and four full
hours of hymn-singing and common prayer on an
empty stomach, was enough to try the temper of a
saint. And Gurney had no illusions about the saintli-
ness of his own temper, even when he was well-fed.

Pringle the lazy, dragging at the stroke oar, looked
up at him and looked hastily away again. "Keep yer
mind on yer oar, man," growled Gurney, seeing the
flash of white eyeballs.

Silence fell over the boat, except for the muffled
creak of the oars in the thole pins. Gurney strained his
eyes into the murk ahead. *Vandal* should be coming
into view at any minute. But he could see nothing.
High on its rock behind him, the citadel frowned over
the harbour. Pray God that the sentries were drunk or
blind. They were unlikely to be on their guard; one of
the traditions of this war, it seemed, was that no self-
respecting Navy ventured within a league of hostile
land after sunset. Gurney crossed his fingers and
hoped that the Turks were as well aware of the rules
as he.

Then he stiffened. From ahead in the darkness came
the groan and thump of oars. Gurney swore. The other

two boats, under Basreddin and McIver, should be standing well off, waiting. This, then, could only be a guard-boat. Cold sweat joined the sea water trickling down his neck. Thank God they had not been patrolling earlier on, to find sixty men sitting like bloody cormorants at the base of the citadel!

"Down!" Gurney hissed. The rowers and passengers lowered their heads, and the longboat, with its low freeboard, was merely a flat hump slopping in the swell. Gurney raised his head. The guard-boat was showing a lantern now, and in its light he could make out bayonets and a bony face with a broken nose. A harsh call floated down the wind. Gurney's Arabic was rusty, but he would have known what it meant had it been in Japanese.

"Who goes there?"

He raised his head. "Boat from *Golden Moon*, brig. Wrecked three days ago many leagues to the south. Allah be praised that we have found land and friendly voices."

The officer in the guard-boat did not sound convinced. "Stay where you are. I am coming alongside."

As the Turk approached, Gurney ran through his boat's inventory of weapons. One boat hook, three knives the Turks had failed to find in their hasty search of the prisoners that evening, and a rusty machete-like bait chopper. Mather, who had joined *Vandal's* crew from an Aleutian sealer, had charge of the boat hook, as was only right; as a knife and harpoon man he was without peer. Gurney had hold of the bait-knife. God knew where the other weapons were.

The guard-boat was coming alongside now. Mather, who as a harpoonist was only truly happy when in the bows of a ship's boat, crouched on the bottomboards, shifting his grip on the boat hook. As the Turk's oars came up and her gunwale brushed the boat's port side, the officer raised his lantern above his head. Gurney was dimly aware of a movement in the lugger's bow as he tried to frame his introductory sentence; then something hummed past his ear and the Turkish officer shot back as if jerked, clawing at the brass-bound shaft of ash suddenly growing from his windpipe.

It was never entirely clear, when he looked back on it, what happened next; there were merely a few flashes that came to him. He remembered turning to see Pringle holding a musket on whose bayonet its Turkish owner stood skewered, and being surprised, when he looked down, to find that he was holding the legs of another Turkish soldier, the top half of whose body was underwater and, it seemed, no longer breathing. Then there were no Turks, merely a reddened patch of sea with a few bubbles rising and bursting in the strong wind, fading astern of the two boats as they drifted down the breeze.

Vandal's lookout was scratching his shaven head under his grubby turban as the guard-boat hove into view. He was in a generally surly mood. Not only had he been set to guard this shot-riddled hulk, but he had acquired some very persistent lice while he was amusing himself with that charming little boy this afternoon. Strange that one so hairless should have been so lousy. He scratched his groin inside his baggy trousers. These raids were amusing enough, to be sure, but they did keep a man away from the steam-bath. The Greeks, damn them for catamites one and all, seemed content with the sea. No wonder they were lousy. Still, there were the rigours of war. He looked across the deck to where Abdul and Mehmet, *Vandal's* other two guards, were squatting under a lantern, playing dice. They had agreed that they would take it in turns to watch; for was it not utter madness to have a sentry here at all? Did the Bey seriously believe that the Greeks would attack in the night? No, the old crocodile was in a huff about the burning of his frigates. It was out of sheer perversity that he had set a guard. And now that jumped-up Suleiman was coming to check that all was well. He called across to his companions, who scrambled to their feet, grabbing at muskets, and came to attention by *Vandal*'s entry-port. The three sentries stared impassively in front of them, their eyes fixed on a spot approximating to the horizon. The officer of the guard, now feeding the fish with a wooden extension to his Adam's apple, had been a fierce disciplinarian, and to allow one's martial bearing to reflect fatigue or inattendance was, with him, a sure route to a painful interview with the bastinado.

It was for this reason that Gurney, his head swathed in the late officer's turban, was able to make his way up *Vandal*'s mainchains, over the gunwale and onto her deck before the watchmen realised anything was amiss. Mehmet, when the face before him resolved itself, was foolish enough to go for his musket; Gurney's fish-knife ripped across his belly from one side to the other, and he fell forward onto the deck with a bubbling groan. His two companions dropped their weapons as one man. The pseudo-Turks, who had followed their captain up the mainchains, grabbed them quickly. Gurney nodded. "Excellent. Mather, get these specimens trussed. Volnikov, stay with me. The rest of you check damage and report to me in my cabin. Hand me up that lantern there." He walked to the seaward rail and worked the shutter of the light three times. From the darkness to seaward, a skua cried.

As Gurney and the Russian carpenter rove the relieving tackles that would do temporary duty in place of the ship's mangled steering-gear, the boats came alongside and disgorged their burden of men. Even through the thickness of planking that separated him from the deck, Gurney could hear McIver giving orders in a hoarse whisper. Volnikov mopped his brow, the lantern throwing grotesque shadows from his bulk in the confined space.

"Should be good. Ah, Captain, I could manage a drink."

Gurney grinned. Volnikov had had a hard night of it, true: he had come down the cliff one-handed, the blinded man clinging to his back. "No drink shall you have, you damned Mohawk, until those tackles have taken us well out of here. Get 'em rove up to the wheel and we'll be out in a trice." He clapped the Russian between the shoulder blades, bruising his hand, and went up to his cabin.

The damage reports told Gurney nothing he did not already know. The foretopmast was a ruin and the leaks would give trouble when they were under way. Gurney deliberated for a moment. To rig a jury mast in their present anchorage would be to court disaster; looking through the smashed plate glass of his cabin windows, he could see that the sky was already lightening with the false dawn. The day would not be far behind. With the wind in its present quarter, *Vandal* would have little difficulty in moving out of the harbour under fore and main.

McIver, standing square and unruffled on the glass-strewn deck, grunted in agreement. "Aye. They're a guid lot, those Norfolk men. They'll have no trouble rigging a new spar at sea. Better go out on the starboard tack, though. There's a nasty one 'twixt wind and water up forrard. I have it stuffed with a sail for now, but she needs a patch. If you're agreeable I'll put one of the boys over the side wi' some sheathing and a mouthful of nails when we're under way."

"Very well. You're sure about the forestay? I don't want to sail the sticks straight out of her."

The Scot's face went blank. "Mr. Gurney, in all our years together, have you ever known me—"

"My apologies. It is merely the presence of those heathen Turks on the hill yonder that makes me wish to get out of here fast and clean."

McIver nodded. "Aye. It's a poor way to go, wi' a sharpened stick up yer arsehole. Well, well. We can send our prayers heavenward." The nearest to praying McIver ever came was to address some purple sentiments to any of the topmen who proved a little slow on the gaskets, but Gurney let it go. "Ye'll be wanting to cut the cable?"

"Yes." The Scot turned to go. "Oh, and McIver. Pass the word for Mr. Basreddin, would you?"

As McIver left the cabin, Basreddin, with his customary near-supernatural timing, entered. "Well, Giorgiou. It seems that Odysseus will escape from the Cyclops' cave."

"Since when have you been a Classicist?"

"Since the abominable chill of that hovel of small stones in which I sojourned in the land of the icy Levanter."

Gurney shook his head. Amazing. "One day you should dine at All Souls' in Oxford. You would make the learned doctors look like schoolchildren. But enough. You can plot me a course to the cove where your ransom lies."

"Indeed. But one thing; it will not have escaped your attention that we are now beyond the reach of my captors. According to the venerable tenets of the Mosaic law—"

Gurney coughed. "I would suggest that such deliberations are best conducted elsewhere. We are still under the enemy's guns, if you remember, and the light is coming up apace." He pulled the chart from its case and spread it on the table.

Basreddin resumed. "I merely point out that we are now under no obligation to the Greeks. They have come near to costing you your ship and your men by their treachery; why should they have your treasure too?"

Gurney paused a moment. "You're right. But there is one thing: I promised Mavromichaelis the gold; and I am sure that he is not a treacherous man."

"But his agent, the reptile Metaxas—"

"Yes. There is no time for this now, however. We shall have leisure to discuss it on our way to the cove. Let's get the ship under way."

Gurney came on deck. The shambles of *Vandal's* deck was coming into view as the sun rolled up under the horizon. He waved at McIver, and suddenly the knots of men lying in cover below her bulwarks were galvanised into action. McIver was bellowing at the men on the halyards. "Haul away there, throat and peak fore and main! Look lively! Slip 'er! Back fore-sail!"

Through his glass, Gurney saw tiny figures running on the ramparts of the citadel and among the drifts of smoke that still obscured the quay. Then *Vandal* slowly gathered way. A single gun boomed from the battery, but the ball fell far astern; the headland dropped away to starboard, and *Vandal* put her nose for the open sea.

At her counter, Gurney was still fretting. "There's nothing except pure cowardice stopping those Turk buggers coming after us. O'Shea! Get me as many guns run out as you can still work, and report back." With *Vandal* in this state; it would be a massacre; but at least, he thought with resignation, it would be a massacre under a clear sky on the clean sea. Better than the execution yard of that stinking fortress.

Basreddin was tugging at his sleeve. "They will not follow us. But nor will we have a clear run to the ransom and the letters. Look." He pointed to seaward. In the circle of Gurney's glass, the sails on the horizon were pink with morning sun. The closest of the ships, a little schooner, was flying a huge banner from her gaff-peak—a blue cross on a white ground. The Greek Navy had arrived.

6

The silence as Gurney burst into the after-cabin of the Admiral's brig was tense with menace. Six pairs of eyes swivelled on him—five with innocent curiosity, and the sixth, those of Pausanias Metaxas, with the look of a tiger-hunter posed with one foot on a carcass which turns out to be still breathing. On his way over to the flagship in the gig, Gurney had been seething with rage; but now, as he faced down upon the six round the Admiral's table, he brought himself under control.

"Admiral. Gentlemen. Mr. Metaxas. Your servant." He bowed.

The Admiral did not offer him a seat. "Well, well." The English was broken but comprehensible. "So you are the brave Captain Gurney, another one come to help Greece find her glories once more. I must confess, it is difficult for me to imagine how you intend to do this by running your pretty ship under the guns of two batteries and three frigates. Cavalry tactics, Captain. Unworthy of a sea officer."

Gurney felt the blood rise to his face. "Damn and blast your cavalry tactics, I say, Sir. Mr. Metaxas, in his wisdom, probably has not told you that he had promised me a landing on that damned island. My sortie was merely a diversion. Nor did he have the grace to inform me that there were three frigates in the harbour. Of which two, I may say, are now burned to the waterline."

The Admiral looked at Metaxas. "Is this true?"

Beads of sweat left little slug-tracks on Metaxas' sallow forehead. "Indeed, yes . . . the first part, anyway. But some of the men would not go, the majority, in effect, so we could hardly make a landing . . ."

"So you left me and my men to face sure annihilation. It isn't your fault that we are not now at the bottom of Ixos' harbour." Which was probably exactly where Metaxas wanted him—and his ship, mythical cargo and all, out of the reach of prying eyes and thieving hands. "I find it hard to believe that a captain can have so little control over his men as to allow them to mutiny openly in time of war."

The Admiral smiled, waved to a chair and poured a glass of retsina. "Come, sit. I see the trouble; you must remember, Captain, that you are in Greece now, in the Levant, where we have little knowledge of your inflexible occidental ways. No, it is fair enough that if Metaxas' men," he threw a scornful glance at the small man, "do not wish to fight, then they need not. We invented democracy, as our apologists in England will have told you, and," he smiled wryly, "we live by it still. Each sailor on each ship has a share of that ship; decisions are made by popular vote. If things were getting hot for you in the harbour of Ixos, the sensible course of action would have been to get out of there."

"And leave Metaxas' landing unsupported?"

"That is different. I heard that he had a hostage to your good faith."

"He did indeed. And it is no thanks to his hostage-taking that we are not now sitting on somewhat sharp seats in the citadel yonder."

The Admiral pursed his lips. "There is obviously more to this than meets the eye. But I fear that in this Navy that is no concern of mine. We are amateurs at best, Captain Gurney, and our discipline is self-imposed, from the cabin-boy to the Admiral, according to the ancient code of the Judgements of Oléron. And now, our task is to throw the Turk into the sea: perhaps in view of the indignities you suffered at his hands, you would join me?"

"My ship . . ."

"Your ship will be safe enough. No Turk will venture far from home when he hears that the Greek Navy, pathetic rabble though it may be in your eyes, is at sea. Let her stand off the island, and come watch our vengeance."

Gurney took a sip of wine, wincing at the resinous taste of it. His eyes brooded on Pausanias Metaxas. "What would you say if I were to go off in the opposite direction?"

The Admiral looked worried. "According to the views of Mr. Metaxas here, I am afraid you would have to leave behind him who rescued you. In Mr. Metaxas' view, there are obligations you are under which he considers are not yet discharged." Down the table, Metaxas' mouth pursed into a sanctimonious *moue*. The Admiral was staring at his fingernails, real pain in his eyes. "Obviously we shall do nothing to hinder you if you wish to leave. But I fear Metaxas has the right to hold on to his prisoner, however I may feel about this personally."

"Yes," said Metaxas. "It was dishonourable of him that he tried to escape. There is also the matter of the stolen boat."

"I suggest you hold your tongue before you cut your throat with it." Gurney caught his eye and held it coldly. "I insist on keeping Mr. Basreddin on my ship. I shall be happy to accommodate Mr. Metaxas and a reasonable escort while I effect repairs to the north of here, if it means that I should otherwise incur the wrath of the Greek Navy."

Relief was in the Admiral's face. "Good, good—now another glass, and we shall tear the Infidel limb from limb and toss him back into the sea."

Gurney, sitting on a bollard near the smouldering wreck of one of the frigates at Ixos, was feeling rather ill. The Admiral, it turned out, had meant every word of his grim threats. The turquoise water lapping at the steps of the quay was edged with pinkish scum. Fifteen feet away from him, a Turk stared with surprised yet sightless eyes at the pink and grey ropes of his intestines, spread round his gashed belly on the limestone paving. Judging by the shrieks from the citadel, the stakes set out for Gurney and his crew were being put to good—well, proper—use. Gurney closed his eyes. Enough, enough, for one day. Closing his eyes, he fell into a state halfway between reverie and doze. A hand on his shoulder brought him back to reality.

Metaxas was beaming down at him. His face was smeared with soot, and there was a smudge of blood on his cheek. The treacherous little eyes shone with a hard glitter. "Ah, Captain, our Greek vengeance is too much for you, it seems. Oh how they squeal, these pashas and their servants, when you tickle their navels with a yataghan." He waved his bloodied sword in the air. "Of course, I am a little past my prime. So I have one of the brave boys cut their hamstrings first, then I move along the line and paunch them like rabbits. So!" The fat man made an elaborate sweep with his sword, as if disembowelling the Sultan himself.

In the water at Gurney's feet a man—a Turk, deathly pale, slack-jawed—floated, clinging to a baulk of timber. Both legs had been hacked off at the knee. Metaxas followed his look. Then, emitting shrill cries of martial glee, he galloped down the steps and began to slash wildly at the legless man's face. The Turk raised a feeble hand to ward off the keen blade, and two of his fingers disappeared; then he seemed to lose his balance and his hold on the timber and fell back, his arms curiously long in comparison with his truncated legs, the water closing over his face with a caressing gentleness. There was an explosion of bubbles, and he sank into the dark green shadow at the base of the quay.

Gurney rose to his feet, not looking at Metaxas, who

puffed eagerly beside him, full of pride at his bravery. He unhitched a boat that lay moored at the steps and began to row to seaward, keeping his eyes fixed on the floorboards rather than look at the reeking red cobblestones, scarred fields and smoke-blackened sky that was Ixos liberated.

*   *   *

The cove in the southern shore of the mouth of the Gulf of Argos lay baking in the clear sunshine of late April. When Ioannis Kallikratides the Klepht had spied down the coast road, the scene had been one of emptiness and desolation, save for the dust-cloud of his quarry bearing the treasure of Osman Bey. Now, the horseshoe of sand and rock presented an entirely different appearance. For one thing, the foreshore was lush with green grass and cheerful with flowers. And the population had grown too. By the steeply-shelving beach *Vandal* lay, hove down on her side by enormous tackles made fast to rocks ashore. Round her exposed bottom a constant swarm of men, directed by Volnikov, scurried like ants. A little further down the beach and slightly inland, a makeshift banner marked the temporary headquarters of the Prussian contingent. Von Kratzstein had insisted, against Gurney's advice, that his choice of site was the best; for were the broken columns on the hilltop opposite not visible in the sunset? His appetite for beauty seemed to be more or less unmarred by the fact that his tent was directly downwind from the reeking fires on which Volnikov was wont to bubble great cauldrons of tar from morn to night.

Metaxas and his escort of twenty Klephts, awaiting the emergence of treasure from *Vandal's* keel, had established themselves on a grassy ledge high on the cliffs over the foreshore. Men working on the beach sometimes looked up from their task to see the sun winking on the brass chasing of a long musket. The tension was exacerbated by the fact that they had somehow managed to drag a six-pounder field piece up there with them, and when in liquor (frequently, as Gurney had discovered during the past three weeks) would indulge in a little target practice. Gurney had complained bitterly of this when a Klephtic shot had landed in a kettle of lobsters he had caught, smashing them to pulp. The shooting had become less accurate since, whether because of deterioration in marksmanship, powder, or wine Gurney neither knew nor cared. All he did know was that in the battery he had established on the headland to the south, to protect the anchorage and its approaches, there was a long twelve-pounder permanently trained not out to sea but on the whitish roof of Metaxas' tent. If another shot came anywhere near his quarters—the quarters of any of *Vandal's* complement—he would pull its linstock with his own hand, and damn the consequences.

But now, from Gurney's viewpoint among the rocky islets three quarters of a mile offshore, the tribulations of a camp as varied as any Peninsular rag-bag were remote. All he could see, as the little rowing-boat glided gently through the transparent mirror that was the Aegean on this clear day, was the wisp of black smoke from Volnikov's fire and the pile of boulders that masked the battery. He sighed, and took the boat alongside the first of the lobster-buoys with a smooth pull. He snagged the rope with a boat hook, braced himself in the stern, and began to haul.

Basreddin, in the bow, grunted. "As I remember, it was about here that she went over for the last time. The lobsters are fat enough, that's for sure."

"But we've been rowing round in circles for a week now, and we still haven't seen anything." Gurney heaved the first pot in over the side, yanked a good six-pounder out by the thorax and slung it in the basket. They he spiked the bait, checked the pot, and put it in its place ready for shooting. "We'll get this lot up, then we'd best take another swim."

Basreddin nodded. "And let us be wily. It is not by brandishing a stick at the field gate that the drover catches his donkey. Think like a wave, Giorgiou."

Gurney looked up at the rocks that hedged them in. "When the lugger struck, you say she hit that ledge there." He pointed at a tombstone of rock that lay just below water-level ten feet ahead of the boat. She must have gone in over, and then straight down. But we've seen every inch of the bottom, and all that's there is a lot of smashed-up crockery and a few trinkets. So today we'll have to try on the south side. If she hit fair and square, her stern might have slid backwards."

Five more fat lobsters were sparring in the basket when Gurney pulled the boat round the south side of the flat rock. Basreddin heaved the pots over the side one by one. As the last of them sank away into the blue gloom, Gurney moodily watched the fifty-foot buoy rope pay out. It disappeared over the side, straight down, and he slung the buoy after it. Instead of floating on the surface when the pot hit bottom forty feet below, the green glass sphere in its little net bag sank like a stone. Gurney stared for a moment. It had shown no cracks when he had hauled it. Then he was on his feet, shouting, the boat rocking wildly, tearing his clothes off.

Basreddin clutched at his thwart. "Sit down, for the love of God! Have you been stung by a bee? I have a salve—"

"Damn your salve! Don't you see? There's a hole under there, a bloody great hole, and the pot's dragged the buoy down with it. Like a funnel. When there's a sea running, it makes a whirlpool under the lip of that reef! That's where she lies, for sure."

"Good." The Sufi was impassive as always, but he also was throwing off his clothes. "Less noise, though. We do not want to let that thieving rabble ashore know that we have discovered the camel that shits gold."

But Gurney was already over the side, breathing deep. He dived, swimming strongly downwards until he saw the buoy glinting green thirty feet below the surface. Catching hold of the rope, he began to pull himself towards the bottom. His ears hurt, and he paused, took his nose between his fingers and blew. The Gulf pearlers had taught him the trick four years ago. As he neared the rock-strewn sand of the bottom, he could see the rope curve away a little and disappear behind an overhang of the rock ledge, down whose sheer side he was moving. His heart pounded in his chest as he rounded the corner and the rope plunged down, down, into a gloomy black pit yawning at the base of the underwater cliff. Lying by the mouth of the pit was a long black cylinder. A cannon! He hung for a moment, unwilling to believe his eyes, then let go of the rope and kicked for the surface.

Basreddin was sitting with his scrawny brown shanks hung over the stern of the boat, feet trailing in the water, when Gurney came up like a breaching whale.

"It's there, I tell you! Bloody great cannon sitting down there. Sternchaser or some such. It's in the hole! The buoy's down five fathoms. There's ten of rope. Fifteen fathoms, near enough."

Basreddin slid over the side like an otter and vanished into the blue twilight below. It was a full five minutes before he resurfaced.

"Fifteen fathoms is a great depth. I came to the cannon, but could go no further." He looked grave. "I fear that to reach the bottom we will need skilled help. Is there any from your village who can dive?"

"No. There isn't the call for it, you know, in the North Sea. In addition to which, you'd perish with cold diving five fathoms, let alone fifteen. What we need is some little pearl-diver who's blind as a bat and dumb as an ox."

"Indeed." Basreddin scratched in the wet mat of his black hair. "Of course, we could find a sponge-diver on the islands nearby, and ensure his silence by simple means . . ."

Gurney shook his head. "No. There has been enough killing. Oh, there will be more sure enough, but not in cold blood. We should be no better than the Turk." Basreddin's disregard for human life—which, to be fair, extended as far as his own—had shocked Gurney when he had first known the Sufi. Now he was used to it, he could see that in the kind of worlds Basreddin had shared with him, it made up in expediency what it lacked in humanity.

He stared down, into the indigo shadows under the ledge. Fifteen fathoms. A depth that would bring the blood pouring from the ears and nose of one not trained since childhood. But there was no one beyond Basreddin and, at a pinch, *Vandal's* warrant officers who he would trust with the secret of the treasure.

Here he was, rocking gently under the forget-me-not sky in a scene from the pages of Homer, and the letters were down there, a mere thirty paces away. Barely more than a cricket-pitch. So near, and yet . . .

Basreddin, staring idly at his Captain from his habitual seat in the stern of the boat, was surprised to see his face break into a broad grin. "What is so amusing?"

"You will see, and soon. Come, let's away. I must have speech with Volnikov."

On a crag above the grassy ledge housing the Klepht's camp, the lone watcher folded his spyglass and began the descent. The watcher was happy, and though picking a way through the tufts and boulders was dangerous work, he hummed a tune. The words of the tune dealt with slaughter, loot and rape in a rather celebratory vein. As he descended his breath shortened, and the tune became lost in a series of wheezing gasps. He stayed in the shadow of a yellow-lichened rock for a moment to compose himself; then he waddled out on to the beach.

*   *   *

Volnikov jerked his head at a small, dry-faced man scurrying past on some errand. "Churchyard. Come here. Talk to Captain for me."

The dry-faced cooper stopped in his tracks and touched the brim of his sailor's straw hat to Gurney. His mouth was a thin line, the lips pressed back over toothless gums, grooved by years of mumbled nails.

Gurney showed him the drawing he had made. It was of a truncated cone, weighted at its larger end with lead. The large end was open, but the small end was closed.

Churchyard's green eyes glinted above his little red cheeks. "Divin'-bell, eh, Sir? Gor swelp me. I mind as how I made one of them things back in '12, Sir, out in the West Indias, after some guns as the capting had ejaculated, so ter speak, pursued by a privateer. Sound as a bell it was, to coin a phrase." He laughed. Quite the wag, Churchyard.

Gurney was pleased. "You've made one before, then?"

"Aye, Sir, and a good'un. Capting got his guns up, and we only lost three drowned a-doing of it." The eye still twinkling.

"Damn you for a canter and a rapparee, cooper. This time, nobody will drown, you will make certain. It'll be Mr. Basreddin and me using it, and we'd better come back safe. Make it good and make it light, so we can take it out in the jollyboat. We'll have the weights separate. Six sixty-eight pound shots should do it. You can hang 'em round the bottom in nets. And Churchyard! Not a word to anyone. Clear?"

"It's a big job, Mr. Gurney." The cooper's face was as lugubrious as his name. "'Twon't be easy to hide, nohow."

"Then you'd better do it right out in the open. I'll send out a party after meat, so it will look as if we're casking up victuals. We'll need it anyway."

"Aye aye, Sir. Three days, I reckon."

"Sooner the better, Churchyard."

For the next seventy-two hours, Gurney fretted and fumed in his tent. He tried to beguile the time by hunting the white mountain goats of the interior, using a long musket borrowed from one of Metaxas' Klephts; but he found the weapon unwieldy with its four-foot barrel, and the goats themselves were as elusive as phantoms. In addition, the sun was already gaining strength as the spring passed towards summer. By the sea there was always cool shade, but here in the hills the asphodels and poppies were beginning to wither. Eventually, by dint of lying in a baking gulley, for four hours, he got a steady shot at a venerable patriarch among goats; the bullet spanged on a hard surface, then whizzed away into the blue. Gurney cursed, then watched in amazement as the goat's knees buckled and it pitched sideways. He ran from his hiding place towards it, hallooing with glee. Rapt in contemplation of its scrawny body and great sweeping horns, he was surprised to see that it was still breathing. He looked closer. On the plate of bone at the base of one horn was a smear of bright lead where the bullet had hit and ricocheted. Gurney stood by, openmouthed, as the patriarch staggered back to its feet, evidently more than somewhat dazed, took stock of its situation, spotted Gurney, and disappeared over the horizon. Gurney had not even taken the time to reload his piece, so he merely stood impotent as the motes of dust from the creature's flight settled in the dead air. Then he grinned, shouldered his weapon, and began the five-mile trudge back to the shore.

When he arrived at the beach, Volnikov sidled across to him. "Is ready," he said. "Done a goot job, Churchyard. Come here." From inside *Vandal's* steeply-canted hull came the sound of hammering. They passed down through the fore-hatch, where two men were putting the finishing touches to a patch of new planking where the shot-hole had been and aft, into the cooper's shop. Churchyard was whistling tunelessly between his gums, his mouth abristle with nails, as he hammered the hoops on the construction wedged to the deck. It was Gurney's sketch come to life, a lovely thing of varnished oak and brass bands, like a harness-cask on an Indiaman in its glory. Gurney nodded.

"Very pretty. Will it work?"

Churchyard nearly swallowed a nail. "Work? Work, Capting? Does a Deptford whore fornicate? Of course it'll work."

Gurney looked at it again, imagined it suspended over that dark, gaping mouth fifty feet below the calm sea among those lethal knives of rock. "It'd better. Get it fast to the main boom. We'll swing it into the jollyboat tonight."

That night there was no moon. The Klephts' watch-fires had burned low, and the singing which had drifted raucously down from the ledge had trailed to silence an hour since. A slight breeze ruffled the surface of the water and played among the grasses of the foreshore as McIver ordered five men to the main boom topping-lift and sheets. The diving-bell rose like a giant limpet-shell from Vandal's main hatch, swung overboard, and descended onto the padded gunwales of the jollyboat. Gurney raised his hand, and the tackles were cast off.

As the two oarsmen pulled slowly towards the rocks offshore, Gurney searched the cliffs with his glass. Not a sign of life, though it was hard to tell in this pitchy black. The bulk of the diving-bell, hiding the rowers, gleamed dully in the hazy starlight. The thought of being ninety feet under water in that conical cell was an uncomfortable one.

Once among the rocks, he spoke words of command in a low voice. As the jollyboat came over the tomb-stone he pulled the bungs from the garboard strake and slid over the side. He waited, waist-deep in water, as the boat began to fill the settle, pushed down by the weight of the bell. When the gunwale was level with the water, he beckoned the oarsmen. They waded to

his side, braced their bare feet on the rough limestone,
and pushed the bell sideways. It held for a moment,
then slid free, floating beside the longboat on the bubble of air trapped in the cone. The boat, relieved of its
weight, rose a little on the buoyancy of the flotation
compartments at bow and stern.

Gurney turned to the man at his side. "Good. Get
bailing." He saw teeth flash white in the darkness, and
the man scrambled into the boat. A bucket began to
throw a glittering stream of water over the side.
Taking a deep breath, Gurney launched himself from
the edge of the tombstone and swam to the diving-
bell. He ducked his head, kicked once, and was inside.

It was not as dark as he had expected; the starlight
reflected from the bottom made a faint luminescence
as he searched for the coils of rope. He found them,
pulled the half-knots that secured them. First one
anchor, then another plunged to the seabed. The bell
stopped its drift and lay to.

Gurney ducked under the edge of the bell and
swam round until he came to the iron loops Churchyard had screwed into its side. He pulled himself up,
put one foot on the loop, and pushed with his fingers at
the flap of the valve at the summit of the cone. Air
rushed out, and the bell sank rapidly until its summit
was awash in the ripples raised by the breeze. He
swam back to the ledge. The boat was nearly dry
when he climbed aboard.

As they pulled back towards the dark line of the
shore, Gurney thought of what the morrow held in
store. There was a chill in the air now, and he began to
shiver. He only wished he could be sure that it was
because of the cold that his teeth were chattering.

Next morning dawned bright and clear. The breeze
that had come up with the sunrise had died down by
the time Basreddin and Gurney took to the skiff and
began to pull for the rocks. Gurney had slept badly,

tormented by dreams of suffocating eddies of water which sucked him, whirling, into black pits. The biscuits and coffee he had forced down at breakfast sat uneasily on his stomach, and the sun burning from a flawless sky seemed to be taking an inordinately long time to warm his bones. As they came between the two islets which flanked the last resting place of Kallikratides' lugger, the pot-buoys bobbing in the slight swell looked to him like the eyes of some frightful seamonster. The bell, hard by the tombstone ledge, only the ferrule of its valve showing above the water, rocked very gently in the sea's heave. Like the remnant of some vast drowned carillon, thought Gurney, tolling a knell for the men who had died in the vain quest for gold. And how many more would die under the curse of Osman Bey? A shadow seemed to fall over the bright day.

He pulled the skiff alongside. Basreddin leaned over, screwed the brass-bound nose of an air pump into the ferrule, and began to work the bellows. Gurney stripped off his clothes and began to rub thick tallow over his limbs and body. It would be cold down there. He strapped a weighted belt round his waist, then sat and watched as the cone rose gradually out of the water, buoyed on the growing bubble of air inside. When bubbles started to burst under the lip, Gurney bent the end of the seventy fathoms of three-inch manila to the ring by the valve, and tugged. "Ready to go."

Basreddin stopped pumping. "Yes. Go with Allah, Giorgiou. And remember: no matter how badly you want to come up, go back to the bell for air. Then breathe out as you rise. If you hold it in, your very bowels will explode within your body."

Gurney nodded, looking down into the water. "I'll remember." He dived over the side. Basreddin watched his white legs kick into the shadow under the bell, then quickly rolled the six sixty-eight pound roundshot into the stout netting bags draped round the bell's lip. He slacked off the rope, and the brass-bound oak limpet shell sank away into the shadows.

In the bell, Gurney hung in the rope handholds Churchyard had thoughtfully installed, and concentrated on breathing as little as possible. Fifteen minutes' air. The circle of light at the open base of the bell changed colour from royal blue to deep indigo, and the pressure drove sharp stabs of pain into his eardrums. He cleared his ears once, then again; he could see quite distinctly the little shards of rock on the bottom, and he grasped the signal line and gave two tugs. The bottom came up more slowly. In the left-hand side of the circle of light, Gurney could see the face of the underwater cliff coming slowly past him. Then there was a black shadow at its base, and a dim indication of a rugged mouth of rock gaping up at him, the greenish filament of the sunken pot-line curving out of sight into its throat. Gurney shifted his hold as the bell sank slowly towards the lip. Too far right. He let his legs drop into the pool and pushed hard against the rock. The bell swung, the darkening circle of water tilting into an alarming oval, the crash of its collision booming in his ears; then it was hanging free again, suspended. Gurney tugged three times, and the bell stopped, swaying slightly, over the narrowing maw of the chasm. He adjusted his weighted belt and took three deep, whistling breaths. Then he slung a coil of rope over his shoulder and dived into the darkness below.

In the bottom of the cave, the guardian of the wrecks moved her tail gently, to balance herself against the strange new turbulence in the water. Last time she had felt such turbulence, it had heralded the arrival of food. Good, dead, solid, putrefying food. Not that she remembered; but in the little bulb of nerve-tissue which animated her twenty foot length of olive-green, slime-covered muscle, a connection was made. She writhed, drawing in on herself, crouching weightless in the stagnant rent in the rock that was her home.

Gurney could see the bottom of the hole after he had swum only five feet: a jumble of objects, rocks; but was there not a regularity of outline about that one there, half-under a projecting ledge of stone? He grasped the pot-line and sank with his weights, slowly but not too slowly, towards it. It was very dark down here, so that shapes were vague and tenuous to his water-blurred eyes. The pulses in him quickened; all thoughts of those ninety feet of heavy blue water above him were pushed aside as he came to his lost lobster-pot, sunk past it, and kicked himself towards his goal. He thrust his hand at the object below the ledge, and his fingers met a complicated arabesque of iron traceries. The body of the chest was of iron, too, metallic to the touch in this work of rock and slime. He stripped the coil of rope from his shoulder and made a quick round-turn and two half-hitches. The last half-hitch was difficult to make; his lungs were tight, and there was a panicky voice beginning to whimper in the back of his mind. Tugging the rope taut, he stripped off his weighted belt and let himself rise out of the dark, towards the dim geometric shape of the diving-bell.

The guardian of the wrecks had come half out of her retreat, and nosed at the unfamiliar object which had attracted the food's attention. It had come tumbling down from above a short time ago in her aeons-long life, at the same time as the last great food; she had sniffed it then to see if it were edible, but it was even less appetising than the rocks. She opened her mouth, taking in water and spewing it through her gills as her sluggish metabolism pumped itself up in anticipation. The food smelt good, even if it was a little too alive for her taste.

Gurney had recovered his breath, and hung in the rope loops, resting. One more line on that box and up she would come. He took another coil, slung it over his shoulders, filled his lungs with the fouling air in the bell, and dived, pulling himself down the rope he had anchored to the ring-bolt in the chest. There was another ring-bolt on the inside, and that should do it. Now that he knew what he was looking for he moved with more assurance, and the rope seemed almost to knot itself. He backed from under the overhang and drifted again towards the bell.

The guardian of the wrecks liked to make sure of her prey. As the white, frog-like figure with the tow-coloured hair swam upwards with futile little kicking movements of its lower limbs, she pulsed a double ripple down her body and rose out of the depths with the slow power of a hydraulic piston.

Gurney made the second rope fast to its cleat inside the diving-bell and prepared himself for the final phase. He was cold now, even through his layer of grease; the air inside the bell was all but unbreathable, cold and clammy; as he drew three last breaths into his lungs, he was aware that he was gasping rather than breathing. He dived out of the bell for the third time, knife drawn, and cut away the garland of shot from its lower rim.

The diving-bell, freed of its weights, shot upwards like a rocket. The ropes which attached it to the chest jerked taut, and with a grinding of iron against rock the treasure of Osman Bey was plucked from its vault and yanked towards the surface.

Gurney rose slowly, allowing the air to dribble in little strings of bubbles from his nostrils. Far above him, as far as the sky from the deck of the *Vandal*, the sun netted the sea's face with light. He smiled, and let the air in his lungs carry him up towards it. Something plucked softly at his right calf. He gave an involuntary kick, and looked down. Two black eyes the size of saucers stared blankly at him from behind a pursed snout set with hooked teeth. His mouth opened and water rushed in, as the little panicky voice became a scream. All the dreams of choking and pursuit he had ever had came roaring and bellowing into his mind as the mouth opened and grinned at him, a hook-toothed grin two feet from side to side. He kicked and kicked again, his mouth burning with salt water, towards that cheerful mesh of light dappling the sea above.

The guardian of the wrecks liked to play with her food. Coiling herself into a spiral, she writhed round its body, rubbing her delicate slime on its hot, greasy surface. Gurney felt the turbulence of her passing against his chest, and kept kicking upwards. His right hand was cumbered. What was it? He made to throw away the thing that weighed him down, but then he remembered. The knife. Long hours Volnikov had spent, first with his stone, then with a leather strop, honing that blade to a sharpness that would cut a hair laid across it. He doubled his grip on its ropework hilt. (Keep exhaling! Slow, exhale.) And, as the death-white belly of the monstrous conger curved past him, he struck.

The skin on the belly of the guardian of the wrecks was a quarter of an inch thick, tough substance close to gristle. Behind it, layer upon layer, were three inches of muscle of the consistency of hard India rubber. Gurney's blade sliced through skin and muscle like paper, and drove deep into the conger's vitals, and round him the sea went mad. The sinuous body thrashed and writhed, setting up currents and vortices, as the knife, dragged by the eel's own momentum, sliced a deep slit in its belly through which guts spewed in a dark cloud of blood. Gurney drew back his knife and kicked free of the thrashing monster, and made towards the surface again, but the panic suffocation-scream was deafening now, and a

red mist was falling before his eyes. *Keep exhaling.*
The strength drained from his limbs, and he drifted
upwards, passive, unresisting, concentrating only on
keeping his mouth shut (mouth filled with water, but
closed) and letting that thin dribble of air trickle
from his nostrils ("lest your bowels burst within you,
exhale, Giorgiou"). Ten feet below the surface he lost
consciousness.

He opened his eyes, then wished that he hadn't. He
felt as if he had been tied to a kicking mule and
thrown over a cliff. The blur that was the world outside the horrid mess of nausea and pain in his head
began to split itself into recognisable parts. A piece of
dried seaweed two inches away from his left eye. A
tiny spider-crab, scuttling out of the orbit of his vision.
And two sledge-hammers, smashing him at regular
intervals below the shoulder-blades.

Gurney groaned, and the sledge-hammers stopped.
He groaned again, hoping that his head might fall
off and leave him in peace. Over the ringing that
filled his ears, he could dimly hear a voice calling his
name. He struggled onto his elbows and looked round.
The world took a great lurch and began to spin and
he vomited sea water all over the rock in front of him.
He hung for a moment, then made another effort.
This time it was better.

"You swallowed about half the Aegean, Giorgiou.
It was as you were making a start on the second half
that I got a grip on you."

Gurney shook his head. "You shouldn't have
bothered. I'd be better off dead." He became aware of
a new, fierce pain. "Christ, my leg hurts. What happened?" The calf-muscle of his right leg looked as if
it had been scored by razors. A piece of flesh about
the size of a crown was missing. Basreddin waved
his hand towards the ledge. On the calm blue water,
something white and flaccid was floating. The white
of a fish's belly. Suddenly it all came back to Gurney.

When the retching had stopped, he looked at Basreddin again. "The chest?"

"Under the diving-bell, safe and sound."

"Come on then. Let's get it stowed and smash the bell. And we'll tow old Hydra here home, too. It will give me great pleasure to see the lads eat that damned sea-serpent for their dinner."

It was no easy task, stowing the iron-bound chest of treasure beneath the lobster-pots in the little boat, particularly in Gurney's weakened state, but somehow they managed it, and Basreddin took the oars to row back, the giant eel trailing astern.

Vandal's careening was finished now, and the heaving-down tackles had been slackened off so they lay on an even keel. As they came alongside, Gurney felt a familiar thrill of pride. She was a good ship, and no mistake. Good men, too; you would have to go a long way to find a gang of dockyard mateys who would do a job like that, and in this little piece of the back of beyond it was well-nigh incredible. He scrambled aboard and passed the word for McIver. When the Scot arrived, his one eye darted nervously over the boat and its cargo.

Gurney winked. "Swing 'er aboard, McIver. We'll be sailing at dawn tomorrow. I've left the pots on board there. See to 'em yourself, would you? We had a goodish haul, and you can bring the proceeds to my cabin. We'll decide which to give the galley and which to keep."

A broad grin spread itself across McIver's face. "Aye, aye, Sir, and with pleasure."

Gurney stomped down to his night cabin and flung himself on his cot. He was weak and queasy, but such was the excitement of the treasure that despite his exhaustion he could not sleep, and after perhaps twenty minutes he returned to his day cabin. Basreddin stood by the glassless stern-windows, gazing out to sea. There came a knocking on the cabin door. McIver was there with three men, carrying with evident difficulty an enormous fish-basket full, apparently, of conger-eel guts. There was a gleam in McIver's eye.

"We have your catch here, Mr. Gurney. Now then, Mather, get rid of them innards." The American picked up the guts and slung them through the window. In the basket, smeared with fish slime, was the iron chest that contained the treasure of Osman Bey.

McIver frowned. "I took the liberty, Sir, of havin' a crack at it wi' a screwdriver. No dice. Have you a key?"

Gurney shook his head. "No. And it's a well-constructed piece of furniture. Yes, Volnikov?" The Russian was making noises in his throat. He was overcome, it seemed, with shyness. "Well, come on, man. Spit it out."

Volnikov rummaged in the capacious pocket of his unspeakable coat. When he drew out his hand, it held a huge hammer. Gurney took an instinctive step back, remembering the chisel incident, and noticed that the other men in the cabin did the same. The giant Russian spat on his right palm, nestled the handle of the hammer firmly in his grip, wound up and let fly at the little keyhole in the ornate iron chest. There was a report like a bomb going off, and Gurney stared, fascinated, the ringing in his ears renewed, at the neat hole that appeared where the lock had been. Volnikov, simple pride in achievement writ large on his battered features, made the deprecating gesture of a conjuror who has just performed a trick too simple to be worth any fuss. Gurney, still a little stunned —the chest was a good inch thick, and solid iron— tugged at the lid. Something gave where the lock had been, and the lid, creaking with the rust in its hinges, lifted in his hand.

The sun was hanging low over the land, gilding the upper billows of the ranks of clouds marching in from the western horizon. The low, clear light which poured through the shoreward windows of the cabin

illuminated the dancing motes of dust stirred by the
refit and blazed like liquid fire in the hearts of the
jewels which filled the chest to its brim.

7

The cumulus which had turned yesterday's sunset
into a baroque Judgement Day had thickened and
spread. Day came up in a sullen flare of muddy red,
briefly crimsoning the underside of the pall of cloud,
then settled into a windy grey with occasional clear
patches pursued by little squalls of drizzling rain.
Vandal seemed more cheered than otherwise by the
dour day, though, as if delighted to be away from her
undignified bottom-up posture at the beach. Gurney,
leaning against the taffrail, felt her quicken to the
brisk northerly that rolled and bounced across the
mouth of the Gulf of Argos, and listened with an
appreciative ear to the roar and bubble of the white
water creaming at her counter.

On the port side the garden of rocks which had
entombed the treasure of Osman Bey slid quickly by,
whipping the sharp waves into a welter of foam.
Gurney realised how lucky they had been to get a
two-week calm at this time of year; had the weather
broken any earlier he might still be on the beach,
seeking some pretext which would convince Metaxas
of the need for further delay.

As the rocks shrank astern, a grey squall of rain
swept across like a curtain, hiding the cove from view.
Gurney pulled up the collar of his pea-jacket and
turned his back to the wind. Not yet time to go below.
He was feeling damned weak, though, since that little
tussle with the conger. He grinned. There had been

some long faces at dinner last night. Try as you might, you could not get a jolly jack tar to dig into a bit of eel. Gurney admitted to himself that his consuming of a couple of pounds of it was more an act of vengeance for the stiffened crater in his right calf than a gastronomic treat. And perhaps it was unfair to ask the men to share his feelings. But they would be sharing the treasure, by God, or at least as much of it as would be left after Metaxas and his jackals had had their portion. And the letters, there was something else. Right as rain, they were, all wrapped in oilcloth, seals attached, pretty as you please. If Jervy did not put through an order for at least two ships, and keep Sea Dalling in work for a year, he was no better than a damned ingrate. Yes, let the weather do what it would, things were looking bright. He let his eyes run down the deck. Metaxas was forward, deep in conversation with one of his henchmen. His mood evaporated as the paunchy Greek felt his eyes, looked up and waved, starting towards him. Not even a sea which foamed up through the lee scuppers and drenched the interpreter to the knees cheered him.

As the little man waddled up to him, shaking his wet feet like a petulant chicken in a puddle, Gurney composed his face into what he hoped was a good-natured smile.

"Good morning, Mr. Metaxas. I hope you are well-rested?"

"Indeed I am, tolerably well. Though I must say that I found my quarters a little, er, *smelling*."

"Dear, dear." Gurney had given Pieter the coxswain definite instructions that he was to put Metaxas in the cabin locker, nearest the rottenest of *Vandal's* salt horse. Now there were black bags under the interpreter's eyes, and his face had a greenish cast, as if from prolonged and painful sickness. "You do indeed look a little pale. Still, fresh air and sea bathing will tone you up beyond measure, I'll be bound." He looked at the Greek's soaking shoes and stockings. "I see you've already had a dip."

The little eyes were suspicious. "The Captain is pleased to joke? Very amusing. I like in the morning to laugh, too much. But as to sea bathing. Some say it is bad for the chest."

Gurney stiffened, then cursed himself for a fool. Even with Osman Bey's hoard reposing beneath the pig-iron of the ballast deep in the bilges, there was no need to be so sensitive about the mention of chests.

But there was a sly spark in Metaxas' eye which did not fit in with his general discomfiture.

The Greek was speaking again. "It will be good to conclude our little affair, so we can go our separate ways about the great work that is to be done. Yes. But I have learnt many profitable lessons during the past few days, not least among them that it is good for the soul to sit on a cliff and watch the sea. In the village of Mavromichaelis, I spend too little time watching the sea." Again that spark of sly malice in the eye.

Exactly how much did this little Klepht know? Gurney bowed. "For me also it has been instructive. And now, as you say, it is over. Within two days, you and your gold will disembark to continue, ahem, the Great Work." Privately, Gurney reckoned he would be a Chinaman before any of the gold lying in bags in the locker in his cabin found its way into the Great Work. It was Metaxas' coffers that would be lined. None of his business though. Provided he fulfilled his end of the bargain, demonstrated the limpet-like adherence to Doing the Right Thing expected of the agents of His Britannic Majesty, he could dismiss Metaxas from his mind as soon as the Mani dropped over the horizon.

The wind freshened steadily as the morning wore on, the squalls becoming sharper and more frequent. There were still long, clear stretches of exhilarating sailing, though, when the sun burned down through a keen and invigorating air, turning the sea a splendid deep blue that surprised Gurney; oceanic blue it was, rather than the kindly turquoise of the Mediterranean. Deep in his bones he could feel that it was coming on to blow. Which was worrying. For while he could as well lie-to and ride out the coming storm under the cliffs that guarded Mavromichaelis stronghold, the memory of the battery overlooking the anchorage was yet green in his mind. Perhaps Metaxas' motives went only as far as personal greed; but Gurney was not prepared to count on it. No, when the storm came up, as come it would, he must have sea-room and plenty of it, though where he would find it in this rock-studded saltwater pond he had no idea. Unless, of course, he were to run for the open water to the southwest of Crete, beyond the Cerigo Straits. But that came later. Now, the important thing was to unload the Greeks and the ransom as soon as possible.

A shout from the foretop broke in on his train of thought.

"Sail! Sail ho!"

Gurney ran forward to the shrouds, scurried up the ratlines, and clambered onto the fore upper topsail yard beside Henry Priest.

"What have you got, Henry?" The wind pulled the words from his mouth almost before he said them. One hundred feet below, *Vandal's* hull, tiny from this elevation, ploughed through the dark blue seas in a lacy arrowhead of foam.

"Hard ter say, Sir. Tricky ol' day fer the seeing." The lookout shifted his eternal quid and spat a looping stream of tobacco-juice to leeward. "But I reckon as she's a frigate. Whose I couldn't say for sure, but I've a feeling as she's one of ours."

Gurney steadied his glass—no easy task, with the mast arching twenty feet one way, twenty feet the other—on the patch of sea Henry's forefinger indicated. Though if Henry said she was a frigate, then a frigate she almost undoubtedly was. The round circle of the glass made sky and sea look curiously flat and two-dimensional, like a puppet-show set. Then Gurney found the sail—three masts, slender and spidery, bearing on the mizzen a single topsail, on the fore and mainmasts courses and reefed topsails. She would be getting more wind out there, thought Gurney. Hard to tell who she was until she came hull-up.

The strange ship's masts came closer together, and even from this distance he could see the yards eased as one, a fluid, controlled movement that spoke of tight discipline and a well-trained crew. "She's seen us, altered course to run down on us. English, for a pound."

Priest shook his head. "No bet, far as I'm concerned. Do you give me that glass." He looked for a moment. "Aye. She's an ensign at her spanker peak. One of ours all right, and she seems to want to chat."

"Good enough." Gurney jumped for a shroud-line and slid down to the deck, shouting for McIver. The mate came forward from the gun-deck, where he had been showing von Kratzstein the approved technique of brightening shot, much to the latter's indignation and disgust. As Gurney walked aft towards his cabin, he gave McIver his instructions; even as he ran down the companionway and banged the door shut behind him, the schooner came up head to wind and he felt her begin to pitch jerkily in the steep waves.

He was tying a cravat—as usual, in the wilds he had cast aside such civilised amenities as collars and ties, and to attain the correct four-in-hand effect was the devil of a struggle—when Metaxas burst in. Gurney did not turn round, but cocked a deliberately supercilious eye-brow at him in the looking-glass.

The interpreter seemed agitated. "Captain," he said. "Captain, for why have ship stop? Is there pirate you have see? We must return, Captain, to the village of Mavromichaelis." He burped. His face now had a distinct pea-green tinge.

"Are you indisposed, Mr. Metaxas?" Gurney gave

the cravat a final wrench, then turned to face his visitor. "Perhaps the motion of the ship disagrees. No, this is no pirate. Merely a ship of His Britannic Majesty's Navy, to whom I wish to report our continuing good health."

Relief swept across the small man's doughy features. "Ah! I see. I feared it was the Turk. So you will tell this English ship you are alive and well, and proceed with me. Tell me something, Captain. Are you yourself a naval man? Does your mission come under the heading of naval matter?"

Gurney frowned. "My mission, Sir, is a matter that concerns me, and me alone."

The interpreter seemed undisturbed by the double edge in Gurney's remark. "Good, good, excellent. Well, it will be pleasant for you to see familiar faces after us barbarians." He smiled his oily smile; then his face turned white and he ran for the door, hand clapped to his mouth. Gurney heard the sound of retching coming from the lee rail. He took his boat cloak from its locker, and permitted himself a grin. Then he wrapped the thick serge round his shoulders and went on deck.

Whoever the captain of the frigate was, he was taking no chances. He had laid his ship to the wind well out of cannon-shot and was now hove-to, main-topsail backed, at a discreet distance. A hoist of flags burst from his signal-halyards. Gurney called for young George Jordan, who came running.

"Bit of practice for you, George. Take the bring-'em-near and read that lot off for me."

"Aye, aye, Sir." Young George braced himself on the deck and steadied the telescope. "Frigate *Fastnet,* Sir. Carrying mail. Captain requests the pleasure of your company on board."

"Acknowledge and accept. Pieter!" The coxswain saluted. "Run me out my gig, and look sharp."

It was a measure of the efficiency of *Vandal*'s crew that it was a mere five minutes later that the first of the steep waves flung its white cap at Gurney's head, drenching his new hat and sending a chill stream inside the collar of his boat cloak. He cursed, then stiffened to attention, clasped his hands behind his back, and resumed a correctly rigid, attitude. *Vandal's* gig-crew, who before now had won many a race over the seven-mile course in the Pit, were on good form. And in the straw hats and blue coats that Arabella had insisted they wear, they looked pretty smart. Smarter by far than the naval rabble, purser rigged and parish damned, who thronged the 'tween-decks of a man-of-war.

As they passed under the frigate's flat stern Gurney caught the sour smell of her, and it transported him instantly back to the midshipmen's mess of the *Egregious*—that blend of powder-smoke, sweat, mildew and rot that was the perpetual, invisible burden of all naval ships. An Indiaman, rolling home from the Orient with a cargo of spices, would sometimes smell like a floating pomander; but a man-o'-war, with its cargo of men and imperial justice, stank like a disused cheese-cellar.

They were alongside now, the frigate's black side with the gunports picked out in yellow rearing above them. Gurney waited until the boat came to the top of a wave, then made a leap for the ship's mainchains and scrambled into her waist. Bosun's pipes twittered as the First Lieutenant greeted him and conducted him down the catwalk above the ship's manoeuvre deck to the quarterdeck where, standing alone in the clear space on the windward side, stood a figure in a blue coat of impeccable cut and condition, a gold epaulette at each shoulder, with a spy-glass tucked under his left arm. Gurney had met him once or twice, in London. A cold enough fish, but solid. He approached and bowed.

"George Gurney, schooner *Vandal*, at your service. Captain Williams, is it not?"

The Captain returned his bow, though less deeply.

"Aye, it is. Gratified to renew your acquaintance, *Mister* Gurney." The "mister" betrayed a fine naval condescension to the private yachtsman, but Gurney decided to let it pass. He himself, seven years ago, would have displayed a similar condescension. "His Lordship at Corfu asked me to keep an eye open for you on this coast. I must say, I am glad we have met. I was beginning to misdoubt me that you had fallen in with the piraticals. Although, now I come to look at your ship and your boat's crew, I am sure those cut-throats would have made but small impression on you."

Gurney bowed again. "You are too kind, Sir. Had you seen us but two weeks ago, however, you would not have been so impressed. Greek treachery and Turkish cannonades had left us a sorry sight."

Little furrows appeared in William's weather-beaten forehead. "Really? Dear me. We, of course, have little truck with such affairs. Neutral as we are, we are merely messenger-boys for their Lordships in these matters." But there were laughter-lines at the corner of his eyes. Gurney decided that he had been mistaken in his judgement. Williams was by no means the strait-laced career officer he appeared. "The day is cold. Will you perhaps join me in a glass of wine before you go about your business? I would ask you to dine, but the wind is freshening and I do not like what the glass tells me."

"Yes. I believe it will be worse before it's better. A glass of wine would certainly be warming."

They went below, into the spacious after-cabin of the frigate. The Captain's steward brought a broad-bottomed decanter and glasses, Williams poured, then looked across at his guest. "I will not drink to the confounding of our enemies, for, as I said, I am—or at least the Navy is—neutral in these matters. So I give you a safe voyage and a happy return."

They drank. Williams leaned forward over the table. "Now. It is none of my affair, I realise, but what brings you to these waters at a time when pleasure-cruising appears, to say the least, fraught with inconvenience?"

Gurney smiled. "Curiosity, Sir, mere curiosity. And the necessity of removing an old friend from the clutches of some murderous brigands. Which enterprise, I hope, is now moving to its happy conclusion."

"And it is this band of brigands which put you to the necessity of rigging a new topmast? A pretty spar, Sir, but new-varnished. And there have been no storms in these parts of late."

Observant devil, this, thought Gurney. He laughed. "No. Not directly, at any rate." And he gave the Captain a shortened and purified account of the raid on Ixos and the refit. He made no mention of the letters on whose recovery his mission hinged, nor of the treasure that had come to him.

When he had finished, the Captain refilled his glass and looked at him narrowly. "Hmm, well. Friendship is a wonderful thing. Judging by the esteem in which you are held by his Lordship at Corfu, that is not the whole story; but it is not my place to press you for details."

"Your delicacy does you credit, Captain Williams. And now, if I myself may ask questions I have no right to ask, what is your errand? It is difficult to believe that one of His Majesty's frigates should be doing mail-packet duty for a yachtsman on his tour—though if this is all, I confess myself much flattered."

Williams pursed his lips. "Yes. Difficult to credit indeed. It is no secret—and it may be of use to you to know—that we have been detailed to keep observation on a nest of pirates in the Sporades. To observe, I say, and no more; for pirate though he may be, this Kapraj Bey is a Turk, and with the Turks we are not at war. Is there something the matter?"

Gurney's face had whitened under its tan, and he was staring at Williams like a man stunned. When he spoke, his voice was strained and distant. "Kapraj Bey, you say. He whom they call the Black Crow of Izmir?"

"I believe he goes under some such disjaskit handle, yes. The man's a mere brigand, it seems. For some ten years now he has looted and slaved in the Southern Aegean, and he continues as before. Quite a fleet he has, by all accounts—"

"And his flagship is a red xebec he calls the *Golden Horn*."

Williams looked at him curiously. "That is correct. You seem to know a good deal about this man."

"And so I should. Four years ago he sank an Italian fishing-vessel on which I was travelling to Alexandria, butchered her crew, and took me captive." Gurney's eyes were fixed on the liquid in his glass, in which the cabin lamp cast lights the colour of fresh blood. "Four months I walked, I and the other wretches in his slave-coffle, into the Torus mountains. He sold us like a flock of sheep and counted the coins as we were driven to the slaughter. Yes, I know this man."

"So. There is a story here, I suspect." Interest quickened in the Captain's brisk tones. "A story I would like to hear at some time."

Gurney made a dismissive gesture with his hand. "Now, I regret, is not the time. Five years ago, it began, at Vernon's; and for three months after that, it was the talk of the town, I have no doubt. But that is past now, stuff for a yarn over a bottle some winter evening ashore. Tell me, would it displease their Lordships if this Kapraj were to take a fall? A fall from which he would not rise?"

A disciplined impartiality fell over Williams' ruddy features. "It is not for me to say." He grinned. "But between ourselves, I can think of nothing that would delight them more. This pirate has not only been making hay with most of the shipping in the Sporades and the Dodecanese, but he's stepped up his campaign during the past three months until it's fair to say that no ship of any nationality save Turkish and Egyptian is safe in these waters. And that's a hell of an area. It's not only the *Golden Horn,* you know; he has five or six others ships, at least as heavily armed if not as fast, and he's a good admiral."

"But if he is sinking English ships, have we not sufficient grounds for returning the favour?"

"He's too clever for that. As I said, he's a fly kind of whip-jacket. He makes devilish sure that when he takes on some unfortunate merchantman, nobody gets away to blow the gaff. And he's as clever a politician as he is a thief, though in my opinion that's one and the same thing. He's well in with the Egyptians, and nobody wants to offend them if they can help it, particularly with that spanking great fleet of theirs at Alexandria. As if that wasn't enough, the Sultan of Turkey pretends to love him like a brother, too. Even the Greeks, or that parcel of ninnyhammers who call themselves a Government, are terrified of hurting his feelings in case he calls the Gippoes out on them."

Gurney nodded. "But an enterprising man, of no recognisable allegiance—"

"Yes. But you'd have to find out where his ken is first. All we know is that it's somewhere hard by Bodrum. That's a difficult part of the coastline nowadays, and I couldn't for the life of me sail in there without some Turk getting up on his hind legs and screaming 'act of war.' Which, while it would bother me not at all, would certainly cause some weeping and gnashing of teeth at the Board of Admiralty."

Gurney drained his glass and rose to his feet. "Suddenly I find myself much interested by Bodrum. They say the ruins there are exceedingly attractive. Perhaps I shall go and see them, and who knows? When I have finished, there may be more ruins to attract rich dilettanti such as myself. If I could trouble you to call my gig?"

"With the greatest of pleasure. I shall follow your progress with interest."

The two men grinned at each other. They shook

hands with considerable warmth; then Gurney wrapped himself in his boat cloak, stumped past the impassive Marine sentry at the door, and climbed to *Fastnet's* pitching deck. When the gig came alongside he climbed down the side and jumped into the stern, turning to catch the canvas mail-bag one of the frigate's men tossed down to him. Then he sat on the thwart and let himself be rowed back towards *Vandal*.

While he had been aboard the frigate the wind had stiffened, and it was now blowing half a gale from the north; but Gurney did not notice. Mention of Kapraj Bey's name had loosed a flood of memories—of the beautiful Greek Helena, once Byron's mistress, who had sheltered him with her body and given him solace on the long road to China; of his first meeting with Basreddin among the roiling glides and foaming rapids of the Tigris gorge; but most of all, of the misery and cruelty of the slave-market. For Gurney's spirit rebelled at the caging of any free spirit for profit. Just retribution for crimes against the common weal, yes; but bartering in flesh and souls, never. As the gig turned into the quieter water under *Vandal's* lee, Gurney decided that he would investigate Kapraj Bey, and investigate him to the death. Last time they had met, it had been a matter of a dismasted Neapolitan trading-vessel against a sleek xebec. Now, as the gig came alongside his ship, Gurney looked up at her hundred and fifty feet of black bulwark and yellow gunports, and decided the odds would be more equal.

According to his invariable habit, he tossed a gold piece to the stroke oar of the gig. The man would share it with the rest of the oarsmen. Then he went up the Jacob's ladder into *Vandal's* entry-port and strode directly aft to his cabin, ignoring the curious looks cast in his direction by McIver and Basreddin. He unclasped his boat cloak and flung it into the corner, pausing as he felt *Vandal* pay off and heel to the wind

as she resumed her interrupted course for Mavromichaelis' stronghold.

The neck of the mail-bag was secured with stout
cord, sealed with the familiar foul anchor. He pulled
out his knife and cut it, upending it over the table. The
letters were not many, which was hardly surprising;
after all, only about ten of *Vandal's* sixty men could
read worth a damn. Now, to be sure, the dame school
in Sea Dalling, which Arabella had insisted on setting
up and endowing, was thriving, and in time the little
Priests, Jordans and Jarvises would probably be as
sharp a clutch of lawyers as ever stole prize from sail-
or. But the *Vandal* had had no such advantages. One
for McIver—probably from the woman who had
turned up at Sea Dalling claiming to be his bastard
daughter, despite his denials. Certainly there was no
physical resemblance. Five or six in a painstaking
copybook scrawl, addressed to various Priests, Jordans
and Jarvises: from the budding geniuses aforemen-
tioned, presumably. And three for Gurney. One, with
an Admiralty seal, probably accounted for the improb-
able honour of mail-delivery by frigate at sea; another,
in the crabbed hand of Gurney's man of affairs, undoubtedly contained depressing news about the state
of his finances and the delivery dates of the Aberdeen
schooners; and finally a fat packet from Sea Dalling,
on the house writing paper, in Arabella's precise,
feminine hand. This Gurney put aside to read last.

He broke the seals on the Admiralty letter. As he
had guessed, it was from Jervy Hutchinson. That bluff
and breezy mariner, evidently in a mood of extreme
discontent with the gout which kept him cooped up in
a room in Whitehall when he should have been
ploughing the raging main, began with a string of
oaths which brought a grin to Gurney's face. He then
proceeded, as Gurney had expected, to give a lot of
advice based on the premise that Gurney's heart ruled
his head under all circumstances. Gurney drummed

his fingers impatiently on the table. Jervy always had the greatest difficulty in grasping that the man he now addressed was no longer the hotheaded midshipman at *Egregious*'s signal-halyards, and the first two pages of his communications were very hard going for one as short-fused as his present reader. On the third page, however, the Admiral arrived at the nub of his message. In short, sharp sentences—Gurney could almost hear him barking at some unfortunate land-lubber to stop tramping the shrouds like a damned Russian bear—he conveyed that the safe recovery of the letters lying in *Vandal*'s bilges would ensure their Lordships' order of at least two schooners from the Dalling yards. He also implied that provided Gurney paid strict regard to the absolute neutrality of England, anything he could do to suppress piracy in the Southern Aegean would be most welcome, and would earn the Admiralty's further gratitude. Fight fire with fire, was the way he put it; Gurney knew that since his demolishing of a French privateer with one of Jervy's treasured prizes, the Admiral had regarded him as a sort of tame Blackbeard. An interesting suggestion, however; suddenly Gurney began to understand why Jervy had gone to the trouble of sending a frigate after him. A fat carrot, and a tempting one. Pleasing indeed that it should coincide with a personal grudge against Kapraj Bey.

Gurney tossed the letter aside, and turned wearily to his business affairs. Matters were better than he had feared, but not much; he occupied half an hour in penning a reply to his agent's more urgent entreaties, though God knew when the man would get it. *Vandal*'s movements were becoming increasingly violent, to the point where it was difficult to write; so it was with relief that he signed his name and pressed his ring into the hot wax that sealed the letter. Then he picked up the packet which bore Arabella's handwriting.

"Dearest George," he read. "Now you have been gone a full month, and without you each day is more tiresome than the last. I have been running about the place like a mad thing, and collect I have quite worn the legs off my horse. Jedediah is in despair with me, for I spend hours mooning round the yards hoping you will pop up under some lump of wood. Misery!

"But I shouldn't whimper at you. All is well at Sea Dalling; your new ships are looking quite beautiful now, Jedediah has put them off the slips and they at least float. They sent down a lot of pelargoniums from Kew last week, so this summer the rockery will be a riot—we've put them in the glasshouse now, the poor little Chinese dears, because the east wind is blowing like razors. Since you left there seem to be a lot more pheasants. Coincidence? If I were you I should lock the ship's chickens up carefully at night in case the Jordans revert to type on the high seas.

"The country has been quiet of late, without you to stir things up. The Buxtons call from time to time, and we trot round the park with our toes freezing off while they tell me about their remarkable turnips and try to hide their suspicion of any gardening that doesn't end up in their stomachs. Barbarians! But there have been some pleasant visits from Mr. Cotman—the painter, you know—and he has done some admirable sketches of the house that will amuse you when you come back. And Isabel came to see me a week ago, calm and collected as ever. Really, I don't think she has an unkind bone in her body. She was in something of a taking, because ever since that evening Paddy Fitzcozens has been bombarding her with letters. I suppose he had nothing better to do in that boggy castle of his in Ireland. But the strangest of it is that I think she is rather pleased! Imagine! Two more unlikely people I cannot conceive of.

"Enough of this tattle, though. Dearest George, I miss you horribly. Every morning I wake up and reach across for you, but all I find is an icy coverlet. Soon I shall have to resort to hot bricks like some shrivelled up old crone. Hurry home, my darling. Your loving Arabella."

Gurney smiled, then realised that there was another page to the letter. The writing here was utterly unlike Arabella's normal precise script: it was filled with flourishes, and the lines ran up and down the page like the oars of a Greek longboat. He frowned and read on.

"P.S.," the page began, "George, the most marvellous thing has happened. Paddy has just come barging in at the door, covered in mud, hotfoot from Holyhead. It seems that Aristotle Gilchrist, a friend of his—and yours, is he not?—has invited him and Isabel to go on his yacht on a tour of the Archipelago. The Isles of Greece! Imagine! And I am to be their chaperone, and Euthymia is to be my companion! So perhaps we shall be together before you know it! We sail from Chatham in three days, bound for Rhodes, and we shall be there by June, Paddy says, and shall wait for you there. And George, don't be upset, or think that I am being rash. Paddy assures me that the yacht has six cannons, and a crew of fully thirty men, as well as the most delightful saloon all done out in satinwood. We shall certainly give any pirates or brigands we meet a very proper lesson."

Gurney threw the letter across the cabin and cursed. He thrust his hands into his pockets and strode to the stern-windows. Damn the woman! What good would six pop-guns on Totters Gilchrist's yacht—and Totters a dipsomaniac if ever he'd met one—do against a determined pirate? And at the height of the season, too. He poured himself a stiff drink of brandy. As if he didn't have enough on his plate without running herd on a bunch of bloody dilettanti!

But perhaps it was not as bad as it might have been. For all his soaking, Totters was as good a man with his mauleys as you would find anywhere. He smiled. There were not many women in England with spirit to leave house and home, and up sticks to the Levant on the spur of the moment. When he had wooed her—gone half across the world to win her, in the teeth of disgrace and public scorn—she had waited. It was not to be expected that she would become a sort of milksop paragon overnight. And it was for that very impetuous streak in her nature that he loved her. With luck, the pirates would sheer away from a well-found ship flying an English ensign. With a lot of luck. But Rhodes. Right on Kapraj Bey's doorstep. He sighed. All there was to do was hope the Black Crow would have better things to do than chase yachts. A forlorn hope, perhaps; but there was little else he could do in the circumstances.

He shook his head ruefully. He would never forgive himself if something happened to her; the only way to prevent that, it seemed, was to get to Rhodes and keep his eyes open for trouble. And trouble there would most certainly be. This was the last week in May. Given fair weather—an unlikely eventuality, judging by the thick swathes of black cloud that pressed down on the chaos of waves in the fading light— they should be able to make Rhodes by the first week in June. Then he could make sure that all was well with the English party and set out after Kapraj Bey, whose base, by all accounts, was reasonably close at hand. Unless, he thought gloomily, Arabella took it into her head to accompany him on the punitive expedition. Which in her present frame of mind was more than likely. God damn and blast all hoydenish women, he thought, pulling his wool cap over his ears and opening the cabin door.

The wind took him in the shoulders like a battering-ram as he came on deck, and he leaned back into it, letting it bear him up. *Vandal* was rushing before wind and sea under a cloud of canvas, the spray hissing back in great sheets from her forefoot, and for a moment Gurney gave himself up to the sheer exhilaration of it. Then he turned to McIver, who was standing by the helmsman, glancing every now and then at the set of the sails. "We'd best take some canvas off her before night."

The Scott nodded. "Aye. Seems a pity, though. Yon new spar's bearing up well."

"You did a good job, you and the lads. But it's a damned tricky landfall by day, and I wouldn't like to have to do it at night, even if there was a moon. There'll not be one this night. So reef topsails, down gaff topsails and foresail. She'll ride easier, too."

"Aye, aye."

Gurney stood by the companionway and watched as the swarm of topmen raced up the foremast shrouds and lay out along the yards, bundling in the flapping canvas and reefing it home. Fifty miles over the starboard bow lay Cape Malea and the Gulf of Lakonia. At the present rate, they should make the cape in about six hours. That would make it midnight. By no means a pleasure-cruise. The man at the helm grinned at him as he came to his side and took the wheel. Gurney jerked his head. "Away with you. Give the lads forrard a tot. I'll take her for a while."

The man grinned again and tipped his horrid felt hat, then scurried away towards the fo'c'sle. Gurney spun the wheel between his fingers, testing the feel of it. Volnikov had done a good job with the new tackles. Then he settled back against the housing, *Vandal* like a live thing under his hands as the storm sent her racing down the troughs towards the deepening dusk that hid the mountains to the south-west.

* * *

The wind was still shrieking in the rigging as the next day dawned. During the night hours, *Vandal* had threaded the straits of Elafonisos and was now pounding through a stiff sea on a close reach, her larboard rail awash, towards the distant jagged line of hills that marked the backbone of the Mani. Gurney had not slept; these were dangerous waters, and though the cloud had begun to break a couple of hours before dawn, the passage through the straits by dead reckoning had been a nerveracking business.

It was evident as soon as Metaxas came on deck that he had not slept either, and that made Gurney feel rather better. The fat Greek was a horrible colour, the black pouches under his eyes like bladders of ink. He walked as unsteadily as a newborn foal.

"How long now?"

"Perhaps three hours, if we can do it at all. I have no desire to hazard my ship on the rocks round your anchorage in this weather; we may have to stand off and wait."

"No, no." Metaxas shook his head. "The harbour is well sheltered from the north wind, Captain. It will not be difficult."

"We shall see."

"You have the gold, ready to take ashore?"

"Yes. Do you want to come below and count it?"

Metaxas shuddered. "Captain, I made a resolution just now. Never again will I go below in a ship, even if the ship is anchored and the sea is flat, flat, flat. I have," he continued, stating the obvious with an air of utter confidentiality, "been sick."

"Dear me," said Gurney, looking away to hide a

grin. "How unfortunate. Some breakfast will do you good. Cookie is even now frying up some nice fat pork; try a bit of that."

The Greek's face turned an unlikely shade of green, and he ran to the rail. Gurney almost felt sorry for him until he remembered the carnage at Ixos.

During the next couple of hours the sea became calmer. The waves here did not have the long fetch which had let them build on the run down the east coast of the Peloponnese, and as *Vandal* approached the shore of the Gulf of Lakonia the rollers gave way to a short chop. Metaxas, inconsistent with his word, had retired below again, and Basreddin, muffled in a woollen robe, was leaning on the rail beside Gurney.

"He is hatching something, that little Greek devil. I saw him just now with his men, huddled together like maidens at a wedding." The Sufi's eyes had an uncharacteristically worried expression as he looked across the heaving blue waters to the now clearly-visible cliffs of the Mani.

Gurney shrugged. "I don't see what he can do. We have fulfilled our end of the bargain, and he wouldn't turn on us now. If that apology for a government of Mavrocordato's heard that he'd been dealing false with his allies, his skin wouldn't be worth a chew of tobacco."

"I shouldn't be too sure if I were you, Giorgiou. As you have already discovered, these Greeks do not have the same sense of loyalty as you English, particularly where gold is concerned. And he is a sly one, this Metaxas."

"No matter how sly he is, he won't be foolish enough to try to sink this ship under us in broad daylight. Now, come on. Enough coffee-housing. Let's try to pilot ourselves into the harbour without putting a stone through the bottom."

As he walked aft to McIver and began to search for the channel-marks, Metaxas appeared on the deck again, followed by his rabble of sullen-eyed Klephts.

"Ah, home sweet home, as you say, do you not?" He shot Gurney what was evidently intended as a winsome grin.

Without taking the glass from his eye, Gurney grunted. "Very good, Mr. Metaxas. By the by, where did you learn your English?"

The Greek spread his hands. "When I was little, an old Englishman with a white beard and a mule-load of books came wandering through our village, and we caught him. I made him teach me his language so I could read the books, and then I killed him. He taught me Italian too, of which I am glad, for it enabled me to read the book by which I have shaped my life."

With every yard *Vandal* made towards the shore, Gurney noticed, Metaxas was gaining confidence. Indeed, he was becoming positively bombastic.

"Fascinating," said Gurney. "What was this book?"

"*I Principe.* By Niccolo Macchiavelli. You know of him?"

"Certainly." Gurney turned away and picked up the next mark. "Starboard five." Dutch Pieter, at the wheel, spun the spokes and hands tailed onto the braces. "Interesting that it should be a favourite of yours." In twenty minutes he would be shot of this little swine for good; until then, he might as well be civil.

"Yes. It has made me the confidant and adviser of powerful men."

"Of one powerful man." Gurney was puzzled. What was Metaxas leading up to?"

"There is more than one powerful man to whom Metaxas is indispensable, Captain Gurney. Yourself, for instance."

Gurney laughed. "Hardly powerful, and hardly indispensable, Mr. Metaxas."

"There are others."

"Who?"

Metaxas gave him a smile of pure self-satisfaction.

"Just others. And you may meet them sooner than you think, Captain."

Gurney decided that while civility was civility, this was no time to be conducting a conversation whose only object was to inflate further this tricky little buffoon's estimation of himself. He walked aft, watching the cliffs unroll to reveal the harbour of Mavromichaelis' band.

"O'Shea!" he shouted. "Fire two guns, wads only, no shot. Then another, thirty seconds after." With the reports, the deck shuddered a little under his feet, and the wind whipped the smoke away. He watched, unmoving, as hands shortened sail and *Vandal* nosed into the anchorage. The third gun roared, the smoke hanging a little longer in the sheltered air under the beetling limestone cliffs, and Gurney waved his hand forward. Water churned round *Vandal's* bow as the anchor dropped to the seabed and held; she came to the end of the cable, stopped, then fell back down the wind and came to rest.

There was no sign of life on the beach. Then across the water from the harbour-cave came the clacking of a capstan pawl. Gurney turned to Metaxas, eye-brows raised.

"It seems that there is no reception committee."

Metaxas chuckled, a nasty, fat little sound. "Do not be too sure of that, Captain. Look there."

A long bowsprit was inching from beyond the rock buttress that shielded the cave-mouth from view. "More of my powerful friends, Mr. Gurney." A pistol appeared in his hand, its barrel trained on Gurney's navel. "Do not make any sudden movement, or you will assure yourself of a slow and painful death."

The bowsprit and the ship to which it belonged were out of the cave now. Gurney found himself staring at a row of eight cannon set in the starboard gunwale of a fast-looking brig. So close were they that he could see the guns' crew standing by their pieces, at attention. Each gunner wore a turban. As Gurney watched, two flags rose to the peak of the strange ship's spanker gaff. The uppermost of the two bore the device of a black crow's head in a golden scimitar; the lower, the crescent and star of Turkey on a blood-red ground.

Metaxas beamed. "More powerful men than two, Captain, more than two. Mavromichaelis died at the same time as you were grubbing for gold up the coast, and with him his men, women and children; long live Captain Gurney, the treasure hunter. And now, Captain Gurney will die, tragically wrecked in waters he does not know well enough; long live Kapraj Bey, the Black Crow of Izmir. And most of all, long live Pausanias Metaxas."

Resignation was in Gurney's voice. "You were watching us from the cliffs."

"Indeed, Captain, indeed. I—or should I say certain powerful men?—was very anxious to get my hands on those letters, and, of course, the pleasing baubles of Osman Bey. But enough. Time presses. If you would be so good as to accompany your men into the fo'c'sle, we shall bolt the hatches over you and be on our way."

8

Metaxas and Gurney sat facing each other across the chart-table in *Vandal*'s after-cabin. Gurney was feeling somewhat constrained, perhaps because of the stout cord which bound his hands and feet to the chair in which he sat. The Greek, however, leaning back with every satisfaction in the high-backed chair which had been Gurney's, was expansive to a fault. He took a sip of brandy from the tumbler at his elbow, and turned a bleary eye on him.

"Excellent stuff, this, Captain Gurney. You have good taste in these matters. A pity it does not extend to your choice of shipmates."

Gurney tried to lean forward, but was brought up short by his bonds.

"The only shipmates about whom I have any reservations, Metaxas, are you and your rabble. I ask you again, what is the meaning of this act of wanton piracy?"

The fat man's fist banged on the oak top of the table, and his mustachios seemed to bristle. "How dare you? Piracy, you say. And what do you call the seizing of the treasure of Osman Bey if not piracy?"

"I would remind you," said Gurney, calming himself with effort, "that the treasure, being below low-water mark, is the property of its finder. You say you wish to remove it from my custody; the only way you will achieve this is by force; I therefore have no alternative but to regard this as an act of piracy."

Metaxas heaved himself to his feet and staggered round the table. Gurney decided that his unsteadiness stemmed more from brandy than from the bucking of Vandal's deck as she flew southeast before the gale. He put one fat hand on each arm of Gurney's chair and bent forward, his nose inches from Gurney's. "Listen to me," he hissed. His breath smelt of vomit and brandy; he had been continuously sick since Vandal had nosed out of the Mavromichaelis anchorage two days previously. Gurney turned his face away in disgust.

"LISTEN TO ME!" roared the Greek. "'Sbetter. Bloody English oafs." His fist came across. Gurney jerked his head back, to avoid the blow and the Greek, unbalanced, staggered. Cursing, he retreated to the safety of the chair behind the chart-table. "Listen to me," he said a third time. "In the treasure you have got

there are letters. You know this. Do not deny it. These
letters will be of great use to Kapraj Bey, my master."
A crafty grin smeared itself across the greenish-white
face. "My master for the moment. He is a powerful
and subtle man, the Bey, and he moves Turk and
Egyptian on his chessboard without their knowledge.
As for the rest of the world, you Greek and English
and French and Russian, he pays no mind to you.
To him you are like flies buzzing round the head of a
master chess-player—to be swatted for the simple satisfaction of swatting."

Gurney's interest got the better of his anger. "Even
the Greeks? Do you feel no scruple about betraying
your people for a master who would annihilate them
all?"

Metaxas belched and leaned forward over the table,
his little eyes buried in creases of fat. "Silence, and listen before you rattle at the mouth to Pausanias
Metaxas. I will tell you the story of my life, and you
will know when you die—which will be soon—what it
is to meddle in the destinies of the great."

"In your destiny, you mean?"

"In my destiny. Imagine, Frank, that you are a
child in a village in the mountains of the north. You
are small and you cannot run as the others do; your
mother loves you—ah, how she loved me!—and she
gives you to eat, protects you from the jeers of your
little friends." Metaxas was lost now, carried along by
the memories that crowded in.

"One day I had been out, with the priest, an old
fool who knew me for a cleverer one than the rest of
those little animals playing in the filth of the street.
I returned earlier than usual to my mother's house;
there was no sign of her. Then I heard the noises
from the chamber where she slept, and I beside her.
Groanings and sighs, and the rattle of the bed; then
silence. In my innocence I thought she was sick and
ran to her. You know what I saw when I pulled aside
the curtain? There, on the bed where I would lie

in the night in her warmth, was Dimitrios Petroboulis, sprawled between my mother's thighs. When
I screamed he rose, laughing, and buttoned his
breeches. Then he tossed my mother a couple of coins,
shoved me aside, and marched out. The next thing I
knew I was bending over my mother with a knife in
my hand, and she was smiling at me. Not with her
face, but with the big gash I had ripped across her
neck." His shoulders rose slowly towards his ears and
he began to shudder. "I killed her, and then, my hands
still dripping from her blood, I went up into the
mountains. Ten days later I came down to the village
in the dead of night and stuck Petroboulis in the
navel with the same knife as he slept. I heard later it
took him a week to die." He buried his face in his
hands. "Mama! O, God, Mama!" Mucus from his nose
streamed down over his mustachios, and he snuffled—
for all the world, Gurney thought, like a pig at the
trough.

A hail came down from the deck, footsteps
drummed on the companionway, and the door burst
open. One of the Klephts ran into the cabin, paused
a moment, then went to Metaxas and shook him by
the shoulder, yelling in Greek. Metaxas looked up,
drew his ridiculously baggy sleeve under his nose, and
stood up, steadying himself on the table. He sniffled
mightily, seemed to recover his composure, and
turned to Gurney.

"You will be taken on deck now. I did not tell you
before, but it is important that the letters you retrieved from Osman Bey should be thought to have
sunk forever. Your ship, therefore, will soon run
aground with all hands in a bay they call the Sirens'
Jaws on the north shore of the Island of Limos. I, with
my men, the treasure and the letters, shall be transferring to one of our escorts in a short time." He
spoke rapidly to the Klepht, who did something to
the rope that bound Gurney to his chair and yanked
him to his feet.

Gurney's ankles were tied in a hobble, so that he could walk if he took little steps; but were he to try to run, he would fall. Staggering, he allowed himself to be pulled to the door. Metaxas spoke again.

"One thing. As I am a man of education, I have decided that your death will be according to Classical precedent. The Sirens' Jaws is said by some to be the rock on which the Sirens would sing, luring susceptible mariners to their doom. So like Odysseus, you will be bound to the mast to assist you in avoiding their wiles. Correctly, of course, your crew should have their ears stuffed with wax, but this being in short supply, I have immured them in the fo'c'sle. But you will not be alone. The unbeliever Basreddin—not that I care what he believes in—will be with you at the last. If, like Odysseus, your will is strong enough to get you out of the Sirens' Jaws, you will escape. Otherwise, and I fear it will be otherwise, you will succumb. Take him away."

Gurney was silent as the Klepht dragged him up the companionway and onto the deck. The Greek prize-crew had taken in sail, and *Vandal* now lay head to wind. As the man slammed him against the mainmast and began to lash him to the spar, Gurney tried to take stock of his situation. Basreddin was bound upright against the foremast, the wind whipping his brown robe, eyes closed. He must have been out there for a day and a night, Gurney realised; but he would be in one of his trances, withdrawn into that hinterland of the mind that slowed the pulse of his being to a state near death. Over the stern, perhaps four miles directly downwind, a streak of foam slashed the boiling sea, darkening now in the fading light. Beyond it, the crags of an island reared against the sky, hidden from time to time by the spray that drifted in feathery plumes from the witch's cauldron of white water that lay between the two headlands flanking the bay. The Sirens' Jaws. He closed his eyes. The gale buffeting at his face pulled his cheeks out of shape when he

opened his mouth, and there was an awful helpless-
ness about being braced to the mast, waved like a flag
on a pole at the ship's lightest whim, the body unable
to compensate for the pitch and roll of the sea by a
movement of feet or legs.

For a long moment he hung in his bonds, his head
lolling, breathing the stink of death that rose with the
spindrift from the foaming waters of the bay. Then
he looked up, and craned his neck round. Metaxas
and the crew were moving fast, dragging the sacks of
treasure across the deck and lowering them into the
boat moored under *Vandal*'s counter. The interpreter,
braced against the corkscrewing rail, waved an oil-
skin packet—the letters—at him in ironic farewell;
then he climbed down the ladder and was gone. A
seaman ran to the jib-sheet and hauled it in, then
dashed aft, lashed the wheel and disappeared. *Vandal*
slowed, turned stern-on to the wind, picked up
speed from the rag of sail. Gurney saw the pirates pulling for the brig hove-to in the offing; then he closed his
eyes.

So this was how it felt, that final moment: the moment of no return, when the duellist feels the steel
pass through his ribs and seek the warm, throbbing life
within. The moment after the trap drops, as the
condemned man, suspended at the start of his fall,
feels gravity begin to straighten the hemp at his neck.

He had expected it to be a moment of calm, a time
for resignation, making a final peace with whatever of
him was eternal. But it was not. It was a moment of
struggle, of bitter stocktaking, a final mustering of re-
sources to smash away the constricting walls of doom
that bore irresistibly in from every side. For perhaps
thirty seconds Gurney, eyes starting from his head
with horror, the screams that welled up from his red
throat where the blood still coursed warm and alive
torn away by the pitiless wind, fought. But he was
fighting two-inch rope, a twenty-inch mast, a three-
hundred-ton ship, driven by a hurricane spun by the

resistless inertia of a planet—he, a puny blob of fragile bone and corruptible flesh. He became slack, and the hope leaked out of him like sand from an hourglass. *Vandal*, dragged by the tiny scrap of canvas drum-taut at her forestay, surged with reluctant purpose towards the slavering fangs of the Sirens' Jaws.

He hung in his bonds, defeated. Then, amid the shriek of the wind in the rigging and the distant boom of the breaks, he heard a shrill, eldritch keening. At first he put it away from him, almost indignant at it for its disturbing of the death-symphony unfolding about him. But try as he would, he could not ignore it. It was a human sound, and it had a strange comfort to it, like the echo of a drinking song over a curlew-haunted anchorage at nightfall. His head came up, and he thought of the men battened in the fo'c'sle, compared his horror with their own. Then it came to him that treachery had put him here, that his death—yes, and the death of his men—was not merely a snuffing out of sixty lives, it was a bloody chapter in the list of treacheries perpetrated by man against man since time out of mind. Treacheries and lies. And lies he would not tolerate. He was damned if he was going to be killed out of hand, like a trapped beast, by a lie. When his time came he would die honestly, face to face with his doom; not as a murky footnote to a petty intrigue. And there was the matter of Arabella, sailing innocently into dangerous seas; Metaxas would have read her letter and he would never pass up the chance of telling his master about such a lucrative prize so close to hand.

The keening stopped, and Gurney felt the hilt of his sheath-knife pressing into the small of his back. He looked up. Basreddin, indistinct in the gathering dark, was looking at him. Even forty feet apart as they were, Gurney could see the whites of his eyes showing all the way round the irises. He nodded, not trying to call out over the howl of the wind, and started to work the small of his back against the mast.

By standing to his full height, stretching up as far as the ropes at ankle, waist and wrists permitted, he could move the hilt of the knife an eighth of an inch in its sheath. He moved again, and found himself starting to grin. To an outsider, he would be looking like one of Monsieur Montfleury's Alarming Contortionist Midgets as seen at Vauxhall, expressed in fractions of an inch rather than yards. He set his teeth, and persisted. After about five minutes, he could feel the knife working free. He shifted his back sideways, which was easier; his bonds had worked up the taper of the mast and there was some give in them now. He reached the point where the knife was hanging from the sheath by its own weight; he could feel it, when he arched his back away from the wood, jumping faintly to the buck and heave of the ship. Then a wave took *Vandal* under the counter from a new angle, smashing her upwards and sideways, and he flung himself backwards as the knife fell between the mast and his body, trapping it with his right thigh.

He paused, bracing himself against the ropes, his legs shuddering with the effort of it. If he could reach it with his hand . . . But his arms were stretched behind him, the rope that linked them at the far side of that cylinder of spruce twenty inches in diameter. He dragged his right arm round, pushing the knife towards it with his thigh, the muscles of his shoulder and neck cramping and knotting with the effort. The rope, wet with spray, gave a little, a tiny relaxing of tension that set his heart thudding. The tips of his fingers felt the ropework of the hilt, and it was better than the touch of silk, than the skin of a woman; then *Vandal* gave another lurch and heave, and the whole hilt was in his palm, solid and real. But his fingers, starved of blood by the constriction of the wet rope, refused to close and the knife jumped free, clattered soundless on the planking, and skittered over the lee scuppers, where it bit into a tangled coil of rope and came to rest.

Gurney slumped forward in his bonds again, the thunder of the surf, closer now, in unison with the blood in his ears. A little later, he looked up again. Were he to be crushed in the Sirens' Jaws, he would at least watch his doom as it claimed him.

He blinked. Where Basreddin's figure had been, stark against the foremast, there was now only a shell of brown cloth hanging in the loops of rope, flapping in the gale like a scarecrow. Came the shrill keening again, this time from behind him. Then something was sawing at the ropes which bound him. As he fell away, Gurney took an incredulous step forward, turned, and fell full-length on the deck as the hobble caught him in the ankles. The scrawny apparition that was Basreddin, naked as the day he was born and holding a long knife in his right hand, swam into focus. Gurney began to laugh. He was still half-helpless with mirth as Basreddin pulled him to his feet and dragged him forward to the fastenings of the fo'c'sle hatch.

Basreddin hacked at the lashings with his knife. As soon as they parted the hatchway burst upward from within, closely followed by the perspiring Volnikov, who had evidently been attempting to repeat his success with the grille in the Venetian fort at Ixos, and the rest of *Vandal's* crew. Gurney looked out over the bow, trying to size up the position.

Whichever way you looked at it, things were not good. The first streak of white water was but a hundred yards off the port bow. Beyond it, perhaps another forty yards, the main tangle of reefs churned the sea to foam. On either side now, the twin horns of land which enclosed the bay seemed to embrace *Vandal*, to beckon her into the shambles within; and the north wind, unabated, howled out of the black horizon like a legion of devils. Gurney turned.

"McIver!" He doubted if even he heard the words, such was the rush of the gale, but the mate was at his side in the blink of an eye, impelled by that strange communication which had grown between them over the years. "Make sail and bring her on to the starboard tack." The headland to starboard was perhaps a little shorter than that to larboard. Easier to weather, though still sickeningly difficult.

"Aye, aye, Sir." The Scot went forward, gathering men to him as a magnet gathers iron filings. The mainsail crept up the mast, the *Vandal* moved round, slowly but surely, head to wind. As she came broadside-on to the troughs a wave lifted her and bore her over on her beam ends until her yardarm hung but ten feet from the water; Gurney watched, fascinated, as the topmen lying out scrambled for a hold on the near-perpendicular yard, then grabbed at the companionway coaming to save himself, as for a gastly moment the ship hung suspended on her beam-ends, over the trough of the oncoming wave. But this one she rode well, settling back onto an even keel, and then she was across the waves again, riding them in a long corkscrew, and canvas was breaking out at her bowsprit and foremast.

"McIver, put Henry Priest in the bow to watch for white water." Gurney's voice was anxious, even though he strove to keep it level. The mate hurried forward and told off Henry Priest and another Dalling man.

Henry, leaning on the viciously plunging bulwark forward of the catheads, stared gloomily into the darkening sea below and in front of him. Look for white water, was it? As far as he reckoned there was enough white water ahead to satisfy anyone, and bugger a bit of it invisible to the man at the wheel. Henry's dignity, which was a larger part of him than at first met the eye, had been sorely tried on this voyage. Not that it was Mr. Gurney's fault, mind; it was what you had to expect from a bunch of igerant wogs like them there Greeks.

Henry turned, and called out. "White stuff dead ahead, helm!" *Vandal* was hard on the wind now, blasting into the waves that came roaring down from the open sea to the northward, steepening to break-ing-point as the bottom shelved upwards.

"Will she go any further?" Gurney yelled at the helmsman. Pieter shook his head, pointing at the luff of the foresail, already shivering as the wind caught its leeward side.

"Right, then. No chance of putting her about. Too tight. Take her between that stone there and the main reef." Pieter swallowed, then put down the helm.

Henry watched in disbelief as *Vandal*'s bow swung and the maelstrom of the shoreline came onto the lar-board bow. "Bloody hell, but he's puttin' her right into the stones." Then he grinned as the bow swung to starboard again and *Vandal* ran on a close reach through a channel only a few feet under than herself between the main reef and its outcrop. Ten feet to starboard, a wave reared and passed under *Vandal*'s flare. Henry felt the bow rise, but he was watching the trough, his jaw slack with amazement. Something pale was coming through the water, light green, foaming with bubbles. A hump appeared at the very centre of the trough, a hump with steep sides of water, and the roar of its draining tore at the very depths at Henry's soul, though Henry would never have ad-mitted that he possessed such a thing. He could see the rock lying naked now, a great molar of stone ex-posed to the air as the wave drew back from it. At the moment when all hung still, Henry spat.

The wind had faded behind the next of the white-bearded walls of water, and his string of mingled mu-cus and tobacco-juice looped through the air and fell, glittering, onto the wet rock. Henry contemplated it with quiet pride for a cat's blink, then hung on for dear life as the next wave hurled itself down over the rock in a welter of foam and *Vandal*'s bow, half-buried in the spume of its ruin, vaulted skywards like a kangaroo. By the time Henry had got the water

out of his eyes the rock was thirty yards astern, and
Vandal's nose was once more pointed for the open sea
a fraction to windward of the headland.

Behind the mantle of racing cloud that cloaked the
sky, the sun must have set. The dark was closing in
fast and the gulls which had wheeled at the mastheads
had gone wherever gulls go when night begins to
sweep over sea and land. Gurney plotted in his mind
the line that *Vandal* must follow to weather the headland. It would be a damned close-run thing. Pieter, at
the helm, brought the wheel up a point, to take advantage of a heavier gust; the gap between the bowsprit and the loom of the land widened, then narrowed again, as the schooner's dolphin-striker knifed
down into a wave and water flowed green along the
deck. Less than a mile to go, and *Vandal* made little
leeway for a ship of her size. But the seas were huge,
and each one as it marched down on the starboard
bow knocked it towards the land like a mastiff harry-
ing a bull. The simplest course would be to take a
tack, and soon; but Gurney, frowning, decided that to
try to bring his ship's nose across the wind against this
sea would be foolhardy. If she failed to come round,
and the chances were that she would, she would be
blown to leeward and lose all the ground she had
made. He gritted his teeth. "Do it in one, Pieter," he
said.

The Dutchman made no reply, his eyes fixed on the
sails. An unnecessary remark, Gurney knew. Pieter
would realise as well as he—as well as every man in
the ship—that they must batter their way past that
blade of rock jutted into the sea or perish miserably.
One attempt, and one attempt only. Roll up, gentlemen, to the awful Duel of *Vandal* and the Elements.
Admission absolutely no charge to Gentlemen and
Sailors. Price of failure: death.

Under the cliffs of the headland the sea was
churned to foam. Henry Priest looked over the larboard bow, whistling, searching the spume fifty feet

away for rocks. There seemed to be none; the turmoil of water was produced, he thought, by the swells
surging up the sloping plates of rock and falling back
into the teeth of the next wave. He felt a little hollow
about the stomach as the billow which had just lifted
Vandal roared up the rock, creaming and leaping,
whitening an area the size of a small meadow.

Vandal's present course was taking her parallel to
the shore of the bay as it edged out to the headland.
The sea was confused here, the backwash from the
cliffs creating a mass of static humps that reared
suddenly from the water and crossed the pattern of
incoming rollers. And while the wind had lost none
of its force, the torrent of air pouring in from the
open sea hammered at the steep places of the cliffs
and rebounded wildly, producing downdraughts and
backdraughts that at times brought *Vandal's* booms
crashing across their horses.

"*Verdommte* plum duffs," grunted Pieter, struggling
at the helm as a particularly vicious backdraught
threatened to take the ship flat aback. Gurney was
lost in admiration for his skill. Trained as he was in
the shallow coastal waters of Flanders and the Baltic,
Pieter had an uncanny sense of the eddies and back-
waters produced by obstructions in the airstream, and
more often than not he managed to use them to his
advantage where a less skilful man would have been
driven to ruin.

Ten cable-lengths ahead the tip of the headland, a
sheer pillar of rock that plunged two hundred feet
straight down into the seething water at its base,
reared like a monument towards the clouds. Long
ages before, this great vein of granite had stood like a
giant fin, vaulting from the limestone of the mountain
range that was now the Aegean seabed. In time,
weather and water had ground away the soft sedi-
mentary rocks that had wrapped it, honing it back until the cliffs round the bay were all that remained
of the great plateau. But the granite, born of fire and

upheaval in the very guts of the planet, had with-
stood the attrition of time, and now jutted, an unbro-
ken wall, directly across *Vandal*'s course. Gurney's
heart sank, and he turned to Pieter.

"What d'ye think?"

The Dutchman shook his head. "Out too far, Mr.
Gurney. Miracle, we need."

"We've had one already, thanks to Mr. Basreddin."

"You'd better ask him for another." Pieter's face
was impassive, as usual, but his voice was dull and
dead. "Jesus Christ himself would have trouble with
this one."

The great wall of the point hung high between them
now, and as Gurney watched the little gap of grey
between the bowsprit and the headland narrowed,
widened again, and disappeared. Heeling under her
press of canvas, the sea spewing in snowy mustachios
from her stern, *Vandal* bore inexorably down on the
blank walls of granite.

Had Henry Priest been of the Catholic persuasion,
he would have crossed himself. As it was, he shifted
the quid in his cheek, spat, leaned back against the
forestay and whistled. Pity, not to see the missis again.
Badgering old stick she might be, but there had been
some good moments. Harvest home in the village, rak-
ing cockles on the wide beach, and one of the Squire's
pheasants bubbling in the pot over the driftwood
fire. He looked at the gloomy slab ahead, the sullen
sea roaring lazily round its foot. Serve him bloody
well right for leaving them nice soft sandbanks for
foreign parts. Mister Gurney'd have to put her about,
then she'd go arse end first into the cliffs.

The whistle died on his lips, and he craned forward.
What was that, that light patch where the fault swept
down the face into the sea? He strained his eyes into
the murk, then ran out along the bowsprit, agile as a
monkey, and looked again.

Henry's hail rang back over the men on *Vandal*'s

deck like a tocsin. "A hole! On the larboard bow! A hole!"

Gurney frowned. What did the man mean, a hole? "Wait," he said to Pieter. "Don't put your helm a-lee just yet." He ran forward, cursing the gaping men who stood staring at death as it soared high above the mastheads. Henry was pointing wordlessly to something a couple of points on *Vandal's* larboard bow.

When the granite of the westerly headland of the Sirens' Jaws had squeezed itself from the bowels of the earth, it had risen, looped over, and spread. As it cooled, the underside of the loop, wrenched upwards by the titanic forces at work in the shrinking stone, had formed an arch; over the aeons the arch had filled with limestone.

At the same time as the sea had gnawed back the land to create the bay, the waves had smashed and battered at the headland until the soft rock had crumbled away. As Gurney looked, there opened before him a great crooked arch, perhaps one hundred and eighty feet high and thirty feet wide, through which he saw the grey sky and the heaving swells of the open sea.

"The hole, Captain." Henry was grinning foolishly, his finger still extended. "The hole." Gurney came to himself and rushed back down the crowded decks, yelling.

"McIver! Topsail yards squared fore and aft and make it damned snappy!" He arrived at the wheel, panting. "Pieter. Port your helm, lay her over as far as she'll go, then put her through that bloody hole. There's a shoal dead ahead—"

Pieter passed the spokes through his hands and *Vandal* paid off, her lee rail biting deep into the sea as the gale took her full in her close-hauled main and foresails. Gurney danced up and down, cursing, as she lay over, lifting her keel away from the rocks passing under her. Then the light water was astern and Gurney was bellowing at the men to ease sheets, to put her on an even keel so she would pass through the arch without losing her topmasts on the side.

As the arch loomed a few rods ahead, McIver drove the men at the braces to haul the yards round, and round they came. *Vandal* entered the arch at perhaps six knots, and the wind, thwarted by the great outer buttress, died. Her momentum carried her beneath the roof, the booming of her sails mingling its echoes with the thunder of the seas. She rolled as a wave surged under her, and the lower yard of her fore lower topsail scraped against the rock with a noise that drew a gasp from the men on deck; then, losing way, she inched towards the wind-whipped foam beyond the sheltering arch. Gurney urged her on as a coachman urges his horses up a steep hill, and she seemed to respond, sliding away on a roll of the water. The wind struck in her flying jib and drove her nose to larboard. Pieter cursed, spinning the spokes to starboard as the rock wall sped towards the larboard bow; then, just as it looked as if she must surely hit, the gale struck firm in the luff of her foresail and she rounded up. Gurney distinctly felt the chill blast of spray that came back at him from the cliff not ten feet from the ship's side. But *Vandal* was sailing again now, hard on the wind, and the rugged shores of Limos fell away from the headland to the southward.

The gale shrieked on unabated, but the waves, undisturbed by shallows, were longer and lower; *Vandal*'s motion eased, and Gurney leaned for a moment against the longboat. There was a dull roaring in his ears, which he attributed at first to exhaustion. A hand fell on his shoulder, and he looked up. Basreddin was smiling at him, and the roaring continued undiminished. It was the crew, the men of the *Vandal*, cheering as though their lungs would burst.

Gurney summoned McIver, and the two of them climbed down the companionway to the after-cabin.

He waved the mate to a chair, lit the lamp, and sat down himself.

"Well," he said. "That was a pretty little passage, and no mistake. Well done, McIver."

The Scot grinned. "Well done yourself, if I may make so bold, Captain Gurney. If ye'd no' let us out of the fo'c'sle we'd have been done for and no mistake."

"You have Mr. Basreddin to thank for that. How was it below, there?"

"Not so good. Verra cramped, you might say. But the lads bore up well." He screwed up his face. "Even they Proosians, rum lot they may be, Captain Gurney, but they've a fair portion of guts to them. Quiet as mice, they were, but no' scared. No' scared. Me, I was bloody bepetrificated."

"Interesting. Perhaps we shall find a use for them soon, though God knows how. Now. To business. In the press yonder you will find the Olivier chart of the Archipelago. Let's cast an eye over it. This blow's not through with us yet, I doubt."

McIver looked through the charts. "Not here, Captain. Perhaps they bloody piraticals took it along with them."

Gurney let his eyes roam round the cabin. The Isfahan carpet Arabella had given him the night before they sailed was much smeared with pipe-dottle, and lockers hung open, ransacked, no doubt by Metaxas and his men in search of valuables. Under the carriage of the twelve-pounder on the starboard side was a crumpled ball of paper. He picked it up and smoothed it on the table.

"Here we are. I suppose they thought it would be of no further use to us. I should say they're in for a shock on that account. Hey, McIver?"

The muscles at the corner of the mate's craggy jaw worked under the skin, and he nodded. "They are that, Captain Gurney."

"And how obliging of them." He stabbed his finger at the chart. "See here, where the dividers pricked.

One northwest of Matapan—the Mavromichaelis anchorage. And here, Limos. The bay." He looked astern, but darkness had fallen, concealing the land. "Another mark." He moved his finger to the eastward, to the peninsula that projected in a splatter of rocks and shallow soundings to the south of the whale-shaped island of Cos. "And it's here that they'll be bound, if we can believe that slippery Metaxas bugger. No reason not to, since he was convinced we'd all be—"

He stopped, and peered closely at the chart. "McIver, have you ever pricked out a course to Cos?"

Mystified, the mate shook his head. "Never."

"Then why is there a dividers mark here?" His finger was resting on a little indentation in the northern shore of the peninsula. "McIver, I do believe we have just discovered the stinking nest of Kapraj Bey. What say you we go after his eggs?"

"If he's the bloody wog bastard, if ye'll excuse the term, Captain, as tried to run us ashore, then I'd like full well to do him a mischief."

"Good. Do him a mischief we shall, and soon." He looked up. "In the meantime, we shall acquire some sea-room and heave to until this lot," waving a hand at the stormy night beyond the cabin windows, "has blown itself out."

Sun was streaming into the cabin when Gurney awoke, and the ship's motion was easier. Rubbing his eyes with his knuckles, he climbed the companionway into the glare of the early morning sun and stumbled groggily to the pump. He worked the handle a few times, and stuck his head under the jet of water. As the numbness of sleep fell away, he took stock. The fingernail he had lost at *Vandal's* bobstay was growing back nicely; but the wound in his calf, where the conger had nibbled him, itched and throbbed under its bandages. He prayed that mortification would not set in—unlikely, after Basreddin's cunning ministrations, but still possible. But the breeze was warm, and the sea blue and kindly. On balance, he decided, it was none too bad to be alive.

He took his breakfast—the perennial coffee and ship's biscuit—leaning against the taffrail in his shirt-sleeves, barefoot, the canvas breeches he affected at sea unbuttoned at the knee. Preoccupied with his thoughts, he did not notice as McIver greeted him with a cheery "Good morning," and waved aside the Scot's offer of a tot to keep out the breeze. The mate had turned the ship as the wind abated and went round to the northeast, and *Vandal* was now flying on a broad reach, studding-sails set at her topsail yards. Far on the southern horizon, an island reared purple from the blue. Gurney looked at it for some time, but did not see it. Then he turned and walked towards the after-cabin companionway, still abstracted. As he started down the steps he turned to McIver.

"Pass the word for Mr. Basreddin, would you. General von Kratzstein, too. Send von Kratzstein down first, then join me yourself."

"Aye, aye, Sir." McIver walked forward, mystified. Mr. Basreddin, yes. But what would that Proosian be doing astern with Mister G?

When von Kratzstein entered, Gurney was standing with his back to him, stooped a little under the low deckhead, looking out over the wake that stretched white on the blue waves to the westward. The Captain did not turn when he entered, and the Prussian cleared his throat. Gurney swivelled. "My apologies, Herr General. I did not hear you come in. Pray be seated. Some coffee, perhaps?"

For weeks now von Kratzstein had been limited to rum and strong tea, the standard fo'c'sle fare. At the mere mention of coffee, the water came to his mouth. "Yes. If you please," he said, trying to keep from dribbling.

Gurney walked across the cabin, stuck his head out of the door, and shouted an order to his steward.

Then he turned and straddled the windward twelve-pounder. "Well, Herr General. I invited you aft because, in my opinion, you and your men have served out your sentence for stowing away. I feel, in fact, that I owe you an apology. I confess that I had meant you to pay for your passage with a little honest labour; but it was not my intention that you should be exposed to such hazards as impalement or being dashed on the rocks while battened below hatches."

The Prussian's face was expressionless. But he rose to his feet, clicked his heels and bowed. "Herr Kapitan." Gurney noticed that his weeks on shipboard had at least taught him to bend his neck when coming to attention. "It is impossible for me, as a Junker, to accept your apology. I shall demand satisfaction at a later date. However." His mouth took on a judicial twist. "It is the opinion of I and my mens that you have been a goot officer. Therefore, we will be to defer to your orders continuing until such time as you put us ashore. We insist, however, that this shall be on the next contact with the Greek mainland."

"Nothing wrong with that." A knock on the door. "Come!" shouted Gurney. The steward entered. The two men were silent as he poured coffee into thick white mugs. Then he withdrew, and Gurney spoke again.

"There is something, though. An errand which I must carry out."

Anger began to build in von Kratzstein's face. "Another errand? Kapitan, I brought my men here to fight for the freedom of Greece, not to assist in your personal errands."

Gurney's voice was low and dangerous. "Von Kratzstein, may I remind you that you are still on my ship and subject to my command? You will kindly refrain from addressing me in that tone of voice." He took a drink of coffee. "And this little job in which I should like your assistance involves taking the war into the enemy's camp. We are going to wipe off the

face of the earth a place on which may depend the
future of the Ottoman Empire."

The cabin seemed very quiet all of a sudden. Von
Kratzstein sat staring, his coffee cooling unregarded in
his hand. "So. Interesting. Tell me more."

Gurney could not fathom the look in the Prussian's
eyes. Amusement? The man had no sense of humour.
Triumph? He had little enough to be triumphant
about. Martial fury? Unlikely, but more likely, when
all was said and done, than anything else. "With
pleasure," he said, and unrolled the map which lay on
the cabin table.

Later, when McIver and Basreddin entered and the
conference became general, he noticed a change in
the Prussian. It was not that during the past few
weeks he had been in any way cowed or cast down; it
was merely that the fire seemed to have gone out of
him. But today the scars on his face once more stood
out like the hackles of a gamecock. His whiskers bristled, and from time to time, when the conversation
did not concern him, he would whistle annoyingly
through the gap left by his front teeth.

Gurney was pleased at the effect his plans had had
on the Prussian, but also a little apprehensive. What
he had asked the Philhellenes to do was perhaps
hazardous, but it was not particularly difficult; but
unless von Kratzstein's boast as to his military suc-
cesses with Blücher had at least some foundation in
fact, there was trouble in store. Fatal trouble for the
Prussians. And while Gurney told himself that he
cared not a tinker's curse whether the blustering Phil-
hellene lived or died, it was a matter of pride with
him that he throw away as few lives as possible.

When the council of war broke up and von Kratzstein had marched up the companionway, chest
puffed up and boot heels apparently lent weight by
martial responsibility, Gurney called Basreddin and
McIver. For some time they looked at the map togeth-

er; then McIver left and Gurney took out the chessboard. Basreddin, winning for the fourth time in as many quarter-hours, realised in full the preoccupation of his Captain. But he said nothing, knowing that for the moment it would be best that way. *Vandal*, the breeze firm in her sails, ploughed on through the azure rollers, towards the white beaches and violet mountains of the coast of Asia Minor.

9

A cheerful sunshine lined the brilliant white walls and the paving-stones of the quay at Mandraki, the port of Rhodes. Though the last of spring had passed into early summer, the sea-cooled island climate had made the transition easy. A little breeze blew off the sea, whining in the rigging of the ships in the anchorage, freshening the winding and crowded alleyways of the walled town and rustling the leaves of the wild roses that covered the coastal hills.

Theodore Polytos, renegade Greek and Harbourmaster at Mandraki by permission of the Turkish Governor, was staring out of the window of his house. It overlooked the busy harbour mole and the narrow entrance which had once been straddled by the Colossus. His low brow was furrowed, and his upper lip curled back from his large yellow teeth in something between a sneer and a snarl. For Theodore was not happy. True, his customary surliness had been something of a byword among the townsmen of Rhodes, a generally cheerful lot before the closing grip of the Turk had squeezed the life from them; but on this smiling morning matters were considerably worse than usual. He was convinced that he had taken a

chill from the little breeze. Which would have been
perfectly all right on a normal day, requiring a minimum of work and a maximum of fuss from his wife,
who had discovered through long experience that it
was as well to sympathise with her husband's usually
imaginary ills. But today did not look as if it would
be a normal day.

Theodore growled blasphemously under his breath.
The big two-masted schooner had come into the harbour half an hour ago, entirely unannounced, and
had dropped anchor and made all secure with a
smooth speed unusual in these parts. He had suspected the worst even without his glass, and his sus-
picions had been confirmed by the White Ensign that
he discerned at the strange ship's mizzen peak. Those
accursed Franks, always sailing into his harbour, refusing to bribe him correctly and using him as a sort
of majordomo who was expected to provide guides,
horses, accommodation, and to know all about the
ruins. As if any self-respecting Christian—and whatever Theodore lacked in Christian spirit, he certainly
made up for in self-respect—would have the time to
trot round a lot of Pagan ruins. Personally, Theodore
was in favour of blasting the whole lot of them into
manageable lumps and using them to build a new
quay. God knew the old one was in a rotten state.
But what could you expect, in a world going mad?

Theodore sniffed loudly, and watched with disgust
as eight men disembarked from the schooner's longboat and began to walk down the quay towards him.
Of the two who led the party, one was undoubtedly a
Frank, tall and square-shouldered, with spiky yellow
hair and the suggestion of a limp. The other—God
knew what the other was. Most of his face was invisible behind a dense mat of black beard, and on
his head was a straw hat. Below the neck he was
clad in a long brown robe which flapped and shivered
in the breeze. A Turk, yet not a Turk.

Theodore brightened a little. If the man was a

Levantine, he might at least have a basic grasp of the little financial courtesies that should be extended to a harbourmaster. Then gloom descended again. If he had so little sense as to sail with the English, he would certainly be into them for all he could get; which would leave Theodore scrabbling for the crumbs under the table.

He turned from the window and plumped down in the chair behind the rudimentary structure of crates and planking that served him as a desk. Two, he decided, could play at that game. Obstinacy would be the best policy. Seized by an afterthought, he heaved himself to his feet and took down the Ottoman flag, hanging on the staff in the corner of the office. He pulled out the blue-and-white flag of Greece and bent it hastily to the pole. Then, as footsteps rang on the paving-stones outside, he lifted the portrait of Sultan Mahmoud from its nail and stuffed it behind a pile of papers in the corner. A knock sounded on the door. As he shouted "Enter," he noticed that where the portrait had been there was a square patch of old paint. The door opened, and he leant in what he imagined to be a negligent attitude against the wall, concealing with his broad shoulders the tell-tale rectangle.

The yellow-haired man's pale blue eyes looked him up and down, and he began to feel uncomfortable. "Good morning," said the yellow-haired one, in heavily-accented Romaic. "You are the harbourmaster?"

Theodore scowled. "I am. Can I be of some service?" His voice said that any service he performed would be begrudged, if not actually refused.

"Thank you, no. I merely wished to ask you a couple of questions. But first, I would congratulate you on the beauty and excellence of your harbour. You keep it well. In fact, I should like to pay a small token of my esteem, though I regret we shall not be remaining long." A purse, clinking with coins, fell among the litter on the desk.

Theodore found himself impressed by the young Frank's excellent manners, and had already started forward to pick up the purse when he remembered the discoloured patch on the wall. He made as if to return, then scowled, scooped up the money and dropped it into the capacious pocket of his shabby waistcoat. The young man was looking at him, amusement lurking in his eyes. "Good. If you will excuse me, I shall come straight to the point."

"But please. A minute. Some coffee perhaps?" The purse was an agreeable weight against Theodore's liver, and the gold—he hoped it was gold, and by its heft it could be nothing else; Theodore was an excellent judge of metals by weight—spread a hospitable glow through him. "Please, a seat, gentlemen. Xanthippe!" His wife, a startled-looking woman with a tired face, stuck her head round the door.

"Coffee, woman, for my guests."

Gurney fretted a little as they sat in the comfortless chairs and made small-talk. Time was slipping away, but in these parts one could not rush to the heart of the matter. There were formalities to be observed. So as the coffee came, accompanied by the inevitable rose-petal jam and glasses of spring-water, they talked haltingly of the weather and crops, and the shocking decline of trade since the beginning of the war. Basreddin remained silent, sipping his water, his eyes roving round the room, as Gurney tried to lead the conversation in the direction he wanted.

It was not until Theodore's wife was pouring the second cup of coffee that he managed to broach his subject. "Have there been many Franks in the harbour this spring? You have a fine lot of shipping in, but all of the Levant, I think."

Theodore spread his hands. "Yes, indeed." He smiled. "There have been four or five ships, a frigate of your navy and some merchantmen. But of cultured men such as yourself, very few."

"No yachts?"

"Yachts?"

"Ships filled with cultured men and women."

"Ah. No. But—" Theodore rummaged among the papers on his desk—"I received a letter three weeks ago, from Kerkyra in Corfu that said such a ship would be putting in." He scowled. "The cultured men and women wished to look at ruins, and I was asked to make ready guides and horses."

"When is this ship due?" Gurney leaned forward in his chair.

"She was due last week, but she never arrived." Theodore's face assumed a hurt expression. "And I had made commitments, spent money for these people. I am a poor man, and I have a reputation to maintain. It is sad that these rich milords should betray an innocent islander—"

"What was this ship's name?"

Theodore peered at the letter, moving his lips. "*Otranto.* A brig. Her owner, it seems, is Milord Aristotle Gilchrist. Doubtless they have found interesting rubble elsewhere. Rich men can afford to be fickle—"

The young man was on his feet. "Thank you. I think that what is in that purse will be compensation enough for your time and trouble, and more besides. As to the horses you found for them. How many are there?"

"Four, and two mules, Milord."

"Good. I shall buy them from you. Lighter them aboard my ship within the hour, if you would be so good. Also, I require what is on this list." He handed him a piece of paper covered in Greek script.

"But—"

"No buts. If you won't do it, then you will regrettably lose the purse of fifty sovereigns that awaits you on board. Understood?"

Theodore's eyes bulged. There was a ringing in his ears that had nothing to do with his cold. "Yes, Milord. If it is your will, Milord."

Gurney nodded sharply. "It is. Now, if you will excuse us. We must weigh anchor in one hour."

Seeing a potential fountain of gold slipping away from him, Theodore expostulated.

"But I can show you the ruins and you can wait for your friends. Most beautiful at this time of year. Even do I know, and very few others, the exact spot where the Sun God himself dallied with the nymph Rhodeia—"

"Deeply as this would fascinate me, I fear I am pressed for time." The two men went to the door and opened it. As he passed out of the room, Gurney turned. "Thank you for your hospitality. And Mr. Polytos. There is a picture of a fat Turkish gentleman in the corner there that would just cover that patch of old paint on the wall. It would improve the look of the room immensely. Now I bid you good day."

As they left the harbourmaster's house and walked back along the mole, Gurney was silent. Round him, the port, filled with shipping after the storm, bustled and hummed with men and boats. But he appeared to see nothing. When a detachment of Turkish sailors from one of the frigates in the roads tramped past, escorting a stout pasha about his business, he hardly looked up. It was not until they had summoned *Vandal*'s longboat from the press of small craft round the stone steps of the quay that he gave voice to his thoughts.

"D'you think the storm would have held them up?"

Basreddin shrugged. "Who knows? That, or they may have put in at some friendly harbour to ride it out."

"We can but hope. Oh, damnation. Had I but the option, I'd wait here until they arrived. But that's out of the question since Ixos. At any minute someone may recognise us, and we'll be done for. I'm surprised it hasn't happened already."

"No. You have little to fear on that score. Our Greek friends let few true believers escape from Ixos.

Truly it is said that it is the gleaners who harvest most, though least there be to find."

Gurney did not bother to try to unravel the Sufi's allusion. He was calculating and calculating hard. They were in the harbour here because they were citizens of a neutral power, and not ostensibly involved in any acts of war. But *Vandal* carried too many men and too heavy a weight of metal to have her peaceable intentions taken seriously by an experienced eye. And experienced eyes there would be, among the shipping that packed the basin. There was also the matter of the treasure, and more particularly the letters. The sooner Kapraj Bey's treasure-chambers gave of their fullness, the better.

He ran nimbly up the Jacob's ladder into *Vandal's* waist, and gave his orders. As soon as the lighters alongside finished their business the schooner came over her anchor, canvas broke out at her spars. Five minutes later, the harbour mouth was under their lee gunwale and the open horizon stretched before them.

In the roads, a brig flying the flag of Turkey passed them, reaching towards the narrow entrance. Gurney played his glass idly over her decks, then stiffened. On her quarterdeck stood a man with a heavy body and flat eyes, set in a face that sloped sharply back from the roots of his nose. The Commandant of the citadel at Ixos. He watched as the man put his own glass to his eye and stared, transfixed, as the lens turned towards him, glittering in the sunlight. Then it was on him, for the space of a heartbeat. On the Turk's deck things began to happen at great speed, and Gurney spun and bellowed "O'Shea! Larboard gunports open, run out larboard broadside." The creak of tackles and the rumble of wheels on wood came from below, together with the crash of bulkheads being knocked out.

The brig had half-turned, come head to wind, and now hung in irons, sails rattling and flapping. Through his glass Gurney could see the Commandant, his face suffused beneath the olive skin, jumping up and down with impotent rage as men blundered about the deck yelling and bumping into each other. Already the Turk was dropping astern. Gurney looked ahead. In the roads, the towering masts and yards of two Turkish seventy-fours were a salutary reminder. He shook his head. "God, how I'd love to give that bastard a good mauling 'twixt wind and water. But I fear discretion is the better part of valour. Eh, McIver?"

"Aye, aye, Sir. Who is he?"

"The Commandant at Ixos. The bloody wog who wanted to spit us."

The Scot's face darkened. "Och, Sir. Can we no' have just a wee crack at him? We'd no' do ourselves any damage, and they buggers," his arm gestured largely towards the great ships of the line anchored in the roads, "will tak' all day to sling their hooks. Can we no' give him a wee pasting, Sir?"

"Your enthusiasm does you nothing but credit, McIver. But if the Lady Arabella turns up and the whole harbour's littered with wrecks and corpses it'll spoil her enjoyment. All the more so if the batteries ashore take it into their heads that any ship that flies the Duster is liable to start popping off at their navy. No, leave 'em. That bloody rogue will get his deserts from his own kind; they won't take kindly to his losing two frigates to a schooner."

The mate nodded, not without disappointment, and went forward to the hatchway. He stuck his head down and bellowed unintelligible orders. There was disappointment, too, in the rumble of the guns as they were hauled inboard and the slam of the ports.

Vandal ploughed to the westward, the castle-crowned heights of Rhodes dwindling astern in the clear air, raising Telos and Nisiros to starboard as night fell. Then, as soon as it was full dark, she turned in her tracks. As the moon heaved its gibbous disc from the inky sea, Vandal's bow came round to the east and she threaded her way along the south coast of the rock-spined Resadiye, the Cnidian peninsula of the ancients.

Next morning the air was hot and still, shimmering over the white sand and glassy water of the bay on the south side of the peninsula. Where *Vandal* lay in the offing, cats-paws of breeze crept across the surface of the sea, but here on the beach, protected from the north wind by the hills of the interior, the heat was intense. Von Kratzstein, buttoned up tight in his canary-yellow uniform, orange cravat swathing his neck to the ears, was finding it difficult to catch his breath.

At the top of the beach, the four fleshless horses *Vandal's* men had brought ashore stood in the sun, lashing morosely with their tails at the flies which buzzed round them. Harnessed behind them was a small six-pounder field gun with its limber. The four members of the Heidelberg contingent were drawn up at rigid attention on the white sand. Von Kratzstein, hands clasped behind his back and sabre dragging, paced slowly down the short line of men, minutely examining weapons and equipment. When he came to Kolonel Albertus, he stopped.

"Albertus, you have sweatmarks on your collar."

"*Ja*, Herr General." The Kolonel's scarlet face clashed horribly with the orange of his neck-cloth, and dark patches of sweat were spreading at his collar and armpits.

"Why? You are on a charge. Not now, but later."

Albertus' military demeanour slipped noticeably. "Gott damn you, Kratzstein, it's hot. What am I supposed to do?"

"A Prussian has self-control. Your duty is evident."

"Damn my duty and damn you, Sir." Albertus dropped his musket into the sand and began to peel off his coat. "And since you imply that my sebaceous glands make me a bastard—for Prussians my honoured father and mother were—I demand satisfaction." He turned to his comrades-in-arms.

"Von Ziehendorf? You will act for me in this?"

Von Ziehendorf bowed. "Certainly. With pleasure."

Someone cleared his throat in an apologetic manner. They turned, and saw Stahlkleber, apparently nerving himself for speech.

"Gentlemen. If you will forgive me. We are now on the Turkish mainland. Can I beg that we put aside our disagreements, well-founded though they may be, until we have gloriously accomplished our mission?"

The three men rounded on him, steaming with fury, their own animosities for the moment pushed aside by the arrival of a common foe. Then von Kratzstein observed that *Vandal*, all sails set, was standing to the westward, and barked, "Silence!" He glowered at the unfortunate Stahlkleber. "You I shall also fight. But it is indeed the Turk whom we should pursue, and we will get no further by discussions on the beach. I shall drive the limber. You, Stahlkleber," he scowled "and you, Ziehendorf, scout ahead. Albertus, walk the lead horses. Understood? Good. March!"

Von Kratzstein climbed onto the limber, took the reins, and gave a practised flick of the whip at the mangy rump of the horses. Stahlkleber and Ziehendorf trudged on ahead, into the dry valley that came down from the hills inland. "Herr Gott," said Stahlkleber. "Kratzstein holds those reins as if he was born to it."

"*Ja*," said Ziehendorf. "It's hardly surprising. Before the Bonaparte wars he was nothing but a Dusseldorf drayman."

"But surely he was a General with Blücher's artillery?"

"Ach, Stahlkleber. Truly, you are an innocent. The uniform, in this case, makes the man. He is no more a General than you are Kolonel."

"Excuse me. A Kolonel I am, and—"

"What you are is a schoolteacher from Breslau. Don't attempt to deny it."

The colour of Stahlkleber's face deepened. "A schoolteacher? You will do me the honour, after our mission is accomplished, of justifying that accusation with your sword—"

"Enough. Why do you persist in these games? What good have they done us? There are no armies of Greek patriots for us to command. All there is is a little pop-gun and a whole village of cut-throat pagan pirates. Save your deceptions for later. If there is to be a later; myself, I think we may say farewell to this life tomorrow at dawn."

Stahlkleber fell silent, and drew away from Ziehendorf. Ziehendorf waited until his comrade-in-arms was a brilliant speck on the far side of the valley; then he looked quickly at the map Basreddin had drawn and began to walk forward, musket at the trail, eyes quartering the land in front of him as he had learned when he had been a private soldier with Von Bülow on the march to Waterloo.

As the day drew on, the four canary-coloured specks, motes in the five-mile strip of dun hillside and grey crag that was the narrow neck of the Resadiye, penetrated slowly into the interior, crossed the divide, and began the slow descent towards the dirt road that snaked along the north coast. They saw nobody; and nothing, save the gulls that wheeled over the barren hills in search of carrion, saw them.

* * *

When the people in the village saw the plume of dust rising from the parched hillside above the mosque, a flurry of fear swept through the little streets and eddied among the old men, blinking like lizards over their coffee beneath the fig-tree in the dung-crusted square. Could it be another visitation from the cove on the north shore? There had been much coming

and going of late, and since Daoud Shnaid had been
found with his throat cut at the beach twenty days
ago there was uneasiness among the people. But
since then it had been agreed that Daoud must have
been asking questions, so he would have deserved to
die. The north shore men were a strange, bad lot,
and even before the Black Crow had come there was
little love lost between their village and the men of
the south. A quiet life and small taxes was all the
southerners asked. Questions, therefore, if they drew
trouble and death, were to be avoided.

Certainly, the two men driving the washboard-
ribbed mules that descended from the hillside and
drew the waggon of hay through the huddle of little
mud buildings did not look dangerous. Their garments, grubby robes over long shirts which had once
been white and baggy trousers of indeterminate hue,
were respectable enough; and though they wore their
turbans wrapped round their faces, it might only be
that they did not wish to choke on the dust that rose
in thick brown clouds from the hooves of the mules.
Also, they did not pause in the village, but passed on
through. True, a woman observed afterwards that she
had seen the eyes of one of them and they had been
blue, the colour of the sky; but the woman had been
the flighty wife of Yusuf the goatherd, and it was
well-known that she was of a fantastical habit of
mind. Yusuf had given her a beating for casting her
eyes at men, and there the matter had ended.

As the village dwindled behind them and the track
steepened towards the mountains, Gurney stared at
the lurching rump of the mule ahead. Basreddin, on
the bench by his side, was humming a tune full of
slides and quarter-tones, his eyes absent. It was the
prospect of blood, Gurney knew, that had cheered
the Sufi. He himself should be feeling a lot more
bellicose; the prospect of spreading fire and ruin in
Kapraj Bey's very nest was one which, a week ago,
would have filled him with delight. But now he was

worried. Arabella on a yacht with Totters and his silly friends was bad enough, even had they been safely ensconced in the harbour at Rhodes. But Totters' yacht at sea in an Aegean gale was another matter altogether, particularly with every pirate on the coast out hawking for disabled vessels to plunder and sink.

He shook his head. There was nothing to be done. The sooner Kapraj Bey's little stronghold was finished with, the sooner he could go and look for her. Anyway, Totters, drunken buffoon though he might be, would undoubtedly have the sense to employ a captain who would know the waters. Yes, they would be in a cosy anchorage somewhere, botanising and painting watercolours of picturesque ruins. He put his worries from his mind and pursed his lips, whistling as he ran over the details of the dawn attack for the twentieth time. There was a tightness in his stomach now, and as always before action, events were slowing, becoming clearer.

Up on the slopes above, where the grass gave way to the bare rock and scrub of the mountains which swelled to the northward, the breeze blew little whirlwinds of dust from the arid ground. Provided that the wind held and *Vandal* could make her rendezvous, Kapraj Bey would have much to think about ere noon tomorrow. If he was still alive. Gurney profoundly hoped he would be; he had much that he wished to discuss with the Black Crow. A slave-auction three years ago in his marketplace was part of it; the letters he had stolen from *Vandal* through the good offices of Metaxas was another; and the contents of his treasure-house was yet another. Aye, that would be a reckoning, and a good one. And at the end of it, the Crow would do a certain dance at *Vandal*'s yardarm that he would find uncomfortable. Fatal, indeed.

Basreddin looked at him, and grinned. "Truly, the wolf slavers even before he has made his kill."

Gurney nodded. "Yes. I trust you're in the mood for blood-letting."

"Only when necessary." White teeth gleamed in the Sufi's beard. "I very much hope it will be necessary. Now." He pointed to a notch in the hills ahead. "That is the pass that will bring us out above his lair. When last I heard it was unguarded, but nonetheless . . ."

"Aye. We'll leave the waggon there, behind those rocks."

"Better still, there." Basreddin pointed to a little hill that stood over the track a quarter of a mile ahead. "Do you see?"

Gurney screwed up his eyes. Above a litter of broken rock a wooden construction, incongruous in the treeless landscape, stood stark from the summit. As he watched, something hanging from the cross-beam between the two uprights swung a little, and down the breeze came a grating creak.

"A gibbet?"

"Yes. One of the hundred gibbets of Kapraj Bey. It was once said, in the medinas and stews of Bodrum, that he prides himself on keeping them always filled. Be that as it may, it seems to me that if we leave our waggon among those rocks, no man will stumble across it. For he stinks, and here they believe a ghost walks while there is yet flesh stinking on the bones."

The mules snorted and jagged at the bit as Gurney drove them up the little hill and into the concealment of the rocks. Basreddin jumped down from the seat and soothed them, whispering in their ears, and they fell silent as he unhitched them and slipped halters over their heads.

The westering sun was smearing long black shadows over the land as they rode back onto the road and made at a trot for the notch in the hills. Gurney looked round uneasily. In the low light, each desiccated blade of grass stood out in sharp relief. It was a dead landscape, a fitting view for the dead man swinging in his creaking chains, staring sightlessly at the harsh tangles of rock and still valleys of the domain of the Black Crow.

The cleft in the hills was close now, indistinct in the night that flowed in from the great continent to the east, and a thin wind sighed down the bed of the valley, swirling chill among the mules' hooves. It smelt of the sea, and Gurney found himself wishing heartily that he was well away from this death-trap, on the familiar decks of the *Vandal*. He closed his eyes for a moment.

Then Basreddin's hand was on his arm. "Hush! You see there, at the summit of the pass?"

Gurney strained his eyes upwards. A red glow flickered on the wall of rock that lined the road. "A fire. Guard?"

"It could be nothing else. Keep your mouth shut and let me do the talking." Basreddin began to sing, a nasal drone punctuated with guttural exclamations. As they approached the crest of the hill, the flickering light grew brighter and Basreddin's voice louder. At the very top, a voice came out of the darkness. "Halt! Identify yourselves."

Basreddin allowed himself to finish his line, then spoke, in a reedy chant. "We are but two poor Mullahs who come bearing the holy word of Mohammed, on whom be peace, into the far reaches of the world."

The sentries—as Gurney's eyes grew accustomed to the light he saw there were two of them, each bearing a musket and a scimitar—relaxed visibly. The one who had spoken was a squat, muscular man with a scarred pit where his left eye should have been. He spoke again. "Peace on you, holy men. You are late, for the durbar began at the sunset cry of the muezzin."

"Late or not, it is as Allah wills, and we shall be beneath the benevolent cloak of the Bey ere long. But as for you, you keep lonely vigil here till dawn?"

The squat guard spat. "No. The night watch comes

at midnight, and remains until the ninth hour. So we shall hear the words of the wise for a span ere the cocks crow."

"Fortunate you are. Now, we pass on. Go with Allah, and may your vigilance be fitly rewarded in Paradise. Truly it is said, the best are they that guard the best." And spurring their mounts with bare feet, Basreddin and Gurney passed beyond the firelight onto the stony downgrade.

After two hundred yards the road curved sharply to the right. Far below, a congeries of lights sprawled at the bottom of the valley. Basreddin turned to Gurney. "Behold the nest of Kapraj Bey."

Once out of the glow of the fire it was not as dark as it had seemed. Though the sun was long below the horizon a wash of pink and violet still hung to the west. A steep-sided valley swept away below, the road serpentine in its bottom, crossing and recrossing a stream that flowed into the distant huddle of white buildings and the sea beyond. The eastern side of the valley flattened out about a quarter of a mile inland, giving way to the coastal plain whence, Gurney knew, came the road from the mainland. To the west of the village the hills rose sharply.

Silhouetted against the sea on the bluff above the houses was a squat structure with a bright point of orange fire on its roof. The blockhouse.

They rode on for a space, the clop of the mules' hooves loud in the silence. Caught at the pivot of day and night, sound and movement hung suspended. The insect-hum had died away, and the creatures of darkness had not yet begun their errands. Gurney shivered. The breeze was cool, and the wavering yellow lights of the harbour seemed somehow menacing— not the warm lights of home that beckon the traveller to surcease after his weary road, but rather the fierce, treacherous eyes of a nest of wildcats, awaiting their moment to spring.

"There is a power in this place that I do not like." Basreddin's voice was grave.

Gurney forced a laugh. "No power that half a ton of gunpowder and a few broadsides won't put paid to."

The Sufi made a sound expressive of doubt. "Let us hope. But I wonder what the sentry meant when he spoke of the words of the wise. Even last year there were reports of strange events coming to pass in these parts. It was said that the mountain Mullahs and certain Black Dervishes were seen to come onto this peninsula; but they were not seen to return."

"Be that as it may, powder and shot will brook no Mullah's logic-chopping. Or is it that you think it sacrilegious to assassinate an entire Synod of Koranists?"

"No, no. By throwing in their lot with the Black Crow they will have forfeited any claim to mercy. But there may be men of power hereabouts, and I must ready myself to meet them." The lids fell over the Sufi's eyes and his breathing slowed into the even rhythm of meditation.

During the next half-hour they rode in silence, Basreddin sitting his mount automatically while his mind flew who knew where, Gurney watching the lights of the village brighten as they drew nearer and the night deepened.

The first of the houses was very close when Basreddin opened his eyes. "Good," he said. "A good trip to the well of being. Wait here." And he slipped away to the left, to the beginnings of the bluff where it rose from the valley floor and merged into the high mountain-mass to the west.

Gurney slid from his saddle, walked the mules into a burnt-out shed, and crouched by the side of the track, hoping that nobody would challenge him. As it turned out only two people passed, both women, heavily veiled in the darkness. And in the nest of the Black Crow, it seemed, women did not talk to strange men.

Sounds of activity were coming from the village now; by the waterfront someone had lit a great bonfire, and the red reflection of the flames danced on the vertical face of the bluff and the domes of the large building that huddled against the side of the cliff. But for the mosque, whose minaret soared skywards in the midst of the little houses, the building beneath the cliffs was the largest in the village. Gurney tried to orientate himself.

Four years ago, he had lain captive somewhere in that group of buildings. In the square he had watched a loyal Sicilian friend crushed, joint by joint, on the wheel; and on the same scaffold Nkudu, the Black Crow's Nubian executioner, had laid bare the ribs on the left-hand side of his body. It came back to him as if it had been yesterday. The sun, brilliant on the white houses round the square, the red blood and white bone on the spokes of the wheel, and the harsh murmur of the crowd as the lash bit home. And then the pain, the awful agony that grabbed the breath from his lungs, and the roaring darkness that covered the world like a shroud. And through it all the black, slippery eyes of Kapraj Bey, mocking him for a useless pawn in a game of the Crow's own devising. The short hairs at the nape of Gurney's neck bristled. Now the Crow was but a quarter of a mile away, waiting unawares in his palace. There would be a reckoning.

Half an hour passed. Gurney, lost in his thoughts, paid no heed to the passage of time; he merely knew that Basreddin was beside him again. "It will not be difficult," the Sufi whispered in his ear. "They will not expect an attack from that quarter. In the blockhouse there are six men. There is a track for the waggon too, a quarter of a mile up the valley. We were right. The village spreads under the cliff like an ant's nest in a dry puddle. And ours will be the heel that crushes it."

"What's doing in the square?"

"As I suspected, there are many holy men in this

place. It seems to be a durbar of some kind. The anchorage is filled with ships, and from what I saw there is some great event which will happen."

"Sooner than they think, too."

"If Allah wills it." Again, there was doubt in the Sufi's voice. "There are many, and we are few."

"Come, come. You are a gloomy old fish, and no mistake. The worse that can happen is that we die."

"Indeed." Ironic. "But what now?"

The old fighting lust had Gurney by the throat. "If we looked like Mullahs to the sentries at the pass, mayhap we shall appear so to others. Let us get to closer quarters with these holy men and see what they are about. There are debts to settle here."

"Yes. But keep yourself well muffled about the nose and mouth; the holy ones of Islam do not take kindly to the beardless. And if any ask, tell them you are from the uplands of far Circassia, where men have blue eyes and yellow hair like yours."

"Very well. We'll leave the mules here."

As they passed down the alleys where mean hovels jostled each other for elbow-room, turning blank walls with high, tiny windows to passers-by, they began to meet people. No one paid any attention to the two Mullahs in their dark robes, however, and as they came closer to the square the press of humanity thickened until it became necessary to hack a way through the crowd with knees and elbows. Such a violent method of passage attracted little comment; the attention of the crowd seemed riveted on the great double doors of the mosque. There was little noise; by the great bonfire in the middle of the square were two or three stalls, selling kebabs of stringy meat and flat loaves of bread, but even these alfresco restaurateurs cried their wares in low tones. Over the whole gathering hung a reverent hush, like the stillness before the deluge.

The smell of roasting meat affected Gurney powerfully. It had been six hours since he had eaten and

what food they had brought they had left in the
waggon. But he could not take the risk of exposing
his beardless face, so he ignored his growling stomach as best he could and looked round him. These
were not the sullen brigands he remembered from
his last visit to the village. Now there were faces and
clothing of all colours and types, from white-turbaned
Nubians to little Tartars, their slit eyes and broad
faces shining coppery in the firelight under great caps
of fur, from heavy-bearded desert Bedouin to almond-
eyed, olive-skinned Bengalis and even, he noticed
with entire surprise, a little man with filed teeth and
a hat like a rounded extinguisher who could only
have come from the East Indies. He looked at Basreddin.

"What d'you make of it?"

"It is strange." The Sufi's lips barely moved as he
spoke. "But those are all holy men, and they have the
air of being on pilgrimage." He inclined his head
towards the doors of the mosque. "If I am not wrong,
the answer lies behind those doors."

A shrill voice cut like a bird's call through the
darkness above the heads of the crowd, and Basreddin
grabbed his arm. High in the minaret, the muezzin
was calling the faithful to prayer.

The double doors of the mosque swung open as
one, and the crowd surged forward towards the
arched portal, from which streamed a soft glow of
lamplight. Gurney and Basreddin, drawn forward in
the press, were dragged towards the threshold and
swallowed up.

Gurney fought to stay behind the Sufi; remembered only just in time to shed his curly-toed slippers
at the door, and then was inside, in the half-light,
where the perforated brass lamps cast little specks of
yellow radiance on the rich mats which covered the
floor and the intricate knots of stone of the vaulted
roof. Basreddin made his way over to a pillar on the
far side. In Gurney's view, it was a good deal too far

from the door, not that that would make any difference if they were discovered. But at least the stone
column afforded some measure of concealment. He
crouched at Basreddin's side, and watched from the
corner of his eye as the throng streamed in.

"What now?"

"We wait. Do exactly as I do." Basreddin half-
closed his eyes and began to move his lips silently,
and Gurney did likewise, rocking a little on his heels.
The only prayer that came to mind was the Twenty-
Third Psalm, however, and that, while encouraging,
was a little too near the bone. The Valley of the
Shadow of Death, thought Gurney, was exactly what
he was walking through. But what came in its place
was worse, bubbling up from God-knew-what Shake-
spearean well:

> The blood of English shall manure the ground
> and future ages groan for this foul act;
> Peace shall go sleep with Turks and infidels.

Hardly consoling. He was trying to identify more
with Byron's Assyrian, coming down like a wolf on
the fold, when Basreddin nudged him in the ribs and
fell to his knees, prostrating himself towards the eastern wall of the mosque, where, Gurney presumed as
his forehead knocked against the carpet before him,
lay Mecca.

After the required number of prostrations the
gathering settled back on its collective heels once
more. Gurney half-wondered if it was all over. He
was acutely aware that he was not only in close
propinquity with near three hundred people who were
his sworn enemies, but also that he was committing
one of the most hideous acts of sacrilege in their book.
It was rather, he decided, as if a Parsee were to come
rambling in out of the blue and start chopping up
sheep on the High Altar at St. Saviour's, Sea Dalling.

A sound between a grunt and sigh ran round the
mosque. Over the heads of the throng, Gurney saw

two figures advancing on the *mirhab* or pulpit which stood high on the East Wall. One, tall and cruel-visaged, clad in a striped robe of sombre hue and a brilliant green turban, Gurney recognised as Kapraj Bey. The other was small and bent, dressed in a nightshirt of grubby white; his jaw hung slack and his eyes rolled crazily in their sockets. The Black Crow helped the idiot up the steps, then descended, his eyes sweeping the crowd. For a moment, as those cold, wet orbs crossed his sightline, Gurney felt an overpowering urge to run for the front and hew him down where he stood. Then the Bey lowered himself fastidiously into a heavily-carved chair, and a yowling screech rumbled and caromed round the vaulting of the ceiling.

Basreddin inclined himself a little towards Gurney. "The Holy Fool," he said. "This is indeed a matter of great weight. Listen, now."

The howl died away, and the idiot in the pulpit began to speak. Gurney's Arabic was rusty, so it took him a little time to get the gist of the words; but when his ear became attuned to the high, cracked voice he understood well enough.

"In me," the drooling moron chanted, "you see the manifestation of the return in the flesh of the Friend of God, the twelfth after the Blessed Ali, he who lay beneath the rocks until the time should come that the word would be fulfilled that the stones themselves should burn with the fire of the Prophet. And my wings are wings of retribution and the light of my eyes is as the light of the angry sun and gestures of my hands are Justice." The little figure in the *mirhab* seemed to have grown, and as he flung his arms in the air it was as if the wings of a great carrion bird had thrown the mosque into shadow. "Justice!" he howled, and the grating of his voice was a vulture's croak. "Justice!" he screamed again, and "Justice!" the whole mosque screamed with him.

Then he dropped his arms to his sides, and a dead-

ly silence crept outwards from the pulpit across the
devotees. When he began to speak again, his voice
was a bitter hiss.

"The Friend and Benefactor of us all, on whom rest
the blessings of Mohammed and of me, the flesh of
the Twelfth Imam, Kapraj Bey, the Black Crow of
Izmir, has received news. News that our wars against
the infidel are twice blessed. News from the Bey of
Mecca, Ali Pasha of Egypt, Mahmoud of Turkey, and
the great Moghuls of India, and our brothers in the
North. Letters, my children, my dear ones, from these
great men and others besides, pledging that there
will be *jihad*. Holy war, my children, against the
Christian, the uncircumcised infidel who tramples the
lands of Allah beneath his horses and ploughs our
fair seas with his impudent keels. In the Greek lands
of the Ottoman a new firmness will rise in the citadels
and hold the souls of men in the iron hand of the
Lord. For did not the prophet say: Strive with those
who acknowledge not Allah and the Final Time, those
who abide not by the laws of the Lord and his Prophet, those who follow the Father of Lies, heeding not
the word of the Book, until their necks are brought
beneath the heel and they eat dust?"

He paused. A long string of saliva fell from the
corner of his mouth onto his robe. His face was fish-
belly white. He stumbled, then recovered himself.
"Now," he screamed. "In the name of Allah, of Mohammed, of Ali and the twelve of whose flesh I am,
I give you this banner as a token!" A great flag of
green silk worked with a motif of red and gold bil-
lowed out from the pulpit and fell into the crowd below.

"Swear on this and by the letters of the Pashas: as
long as it shall persist in the circles of the world, let
strife not cease." His head arched back, teeth bared,
and he fell backwards, heels drumming on the boards
of the *mirhab* in an epileptic fit.

But the deed was done. The green banner passed

from hand to hand, and, as it passed, each of the Mullahs pronounced his blessing. It was perhaps twenty minutes before it arrived where Basreddin and Gurney were sitting, and Gurney's legs, unused to the long crouching, were almost numb. As the silk passed through his hands, he stared at it, mustering every curse he could think of. What emerged, however, was a growled expression of his unwillingness to blow his nose on it even if his nose was running like a dozen hares.

When the banner had passed back to the *mirhab*, Kapraj Bey folded it reverently and left the mosque through a side entrance, supporting the semi-conscious Fool. This signalled a general rush for the exits; Basreddin and Gurney waited until the crush had thinned, then collected their shoes and left. For twenty minutes, Gurney prowled the three streets of the village, familiarising himself with its layout; then he returned to the burnt-out stable, where Basreddin was waiting with the mules.

As they rode up the valley in the bright moonlight, Gurney broke the silence. "So. What, besides the obvious, was all that about?"

Basreddin shrugged. "Holy War. Though it is strange that it should be called here, in a nest of pirates. But the word will undoubtedly travel, and there will be risings."

"Under that banner?"

"It is usual, in these cases, for the banner to be cut in pieces and distributed. It is a valuable talisman."

"Who is the Fool?"

"No man knows. He comes out of the hills, from time to time, claiming to be Flesh of the Twelfth Imam. An anchorite."

"And why would the Crow suddenly see himself as the Defender of the Faith?"

"The Crow has much to gain from Egypt's taking sides in this war. And the Egyptian needs a sense of mission."

"You mean that if he can get the Egyptians stirred up enough against the Greeks they may get the better of the Turks too?"

"Not exactly, Giorgiou. But close. The Egyptians are the vassals of the Turks, but they are strong, and their strength increases daily. The Russians hang at their frontiers—"

"So it would be in the Russian interest to encourage Egypt in her aims, the more to weaken Turkey."

"Precisely. We are at the very hinge of events, Giorgiou, and the door is opening."

They fell silent as they came to the pass. The guards challenged them languidly, without interest, and waved them by after some appropriately high-flown religious rhetoric from Basreddin. The waggon was where they had left it. As they spread their blankets underneath the wheels the moon was setting, and a little breeze sighed through the boulders, setting the dry grass to rustling. Gurney fell asleep lulled by the grating of the gibbet's chains.

10

Arabella was lying on the filthy stone floor of a cell, her bodice torn and her feet bare, arms chained to the wall. Her face was smeared with grime, but her blue eyes were proud as the heavy door crashed open. In the threshold stood Kapraj Bey, his eyes caressing the curve of her breast, the line of her thigh under her ragged dress. His tongue ran round his cruel lips. "Come, my fine beauty," he said. "Come, for first you will sport with the executioner Nkudu for my delight, and then we will sell you to the Bey of Dyarbakir for a king's ransom." Gurney, spread-eagled on the

wall, manacled at wrists and ankles, roared desperately, struggling in his bonds as Arabella, kicking and
struggling, cast him a beseeching glance. Then she
was out of the cell door, and a guard was pressing,
pressing the blunt tip of his spear into the hollow
under Gurney's ear ...

He groaned and opened his eyes. Basreddin was
crouching by his side, watching him. "A dream?"

It was cold, and his legs were stiff. There was an
ache behind his eyes and a metallic taste in his
mouth. He grunted. "Aye, and a nasty one. There's
something about this village—"

"I know. I also have slept badly. The wickedness of
the mosque poisons the air as an octopus spreads its
ink through the water. But enough of that. It is time.
Here, drink this."

Gurney drank, and his aches and the memory of
the foul dream slipped away. Warmth and energy
spread to his fingers and toes, and he climbed to his
feet. "Good. What was that?"

The Sufi, a dim figure, in the starlight, shrugged.
"It matters not. The effects will last for a day, then
sleep will take you and it will be as if you died for a
little."

"Hmm." There remained two and a half hours
till dawn, Gurney guessed. The wind had dropped
now, and the corpse on the gibbet hung still in its
chains. "Good. I'll take the sentries. When I show a
light, bring the waggon through." He began to run
towards the notch in the hills. Damn that wind. If
Vandal was becalmed, it would mean nothing but
trouble. Timing was of the essence, and if one part of
the plan was delayed the others would be entirely
useless. By now, *Vandal* should be lying about five
miles off, hidden from the lookouts. But if this calm
persisted, it would take her five hours to make the
last five miles. Five miles, rowing and towing. Too
long. Too bloody long.

The ground was rising under his feet now, and he

turned off the track, climbing the steep bank and traversing the side of the mountain until only a projecting bulge of rock hid him from the sentries' campground. Moving very slowly, he reached his head round the bulge and looked down.

The watchfire had died to a red glow, but to Gurney's eyes, accustomed to the dark and further stimulated by the drug on which he had breakfasted, the little arena in the rocks was lit up as if by a flare. One of the guards lay sleeping, huddled under a threadbare rug in the shadows on the far side of the fire; the other sat, musket propped against a rock, staring into the embers wheezing in the hearthstones.

When he heard the little sound behind him he jumped, then reassured himself. The rats ran through the rocks here often, attracted by the bits of food and the sentries' latrine. But he reached for his musket nonetheless, and looked round him, eyes dazzled by the glow of the embers and the opium he had smoked during the revels the evening before. There was no other sound, and he fell to musing again, arms wrapped round his musket.

Death plummeted onto his shoulders from vertically above. Gurney, landing with his knees into the man's shoulder blades, crooked an elbow round his neck and let himself fall back. There was a moment of resistance, then a grating click as the vertebrae separated. The sentry went limp. He looked round. The other man had come awake and was reaching groggily for the pistol that lay on the ground at his side. Gurney's foot scooped up a shower of ashes and the sentry choked back a scream and staggered to his feet, beating at his blazing beard. Then the knife caught him in the navel and ripped upwards, shearing a track round from the right lung to the heart. Breath sighed out through the wound in his chest and he collapsed into the ruins of the fire.

As the hooves of the mules came up to the pass,

Gurney was using the remains of the guards' water-supply to extinguish the smouldering embers that still stuck to the second guard's clothing. He heaved the bodies into a crack in the rock, tossed ashes over a dark bloodstain. Then he waved a burning brand inland. When the waggon clattered up he mounted the box beside the Sufi. "Drive on, coachee," he said. "Things to do." His fingers drummed nervously on his knee and his heart was thudding in his chest as the waggon bumped and rumbled round the hairpin bend towards the village. Down there all was quiet. The only light came from the blockhouse on the cliff, on whose roof the fire still burned.

Basreddin was silent for a time. Then he began to mutter, and turned to Gurney. "The spirals. Spirals of great events." His voice became clearer. "It is curious, Giorgiou, that our travelling is moving in a spiral, upward and outward. At first, your journey was in pursuit of my liberty and certain letters; then, in pursuit of the treasure of Osman Bey, the consequences enlarge, spreading out from that one original cause. And now, where are we?" He was silent for a little. Then, "I shall tell you," he resumed. "We are touching the fringes—the merest fringes—of a plot whose darkness is inconceivable to one who looks merely at the politics of the body and mind. A plot of the spirit, that can plunge the processes of reason and good magic into a dark age from which they may never emerge. A plot forged in the mosque by the Black Crow and his twisted Hell-disciples, before our very eyes. A plot whose only outcome can be death and chaos. You know of Ali Pasha, he of Albania?"

Gurney swallowed. "The name is familiar."

"It was he, first of the great Albanian rulers, who set the tradition that the Black Crow and Mehemet Ali of Egypt now pursue. It is they who, if they succeed, will have the empires of tomorrow between their hammers and their anvils. For they are men of no scruple, no honesty; in power lies their only satisfaction, raw power for its own sake; and their delight is cruelty. Let me tell you a story."

Gurney looked at the horizon to the east. No light in the sky yet. Plenty of time. But Basreddin did choose the oddest times and places for his essays in storytelling, damn him. Once he had the bit between the teeth there was no stopping him.

"It is said that once, when Ali Pasha was but a child, his mother was travelling through a certain town in the mountains. They stopped at the inn in this town, and food was brought to them. In one of the apples that finished the collation there was a wasp, and when the mother of Ali Pasha bit into the apple, the wasp not unnaturally stung her. She arrived at her son's side a day later with her lip swollen; he asked what had happened. When she told him he flew into a rage.

"Now the rages of Ali Pasha were not as the rages of other men, brief and thunderous. The rage of Ali Pasha was a slow, brooding thing, a pustule filling with bile, festering in the dark. It was not until forty-five years later that Ali Pasha went to this town. He caused it to be known that he wished to speak of the question of military service with all males over the age of six, and that to this end he would give them a dinner in a great walled courtyard. Near seven hundred men there were, from tiny children to ancient dotards, sitting at the long trestles beneath the trees of that courtyard, waiting for the Pasha. But he never came. Instead his soldiers swarmed over the battlements and poured bullets into that crowd of men and children until the cobblestones were deep in blood and no living soul remained. Then they walled up the entrance, erected a plaque for the edification of passers-by, and left all to rot.

"The women of the town they sold into slavery, having first shaved their heads; the Pasha's sister slept for the rest of her days on mattresses stuffed with their hair. If it is thus that these Albanians revenge themselves for the sting of a wasp, how much more hideous will they be in Holy War?"

Gurney shook his head. "Not a pretty tale. He seems indeed the spiritual forebear of our friend the Crow."

"Aye. His brood is Legion. But as for the Crow, he lies under the malediction of Osman Bey. Our motive is more vengeance than avarice; but his is avarice unalloyed. Let us hope it works for us. But enough, now, of talk; the time is come for action." He halted the mules and jumped down from the seat. Gurney went to the tailboard of the waggon.

Under the mound of hay lay perhaps forty kegs. It was getting lighter now, and Gurney worked with feverish speed, pitching the hay into the ditch by the side of the track. He looked for a moment, came to a keg marked with a cross. Basreddin had worked long at that keg, filling it with a compound of his own devising, made up of herbs and liquids from the list he had given the harbourmaster at Mandraki. Gurney knew the chief ingredients were pitch and opium, but beyond that he had no idea. He picked it up and tucked it under his arm, the fuse dangling from its end like a pig's tail, and set off for the blockhouse. Basreddin paused just out of sight of the guards, holding the mules by their heads. Gurney went on until the square stone redoubt was plain to view in the half-light. He covered the last hundred feet on his stomach, wriggling like a snake, and crouched behind a boulder. There was more light, here on the summit of the bluff, than there had been behind the village below, but the blockhouse, a low structure of grey stones bound with mortar, had no embrasures on its inland side. And why should it? It was from the sea that trouble would come to the harbour of Black Crow; the village was heavily walled on its eastern side where the road from the mainland came in, and the sentinels at the pass in the mountains could deal with any enemies coming across the peninsula. If anyone was foolish enough to attempt that route in strength.

Loosening his knife in its sheath, Gurney pressed himself against the boulder and pulled flint and steel from his pocket. Then he froze. On the roof of the blockhouse a man dressed in baggy trousers and a tattered wool coat heaved himself to his feet and put another log on the fire. Then he stretched, spat, and busied himself with something Gurney could not see but which he guessed from its clatter must be a coffee-pot. He left the keg behind the boulder and crept to the stone steps which led to the roof. The sentry had his back to him and his head was tilted back as he drained his cup. Gurney pulled the knife from his belt, sighted on a spot below the sentry's left shoulder blade, and threw, running forward as the knife left his hand.

The Turk felt the awful pain that clove his chest and drew breath to shout; but his mouthful of coffee rushed into his lungs as the knifepoint reached the left ventricle of his heart, and he collapsed with a gurgle. As Gurney turned him over, pulled out the knife and wiped it on the dead man's coat, a black fluid flowed from the mouth. Gurney, wondering dazedly if it were blood or coffee, slipped down the steps and retrieved the keg. Then he began to shake.

The killing of the sentry had taken perhaps thirty seconds, and it had been entirely soundless. Gurney clamped his jaws to stop his teeth from chattering and stared at the blockhouse, hoping desperately that all would be asleep. No movement came from the squat building, though he waited five minutes, and after a while Basreddin's drug took hold and he was calm again. He groped in his pocket for flint and steel and struck. The tinder caught on his third attempt and he applied it to the slow-match, blowing the little coal to cherry brightness. When all but an inch of the match was burnt down he started from his hiding-place, skidded round the front of the block-house, and hurled the keg into the central embrasure.

Startled snorts came from within, muffled by sleep. Then there was a great *whoosh* and a flurry of cough-ing. As black, pungent smoke began to seep from the embrasures and the chimney, the coughing stopped and silence fell. Gurney was still standing there, un-believing, when Basreddin appeared beside him.

"They will sleep, and when they awake it will not be in this world."

"Poor devils." The reaction was with him again, and he clasped his hands behind his back to keep them from trembling. "Come. To the roof."

"No. Not until the fumes have cleared. In five min-utes it will be harmless; until then, one good whiff and you'll be—how do you say?—flat out, without sense or motion."

"What is that devil's brew, anyway?"

"An old hunter in the mountains of Anatolia gave me its secret, when we were after furs in the winter. He used it to subdue packs of rabid wolves."

"Very effective."

As the light slowly grew, cocks began to crow in the village below. Gurney and Basreddin busied themselves assembling certain machines that they took from the waggon on the lip of the cliff over-looking the domes and courtyards. A breeze began to blow from the land, rustling in the dry grass, and the fumes from the blockhouse dissipated down the wind. When they had finished their preparations they went to the roof of the blockhouse, and Gurney ex-amined the heliograph that stood at its seaward end. He looked along the coast to the westward. High on the shoulder of a mountain that plunged into the sea perhaps three miles away was another blockhouse. Kapraj Bey's sentinels were well-spread; but the final link in the chain was now cut, and the village lay incommunicado. Even as Gurney watched, a beacon blazed up on the blockhouse roof, and he reached for the glass in his pocket. Two miles out to sea, her sails grey in the burgeoning light, *Vandal* was standing close-hauled towards her dawn rendezvous.

Beneath the pointed arch of masonry that framed it, the gate of Kapraj Bey's village was closed. To General von Kratzstein, it looked daunting. Very daunting. Above the iron-bound wood, the stone of the wall swept twenty feet to jagged crenellations of stone, and on either side a tower flanked the area of stones and trodden earth where the road disappeared into the village. Von Kratzstein had pictured a Turkish village as a place of mean huts, with perhaps a filigreed tracery of stone here and there, a relic of a great empire fallen into decay. The rude curtain-wall that now met his eyes, a structure as solid and inflexible as the Crusaders who had built it in the thirteenth century, came as a disagreeable shock.

Stahlkleber, at the head of the nearside lead mule, whimpered. Von Kratzstein's resolution, which had for a moment metamorphosed into an overwhelming desire to strip off his uniform and start running like a hare in the opposite direction, stiffened. "Unharness!" he barked, and the hills inland threw his voice back at him tenfold.

A head appeared on the ramparts above the gate, and Albertus, ensconced with his musket behind a ridge of rock a hundred yards to the left, fired. The ball spanged on the stone near the Turk's head as the echoes of the shot bounced from hill to hill. Moving with terrified speed, the Prussians unharnessed the horses, and by the time the dawn watch ran out onto the catwalk behind the battlements the field-gun was positioned with its limber in a clump of boulders and scrub on the seaward side of the road.

Sweat was running down von Kratzstein's face and into his eyes as he crouched in the sand by the gun. Behind him, the sound of the horses' hooves died

away as they left the straight road for the shelter of
the hills. He wondered if he would ever see them
again. Then he sighted down the gun, adjusted the
elevation screw, and pulled the linstock. At the roar
of the field-piece a flock of gulls rose screaming from
the harbour and shouting broke out on the ramparts.
Von Kratzstein cursed; the bushes in front of his hiding place were burning, set afire by the muzzle-flash
of the six-pounder. Still cursing, he grovelled his way
to the muzzle, swabbed it out, shoved cartridge and
shot home, pricked, primed, and pulled the linstock
again. This time the roar of the cannon was accompanied by a thin, widely-spread rattle of musketry
from the hills before the walls, and when the smoke
cleared the Turks were running round like ants in
the nest. Something zipped past his ear, and he
swatted at it with his hand. Then he realised that the
little men on the walls were shooting at him, and his
stomach turned to water. It seemed to take him a
terribly long time to put his awl through the touchhole, and as he pulled the linstock for the third time
a bullet smashed his kepi from his head. It was at
that point that von Kratzstein began to get angry.

At the third cannon-shot from the eastern end of the
village, Gurney began to move. He went to the last of
the line of little catapults he and Basreddin had as-
sembled at the edge of the cliff, a burning brand from
the guards' fire in his hand. As he lit the fuse, Basreddin triggered the mechanism. The keg of gunpowder looped thirty feet up and outwards, and fell, the
plume of smoke from its fuse arching in an airy parab-
ola behind it, into a narrow alley that cracked the
white roofs below. A flash and a roar, and a moment
of stunned silence; then the shouting began again, and
swarms of men began pouring into the square.

On the walls the Turks had brought their cannon
into play, but so thick was the smoke that drifted

across the road that there was nothing to aim at. Ignoring the chips of rock that whizzed round him, von Kratzstein worked his gun like a madman, hammering shots into the wood of the gates. In the hills to the left, the Prussian Kolonels kept a continuous stream of musket balls whizzing among the bunches of Turks on the battlements. From his vantage-point Stahlkleber could see four men down. He was desperately frightened, but a strange elation was building up in him. A Turk walked into his sights and stood indecisively, looking into the dense smoke, searching for a target; Stahlkleber squeezed the trigger, heard the hiss as the priming caught and the crash as his musket fired. When the smoke cleared, the Turk was sprawled half-out of one of the embrasures, twitching feebly. Stahlkleber giggled and slid back behind the ridge, running for his next firing-point. As he dropped to his knees and began once more to crawl into the sightline, heavy explosions began to sound from behind the wall.

From behind the cliff the square looked black with men. Gurney, playing his glass over them, was delighted to notice that only about half of them bore arms; those who did not, some of whom he recognised from the mosque last night, were getting badly in the way. He reached for a keg with a circle painted on it, trimmed its fuse and placed it carefully in the catapult. The keg arched into the air, began to fall and exploded with a roar about ten feet above the square, the musket-balls it contained hissing like a deadly scythe into the packed bodies. Basreddin, at his side, was humming one of his tunes. Gurney recognised it as an Anatolian reaping-song.

The sun was well up over the mountains to the east now, shining straight along the road and the mainland. The Turks at the cannon had fired four shots into the smoke that lapped the shadows under the gate, and the gun-captain was gnawing his nails. There was nothing to shoot at. One thing was certain, though; they were under attack by a sizeable expeditionary force. He was a man experienced in mountain warfare, and he knew full well that you did not simply drag a single cannon to a well-fortified town and open fire. And the musketry from the hills inland was coming from a lot of different directions. When they had pounded the gate open—and it would be soon—there would be an assault. But where was the main body? He grinned. Try to bluff him, would they? He would see about that. "Full elevation!" he shouted. "Fire shell over the ridge!" The cannon roared again, and explosions began to leap from the dry, gravelly soil on the other side of the hill, disturbing some grazing goats but in no way incommoding the four Prussian sharp-shooters.

"Boats away!"

Vandal came up into the wind and McIver watched as her boats, each one jammed with men, put out for the shore. The bower anchor plunged to the bottom and she fell back; then, as the cable came taut, the three westernmost boats let fall the kedges.

Fifteen pairs of hands slapped onto the capstan handles, and the schooner's broadside came slowly round until O'Shea, peering down the barrel of the larboard sixty-eight pounder, saw the minaret of the mosque behind the square. He raised his hand, and the man at the hatchway shouted. "'Vast hauling." The clacking of the capstan stopped; O'Shea wiped his hands fastidiously on his filthy handkerchief, stepped aside half a pace and pulled the linstock.

For a moment Gurney wondered what had happened. One moment, the square had been almost solid with struggling men, some running for the quays and the ships moored there, some for the walls, and some merely racketing round like so many chickens with their heads cut off; and the next, there was a broad avenue, carpeted with red, running from the doors of the mosque to the sea. Then he looked towards *Vandal*, and he realised. Half a hundredweight of grapeshot from a sixty-eight pounder had a magical way with flesh and bone. He bent, and released another keg of powder. Keep 'em guessing.

The village of Kapraj Bey was beginning to look a little the worse for wear. Among the hovels on the far side of the palace, smoke was rising. The fire would soon be out of control, he guessed. On the eastern side of the square the slave barracoon was untouched, as he had ordered. Directly below his feet, the palace of the Bey was a pristine white. And the shipping.

Vandal's boats were nearly at the quays now, and in the confusion it looked as if they would have little opposition. Gurney let his eyes travel over the ships anchored near the shore. The red hull of the *Golden Horn*, the Black Crow's personal flagship, gleamed in the morning sun. Volnikov would look after her. Three other brigs. No trouble there. None of them was awake, and anyway, the men would all be ashore. He trained his glass on the last ship in the harbour, a little further offshore than the others. The figurehead was a young man who looked vaguely familiar rising from battlements of cunningly-carved wooden masonry. The name, its gilt bright, looked Italian. *Otranto*.

Otranto! Gurney's heart stopped. Then he whirled, picked up a keg with a circle, lit the fuse and hurled it into the courtyard of the palace. Basreddin watched appalled as he tied a rope to the catapult and went swiftly hand-over-hand down the cliff onto the roof below. He crouched there until the crack and boom of the explosion, then dropped out of sight into the shadowed lair of the Black Crow.

Mather, at the head of *Vandal's* landing-party, lay flat on the quay as the third blast of grape from her broadside tore over his head and into the carnage in the square. Then he got up and began to run, a cutlass in his right hand and a long, keen skinning-knife in his left. At his back, forty good men of *Vandal*'s complement, each with cutlass and pistol, pounded across the grey flags of the quay towards the bright stripe of blood splashed across the white façade of the mosque. The air zipped and hummed with musket-balls, mostly from the wall; little moved now in the square, carpeted with death. When they reached the square, twenty men peeled off towards the wall, with the slave-quarters and the squat hulk of the magazine nestling at its base; the other twenty split, ten men running for the alleyways that debouched like tunnels on either side of the mosque, and ten for the little knot of guards at the wrought-iron gates of the palace under the cliff to the right.

In the harbour Volnikov, roaring a shanty, tossed a keg of burning pitch into the *Golden Horn*'s gundeck and jumped into the waiting boat. As the oarsmen pulled him away he continued to sing mightily. A wisp of smoke rose from the xebec's hatches, and flames began to lick at her rigging, running along the pitch in her planking. The Russian took another swig from the keg at his feet and wiped his mouth with the back of his hand. Before embarking, he had taken the precaution of raiding *Vandal*'s grog-locker—an easy thing, with Captain Gurney ashore. And Volnikov was sure that Captain Gurney would not, in the circumstances, have minded. For when Volnikov got drunk, Volnikov got dangerous, and he had the feeling that on this day of all days the more dangerous he was, the better. Burping, he applied a slow-match to the next pitch-barrel, stood up in the boat, wound up, and hurled it into one of the brigs. It burst with a satisfying crash, and after a little while the ship began to burn.

The smoke before the gates was very thick now, and it was making von Kratzstein's eyes water. This did little to soothe his anger. But despite his rage, he was aware that his position was becoming untenable. The sounds from the other side of the wall were gaining in intensity, too, though his ears were ringing from the concussions of the six-pounder. The time, he decided, had come; and being a great general, what could he do but seize it?

He rose to his feet, cupped his hands round his mouth, and roared "Heidelbergers! To me!" Then a bullet passed across his cheek like a red-hot poker, and he fell back towards the gun. While he was there, he decided he could as well fire another shot; and, as luck would have it, the ball smashed into the very latch of the gate, driving out one of the iron clamps that held the bar in place. The timber fell to the ground, and the portals of the village hung ajar.

Three canary-coloured figures materialised in the fog of smoke at his side. "Goot!" he roared. "Frontal assault! Charge, for the glory of Greece!"

Stahlkleber giggled again. Like Volnikov, he had been refreshing himself liberally, and while his aim had grown increasingly poor his martial enthusiasm had been swelling like a bladder. Without further ado he drew his sword, screamed a terrible Teutonic oath, and began to run for the gate. Von Kratzstein, deeply conscious of the necessity of being at the head of his men, lumbered after him, and the other three, brandishing their blades rather more half-heartedly, followed at a fogbound canter.

The advance of the Heidelberg vanguard was beginning to take on the air of a vulgar foot race when the puff of wind from the sea blew the smoke away. Stahlkleber, distracted, got his scabbard between his legs and crashed headlong into the dust; von Kratzstein, sensing the sudden lack of competition, looked round and put out a hand to pull the Kolonel to his feet; and a Turk on the wall above leaned over and

aimed his musket at the yellow centre of von Kratzstein's back. But the shot never came. Instead the
Turk, a look of great surprise on his face, gargled a
stream of arterial blood down the wall and fell into
space, a rope-handled knife locked firmly between
his sixth and seventh vertebrae as *Vandal*'s landing-
party dealt swiftly and neatly with the defenders of
the wall. The Prussians scurried into the overhang of
the gate, pushed, and ran through into the press in
the alley leading to the village square.

Before the gate to the Bey's palace, things were not
going so well. On the cobbles before the entrance two
of *Vandal*'s men lay limp and lifeless, and Mather
had dragged two more back with him to the meagre
cover of the stream where it emerged from the arch
under the palace and flowed into the harbour. Face
down in the stinking water, the American raised his
musket to keep his powder dry and stared gloomily
at the loopholes in the walls to either side of the
gateway, whence came flashes, puffs of smoke, and
the reports of musketry. Of the five fit men who remained to him, one was too young to be of much
use—George Jarvis—and the others—well, you
couldn't expect a sailorman to jump up in that hail of
lead and tear the gates asunder with his own hands.

A movement on the palace roof caught his eye. He
raised his musket and took aim at the turbaned figure;
then the Turk waved and shook his head, and he
recognised him as Mr. Basreddin. Basreddin was
performing an elaborate exercise in dumb show, and
Mather was puzzled for a moment; then, as the Sufi
lit the fuse on the keg under his right arm, he
grinned.

The keg fell directly in front of the gates and spun
on its axis, a little plume of smoke rising from its
touchhole. Mather quickly checked the priming on the
pistols at his belt and braced himself for the charge.
The bomb exploded with a roar, and the loopholes

fell silent. Mather waved his men forward and they
rushed for the blank wall on either side of the gate.
When the smoke cleared they were pressed into the
angle of wall and paving-stones, out of the line of fire
of the loopholes. Mather looked across at the gates.
They still held. He reached carefully to his belt and
drew a pistol. Inch by inch, he stole it up to the
nearest loophole. The musket inside fired, spitting a
cloud of smoke across the square; then Mather
jammed the pistol to the hole and pulled the trigger.
Someone screamed and, by the sound of it, fell into a
stack of muskets inside. Mather grinned and reached
for his next pistol. Where Mr. Basreddin had gone,
God only knew, but he'd be up to something. In the
meantime, good enough to sit here picking off the
darkies one by one, so long as their backs were covered. What they needed was more powder for those
goddamned gates.

Basreddin, after his good deed with the powder keg,
had bethought himself of problems more pressing
even than those which faced Mather and his men
under the loopholes by the gate. It had been a good
ten minutes since Gurney had disappeared into the
courtyard, and the Sufi was commencing to be a
little worried.

He was right. When Gurney had dropped from the
half-roof of the courtyard into the scene of devasta-
tion left by the bomb, he had realised that once again
he had dived head-first into a hornet's nest. He looked
up, once, resigned himself to the fact that there was
no chance of getting out the way he had got in, and
began to run. Then he stopped. Lying in the middle
of the courtyard, head dripping blood into the ornamental fountain whose trickle could be heard even
through the gunfire and shouting outside, was the
body of a Turk. And the scimitar and breastplate he
wore were those of the personal guard of Kapraj Bey.
Gurney stripped sword and breastplate from the

corpse and buckled them on. Then he put his hand to the dead man's wound, took a smear of blood and wiped it over his face. He strode to the arched doorway that led into the inner depths of the palace.

The next room was full of men. As Gurney saw them he changed his walk to a stagger and let his head fall forward so they would not see his eyes; but they seemed too panicked to notice. He went to lean against one of the walls—by the weapons piled in the corners and the lockers and pegs on the walls, this was the Black Crow's guard-room—and edged towards the far door. Explosions were coming from the direction of the front gates now, and the guards were putting on equipment and running across the ruined courtyard to reinforce the defenders.

The door into the inner quarters was guarded by a huge man wearing the same breastplate and turban as the man in the fountain, but his face was coal black. He turned incurious eyes on Gurney as he stood slumped against the wall.

"No closer, please. We do not want the wolf-pack savaging their leader, now do we?" The voice, terribly soft and gentle, was one that still visited Gurney in his dreams and woke him screaming. The voice of Nkudu, the Nubian executioner of Kapraj Bey.

Gurney let himself slide down the wall until he was squatting on his hams, letting his head loll forward. Arabella was in there. That bloody fool Totters. But the rage he felt against Aristotle was a pale glimmer beside his blazing fury at Kapraj Bey and all his creatures. It was, he supposed, reasonable in some sense that he, George Gurney, should have his contest with the Bey, but that Arabella, whose only crime was her curiosity, should suffer the attention of that reptilian Levantine was intolerable. His hand crept to the pommel of his scimitar, and with a hoarse bellow of pain and anger he pulled it from its scabbard and brought it swinging at the Nubian's waist. The Nubian seemed to flicker slightly, and the blade clanged against the wall in a shower of sparks. The black man drew his own sword, and fell into a defensive posture. "Dear me," he said mildly. "I thought that all you little ones knew it was not clever to try things with Nkudu." He sighed. "Ah, well. Before you die, let me see your eyes. I love to look at the eyes. Particularly pretty blue eyes, like those of the new plaything of the Crow my master. But yours will be black, pig."

Gurney raised his head. Under his turban his forehead and cheeks were crusted with dried blood; but below the level brows his eyes were twin arrowheads of blue steel. "Black?"

Nkudu faltered a moment, and in that split second Gurney drove the curved blade into the triangle of black skin between the breastplate and the cummerbund. His mouth opened in a soundless O of surprise and he doubled up, sprawling forward onto the marble floor, fingers twitching. A pool of blood began to spread about his belly.

Wiping his sword, Gurney stepped over the body and pushed open the door.

The stained glass set in the dome made little splashes of brilliant colour on the walls and the floor, and cloying perfumes hung heavy in the air. Gurney walked in, his footfalls deadened by the thick carpets that covered the floor, and stood for a moment, trying to accustom his eyes to the gloom. A voice came from the pile of cushions at the far end. "So?" it hissed. "What do you want? I gave orders that nobody was to disturb me."

Gurney feigned confusion, advancing nonetheless. "But Nkudu told me that you were to give orders to us—"

"Stop there. Your voice is not familiar." Into one of the dim shafts of light came a face, black-eyed, hooknosed, long-cheeked. The stained glass painted half of it a deathly green and the other half a cheerful orange. "Who are you?"

Gurney held his peace and walked onwards. Then, "That does not matter," he said. "What does matter is the whereabouts of my wife, the Lady Arabella. They say she is your new ... plaything."

The sword was in his hand now, and Kapraj Bey rose from his nest of cushions and backed towards the wall, his face suddenly sallow with fear. Gurney stopped, but the Crow still backed away, arms spread in terror. When he reached the wall he started, as if he realised he could go no further; Gurney advanced again, eyes fixed on the slitted black orbs of his enemy. Then the Bey's left hand blurred into motion behind a hanging. Gurney flung himself sideways as a pistol bellowed, and felt the wind of the ball on his cheek. He hit the floor and rolled. The Crow was coming at him now, a scimitar in his right hand, the lipless mouth stretched back from his teeth in a skull's grin. "They say correctly, Captain, ah, Gurney, is it not?" He spoke English now, with a thick, guttural accent. "The Lady Arabella has told me much about you. She seems to think you will be the death of me. Alas, she is wrong." The blade in his hand flicked out and Gurney, barely on his feet, only just made his parry. "I have always loved widows," said the Black Crow.

When Volnikov's boat came alongside the quay he ran up the steps and stood swaying at the top, trying to bring the scene into focus. Behind him, the ships in the anchorage were throwing up gouts of smoke and flame, rippling the air with the heat of their burning. He was conscious of the deep satisfaction of a job well done, but he had a feeling that there were other avenues remaining to be explored. Throwing his head back, he drained the keg of rum and sent it spinning into the littered water; then he began to lumber towards the palace under the cliff. Most of the fun seemed to be there, he decided. By the look of things the fighting on the wall had degenerated into simple skirmishing, unworthy of his attention. But the battle at the palace gates looked tailor-made for him. Opening and closing his huge hands, he tightened his grip on his weapon, a sixty-eight pound cannonball drilled and threaded on a four-foot rope, and strolled towards the gunfire.

Mather, struggling to reload his pistol at the bottom of the wall, looked back and rubbed his eyes. The Russian had accelerated, and was now advancing at a lumbering trot, the huge cannonball swinging round his head at the end of its rope. As he watched, the Russian broke into a crouching run, pounding towards the gate, weaving a little as bullets sang round him. Mather shook his head, made a sign to the other men under the wall, jammed his pistol to the nearest loophole and fired.

The Russian was close now, and Mather became aware of a roaring. He grinned. Volnikov, pounding down on the palace of the Black Crow, was singing.

Ten yards from the door a red flower bloomed at the Russian's left shoulder, spinning him round, and Mather held his breath. But Volnikov merely jacked up his roar half an octave, starting a glissando bellow that took him to within five feet of the gates.

Above Mather's head a musket poked out, trying to swivel onto the giant figure of the Russian. Mather pulled a wad from his pouch, reached up and tapped it home in the end of the barrel. The gun exploded, but no smoke came from the muzzle. Screaming broke out inside the gatehouse, and Mather turned his attention to Volnikov once more.

Feet firmly planted, the Russian stood in front of the gates, the cannonball a blur at the end of its rope. For a long thirty seconds the ball gained speed; then, his glissando touching a note uncomfortably close to a high C, he lowered his right shoulder. The cannonball struck the gate like a bomb, and the lock gave. Dusting his hands and smiling with pleasurable surprise, Volnikov pushed, hard. The gates grated open. Picking up his weapon and whirling it a couple of times, he lumbered into the gatehouse, from whose interior came a racket of panicky shouting.

The Black Crow was a superb swordsman, fighting for his life with a weapon he knew. But Gurney had more than his life at stake, and he was angry. Bitterly angry. He pressed the Turk back towards the hangings, slashing and hacking at him, the blood singing in his ears with the cool joy of good swordplay. The Crow felt the wall against his back, and smiled, parrying Gurney's stroke. But Gurney feinted, and the blade came whizzing from the left when it should have been met by the Crow's steel at the right. Too late, the Turk tried a clumsy parry: the blade sliced into the muscle of his left shoulder, and as Gurney drew it back he felt it grate on bone.

As the Crow slumped back, white-faced, Gurney took a step to the side, the better to administer the *coup de grace*. His right foot landed on a little bottle that spilt and rolled, bringing him crashing full-length into a puddle of attar of roses. And by the time he looked up, the Crow had gone.

Gurney cursed, wrinkling his nose at the sweet-smelling liquid soaking his right sleeve. Then he ran for the wall, grabbing great handfuls of hangings and tearing them away. Sure enough, there was a little door there, cut into the living rock of the cliff that formed the chamber's west wall. He hesitated a moment, then booted the door open. A flight of steps ran down and away, lit by torches flickering in cressets to either side. The air was damp and smelt of salt, lightly tinged with decay; the sea. Taking the steps four at a time, Gurney raced down into the guttering torchlight.

Von Kratzstein waded through the crowd like a scytheman, his sword-arm rising and falling with a methodical chop, at the head of his men, who followed him in arrowhead formation. That the people he hewed down were unarmed mattered to him not at all. They were Turks, and in the anger that gripped him, that was enough.

To the crowd of holy men and others attempting to retreat from the horrors of the square, through the eastern gate, the little phalanx of canary-coloured men was a nightmare incarnate. The brilliant yellow uniforms were splashed with bright blood now, and the eyes raw from dust and smoke. Their blades, spraying gore in great fans in the air, hacked and chopped, sparing none, until there were no more to chop at and they were in the square.

Von Kratzstein raised his weary sword-arm to strike at the last of the figures that confronted him, and was greatly surprised to receive a buffet in the stomach that knocked the breath clean out of him.

"Watch who you're waving that thing at, yer silly Proosian bugger." The voice was Henry Priest's, though the speaker was by no means immediately recognisable as its owner. Henry's stocking-cap hung over one ear, his coat was torn half off his back, and his right arm with its cutlass was dyed red almost to the elbow.

Von Kratzstein, when he recovered his breath, found that his anger had gone, and in its place was something very like relief. He dropped his sword and took Henry by his bloody hand, shaking it warmly. "So! The city is fallen to the siege! Felicitations, mein Heinrich. A great victory against awful odds."

Priest wrinkled his nose at the carnage by the gate. "Aye. Terrible hard work, fighting old men with no weapons. As to the city having fallen, I'm not so sure about that either. There's warm work afoot yonder" —he pointed to the open gates of the palace—"and they may reinforce at any minute. Well. I'll go and loose them poor devils of slaves. You'd like, perhaps, to see if you can lend a hand over there?"

Von Kratzstein looked at the palace with apprehension in his eyes. Then he began to walk towards it, his sword trailing on the cobbles, his men straggling behind like ducklings after a duck. Priest turned to the rough stone shed with little barred windows that the Captain had told him was the slave barracoon, drew the heavy bolt on the door and flung it open.

It was warm work indeed in the palace. Mather and his contingent, following hard on Volnikov's heels, had rushed through the gates to find the guard-house thick with smoke and very dangerous. Though it was fair to say that most of the danger came from the Russian, who, cannonball firmly fixed to his right fist, whirled uncontrollably among the garrison, cutting a horrid path of crushed heads and smashed limbs.

Basreddin, searching the upper rooms of the Bey's quarters, heard the crash as the gates gave and Volnikov's singing. Then the noise grew louder, and he hopped out onto the roof above the courtyard. The mêlée below was thickening, but it seemed that the Black Crow's men were being pushed back towards the guard-room. Basreddin picked up a couple of loose tiles and spun them at two soldiers below, noting with approval that both of them found their marks; then he climbed in through the window again and resumed his explorations.

Many of the rooms were furnished for women, but of their inhabitants there was no sign. In time of siege, Basreddin guessed, the principal wife and her attendants would be swiftly whisked to a place of safety. He strolled on through the little interconnecting rooms, relaxed but alert as a quartering hawk, but found no one. Then, as he was returning towards the stairs, he stopped and looked at a rack of hanging shirts. There was no movement in the air here, so why were the long shirts swaying gently, as if to an invisible breeze? Moving slowly, Basreddin crept towards the rack, then hurled himself into the shirts, scattering them in all directions. He backed out with his arms round a bundle of fabric that struggled and cursed in highly-coloured Romaic, and dumped it on the floor. Then he drew his knife and kicked at the bundle. "Up, you." The bundle shook itself apart, and Pausanias Metaxas, trembling, climbed to his feet. Metaxas stood gaping for a moment, then his eyes grew cunning and he recollected himself. "Mr. Basreddin! Well, well, providence has been kindly to Metaxas. Fierce Kapraj Bey had Metaxas quite captive, and it was only by dints of superior braveries that I managed to escape his clutch. It was nothing, really," said Metaxas, beginning to believe in his own heroism.

"Enough of your clacking." Basreddin stopped, put his face close to the Greek's and backed him into a corner. "You will feel that my knife is at your belly. Now, you will tell me, where is the Lady Arabella? And the secret stronghold of the Black Crow?" The interpreter whimpered, and Basreddin's voice deepened. "Tell me, I command you: where is the English lady and where is the stronghold of the Crow?"

"I don't know. Aaah!" Metaxas screamed as the knifepoint sank a quarter-inch into the blubber of his stomach. "Yes! I tell you! English lady in all down tunnels behind Bey's room! And in tunnels is Bey's bolt-hole. He has boat! Quick, quick, you catch him!"

Basreddin did not release the interpreter. "I have no time to put you to the question of the Third Order, but I tell you this: if you are wrong you will surely die. You have told me everything?"

"Oh, yes, yes, everything."

"Good. We shall go together, you and I, into the stronghold of the Bey, and seek out Captain Gurney. Is there something wrong?"

Metaxas was huddled in the corner, sweat streaming down his greenish face. "No. Not me. I come not down."

"Metaxas. I think there is something you are hiding from me. Tell."

"Water. There is a system of levers that will flood the tunnels."

"How controlled?"

Metaxas shrugged. "Only the Bey know."

"Then we had better follow him." Basreddin threw a quick glance out of the window. The fighting had stopped, at least in the courtyard, though the clash of weapons still came from within.

"Volnikov!" he shouted.

The Russian paused to throw a Turk at the wall, then looked blearily round him. "Who wants me?"

"I, Basreddin. We go in search of the Captain. Catch this." He bundled Metaxas out of the window and shoved him into the courtyard, dropping lightly after him. "Lead the way," he said, prodding him ahead with the point of his knife.

The din of battle died away, muffled behind walls of living stone, as the three men entered Kapraj Bey's chamber and passed through the secret door.

The slaves streamed out into the sunlight, blinking and screwing up their eyes against the glare. The yachtsmen came last, Aristotle leading, fiddling with his filthy cravat and peering to left and right like a myopic crane; then, after him, Euthymia Henry, her hair full of straw and her face pale, her eyes flickering round her, presumably in search of local colour, leaning on Paddy's arm; and last, Isabel, her dress amazingly clean and crisp, pity and concern on her face, assisting a little old Macedonian with a great running sore on his leg. Henry Priest knew Miss Euthymia and Miss Isabel, and he had sunk a tankard or two with Sir Patrick in the Dun Cow at Dalling; but he was damned if he knew any of the others. A sorry rabble they were, save for the gentry and the thirty men who must have been the brig's crew. Dredged up from all over the Aegean, no doubt. Then Henry caught a whiff of the atmosphere inside the barracoon, and decided that their pallor and filth were not to be wondered at. He went up to the tall, shortsighted man.

"Beggin' your pardon, Sir, Mr. Gilchrist, is it? Henry Priest, Topman, *Vandal*, Captain Gurney, at your service, Sir."

The tall man looked down from his great height, appearing to notice Priest for the first time. "Ah. Glad to see you, Priest. Warm weathah we are having, are we not?"

Henry shifted his weight nervously. Undoubtedly this seven-foot streak of piss was off his napper. "Issir. Most clement, Sir."

Paddy burst in. "Henry. Where's Lady Arabella?"

"Dunno, Sir Patrick. Thought she was with you, Sir Patrick."

He shook his head. "Not with us. Damned rascally Turk pirate took her away. Very little we could do." From the gash on his temple, Henry guessed he had tried something. "Never forgive self. Quick, quick. To the palace. Sword, someone?" And seizing a cutlass from a watching tar, he hobbled and limped his way across to the palace of the Bey.

Aristotle made to follow him; then something caught his eye and he stopped, staring. Out in the harbour, the brig *Otranto* heeled steeply to starboard, fizzed steam, and slid beneath the blue water.

Henry Priest's amazement deepened. Aristotle's pallid features were for a moment contorted with some emotion—grief or fury Henry could not tell. Then he was once again impassive, slightly amused. But he muttered something to himself, and, looking round, picked up an abandoned musket.

"You'll be needing powder and ball for that, Sir," ventured Henry, proferring his pouch.

"What?" Totters looked surprised. "Oh. Powder and ball. No, never mind that." And, grasping the musket by its barrel as a cricketer grasps his bat, he made a couple of experimental swings, frowned, and stalked off in the direction of the palace.

Euthymia was looking in fascinated horror at the scene about her. Even in her wildest dreams of lechery and slaughter she had never conceived of anything like this. While part of her wanted to be sick, another part of her was calculating that from this would come something that John Murray, the publisher, simply could not ignore. She was wakened from her reverie by Isabel, who was calling her sharply.

"Euthymia! Stop mooning and come and help with the wounded. Really, this is quite ghastly of George. I am sure there was no need for this horrid slaughter." She tore a strip from her petticoat and staunched a pulsing gash in the neck of a broken-nosed pirate, whispering soothingly to him. Euthymia, who had seen her savagely kicked in the stomach by that same pirate only yesterday evening, marvelled at her kindness. Then she, too, sorted through the corpses until she found a body that still breathed and set about patching it up as best she could.

At the bottom of the slippery stone steps was a landing; from it, two tunnels branched off. Gurney hesitated a moment, undecided. From the right-hand tunnel, lit with torches, came a slight draft of cool air. The sea. The left-hand entrance was dark. He started into the entrance on the right, eyes fixed on the ground. If the Black Crow intended to escape, this would be his bolt-hole. But after twenty yards Gurney had still not seen any blood-spots. And the Crow had been bleeding, heavily. He turned and retraced his steps to the landing, examining the rock floor. Sure enough, into the left-hand tunnel led a trail of little drops of a liquid that shone black in the light from the brands of pine. Then it fell into place.

Nkudu had said that the Bey's new plaything was within. And he would not have kept her in the open, for all eyes to see. No, somewhere beyond the mouth of this hole in the living rock was the dungeon—bedchamber?—in which Arabella lay captive. And the Bey, crazed with the fear of a hunted beast, was in there with her. Gurney snatched a torch from one of the cressets and started into the black maw.

His blood was up now, but he moved slowly. For who knew what pitfalls the Bey would have installed in this, his most secret sanctum? The red torchlight threw stabs of light into the darkness ahead, casting his shadow huge and grotesque on the rough-hewn vault of the roof as he pressed warily on down the steepening tunnel. Water splashed under his feet; a little brook ran down the side of the tunnel, and over the quick padding of his steps there sounded an irregular dripping of water. There were no more bloodstains, but then on this wet surface they would not show.

It was five minutes later that he came to a right-angled turn in the passage. He inched cautiously round it, aware that his torch would give him away, but conscious that without it he would be helpless. Twenty-five yards further on, the tunnel widened into a great chamber. He strode forward, holding the scimitar before him in his left hand, and came into the cave.

The size of the place took his breath away. Above him, the light of the torch bounced and glittered on rank after rank of stalactites, marching away into velvety darkness; on either side of him the stalagmites rose like the dragons' teeth of Jason, each one ready to spawn its harbinger of death. The water-noises were loud now. Gurney stopped. All round him the air boomed with falling drops, each with its cargo of liquid rock. Drops which would in time build up these fangs and pendant lances of stone until the cathedral would be a forest of slimy pillars. Somewhere a stream trickled, loud in the blackness; and somewhere, more remote yet, a bolt grated in hasps of iron . . .

"No!"

The scream caromed and tumbled down the cave,

waking echoes that had slumbered since the Creation.
Gurney began to run, stumbling on the slippery
ground, the torchlight leaping wildy round him.
"Arabella," he yelled. "Arabella!" Then his feet slipped
away and he fell, coming up against a rock with a
crash that made his head spin. His torch arched
away, plummeted to the ground, and went out. As
the blackness of the cave closed round him like an
icy shroud, the drop and gurgle of the water came
back, blotting out all other sounds.

Gurney climbed slowly to his feet, cursing silently.
The scimitar was still in his left hand, but otherwise
he was lost. Hopelessly lost. He leaned against a pillar,
trying to accustom his eyes to the inky darkness. But
where there was no light, no one—not even Basreddin
—could see. Somewhere in this cave was Arabella;
she might as well be a thousand miles away. Gurney
raised his eyes to the roof, as if in search of a sign in
the heavens; and a sign was vouchsafed him. High
and to the left, a red gleam of torchlight shone for a
moment on the wet surface of a stalactite.

He began to pick his way forward. It was a hellish
business. He soon found that the only way he could
make progress was to go on his hands and knees,
groping his way across the water-smoothed boulders by
touch. Once he put his hand forward and there was
nothing there, only an emptiness from whose depths
came the sound of rushing waters; but inch by inch,
breath by sobbing breath, he crept towards his goal.

As he crawled, his mind was on that glint of torchlight that had flickered on the roof. Over there was
Kapraj Bey, a wounded beast at bay. And there, too,
was Arabella. Cold rage steadied him as he worked his
way forward, and his thoughts were very clear. The
Black Crow had heard him, knew he was on the hunt.
Therefore, he would be on his guard. How to make
him unwary? For unwary he must be made, with so
valuable a hostage.

A blast of cold air struck Gurney's face, and he

groped for its source with his hand. Another pothole in the floor. From far below the smooth hiss and whoosh of the subterranean torrent came to his ears. On the lip of the hole was a boulder the size of a football. Gurney rolled it to the very edge, and tipped it over. As it fell, he clashed his sword against a rock and loosed a yell of surprise, giving it a sharp diminuendo; then the rock splashed with a hollow boom into the water and the echoes died away into dripping silence. Someone laughed smoothly in the far corner of the cave, and Kapraj Bey's harsh voice, broken by the pillars, rose in triumph. Then it stopped. Grinding his teeth, Gurney pressed on.

When he arrived at the fringes of the glow of torchlight he lay flat and wriggled forward. The Black Crow, his torch jammed in a crevice behind him, was using his turban to bind up his left shoulder. Behind him stood an uneven row of limestone pillars, six inches apart; in the centre of the row was a crude doorway with a great iron bolt. Gurney's fingers tightened convulsively on the hilt of his sword. At the base of the pillar next to the door, the torchlight flickered on golden hair. Arabella's hair.

It was at that moment that he lost control. Shock showed in the Black Crow's face as he looked up at the ragged figure bounding out of the rocks, sword in hand; but it did not slow his reflexes. He grabbed for his sword, backed up against the pillars, and fell into a defensive crouch. Gurney, technique thrown to the winds, came at him in a blur of steel, raining a dozen blows at him in as many seconds. The Bey parried them easily, and as Gurney fell back he spoke.

"You are really most persistent."

"And with reason." Gurney was getting himself under control.

An ironic smile played about the Bey's cruel lips, but it did not touch his eyes. "Really. All this for a woman? A mere plaything? You have sacrificed your life in vain, Captain Gurney."

"You are mistaken. It is not my life that is to be sacrificed."

"Then whose? Your woman, I fear, has paid dearly for your intrusion—"

Gurney's heart went cold within him. "You have murdered her?" Despite himself, he looked down at the golden hair that crept between the pillars. As his attention strayed from the sword-point in front of him, the Bey sprang. But he was slow, weakened by the loss of blood, and his blade sang past Gurney's ear.

"So, tricky, eh?" Gurney regarded him through slitted eyes. "Let's see you fight, you cut-throat dog. You've had it easy; but you've been proving your valour on women and unarmed men for long enough. Come, Crow, and be plucked." He lunged and the Crow parried, falling back; but his wounded shoulder banged into the pillar and he gasped with pain. Gurney followed up, and was parried again; then the Crow loosed a cut which missed him by a full foot and sent the burning end of the torch spinning away into the darkness. Black night descended again, and Gurney's final thrust smashed ringing sparks from the stone where the Bey had been.

A harsh laugh came from the darkness behind him. "Farewell, Captain Gurney. I wish you joy of your woman. Use what time remains as best you can; the waters that flow here drop to Hell. They will take you with them."

Gurney fell to his knees, feeling through the prison-pillars for Arabella's face, heedless of his enemy's flight. The silky skin was chill, but a pulse still beat at her throat. Relief dizzied him.

"Arabella!"

No reply.

He felt his way to the door, drew the bolt, and went into the cell, stumbling on the threshold. Fumbling in his pockets he drew out flint and steel. After three attempts he succeeded in lighting a handful of the straw that covered the ground. In its smoky flare he looked at Arabell's face for a long moment, caressing with his eyes the delicate features and the smooth, pale skin. Then he ran out and plucked the stub of the torch from the crack in the wall where the Crow had left it. He lit it from the straw, gathered up Arabella in his left arm, and staggered off along the path towards the palace.

She was heavy in his arm, but he hardly noticed the weight. Her head on his shoulder breathed warmth into his ear. As he walked through the rioting shadows of the cave, racing the guttering butt of pine-resin, he was for a moment transported home. Home to the great bed at Sea Dalling, where they lay together watching the dawn spread golden fingers across the icy Norfolk sky; where she would turn to him, her breasts soft against his chest, and twine her body round his until the birds sang in the hornbeam by the window.

As he stepped into the tunnel the torch died and went out. But the slope of the floor signalled the right direction, and soon they were on the landing at the bottom of the stone stairs. Gurney laid his wife against the wall and paused for a moment to catch his breath, looking at her as she lay, breathing slow but easily. There was a purple bruise at her temple where the Bey must have struck her, but she had none of the waxen look Gurney had seen on the faces of those whose skulls were cracked.

Footsteps sounded on the stairs above. Gurney drew his scimitar again from his sash, and pressed back against the wall. The intruder carried before him a penetrating reek of rum and a basso sea-shanty.

"Afternoon, Volnikov."

The Russian stopped singing and his mouth fell open. "Captain Gurney. And Lady Arabella? What happened?" He stood swaying, a top-heavy colossus, over Arabella's motionless form.

"Tell you later. Pick her up now, you drunken oaf, and we'll get her out of here."

Volnikov, hurt by the suggestion that he was anything but sober, began to expostulate. Then he remembered that he was in the presence of the Lady Arabella, and checked himself. He picked her up, transferring his cannonball to his unwounded hand, and started to lumber up the stairs.

Gurney, standing at the point where the tunnels divided, mopped his brow and gave silent thanks that Arabella was alive. Now there was the matter of Kapraj Bey's continuing survival.

He leaned against ths wall, resting, drawing long deep breaths of the damp air, and closed his eyes for perhaps a minute. When he opened them, Basreddin was standing there, Metaxas beside him.

"Well?" said Basreddin.

Gurney pointed down the tunnel. "It seems that the Crow has a back entrance to his nest."

"Yes. This hound tells me the same." Basreddin prodded Metaxas with his knife. "What do you intend to do with him?"

Gurney shrugged. "At least we will give him a chance to say a word for himself. Then we will decide if we kill him or not." Metaxas' teeth clacked together, once, loudly, before he took himself in hand. "Sirs, I beg of you, do not stay here. One mile and a half down that passage is the machinery that controls the water—"

"The Crow is in no condition to run. We have time yet. Speak, Metaxas. You have endangered my ship and my crew, caused my wife and my friends to be endangered and inconvenienced. And by your own admission, you have turned traitor on my allies. You deserve to die thrice over, Metaxas."

"No!" The Greek fell on his knees, blubbering and wringing his hands. "No! All I did, I did honestly, for the great good of all. Can you not see?" Above him, the blond Englishman and the hawk-faced Sufi were judges graven from stone.

Fire flickered in Gurney's blue eyes, and his voice

was chill with doom as he spoke. "There is nothing to see but the fact of your guilt. However, a double choice. You can, if you will, meet your end now." He put both hands on the hilt of the scimitar and held it before him. "A quick, clean death, Metaxas. Or you can run to your master, Kapraj Bey, down the tunnel yonder. But remember, Metaxas, not only have you betrayed me, you have failed him; and I think he will not take kindly to it. Choose, now."

The Greek's eyes rolled back until only the whites showed, and he gobbled like a turkey in the extremity of his panic. Then he got to his feet, and, weaving drunkenly on knees turned to jelly, staggered towards the tunnel that led to the sea.

"Farewell, Metaxas," said Gurney. "You take the coward's way, as always; much good may it do you."

Metaxas half-turned, as if to say something; then he ran into the tunnel and vanished from sight round a curve. The slap of his feet on the wet stone rang for a short while, then faded into the distance. Gurney slumped against the wall again. "We'll deal with them in a moment. They'll not be hard to find. Unless, as I think likely, the Crow kills him first."

Basreddin shook his head. "He will not reach the Crow, and Allah be praised that you did not try. Listen."

Under their feet, the rock seemed to tremble a little. A wind was freshening from the mouth of the right-hand tunnel, and the trembling came again. This time it was no hallucination, of that he was sure. From the bowels of the earth came a thundering roar, a roar like a waterfall. Gurney was already climbing up the stairs when the first great fist of green water tipped with foam hurtled out of the tunnel and smashed into the landing where he had stood moments before. Wearily, he kept climbing. Behind him the dirty water that filled the tunnels and caves swirled upwards.

In the grime and scum something rolled, an arm flopping into the air, then splashing back. Gurney looked round. Metaxas, mouth open and eyes glazed in death, stared at him for a moment. Then the body turned face down and sank.

The village of the Black Crow was quiet as a charnel-house as Basreddin and Gurney walked across the quay. Death hung over the white houses and the blue sea, and Vandal's men moved through the ruins like ants over a corpse. Most of the pirates were locked in the mosque, whose doors were guarded by five men with muskets. The slaves—even Isabel, protesting that she was needed in the village—had embarked on Vandal, where they were uncharacteristically quiet.

As the longboat rowed them out towards Vandal, Gurney was quiet too, worrying about Arabella. Nothing wrong with her body, Basreddin said. But what of her mind? What nameless cruelties had the Black Crow practised on her? Gurney looked to the southward, in the direction of his flight, and vowed that he would exact full retribution, and soon. Meanwhile his nest was not going to be the cosy little retreat of past years.

He stood at the larboard rail, watching abstractedly as Mather's party brought the sacks and chests of gold and jewels up over the side and stowed them in the main hold. When they had finished, he nodded to young George Jarvis, who was dancing with excitement. George had done well today; he had hardly a scratch on him and, it appeared, had accounted for his share of Turks. Now he ran to the signal halliards. A little square of bunting broke from the main peak, fluttering bravely in the breeze, and the last of Vandal's men ashore, the party by the magazine, finished their work and took to the boats.

As they came alongside, Vandal was already over her anchor. Henry Priest jumped through the entry-port and gave a wave of his hand to Gurney, then sprang to the shrouds. Gurney trained his glass on the village.

The mosque doors were open now, and tiny figures were spilling out through the gates and up from the valley behind, spreading out in flight towards the distant mountains. A slender plume of smoke—no more than a wisp—was escaping from the magazine. The last of the fleeing figures from the mosque was barely out of the door when there was a great flash, followed a little after by a sound like a thousand thunderclaps rolled into one. Thick smoke rolled over the village. When it cleared away, where once the mosque and the houses had stood was an untidy pile of rubble.

Swallowing to clear his ringing ears, Gurney folded his telescope and went below to Arabella.

11

Turning the handle of the door carefully, Gurney went into his night cabin. Arabella lay in his cot, her hair spread about her on the pillow, her lips slightly parted. The bruise on her temple had darkened, but there was colour in her cheeks where there had been none an hour ago. Gurney pulled up a chair and sat down by her side, watching the rise and fall of her breast as she breathed. He took Arabella's hand and held it in his own. It was warm.

The song of *Vandal*'s passage through the sea, the working of her timbers and the distant hum of the wind in her rigging, was a comforting sound. A cheerful beam of sunlight shone through the porthole, casting on the coverlet a splash of gold that swayed as she met the rollers. Gurney found it hard to believe that in the midst of the humdrum realities of an easy sea passage his wife should be lying unconscious, at the gates of death for all he knew, while the life of the ship went on round her. Revenge was one thing; Metaxas was dead, and sooner or later he would catch up with the Bey; but were she to be taken from him, the Furies themselves, could he but enlist their help, would not bring her back. He had not yet been able to face Totters and his companions, fearing that his ire would get the better of his good sense. For it was not Totters' fault—it was nobody's fault but his own. He vowed that ruin or no ruin, he would never again go chasing off to the ends of the earth, leaving Arabella behind, if she did but recover. But even as he made the vow he knew he would break it.

He had been there for some time—exactly how long he did not know—when he heard Basreddin's footsteps in the day cabin. He rose and went out.

The Sufi was leaning against the chart-table, hands thrust deep in the pockets of his brown robe. As Gurney came in, he looked up sharply.

"I put the question to him." He paused.

"To whom?"

"Metaxas, before he perished."

"And the answer?"

"It was buried deep. I think that the Bey or one of his creatures must have knowledge of the use of the Third Order, for it was hid by commands of power. What I have is garbled; the Crow has flown south, he said, and will return in the guise of a flock of vultures from the Great Sands."

"Mehemet Ali's fleet."

"Indeed."

"Damn." Gurney paced to and fro, thinking. "We are not going to confront them in this state, that's for sure. No. We'll leave them to stew while we deliver these cursed letters to Nauplion; then we'll see what we will see. We'll need help, though."

Basreddin bowed gravely. "You must be getting old, Giorgiou. To refuse to pursue your enemy to the death simply because it involves sailing bullheaded at an entire fleet? What has become of you?"

"Senility, certainly senility. But I must look to my wife." And he returned to the sleeping-cabin and resumed his vigil.

Outside, the sun rolled round the sky and dipped towards the western horizon. Gurney sat on, never taking his eyes from Arabella, the thoughts rolling through his mind as the cabin grew dark. He rose once, to light the lantern; then he sat again, watching the shadows play over the counterpane, until the dim tintinnabulation of six bells of the evening watch found its way through the planking.

Arabella heard the bells too, far away in the dark. Suddenly, out of the darkness, she knew who she was. With the knowledge came the pain, ringing through the front of her head like a saw on stone.

"George," she said. "George." Then memory returned, and she knew she would never see him again, that his drowned corpse was tumbling down the underground torrents to the centre of the earth. And she was at the mercy of the slime-eyed warlord who called himself the Black Crow.

Then she felt a cool cloth on her hot forehead. She opened her eyes. The blur of yellow and black resolved itself into a ceiling of lamplit planks, the light terribly bright. And bending over her was that square-jawed face, the blue eyes pools of worried shadow. "George," she cried again, struggling to raise herself. But a great whirl of nausea gripped her and bore her away, and she fell back, fainting, onto the linen pillow.

When she came to herself again, she did not open her eyes. So it was true, she thought. Loved ones did wait on the other side to guide their partners over the plains of heaven. Grief took her, for all she had left behind, and the tears began to stream from between her closed eyelids.

Gurney, seeing them flow, bent forward, his heart thudding.

"Arabella! can you hear me?"

"Is that really you, George?"

"Me and no other. Welcome back, my love."

"George. Did it hurt to die? Oh, but it is so beautiful to be dead and with you."

Gurney frowned. Rambling. The blow on the head must have affected her mind. "Dead? What do you mean, dead? Here." He bent over and kissed her on the lips.

"But I was in the cave with the Bey, and I heard you—"

"Not me. A rock. And now you're aboard *Vandal,* the Bey is God knows where, and Metaxas is carrion. Now rest. There's all the time in the world."

Arabella closed her eyes. Then she said, "George?"

"Yes, my love?"

"Don't be angry with Totters. It wasn't his fault."

"Not his fault? He should know better than to come pleasure cruising in these waters—"

Arabella rolled her head from side to side on the pillow. "No, we made him. He was never going to come this far east, but I persuaded him it would be amusing to track you down."

"So." Gurney smiled, despite himself. "I should have known. Poor Totters. His weakness of resolve has cost him his ship."

The eyes opened. "Perhaps you will build him a new one, then."

"Perhaps. That depends. Tell me, Arabella, how was it that you were caught by Kapraj Bey?"

She closed her eyes again. "It happened very quickly. After the storm. We all saw this red ship some way off. Totters had the guns run out, but when the red one came close he said she had too much metal for us, so we struck. Totters would have fought, George; I am sure of it. It was merely that he was worried that we should be hurt."

Gurney grunted. A terrible choice to make. But

there was something else, more serious, on his mind. "When you were ashore, there, what did they do to you?"

"They herded us into that beastly shed. Then they came, that night, and fetched me away to the palace." She struggled upright. "Oh no, George. Nothing happened. Nothing like that."

"Lie down, my love."

When she spoke again, her voice was small and far away. "But he tried. He said that have me he would, but that he would wait until I came of my own free will. Then he took me into that cave, and every day he would come down with my food, and ask me again." Tears ran down her cheeks. "God, that cave. The water. I began to hear voices in that water, and then he would be standing there. Day after day. Do you know something, George?"

"What?"

"Another week, and I would have broken. I am sure of it. And then how could I ever have looked you in the eye again?"

Her hair was soft under Gurney's hand. "The fault would have been mine. To have let you fall in with that damned cut-throat. I shall never forgive myself. It is I who should be shamed before you."

She shook her head, beyond words, and pulled him down to her. He breathed the scent of her for a little while and then drew gently away.

"Now you must sleep, my love. If you can bring yourself to forget . . ."

"And you, George?"

"There is nothing to forget. Sleep now. And then we will see about a retribution for this Kapraj Bey. Here, drink this." He put his arm about her shoulders and lifted her, putting a bowl to her lips.

She drank. It was a bitter brew with a tang of crushed herbs. Even before she lay back the cabin had shrunk to a little point of light; then the blackness closed in again, and she slept.

The night was warm, the sky clear as *Vandal* nosed slowly up the Gulf of Argos towards Nauplion. What breeze there was was enough to cool but not to chill. The schooner ghosted through the tepid water; her helmsman leaned negligently against the housing, her deck ablaze with lights.

In the waist forward of the mainmast, Gurney had had a table rigged. Now he sat at dinner with his guests. Forward, hands were dancing, the scrape and wheeze of fiddle and squeezebox lilting into the *Devil Among the Tailors*, bare feet slapping on the white deck.

Gurney leaned back in his chair, filling his nostrils with the land-smells that rolled in from the mountainous shores to north-east and south-west. He looked round at the company. They all seemed to have come out of it remarkably well, he thought. Euthymia was in her usual tizzy of romantic aspirations fulfilled, and Paddy was attempting once again to breach the unbreachable walls of Isabel's self-control. Totters was draped forward like an animated question-mark, addressing some observation to Basreddin; pixillated again, of course. And Arabella, at his right hand, was leaning back too, drinking in the warm air and the sounds of the night. She had made a swift recovery, but there was still something worrying her.

As if he had spoken his thoughts out loud, she turned to him. "What now, George?"

"Nauplion, where you will be interested to see the variety of the brigands; then a last little errand, and home."

"What errand is this?"

"A reckoning with Kapraj Bey."

Arabella sighed. "Excellent. I shall enjoy watching that."

"Unfortunately, you won't get the chance. I shall leave you ashore, with Paddy and the rest, where you will get into no mischief."

"What?" Arabella's eyes blazed. "That you will not,

George. I entirely insist that you take us along, too."

Gurney shook his head. "It will be a damned close-run thing, I think. You will be in danger, and what is worse, in the way."

Arabella's jaw was set in the firm line Gurney had come to know well. She would not move unless physically carried away. "No I shall not. I and Isabel and Euthymia can look after the wounded, if there are any. And Paddy and Totters are devilish pugnacious. Really, George, it is the least you can do."

They fell silent. Gurney realised that conversation at the table had come to a dead halt. "Out of the question," he said.

"Oh, come now, George," said Paddy. "Be fair. You might let us watch you undo that damned Turk, even if you won't let us join in."

"Rathah." Totters finished his glass and poured another from the decanter before him. "Sank my ship, George. Only fair, after all. Could lend a hand. Man a gun, read signals. Scrub a deck, even."

Gurney bowed to him. "A touching display of enthusiasm, Totters, and I thank you for it. But even if each and every one of you wants to come. I must insist that I cannot willingly ask you to come to your deaths."

"Our deaths? Who said anything about death?" Arabella was incensed. "If it is a matter of death, then I shall certainly come, and die with you."

A ripple of laughter passed round the table, but Gurney's face was grave. "What I propose to do is to attack the fleet of Mehemet Ali of Egypt. A large fleet—the largest in these parts for years; and Mehemet Ali is not the kindliest of men. Should we fail, the price will be one which will make Kapraj Bey look almost charitable by comparison."

"Good." said Arabella brightly. "Then we'll make sure that we don't. Is that not so, Paddy? Totters? Ladies?"

Basreddin had been silent thoughtout, but now he

spoke. "There is a means of healing used by certain mountain men. They take the blade that causes the wound and destroy it before the eyes of the wounded man. In this case, to see the undoing of the Bey would be to purge the wrong he had done you, and leave minds clear and unfettered by base desires. For though ye may think it but sport to watch the Bey, it is blood ye crave, the blood of him who wronged you."

Gurney shrugged. "*Et tu*, Basreddin? Well, I see I am outvoted. Totters, now I understand the pressure you were under to come east. My sympathies. Come, if you will, then; and pray God we get out of it safe."

He filled a brimming bumper of cognac and tossed it back. Then he rose. The fiddlers' measure was getting into his toes, and he pulled Arabella to her feet. "Come, my love." And he towed her forward, followed by Paddy, Isabel, Euthymia and Totters, the latter protesting with a positively narcoleptic languor entirely belied by his twinkling feet.

They danced until they were panting, then they drank and danced again. *Vandal*'s men danced too, and the whole ship resounded to the clap of hands and the thump of feet on the deck. Then finally, Arabella came to Gurney from a Grand Chain and he caught her round the waist and whirled her.

Her eyes met his in the dark, held them. "Your cabin," she said, and laughed. He danced her away, towards the hatch astern, followed by the cheers and whistles of the crew. As they passed the companion hatch she waved her handkerchief to those on deck, then turned to Gurney in the lamplit after-cabin, threw her arms round his neck and drew him down into a deep, melting kiss. They stumbled towards the cot in the sleeping-cabin, shedding their clothes in a long trail behind, and fell on the covers in a tangle of arms and legs.

It was later—much later—that Gurney pulled the covers over the sleeping Arabella and closed his own eyes.

* * *

Von Kratzstein had a fearful hangover. He could not remember much about last night, except that he had drunk a lot of rum and indulged in a head-knocking contest with Volnikov from which he had emerged covered in glory. But from the rasp in his throat which he could feel whenever his head stopped throbbing he guessed he must have been singing. The sight that greeted his eyes as he dragged himself to his knees and staggered towards the pump in the ship's waist did little to cheer him. *Vandal* lay at anchor in the Nauplion roads, and round the harbour the city's three fortresses rose into the blue sky of early morning. He knew that the sight of so much dry land, populated in the main by friendly folk, should be a welcome sight; but somehow, now that the Greece he meant to save was within his reach, his enthusiasm was waning.

He put his head under the pump and stumped into the galley, searching for coffee. He found some, lukewarm, and sat in the sun, soaking it up like a lizard until he saw Captain Gurney run from the after-cabin and on deck, shrugging into his coat as he came.

"Morning, Herr General."

Von Kratzstein scowled, suddenly mindful of his honour.

"*Morgen*," he said, and would have continued, but Gurney was already over the side and away towards the city in the gig. The Prussian sat for a while deep in thought. Then he rose, went below, summoned his henchmen and began to talk.

Two hours later, Von Kratzstein and the Heidelberg contingent, ditty-bags over their shoulders, filed over *Vandal*'s side into a dirty bumboat and disappeared into the stews of the waterfront at Nauplion.

Gurney had left Arabella lying in his cot, drowsing over a cup of coffee, and as the rowers took him ashore he hardly noticed his surroundings. Bad luck or no bad luck, it was certainly a comforting thing to have a woman on board ship, particularly when that woman was Arabella. He smiled, remembering, then came to himself as the gig came alongside the quay steps. Basreddin, who had earlier slipped ashore on God-knew-what mysterious errand, met him at the top.

As they walked up the steep steps of the city, Gurney looked round him in amazement. The scene was closer to the Arabian Nights than anything he had seen in Baghdad or Bombay, and he had to remind himself sharply that he was still in Europe. Or, for that matter, anywhere but on a stage, and a damned gaudy stage at that.

The inhabitants of Nauplion, it seemed, were in carnival mood. Most of the men were dressed in Albanian costumes of eye-aching whiteness, topped with waistcoats and short jackets whose embroidery of precious metals looked to be measurable in pounds. Some of those in this uniform looked at home in it; the metal of their weapons had the soft shine of long handling, and there was that wary pride in their eye that Gurney had first noticed in the late Nicholas Mavromichaelis. But others—usually the most richly dressed, and those with the largest retinues—looked as if they were bound for a costume ball.

A short man of great girth, hung about with richly chased weapons which had obviously never been used, attended by two pipe bearers and four grim, mustachioed Klephts, passed. Gurney leaned against a wall and watched. The little man looked haughtily at him, and his fez fell off. One of the brigands picked it up, but the mock-pallikar, tripping over the skirts of his overlong fustanella, fell headlong into something steaming evilly in the gutter.

"Come," said Gurney, laughing, "I need wine. What on earth is going on here?"

Basreddin smiled. "It is the loan raised by your countrymen. Now everyone in Nauplion is rich, all the

Klephts are generals, moneylenders are Klephts, and no man fights. Except, of course, among themselves. For why fight when you can buy?"

Gurney turned into a taverna, and ordered retsina. They drank for perhaps half an hour; then they resumed their walk up the hill.

* * *

Of all the joys of life, reflected James Strathcona, the sheen of morning sunlight on maiolica must be the foremost. He took a small sip from his eggshell cup of sweet, thick coffee scented with rosewater, and turned the Izmir plate in his hand to catch the faint iridescence of its lustre glaze. Round him, in the courtyard of his house behind Syntagma Square, bougainvillea and hibiscus poured down the pillars in brilliant festoons. Swallows hawked for insects in the blue square of sky above and twittered in their mud nests in the eaves of the red-tiled roof. The air was redolent of flowers.

Beyond the courtyard, the bustle of the city was not yet properly under way. Strathcona loved with a passion these few cool, hushed moments before the shambles that was Nauplion cranked itself into motion.

This was the time when he could devote himself to the pleasures in pursuit of which he had originally come to the Levant. For he liked to pride himself on the fact that his love for Greece and the Greeks was not, as Byron's had been, a pretentious fascination for the wild and brutal veneer that a three-thousand-year Dark Age had laid over the cultural heartlands of Antiquity. His love was for the place itself, unalloyed by fanciful nostalgias. The sensations he sought were small ones, but none the less poignant by reason of their smallness ...

High on the south wall of the courtyard a tiny door opened. From it emerged a minute bronze Alexander, mounted on a minute bronze Bucephalus. Alexander

raised his mace and banged it ten times on a great
bell, hung from a bracket on the white stucco. It was
seven years since Strathcona had commissioned his
Austrian clockmaker to make the tiny automaton, but
the pleasure he experienced as he watched Bucephalus rear and caper back into his clockwork stable was
as keen as the first time he had seen it. Alexander, he
reflected, a bragging, brawling sort of fellow. Ghastly
empire-builder. The fussy folds and pleats of those
great cowlike Hellenistic statues were all his fault. All
the sensitivity of a peasant ploughing up a formal
garden to plant turnips. Strathcona shuddered deli-
cately, feeling, as he always did, that the little automaton was hardly sufficient revenge. But enough. Time
for the business of the day. He rang the little bell at
his side.

A Greek youth of some sixteen years, implausibly
clad in a white belted tunic which fell to just above
the knee, came to remove the coffee apparatus. Strathcona sighed, his eyes travelling from the servant to a
marble head and torso of the Classical period that
stood in the south-east corner of the courtyard. Such a
pity that Menander had to go clad nowadays. But
those awful jack tars at Corfu had insisted that the
head of His Britannic Majesty's intelligence service
in Nauplion should at least dress his servants properly.
It had been after the Commodore had dined with him
in '20. His boy at that time habitually went naked,
and as a special concession to the Commodore, Strathcona had told him to wear a figleaf. But even that
dreadful sop to Admiralty prudery had not sufficed.
Really, those great red-faced buffoons had no appre-
ciation of the little things that made life worth living.
He sighed again, and became aware that his majordomo was at his side.

"Good morning, Lycurgus," he said. Actually, the
man's name was Stavros, but so forbidding was his
attitude to strangers that Strathcona had renamed
him in honour of the great law-giver of Sparta.

Lycurgus scowled. "Mornings, Mister."

"What have we today?"

"Quite usual stuffs. Three pallikars, want money. Four little spies, information false and expensive." Lycurgus, using a talented mixture of cozening and bluster, habitually weeded out the petty sneaks who thronged Strathcona's outer halls trying to peddle useless tidbits at high prices. "Reports on pirate activities, Dodecanese. And a sea-captain, English, with a good Turk."

Strathcona's eyebrows rose a little. Lycurgus describing anyone as a good Turk was tantamount to Torquemada describing Calvin as a good Dissenter.

"Really. Well, I think we shall have the pirates first, then the sea-captain and his friend. Tell the rest to come back this evening."

Lycurgus handed him a packet on a silver salver, grunted and strode away into the shadows of the house.

Drawing the packet towards him, Strathcona slit it with a bronze Minoan spearhead and began to read. Then he rose to his feet and began to pace to and fro, his long dressing-gown of oyster-coloured silk trailing on the gold lustre tiles of the courtyard, his high white brow creased a little in thought. It was not until Alexander struck the half-hour that he reseated himself in his marble chair and rang once more for Lycurgus.

When the Turk and the tall, fair-haired young Englishman came into the courtyard he rose and went to greet them. "George Gurney, is it not?"

"Indeed. Mr. Strathcona—Haji Basreddin, whom men call the Eagle Owl."

Strathcona waved them to seats, called for coffee, and settled back into the comfortable grooves that ten years of his alfresco *levers* had worn in his marble throne. "Well, well," he said, "I am glad you have arrived. Admiral Hutchinson sent word of your coming, but I confess I had almost given up hope. He also spoke of you, Eagle Owl."

"Please call me Basreddin."

"If you wish, certainly."

Gurney was by no means convinced of the genuineness of Strathcona's welcome. He had the impression that he had blundered in on a dilettante about to start on the aesthetic frittering of another day, for whom the commonplaces of espionage and diplomacy would be demeaning and tedious. And indeed, it was exactly this impression that Strathcona, certainly the most knowledgeable Briton in the Levant at this time, strove to make. There was a silence as the coffee arrived.

Then, "I understand," said Strathcona, "that you have been in search of certain documents. May I make so bold as to enquire whether your search was successful?"

"It was." Gurney thought he saw a look of relief in Strathcona's eyes, and wondered if he had been wrong about him.

"A lengthy search it has been, however."

"Yes. We were sidetracked by the necessity of removing a nest of pirates from—"

"From the Resadiye, Captain Gurney. The nest of Kapraj Bey." The mask had fallen from Strathcona's eyes now, and he leaned forward a little in his chair. "Do you by any chance have the Black Crow with you now? I know their Lordships would be most interested in questioning him on various matters."

"Alas, no." Gurney's face was grim. "He is fled, but I shall have him soon; his henchman, one Pausanias Metaxas, is deceased."

"Fled and dead, by Jove. Well, this is capital, capital. But do not spread the news round, or the good citizens of Nauplion"—he made a face—"may rend you limb from limb. Nicholas Mavromichaelis was a popular man, and it was only a fortnight ago that the sole survivor of his village crawled into the city and let it be known how he was betrayed. The Greek Government—Nauplion, as you doubtless know, is now the capital city of the Republic—would have dearly loved to make an example of him."

Gurney frowned. "Yes. But now, if I may come bluntly to the point? I was told that you would be my contact here, and that it was to you that I should deliver the spoils of my victories, if any. I hereby deliver them." He reached into the breast pocket of his coat of blue broadcloth, pulled out the packet of letters, and laid them on the table. "Am I now to consider that my task is at an end?"

Strathcona smiled, with the air of one who deals with a child whose manners have not yet reached their final polish. "Perhaps, Captain Gurney, you would like to know the significance of these letters you have retrieved? You would? Excellent." He took a sip of coffee. If there was one thing that he enjoyed more than being at the hub of His Majesty's intelligence network, it was explaining the meaning of the network's activities to the uninitiated. "As you already know, the events currently unfolding in Greece are of interest to more important forces than Greeks and Turks alone. Frankly, His Majesty's Government is not over-concerned with the fate of this charming country for its own sake. On the chessboard of international politics, however, Greece is a pawn which could, in the hands of a subtle player, become a queen. Crudely, the position is as follows. The Russians, who identify strongly with the Greeks for what they claim are religious reasons—their priests wear the same sort of beards, and so on—are anxious to use Greece as a thorn in the side of the Ottoman. The Austrians have also acquired a sudden interest in the Classics, but their ambitions can be safely discounted. And the Egyptians," he sighed and waved a slender right hand in the air. "Who can ever tell with the

Egyptians? But two things are certain. Despite the fact that they are a vassal state of the Turks, Mehemet Ali, their ruler, is ambitious. And they are, apart from the Turks, the only nation who will risk using such blunt means as conquest by force of arms. Once they are entrenched here, life will become damned difficult for the rest of Europe." He leaned forward again, and now there was no trace of languor on his delicate features. "It is not for nothing, Captain Gurney, that Mehemet Ali's army and navy have a strong French element in their commands."

"A French element? Surely you don't mean Bonapartists?"

"I do. I'm afraid I do."

In the silence that followed, Alexander bonged the hour.

"Which brings us to the letters, and to your friend Kapraj Bey. First, I would make it clear that the, ah, French element in the Egyptian forces is a threat, not a promise. For all anyone knows, these men may be honest warriors, scraping a living the only way they know how. But that is by and by. The letters, now. They are merely a token of support for holy war, which would bind the Turk and the Egyptian in a bond stronger than any political alliance—"

Gurney nodded. "I know. The Haji Basreddin and I witnessed the consecration of the banner in the mosque of the Bey, three days ago."

"Did you, by God." Respect was in Strathcona's voice. "Then you have undoubtedly already guessed much of what I have told you. But let me put one more thing to you. What will be Turkey's reaction when the Egyptians land—as they will—in the Peloponnese, in huge strength?"

"I suppose the Sultan will be delighted."

"At first, yes. But it will also be a considerable threat to him. Once the invasion is consolidated and Egypt is the stronger, as she is already, one can see the vassal overwhelming the master. But tell me something, Captain Gurney. Who, in your opinion, really wrote those letters?"

"Damned if I know. But they seem to have served their purpose well enough."

"Not yet. I'll tell you who wrote them. Canning."

"Canning? The Foreign Secretary?" Gurney could not believe he had heard aright.

"The same. Very soon, Captain Gurney, there must be an agreement made on the future of Greece. It goes without saying that neither the Greeks nor the Turks will be consulted. We have been trying to sit down with the Russians for some time now; but we have been in dire need of a, ah, *locus standi* which would tip the game in our favour. When it is put to them that these letters have been in circulation—there is another, from a highly-placed Russian whom we, ah, suborned, which admits their complicity in the affair—they will be embarrassed, and will have to take their medicine like good little bears."

"Good Lord." Gurney's head was whirling. "But how the hell did Osman Bey get hold of them in the first place?"

"Perhaps I should explain, Giorgiou." Basreddin's voice was as nearly apologetic as Gurney had ever heard it. "Osman Bey died largely through my agency. I had the letters with me at the time, and it was not difficult to put them by him with the treasure, and then let it be known to the Klephts. Subsequently, it was an easy thing to secure its capture and sinking."

A numbness was starting to make itself evident between Gurney's ears. "You really mean to say that you planted the treasure in that bloody hole, persuaded Metaxas to betray me and my ship, and exposed us all to death and worse?"

"Not exactly. It was a mischance that led me into the prison of Nicholas Mavromichaelis, but happily I met Metaxas. He was always corrupt, so it took little for me to suggest to him that he contact Kapraj Bey and

his creatures. Obviously, he jumped at the chance. I
. . . suggested to him that he would never find the
letters without me, and I further suggested that he
would find with them a great treasure. But the means
I used for this suggestion were such that he afterwards
forgot entirely. All he knew was that he must follow
me, why he did not know. He was convinced that he
merely wanted the ransom-money; I triggered his
knowledge of the real reason at the beginning of our
hunt for the treasure."

"Carry on." A chill had crept into Gurney's voice.

"I confess, Giorgiou, that I had assumed that once
Metaxas had what he wanted he would let us go on
our way. I did not reckon with the evil in the man,
and for that I am bitterly sorry. Never shall I forgive
myself for my part in endangering the Lady Arabella
and her friends."

"And as to endangering my ship and my crew?"

Basreddin spread his hands. "I know you of old,
Giorgiou. There is no-one else in the world I would
trust to come so swiftly to the aid of a friend, or who I
would rather have by my side when it is a matter of
cold treachery and colder steel."

There was a silence. Basreddin sat with his eyes
downcast. Gurney stared at his hands, unable to believe his friend's betrayal. Or was it betrayal? Jervy
Hutchinson and his hellhounds had dealt harshly with
Gurney; they must have snapped at Basreddin's heels
for a long time to get him into something like this. The
wheels of power turned, and in their turning they took
little account of soft flesh and brittle bone. Finally,
he spoke.

"Well, you could knock me down with a priming-
awl. But I suppose, when all's said and done, we still
have the treasure."

"The treasure." Was there a hint of laughter in Basreddin's voice? "As to that, I'm afraid that His Majesty's Treasury baulked at dropping a king's ransom
into the Aegean, where if not moth, rust may corrupt,

and thieves break in and steal. A fakir's ransom there was—one thousand gold pieces; the rest, those pretty jewels and so on, are no more than coloured glass."

Gurney's face went purple and his mouth fell open. Peculiar gargling sounds came from his throat. Strathcona, smelling violence, rang his little bell, and Lycurgus appeared out of the shadows. Then the Alexander clock struck the first stroke of noon and Gurney, falling on hands and knees on the courtyard tiles, began to laugh, roaring and guffawing. The swallows rose twittering in annoyance into the clear blue sky, weaving and looping in an airy pillar above the fortresses and the harbour of Nauplion.

When the party from *Vandal* returned to Strathcona's house in response to his dinner invitation they rode in force, escorted by a surly gang of kilted Greek brigands who had caught Arabella's fancy at the quayside. A couple of gold pieces had secured their services, and though Gurney would have chosen a couple of good Norfolkmen any day, they seemed to be keeping his guests happy. Which was important, at the moment, because Gurney had things on his mind.

Part of what rankled was his failure to catch up with Kapraj Bey and give him his deserts. It was intolerable, and there was an end to it. Strathcona had been most understanding that morning, but he had declared himself irrevocably opposed to any Naval interference with the Egyptian fleet. Like it or not, the English were neutral in this matter; Strathcona's diplomat's soul rebelled against anything so blunt and brutal as stopping and boarding at sea. No matter that Gurney pleaded that the Bey, a molester of British nationals and a known pirate, was aboard the flagship; the spymaster remained adamant. But Gurney had spent the afternoon brooding over a scheme. The stratagem he had devised would, he thought, appeal to the thief in Strathcona; he planned to put it to him over the port this very evening.

Arabella, dressed in a long gown of something white which looked cool and inviting against the honey-brown of her skin, was in animated conversation with Basreddin. Gurney fingered his collar and shifted uneasily in his coat. Really, it was a damned nuisance, having to cram and jam oneself into a dress coat on a night as warm as this. Particularly when the fashion dictated that it should take two strong men to get you into the bloody thing. He looked round. How the hell did Totters do it? The tall man was shambling along, chatting in his usual languid manner with Euthymia, who looked as if she was badly distracted by the mustachios of the escort. Totter's sky-blue broadcloth hung across his stork's shoulders without a wrinkle, his collar and cravat were white as snow, and his artistically-disarranged hair was exactly as it had left his valet's comb. He seemed entirely untouched by the loss of his yacht, though Henry Priest had told Gurney about the frightful execution he had wrought with a reversed musket in the palace of Kapraj Bey after its sinking.

Gurney returned to matters of more moment.

They were at the door of Strathcona's house, a door of dirty planks set in a wall whose paint was peeling off in a score of places. Gilchrist wrinkled his nose.

"Lord! Is this where Strathcona lives, now? He must have fallen on deuced hard times."

"Wait and see, Totters," said Gurney, signalling to one of their Greek escort, who hammered thunderously on the ancient wood with the butt of his pistol. "Paint and varnish don't last long here."

Lycurgus swung the door apart with the air of a gaoler admitting a new group of prisoners, but his black brow lightened perceptibly when he saw Gurney, and his bow to Isabel, Euthymia and Arabella brought his huge mustachios almost into the dust. Strathcona was waiting for them in the courtyard, dressed now in a faultless fustanella with a long yataghan at his waist. If Euthymia's response to the escort had been admiring, the sight of the tall aesthete, who bore his five-and-forty years as if they were ten fewer, near bowled her over. Her fingers dug uncomfortably into Gurney's arm, and a deep flush rose from her bosom over her neck and face.

The young Menander served the company cooling drinks, and Gurney, watching Strathcona's face as he followed the Greek with his eyes, decided Euthymia was out of luck, at least as far as Strathcona was concerned.

"We are not all here yet," said Strathcona. "We are waiting for five more." And as he spoke, Lycurgus led them through, two men and three women. "And here you all are. How lovely."

One of the men was the Greek Admiral Gurney had met before the raid on Ixos, and now he came over to him and shook him warmly by the hand.

"My dear Captain Gurney! How I am delighted that I can meet you beyond the committee of my captains. We owe you a debt of gratitude we could never in a million years repay."

Gurney smiled at him, and the Admiral grinned back, his teeth surprisingly white in a mahogany toper's face. Then Gurney looked up, towards the women, and it was as if the breath was driven from his body.

In the light of the candles that gleamed, beset by moths, in the sconces of the courtyard walls there was something familiar about her figure; then she stepped forward, the shadow falling from her face like a veil. He excused himself and half-ran to meet her, unconscious of the curious eyes upon him.

"Helena."

The dark-haired womna raised her eyes to meet him, and smiled.

"Hello, Giorgiou."

Words failed him, and he lowered his head. "Helena," he said again, stupidly. Three months he had spent with this woman, on Basreddin's raft on the river Tigris, and then in a filthy pearling dhow, trudging across the Indian Ocean to Bombay.

"You are very beautiful, Helena." And so she was, the skin flawless as ever, the full mouth wide, the great eyes dark and soft, deep wells of calm. But before, she had been merely beautiful. Now, dressed in a mantilla and an embroidered velvet caftan over boots of soft red leather, she was more than that. There was a poise to her, a balance, that was new. He swallowed. They had been staring at each other in silence for a full minute. "You have changed," said Gurney.

"So have you. You are older now, and married to the one you used to speak of in your dreams."

"Yes." Gurney realised that Arabella had been watching the exchange, and felt a moment's trepidation. In the account of his travels that he had given her, Helena had figured as somewhat older and considerably less attractive. Loose references to his sleep-talking might raise questions which, while they were no longer strictly germane, could be very embarrassing. "Would you like to meet her?"

"Yes. But first, what of you?"

Gurney shrugged. "As ever. But as you see, I am married now, and I build ships. Very respectable."

Helena laughed her deep laugh. "Yes, I see. No longer the madman chasing half across the world in pursuit of chimeras. But that is not fair. It is only that it is so strange to see you, the English gentlemen in your coat of good cloth, shaved and with your hair cut. The Giorgiou I knew was thin as a stick, burned black by the sun, with a beard and a smell that would kill a goat at fifty paces." She reached up and touched his forehead. "But the scars are the same. The scars and those mad, mad eyes you have, cold and burning at the same time. It was your eyes that made me notice you."

He shook his head. "We have both changed. Who

would have thought it? Two filthy slaves chattering in polite society in Nauplion? A pretty pass the world has come to. But tell me, what are you at now?"

Her face cracked into its grin, her black eyes laughing at him.

"Would you believe that Helena, the butterfly, the pleasure-seeker, is now dedicated to Greece? No more do I dally for the sake of dalliance; now I am the companion of generals, the consort of admirals, and the mistress of brigands. Even the odd priest. I am a loose woman, George; but I have a purpose now, and it is easier. Now, your wife."

She took his arm and he led her across to where Arabella stood, slim and arrow-straight.

Having made his introductions Gurney backed away, and took a glass from a tray Menander held out to him.

"I thought you would be interested to meet our Helena." There was a hint of malice in Strathcona's tone. "She also, I believe, was one of Kapraj Bey's victims?"

"She was."

"A beautiful woman. It must have sensibly diminished the hardships of slavery to have her by your side."

"Not by my side, Strathcona. In the coffles of Kapraj Bey one does not walk in crocodile, as if on a dame-school outing."

"Have it your way, then." Strathcona looked almost disappointed. So the spymaster is a gossip, thought Gurney. "She is a prominent figure now at Nauplion. She moves in the highest government circles, and it is surprising how much some of our leading politicoes let slip in her presence. Beside their breeches, that is." Strathcona grinned like a pleased wasp and turned away in a swirl of pleated linen, addressing himself to the ladies. "Now, Lady Arabella. Perhaps you will do me the honour of accompanying me in to dinner?"

Arabella curtsied, not without irony. "The honour will be mine, sir."

The Admiral executed a gallant cutting-out on Helena, and Gurney and the others followed, into a high-ceilinged white room that led off the courtyard. In a fireplace at the far end, a fire of charcoal burned, but the room was cool, open to the courtyard on one side and to what must be a garden on the other. The air was full of the smell of herbs, and as Gurney sat down between Helena and Euthymia he realised that whatever storms of emotion might rage over his head, he himself was damned hungry.

As the dinner wore on and the talk, warmed by wine, became more animated, he realised with some relief that there would be no storms. After her initial coquettishness, Helena seemed to forget that she and Gurney had never shared anything more intimate than a long journey under difficult and dangerous circumstances. Their conversation was confined, as if by mutual consent, to reminiscences of the river and the vicissitudes of their travels. Later, as he described to her the sacking of Kapraj Bey's village, her eyes sparkled with delight. At the head of the table, Arabella was involved in a lengthy argument with Strathcona about the relative merits of two geranium hybrids; further down the Admiral, speaking English in deference to the majority, was flirting outrageously with Euthymia, who was becoming more breathless by the minute. Paddy, as usual, was locked in close conclave with Isabel, their voices low and intimate.

As the hors d'oeuvres were cleared away and Lycurgus set about the spitted lamb with his yataghan, Helena became suddenly inattentive.

"George," she said. "I heard news today which will be of interest to you. A friend of mine—never mind who—tells me that the Egyptians are at sea. There was also a rumour that our friend the Black Crow is on the flagship itself with his master, the Pasha. I do not know how you will do this thing I ask, but I ask it nonetheless. In the name of all we have shared, and in the name of Greece, you are to destroy that man, and destroy him utterly."

Gurney's face was grave. "In the name of those things and of others beside, I will do this." He filled their glasses, and as he raised it in a toast he caught Basreddin's eyes across the table. The Sufi inclined his head, and both Helena and Gurney knew that though they had spoken in low voices, he had heard.

Later, as the covers were drawn and more wine appeared on the table, Gurney drew Strathcona aside and spoke to him long and earnestly. The spymaster looked doubtful at first; but as Gurney went on, his scepticism ebbed away. And when he had finished he shook him warmly by the hand.

Then they all went out into the courtyard, and the bouzoukis began to clang and buzz, and the wine took over their feet, and all of them, dilettantes, steeplechasers, mariners, even Basreddin, danced until the bats fled squeaking to less noisy parts and the dawn lightened the mountains to the East.

Someone was banging violently on the door. Gurney opened his eyes with an effort and took a strand of Arabella's thick golden hair out of his mouth. The banging started again.

"All right! Hold on!" he croaked. "I'm coming." The chronometer screwed to the bulkhead said 8:30. Gurney seemed to remember dancing down the cobblestones with Arabella, the rest of the party, and a fairsized portion of the bouzouki band when the sun was already well up in the sky. His head felt as if he had been in a nasty carriage accident. Still with his eyes half-shut, he slid into a shirt and a pair of breeches. Arabella, breathing slowly, did not stir; she could sleep like a log through a sea-battle. Gurney, envying her in a muzzy sort of way, opened the door and stepped into the after-cabin.

McIver, looking offensively cheerful considering the hour, came to attention, the crash of his heels making Gurney wince.

"What is it?"

"I'm sorry to disturb you, Captain. But ye should know that yesterday, it seems someone helped himself to a chest of the treasure."

"How could they do that?"

"Well, we have no watch on the holds, Captain. We reckoned that if anyone was after it they'd no' be from the crew, so a man with a cutlass at the entry port should be enough."

"My sentiments precisely." Gurney's head was clearing now. "So what happened?"

"Well, sir. It seems that yon von Kratzstein and his Proosians have, er, decamped. Last they were seen was yesterday morning, airly, sir. And they each had a ditty bag."

Gurney sighed. "All right, McIver. Let me get a cup of coffee, then we'll have a look."

Ten minutes later, Gurney and McIver were standing in *Vandal's* forelocker. The great bales and chests that Kapraj Bey's treasure-houses had yielded stood round them, piled one on the other in a rampart of riches. On the deck, lying open, the hole where Volnikov had smitten it ragged among the ribs of its iron binding, was the chest that had held the treasure of Osman Bey. Empty.

Gurney grinned. McIver stared at him, puzzled, as the grin became a chuckle. Then the Captain ran to the ladder and climbed on deck, shouting for Basreddin and his gig.

* * *

The keeper of the town gaol at Nauplion was a tall man, proud of his gaol and his mustachios but otherwise a fatalist. There was much illegality in the town, but he was gloomily resigned to the fact that every miscreant thrown into his evil-smelling cells was a

mere bird of passage. Most of his guests today were
drunken Klephts who would shortly be rescued by
their pallikars. If he was lucky, the pallikars would
grease their men's liberation with a gold piece or two;
if he was not, he would be backed up against the wall
of the guard-room at knifepoint while some kilted
brigand opened the doors to his henchmen. Even the
gold did not ease his conscience. He was a man of high
professional standards, and his ideal prisoner was one
whose acquaintance with him would deepen over a
period of say, twenty years. And this Frankish sea-
captain and his Turk-looking lieutenant, despite the
impressive seal of the Government on the release
order they carried, were about to dispossess him of
some really interesting prisoners.

Gurney, following the stoop-shouldered Greek down
a long passage whose walls ran with moisture and
whose stink bore witness to a certain apathy in the
changing of slop-pails, wrinkled his nose. Gaols, as a
general rule, were places he would rather avoid than
otherwise, and this was certainly the dirtiest he had
ever seen. At his side, Basreddin would be experienc-
ing a similar reaction, though the eyes below his bushy
eyebrows were, as usual, impassive.

They arrived at a door of massy iron, and the gaoler,
sighing, took a huge ring of keys from his belt and
thrust the largest into the keyhole. The tumblers of the
lock turned without a sound. Evidently the man's
disregard for his guests' personal comfort was bal-
anced by a healthy concern for their security.

As the gaoler opened the door Basreddin and
Gurney stepped inside.

"Thank you," said Gurney. "We would be alone
with these unhappy miscreants." The gaoler shrugged,
slammed the door, locked it, His shuffling feet receded
in the passage.

Von Kratzstein, who had been sitting on the stone
bench that was the cell's only furnishing, barked an
order. Kolonels Albertus, Ziehendorf and Stahlkleber,

sitting beside him, leaped to their feet, crashed their heels together, and stood at quivering attention, Gurney, feeling that it was expected of him, walked slowly down the line in the manner, he hoped, of a Caesar inspecting the Praetorian Guard. As usual the Prussians bore an irresistible resemblance to a row of canary birds waiting to migrate. If canary birds migrated. He made a mental note to ask Arabella, who knew about that sort of thing.

When he reached the end of the line he nodded, as he had once seen the Duke of Wellington nod at a review. "Good," he said. "Stand easy." A general shuffling of feet. Basreddin's beard twitched, and he looked hard at the little barred window that provided the cell's only light. Gurney felt the laughter beginning to take hold, and coughed harshly.

"Sorry state of affairs," he said. "How do you come to be here, my bold freedom fighters?" He knew damned well how they came to be here, but he was determined to see von Kratzstein wriggle a little. And sure enough the Prussian's face turned the colour of a ripe beetroot.

"Hrumph," he started, glaring at a spot on the slimy wall in front of him. "Well. When we left your ship, Herr Kapitan, we took with us a chest of treasure. As pay for our services. We were sure that you would not begrudge it us."

Gurney grinned. "As it happens, I do not."

"*Ja*, I see." Von Kratzstein's jaw thrust forward. "When we these chewels for money with an American merchant attempt to negotiate, we find that they are glass, no more. Zo. They put us in this stinking chail." The colour of his face deepened. "It is a most abominable insult, Kapitan, to a Prussian officer put to the humiliation of condemned being a vulgar counterfeiter. This is further cause for me satisfaction to demand, when my sword is returned."

"May I point out to you, Herr General, that your sword may never be returned?" Gurney's voice cooled.

"The Greeks, I hear, tend to hang forgers high as Haman. And as to your original premise; it is not the act of an honourable man, even a Prussian, to sneak away with a chest of jewels, real or counterfeit, that is not his."

"Truly it is said." Basreddin paused. "Aye, most truly: if a man steal a bell-wether and the flock be thereby lost to the shepherd, shall he not suffer as a thief of many, though he wished only to be a thief of one?"

"Indeed. So Herr General, you stand condemned out of your own mouth—"

"But—" von Kratzstein spluttered—"But ve work on your ship for you, without pay, for three months. The labourer is worthy of his hire—"

"But he does not usually steal the wages of his fellow toilers. And surely you would not describe yourselves, you and the Kolonels, as labourers, Gentlemen, but rather, devoted to the cause of freedom in Greece. And by your assault—your most valiant assault—on the citadel of the Black Crow, you have achieved much to that end. Is this not sufficient reward?"

"Ach Gott." Stahlkleber sounded as if he had had enough. "It is true. We came to Greece in search of plunder. I have a bellyful had of being a Kolonel—"

"Silence," roared von Kratzstein. "Court-martial talk! Stahlkleber, you are under arrest!"

"And so, it appears," said Gurney mildly, "are you. But we have wasted enough time. I have a letter from the Government, which will secure your release. There is need for good men to fight for Greece, and good men you have proved yourselves to be. The Government asks that you accept commissions in the Army of Greece. You are all, if you accept, ensigns to that fine body of men. I would point out that if you do not accept, the noose is all that awaits you."

There was a long silence. The colour drained from von Kratzstein's face slowly, and he hung his head.

"Truly it is said," Basreddin pointed out, "better to shovel dung in the gutters of Trebizond than to swing from a gibbet in Mecca."

Finally, von Kratzstein raised his eyes to Gurney's. "Very well," he said. "If my men agree."

"Your men no longer. You are at last in the service of Greece."

And at length von Kratzstein bowed. "Goot," he said. "After all, it seems you are a fair man, Kapitan. I accept this demotion. But our original quarrel remains."

Gurney sighed. "So be it. But I cannot meet you in prison. Let us get you out of here first; then we'll see what satisfaction can be arranged."

The gaoler was summoned, and Gurney returned with him to his office. After the formalities for the release of the Prussians were complete—for a Government in its infancy the Democracy of Greece had spawned a snowstorm of paperwork—the six of them made their way through the thronged streets to the harbour. As they left the gloomy battlements of the gaol, Gurney spoke briefly with Basreddin. Then he walked on, and Basreddin fell back a little, chatting with von Kratzstein. The ex-General looked a little surprised at first, but then seemed to decide that Basreddin could bend the sympathetic ear he needed. Soon, Gurney heard von Kratzstein's voice waxing confidential in an English broken with emotion.

As usual, the waterfront was bustling with people. If bustling was the correct word for the bands of brigands lounging on corners smoking, or crouched out of the hot sun in noisy card-playing clutches. Prosperity had come as a shock to Nauplion, and the gold the Greeks so strenuously acquired from the English with one hand was freely wagered on any proposition, however unlikely, with the other. Among the brigands the inevitable gangs of small boys roved in search of excitement and plunder. The occasional political man, dressed in dark coat of good broadcloth and sober nankeens, passed through the throng with the purposeful air of a foraging crow in a treeful of parrots.

Basreddin came up with Gurney at the quayside, and winked.

"All is prepared," he said quietly. Gurney nodded and turned to von Kratzstein. "This is the parting of the ways, then. As to this affair of honour of which you spoke. You are sure you do not wish to let bygones be bygones and part friends?"

Von Kratzstein, delighted to be in the limelight, drew himself up to his full height and stuck out his chest. "Among gentlemans, Kapitan, this cannot be." His right hand went to his sword-hilt. "Please. Draw your sword, and yourself like a man defend."

Gurney let out a sorrowful hiss. "If you insist. Though I must say that this 'affair of honour' could easily be confused with a waterfront brawl."

On von Kratzstein's cheek the duelling scars stood out like pink caterpillars. "How dare you sir!" Saliva sprayed from the gap where his front teeth should have been. "Satisfaction I will have." His heavy cavalry sabre leaped into his hand.

Even a dogfight was a major attraction on the waterfront at Nauplion. When the loungers and cardplayers realised that the two Franks were about to indulge in some genuine bloodletting, a crowd, complete with self-appointed marshals, homed in like bluebottles to a dead goat. Gurney took his time about drawing his own hanger, jockeying fussily for position, pretending the sun was in his eyes, then taking out his handkerchief and blowing his nose. By the time he appeared satisfied with his spot, there were eighty spectators and three fights had already broken out among brigands whose toes had been trodden on by other brigands."

When Gurney drew, a hush settled over the crowd. But when he stepped forward and aimed a cut at von Kratzstein's head, the shout broke out in earnest.

Von Kratzstein parried the cut with an ease that surprised him, and riposted. He had been more than a little nervous about his encounter, for the English captain was a good swordsman; but that first cut had been slow and careless. He would not kill him though; merely maim him a little. He looked at Gurney as they circled, seeking an opening. The cool blue eyes met his. Below the broad brow they held a disturbing hint of mockery. Von Kratzstein's colour rose. Damn the whelp! He would learn to kidnap a Prussian! He sprang, aiming his heavy blade like a meat cleaver at the Englishman's right shoulder. The sabre rang on the cobbles and he stumbled, drawing a chorus of jeers from the bystanders. As he recovered himself, he felt a tug at his breeches and whirled. Gurney danced back, grinning. "End of contest, I think. Herr General." And he sheathed his sword and walked away.

For a moment von Kratzstein could not believe his eyes. Then he began to follow the Englishman, who was shrugging into his coat. Something caught him around the ankles. He tripped, and sprawled headlong on the dirty cobbles. He tried to get up but could not.

Someone in the crowd sniggered. The sniggerer was joined by others, and soon the houses rocked to a great roar of mirth. Von Kratzstein, looking down, saw what had tripped him was his breeches, which lay round his ankles. He grabbed for them and pulled them up, searching for the braces buttons with his fingers. It took him ten seconds, which seemed like hours, before he realised that the two back buttons had been neatly cut away.

Gurney and Basreddin looked shoreward from *Vandal's* gig, which had been awaiting them at the bottom of the steps. The laughter had died down now, but the crowd had not dispersed. Instead, the mass of men was following one man, dressed in canary yellow, who ran before them, waving a cavalry sabre in his right hand and apparently holding up his breeches with his left.

"Genius," said Gurney to Basreddin. "Sheer genius. To remove one button entirely and to leave the other hanging by a thread. You are a Newton among pickpockets, Basreddin. Entirely wasted on His Majesty's service."

Basreddin spread his hands in self-deprecation. "A mere nothing. Have I ever told you, Giorgiou, of the time when I took from the navel of the favourite dancer of a certain keen-eyed Pasha a ruby beyond price? The occasion was fraught with greater difficulties than this. For one thing, the dancing girl in question was in coition with the Pasha at the time." He paused, remembering. "And for another, I was eight years old."

12

Vandal had been at sea for nearly ten days before Mehemet Ali's fleet hove into view. The first Gurney knew of it was the long-drawn-out screech from Henry Priest in the foretop. Henry's rendition of "sail ho" sounded a lot like a baritone pig being killed, and under normal circumstances it rather amused Gurney. But now, as he ran up the shrouds and swept his glasses along the white line of topsails that stretched across a 120° quadrant of the horizon, he was far from amused.

He slid down the backstay, the cable burning at the sole of his foot, and ran aft, shouting orders. George Jarvis ran for the ensign halliards, the red ensign came sweeping down from the gaff-peak, and up went a great white flag, bearing the cross of St. George with the Union Jack in its top right-hand quarter. McIver chased the ladies below decks, refusing to listen to Euthymia's protests that she wanted to see what would happen; and the ship rang with the crash of mallets on bulkheads as they cleared for action below. Gurney donned white duck breeches, a gold-braided coat of dark blue serge, collar and cravat and a cocked hat. It was the first time he had dressed in the uniform of His Majesty's Navy for nearly seven years now, and he felt a pang of nostalgia. But in the August heat of the sun that beat down from its noonday height above him, nostalgia was soon forgotten, and in its place came discomfort. The coat scratched like the devil, the dark stuff of the hat attracted the heat and turned the crown of his head into a rain-forest, and the collar began to wilt. The only satisfaction was in watching McIver, Basreddin and Mather, crammed into similar rig but with a good deal less gold braid, attempting to play the part of naval officers.

Paddy and Totters, for their part, looked as bizarre as the others were uncomfortable. Fitzcozens' jockey-like frame might have done for a cavalry officer; but his stoop shoulders and bow legs were distinctly incongruous on the quarterdeck of a man-o'-war. And Gilchrist, who fitted nowhere but in a drawing-room or a carriage, was made yet more scarecrowlike by the fact that his uniform had been built for a man five feet ten inches tall and stout, while he was a full six feet five and emaciated. Between them they were putting on a gala display of overheated itching. Particularly Basreddin, whose predilection for loose robes must be subjecting him to the tortures of the damned. Serves him right, thought Gurney. If it wasn't for him we wouldn't be here, not only going for the biggest fleet the Mediterranean had seen for fifteen years with a twelve-gun schooner, but impersonating His Majesty's Navy in the process.

Stumping to the windward side of the quarterdeck, he explained the rules. "I, as Captain, have this as my

stamping ground. You lot had better keep well to leeward if you know what's good for you. Can't have the
horrible Egyptians thinking that the great traditions of
the Navy are breaking down. Also, I would point out
that Egyptian guns are reputed always to fire high, so
to windward I am in the most exposed position." His
face went grave. "Pipe hands on deck."

The bos'uns pipes that twittered were woefully un-
synchronised, and Gurney frowned. One could expect
little else, however; if they were to masquerade as a
King's ship more often, the pipers would get more
practice. He ran his eyes over the men assembling in
the waist. A cheerful bunch they were, this crew. As
well they might be, considering the fact that under
their feet was enough gold and jewels to set all of
them up with a good independence for life.

Gurney raised his eyes. Vandal's crew was assem-
bled now, waiting, crammed into the deck, the
younger ones hanging from the rigging like so many
apes. At his back, Paddy, Totters, Mather, McIver and
Basreddin stood, feet planted apart, hands clasped
behind backs.

"Boys," shouted Gurney. "Boys, yonder lies the
Egyptian fleet. It is not a small fleet. In fact it is a
bloody enormous fleet. But have no fear. We are not
going to fight them. We are now, for long as we are
in sight of them, His Majesty's Schooner Vandal. And
no bloody Gippo is going to interfere with one of
His Majesty's ships, because they know that if His
Majesty's Navy were to hear about it they would be
seeing Davy Jones and that right speedily." A rumble
of laughter from the waist. "But if it so be that they
open fire, remember that they can't shoot straight.
And we can sail three feet to their two.

"The reason we are dressed up like monkeys is
that I am going aboard the flagship and do not wish
to be recognised. You will all behave yourselves in a
manner befitting the Navy. And by that I do not mean
smashing the locks off the lazaret and making animals

of yourselves with the spirits." Another laugh. *Vandal*'s men had little time for the Navy, which had within memory pressganged friends and relations.

"All right. That's all."

He looked round. From the after-cabin scuttle there emerged a figure he did not recognise. A young naval officer, apparently, but even in comparison to the pseudo-Navy men on *Vandal*'s deck, an unusual sight. Under the cocked hat the face was smooth and, beneath a delicate tan, pale, the lips full and red. Beneath the coat the body curved in a manner not usually seen in His Majesty's officers.

"Arabella!"

"No, no. Lieutenant Mountolivet, at your service, Captain."

"Good God, my love, what are you doing?"

There was a grim resolve in her voice when she answered. "If you think I am going to crouch below with Euthymia and Isabel while you take on the Fleet single-handed, you are entirely mad."

"But if they should open fire—"

"You know perfectly well that if they open fire we are done for, above or below decks."

Gurney stood for a moment, at a loss. Then he smiled. "Very well, my love. Lieutenant, God help us. But please, go below for the moment or you will cause a riot." He took her by the arm. "And Lieutenant. Whatever may happen, remember this; I love you."

Butterflies began to flutter in Arabella's stomach as she watched George clasp his cocked hat on his head and stride to the entry port in the waist. She could hardly believe it was happening—it was the maddest thing she had ever heard of: it could not be true. But Gurney paused a moment, and did something to the sword at his belt. With a lurch of the heart, Arabella realised he was loosening it in its sheath. She wanted to shout at him not to be so damned stupid, to come back; but she knew it would be worse than useless. So she choked back the lump that rose in her throat,

and forced a smile in its place. He turned; she waved,
and his white teeth showed in a smile. Then he disappeared over *Vandal*'s side.

To all appearances, *Vandal* was merely one of the
ships of His Majesty's Navy that cruised the Eastern
Mediterranean, week in, week out, all year round.
Their function was not exactly peacekeeping, for England did not concern herself, at least not overtly,
with the wars of Asia Minor. Nor was it simple observation, for observation implies intervention, in that the
observer must report back to somebody, who will
then presumably act on the report. No, it was a curious
sort of presence—for a presence was all it was, neither
active nor passive; but it had a salutary effect. As a
large man with a broken nose and scarred knuckles,
watching a street-fight between two skinny pimps, has
a salutary effect; the contestants know that whoever
wins may not have to face that nose and those
knuckles, but his presence reminds them that their
fight is second-class stuff. This, though it does not
stand in the way of their fighting, keeps them in their
place.

Ibrahim Pasha, son and Admiral of the Fleet of
Mehemet Ali, had been running this state of affairs
through his mind since his flag captain had informed
him that there was a British schooner in the offing,
signalling that she wished to send over a boarding
party. Mehemet Ali had little love for the English,
having rewarded them for an ill-judged expedition
into his territories in 1807 with an avenue of their
severed heads on pikes in Cairo. But his son knew
that close and clever handling was the essence. He
therefore gave instructions to his captain to heave to
and await the Englishman's arrival. From crosstrees to
crosstrees the message sped, and soon the entire fleet
lay passive.

To Gurney, as he climbed down *Vandal*'s side into
her gig, there was a good deal that was awesome
about the fleet that now stretched on either side, sails

backed, hove-to at his pleasure. Such was the power
of the Navy that one schooner could stand in the way
of this mighty armada. But if it was discovered that it
was a mere imposture that was delaying the fleet, then
. . . Gurney did not like to think what would happen
then.

It was a long pull over to the flagship. The Egyptian fleet was sailing in a sort of flattened arrowhead
with the flagship at its point, and Gurney had given
instructions that Vandal should lie up-wind, well out
of cannon-shot, in case anything should go awry.

Even with the fine oarsmanship of the gig's crew
sliding her through the little waves, it was twenty
minutes before the painted side of the flagship, her
three tiers of gunports picked out in red and yellow,
loomed over him like a wall. Gurney was conscious,
as he looked back from halfway up the Jacob's ladder
at the gig pulling away into the offing, that his heart
was beating a little more quickly than usual; and that
the thudding was not entirely attributable to the height
of the ladder. But as he climbed on, the calm that always came before a set-to steadied his pulse, and the
world began to slow down as his reflexes geared up to
crisis speed.

The quarterdeck of Ibrahim Pasha's flagship was
structurally like many another quarterdeck Gurney
had walked in the uniform he now wore. But the resemblance ended at the structure. For underfoot were
rich carpets overlapped, and upon them Gurney's
buckled shoes sank in near to his ankles. A rank of
marines in huge turbans and baggy breeches, each
with a curved scimitar naked in his right hand, stood
at either rail. And on the final upward sweep of the
deck to the ship's taffrail was pitched the silken pavilion, embroidered in gold with choice sayings of the
Prophet, of Ibrahim Pasha.

There were so many people in the pavilion that
Gurney could not at first see the Pasha. Besides the
Nubian boys with the giant ostrich-feather fans, there

were two fat eunuchs with writing-tables, three sallow-skinned men in uniform arguing volubly, and a little man who seemed to be attempting to rescue coffee-cups from underfoot. As Gurney approached, a shout came from the middle of the crowd and it dispersed onto the deck and vanished. And there, on a rich brocade sofa, his feet tucked up beneath him, sat Ibrahim Pasha.

The Pasha was one of the fattest men Gurney had ever seen. The sofa on which he sat looked, next to his vast bulk, like a rather flimsy armchair. But his skin was not dimpled and grained with the fat; it was smooth and sleek, and it gave him the look of a giant seal, sunning itself on a rock. And when he moved his hand, beckoning, it looked so like a seal's flipper that Gurney reflected that had he a bucket of fish with him he would have fed him one. As he drew closer, he saw that the coarse-featured face and ballooning hands were much pitted with smallpox scars. But the eyes were shrewd. Gurney reminded himself that, neutral or not neutral, he would have to watch his step.

He bowed deeply, and in the good Arabic he had learned from Basreddin, he introduced himself. The Pasha acknowledged his presence with a sleepy lowering of the eyelids, and waved him forward. The sensual lips rolled back from the rotten teeth in a smile, and he patted the sofa beside him. "Come, Captain, be seated."

Gurney bowed again and sat down. The fat man smelt of too many sweet perfumes, and he felt a curious reluctance to let that gross flesh touch him. "A delightful day and an impressive fleet, Excellency," said Gurney.

"Aye," the Pasha replied, signalling to an attendant. "Allah has been good to our enterprise. Since we sailed from Alexandria, he has smiled upon us."

Etiquette demanded a certain amount of polite chatter about the weather and an exchange of compliments about ships, as well as a rapid bulletin on the

health of their respective Heads of State. As Gurney
went through the motions, coffee was brought in the
inevitable filigreed egg-shells, and two narghiles were
placed at their feet. Then there was a short silence.
The Pasha gazed unseeingly down the broad decks of
his flagship, smoke trickling from his nostrils. Gurney
could see *Vandal*, tiny in the distance, her sails very
white against the deep blue of the sea. As he looked,
the sun flashed on a glass. They were watching. Arabella was watching. So close, but at such an immense
distance! He wished heartily that he was aboard at
this very moment, preferably sailing away from this
floating palace as fast as sails could carry him.

The Pasha seemed to recollect himself. "But tell
me, Captain, if I may be so blunt; to what do I owe
the honour of this visit?"

Gurney drew deep on his narghile, then turned to
the Pasha and smiled sweetly. "It is merely that I was
asked by their Lordships to greet you on your way to
the Peloponnese."

"And discover my exact intentions, no doubt." The
fat brow-ridge lowered a little. "Come, come, Captain.
This is unworthy of your British diplomacy. I know
you have spies here who have given you precise information on my intentions, or as much of them as
they can discover . . . I fear that I must leave it to
them to inform you of my plans."

"So be it." Gurney shrugged. "But those were my
orders. There is one other thing, however."

"Which is?"

"It is known that on your ship there is a man who
has made unprovoked attacks on the loyal subjects of
His Britannic Majesty George IV."

"Whom may God preserve." There was irony in
the Pasha's voice.

"I shall make sure that your good wishes reach
his ears." Gurney swallowed. "The name of this man is
Kapraj Bey, otherwise known as the Black Crow of
Izmir. I have been instructed to take him into custody

on the charge of piracy on the high seas." Now for it. "Failure to render up this man may result in the severest consequences to England's continuing amicable relations with the Pashalik of Egypt."

The Pasha picked at his lower lip. "I see. Large words, Captain. Strange days are upon us when His Majesty despatches a mere schooner to threaten a fleet. But with you English it has always been so." He paused, and time seemed to pause with him. "Kapraj Bey is one of my most trusted men. I will not lightly part with him. On the other hand, if England is offended, then England must have justice." The heavy-lidded eyes bore into Gurney's. "Are you sure, Captain, that you are not exceeding your authority? Of course you are."

Exceeding his authority? Or sure? Looking at those eyes, Gurney could not tell.

"Let me give you a little demonstration, Captain, of what happens to people when they exceed their authority." He snapped his fingers at one of the eunuchs standing by. The eunuch bowed and left, taking with him two marines. A servant brought a little brazier of charcoal and placed a pan of water on it. "Yusuf, whom you will shortly meet, is charged with heating the water for my bath. This morning, he exceeded his authority. The water was five degrees too hot. Happily, I experienced only slight discomfort. But Yusuf must be taught that the lines that limit his authority are strictly drawn." He lapsed into silence, drawing tubercular wheezes from his narghile.

The water on the brazier was boiling fiercely by the time the eunuch and the marines returned. Between them was a soft-faced youth with kohl-rimmed eyes. Evidently the temerarious Yusuf. When he saw the pan of water, he started to tremble. The colour left his face, and two patches of rouge stood out on his cheeks.

"Yusuf, my dear boy." The Pasha's voice was silky.

"I am intending to wash my hands. Perhaps you would test the water for me."

"But Excellency, my thermometer—"

"Oh, never mind your thermometer. If your right hand was good enough for my bath, surely it will be sensitive enough for this purpose." The Pasha nodded curtly to the marines. "Roll up his pretty sleeves."

The unfortunate Yusuf tried to run, but his captors held him fast. One of them rolled up his sleeve to the armpit. His arm was white and soft as a woman's. Gurney, hardly believing his eyes, watched as he was dragged forward and his hand, twitching and wriggling as if possessed of a life independent of its owner, was thrust into the boiling water half-way to the elbow.

The screams were high and shrill, and Gurney fought for control of his face. A full two minutes passed before Yusuf's eyes rolled up and he pitched sideways in a dead faint. The Pasha nodded again.

"A little warm, it seems. Take him away."

When the soldiers withdrew the hand from the pan, the skin hung from it like an obscene glove.

At his side, the Pasha sighed, his body wobbling like a jelly.

"Such talented hands he had, too. Poor Yusuf." Then the little eyes swivelled to Gurney. "But he had to learn. My convenience is paramount, and anyone who acts beyond his authority threatens me. I do not enjoy being threatened. Now let us hear your case against Kapraj Bey. You have seen that I am a just man. I shall listen to his side of these matters, too."

He barked a command at one of the viziers, and the man scurried away.

Gurney braced himself. This was the part of the ordeal that he dreaded above all else, depending as it did on pure bluff. Two less gullible cases than his present opponents would be hard to come by. But it was not as if he did not have the foundations of a case.

Kapraj Bey's seizing of *Otranto* was an act of pure
piracy, and the Navy could, Gurney supposed, quite
reasonably be expected to act in protection of British
subjects. But if Kapraj Bey managed to call his *bona
fides* into question, then ... Having witnessed Yusuf's
come-uppance, Gurney decided he had no wish to find
out what would happen then.

He looked up. Ibrahim's eyes were staring at him
incuriously, the whites tinged with yellow. Gurney
had a nasty feeling the reason for their lack of curiosity
was an excess of certain knowledge. He was worried
now, and there was that hollowness in his stomach that
was sure warning of warm times in the very near future.

His musings were cut short by a little commotion at
the break of the poop. The figure that strode across
the carpets and bowed deep before the Pasha was a
familiar one; as the Black Crow straightened himself
and turned eyes like twin gun-barrels on Gurney, his
mind went back to the last time he had seen the Black
Crow on board ship. On that occasion, as now, the
sun had made rainbows in the diamonds that crusted
the pommel of his scimitar, and his garments had been
of white silk. But last time, Gurney had been clad in
rags, exhausted after the storm that had destroyed his
ship; now he was dressed in a uniform that com-
manded respect in all but the most uncivilised corners
of the world, and despite his apprehensions he was
calm and rested. As their glances met it was as
though two swords clashed, then bounded away; but
Gurney had time to see that his enemy had recognised
him.

Ibrahim, as was proper, was the first to speak. His
voice was hard and flat, the voice of an impartial
judge, and Gurney, looking around him at the monstrous fleet, once again felt a great sense of his own
temerity. "Kapraj Bey, this is Captain Gurney, of His
Britannic Majesty's Navy. He makes allegations that
you did, without provocation, make captive and sell

into slavery subjects of his King; and he therefore asks me to deliver you into his custody. What reasons can you give me as to why I should not accede to his demands?"

The familiar smile spread itself across Kapraj Bey's face like butter from a hot knife. The eyes were slippery with deceit, and something else. Triumph? Gurney could not tell. "Two reasons, O Pasha. First, the ship I captured was an armed merchantman, and I made the reasonable assumption that since she was sailing under the Greek flag she was hostile. Second, and this is undoubtedly the more pressing: I have reason to believe that Captain Gurney, as he calls himself, is no more an officer of the English Navy than you or I."

The Pasha turned to Gurney, his face mildly surprised. "Well, well, Captain. This is certainly a serious allegation. I would not for one moment suggest that the burden of proof lies with you, but I feel in duty bound to examine closely the last of the Bey's suggestions."

Here it is, thought Gurney. The moment of truth. "There is little to examine," he said. "Would you take the word of a man who for years has been a pirate against my word as an officer and a gentleman?"

"Come, come, Captain. The Bey's piracy and the rank you claim are exactly the points at issue." The Pasha's expression hardened. "I am aware that in the past the Bey has at times made a livelihood from the unwary on the high seas. But in the East, as elsewhere, the distinction between piracy and enterprise has always been hazy at best. And I have a little confession to make. When you signalled me, I took the precaution of checking the Navy list—which I have remarkably up to date—for your ship. And later, when you told me your name, I had that checked too. Neither appear in that useful volume, though it seems that there was one of your name who resigned, after the rescinding of a dishonourable discharge, some three years past. It seems to me, *Mister* Gurney, that you have exceeded your authority."

There was a short silence. Then the Bey spoke. "It was a mistake to mention, when we fought in my palace, that it was your wife that was at the root of your ah, dislike for me. Navies are not usually swayed by the personal animosities of their officers."

So that was it. Gurney cursed himself for a fool. He had walked into a trap, and now he was to be taken. But there was one manoeuvre left to him.

"This is outrageous," he said, letting the anger he felt begin to come into his voice. "You doubt the word of an officer, simply because your list is out of date? Preposterous. You must know that in times like these commissions are swiftly bestowed—"

"And as quickly taken away." The Pasha smiled. "It is a risk I am prepared to take. For when I have dealt with you, I shall deal with your ship. Unfortunately, the schooner *Vandal* and her complement will disappear. If you are indeed in His Majesty's Service, then it will be unfortunate that you were shipwrecked, and that my men found one of your lifebelts. If not, then who will blame me for protecting myself against a common pirate?"

Gurney stayed where he was for a moment, waiting. Once again he thought of Arabella, watching him there, not two miles away, and bitterness filled him. Weak fool that he had been, to give in to her demands that she witness the undoing of the Black Crow! Now it bid fair to cost her her life. For himself, the end would come quickly. And God send that *Vandal* would sheer off before she was sunk. But nothing happened, and dimly he realised that the Pasha was speaking again.

"As I have already demonstrated, I am a fair man. And it seems that if the Bey indeed enslaved your people, you have a fair grudge against him. I therefore propose to let you have it out with him, man to man. But do not expect to escape with your life. If he is the victor, it will be as if nothing had happened; if you conquer him—and I hope that you will not— you will die, slowly and badly, and your ship with you." The Pasha folded his hands over his gross stomach, smiling. "A delightful spectacle for such a fine morning, with the added spice of justice. Set to, gentlemen, set to."

Almost before he knew it, Gurney was on his feet. The two swords hissed from their scabbards as one, and the two men faced each other, the yellow-haired Englishman and the hook-nosed Turk. Over the point of his hanger Gurney watched his enemy's eyes, narrowed against the brightness of the sun's reflections from the sea. On the Crow's face there was that snarling grin, the twisting of the lips revealing canine teeth pointed like an animal's. Gurney forgot the Pasha, gross in his pavilion, forgot the twin ranks of impassive guards, the crew, standing mute in the waist and on the fo'c'sle. His mind was quiet now, his whole being centred in his sword-arm, waiting.

Then he sprang—not for the Bey, but for the rank of marines at his back, hewing down a man who stood in his way, kicking the body aside, and swinging into the mizzen shrouds that ran to the platform of the top fifty feet above. He turned. Below, the marines gaped up at him, several of them with muskets half-raised. Kapraj Bey still stood on the deck, the point of his scimitar lowered now, a look of something like surprise turning slowly to anger on his thin features. Gurney smiled.

"Well, Crow?" he called. "Can it be that you are afraid of the height? Come a little closer to heaven, my cowardly bird, and you will feel cold iron in your guts. Or will it be too rich a meal for your yellow belly?"

Slowly, Kapraj Bey walked across to the ratlines. There was a flicker of fear in his eyes. His left arm had been badly wounded when he had fought Gurney last, and he would need it for the rigging if he was to keep his sword-arm free. As he began to climb, Gurney stayed ahead of him; then the shrouds began to narrow, and when he looked up he saw the half-moon platform of the top. The deck was a sea of faces now, all turned up, expectant. As the Crow came up to him Gurney scrambled onto the platform, then leaned over and slashed at the green silk turban. The blade, ground to razor-keenness by Mather, sliced through the cloth, and the Bey's headgear fluttered away in the breeze. His shaven head gleamed white, horribly naked in the sun.

"Come up, you dog, and I will fight you fair." Gurney stepped back, onto the crossjack yard, balancing on the spar like a tightrope-walker, watching the Crow haul himself laboriously onto the top, favouring his left arm; then, as his enemy rose to his feet, Gurney danced forward, the heavy cutlass flickering out towards his belly. The Crow parried, and at the first ring of steel on steel a murmur rose like vapour from the deck fifty feet below. Gurney staggered, as if unbalanced, and the Crow came forward a little, smiling again.

"This is the end of you, infidel scum. And when you are carrion, I shall find your woman again. This time I shall not be so gentle with her." The scimitar came down in a blue of steel, and Gurney caught it on his blade, then backed away again, aiming a clumsy swipe at him. Inching his body a little to the right, the Crow came on.

"Really, Captain. I thought you more of a swordsman. Or is it that you wish a quick death now rather than a slow one later?" Another sweep, with a cunning feint. Gurney's parry met empty air, and he dropped almost to his knees to avoid the blade as it fanned his right cheek. Backing away again, the light of anticipated victory began to show in the Crow's face. They were halfway to the yardarm now. Gurney decided it was time to make a gesture. He jumped forward, thrust, was parried in tierce, thrust again in quarte,

and ducked as the Bey responded with a great looping slash which nicked his arm. Another sigh rose up
from the deck below. He moved backwards again, no-
ticing as he went that the ship's bulwark was below
him now, then the sea, ruffling at the waterline eighty
feet down.

The Bey's grin had faded a little. Gurney decided it
was time to act. Rushing on the Bey, he hacked once,
parried the riposte, then reeled, as if losing his balance,
and toppled into the gap between yard and sail. As
he plummeted downwards, he shot out his hand and
grabbed the footrope running along the bottom of the
yard, muscles cracking as his weight caught and
swung, then turned in mid-air, released his hold, and
landed with his foot on the footrope, hard against the
yard on the side opposite to that from which he had
dived. His right hand locked on the jackstay and his
left, still holding the sword, drove upwards at Kapraj
Bey's kidney.

It had been a considerable surprise to the Crow
when Gurney, unwounded, had fallen into space. His
astonishment became complete when he felt the awful
pain in his left side below the ribcage, and it was the
shock as much as anything else that sent him toppling
forwards, Gurney's blade locked where it had penetrated between the fourth and fifth ribs on its way out
of the front of his chest. Salt blood rushed into his
mouth and nose; he was dead before he hit the deck.

Gurney swung himself onto the top of the yard
again, and ran towards the place where the spar gave
way to blue space. As he launched himself outwards,
he saw for a moment that seemed years long, the
Black Crow's body sprawled on the rich carpets of the
poop, the white robes stained with blood, the cutlass
angled from its back like a pin in a moth; then the
water came up at him and he was diving deep, deep,
the blue of the sea darkening into indigo over his
head.

He swam away from the ship underwater. He

would have shed his blue coat which hampered him as he swam, but he knew that the white shirt he wore beneath would give away his position as surely as a beacon. By the time he began to swim upwards, his lungs were taut to bursting; but he felt little fear of drowning. It might even be preferable to that iron rain which would start to fall around him as soon as his head broke water. Then he came up.

The side of the flagship was enormous, a great wall of wood rearing from the water perhaps fifty yards away. As he breathed once, twice, the rail was suddenly studded with the heads of men, and someone shouted, voice curiously indistinct considering the small distance that separated them. And then it started, the first musket-ball kicked up a little fountain of water three yards from Gurney's ear. He looked quickly around. The gig was perhaps a thousand feet off, out of accurate musket shot from the flagship but still running a considerable risk if she brought her broadside into play. He struggled out of his coat, feeling a ridiculous surge of regret as it sank away. There had been days when such a coat would have been worth more than life itself. Then he dived again, towards the gig, in the midst of a hissing shower of bullets.

When he resurfaced, he was an easy hundred yards to weather of the Turk. This time there were no bullets, and he trod water for a second, grateful for a chance to catch his breath. As the water cleared from his ears, he became aware that a voice was hailing him from the flagship. Straining his eyes, he thought he made out a megaphone at the mouth of one of the tiny figures at her poop. "You will die," the man was crying, "for acts of aggression against His Excellency Ibrahim Pasha." A pause. "The Pasha sends his farewells. He decrees that his broadside will be your firing-party, as befits a brave seaman. Even if he is a pirate." And while Gurney watched, the covers of the Turk's sixty-five starboard gunports rose like the lids of so many eyes. Even from where he was, he could hear the rumble of carriages as the great guns trundled up on their tackles. Then he dived again.

He was underwater by the time the first gun boomed, at the Turk's bow; and when the main part of her battery went off, though he felt the mighty concussions as the iron balls smacked into the water, there he stayed. Eventually, desperate for breath, he came up again and looked around.

The side of the ship was wreathed in smoke, and great wisps and banks of the stuff rose from her hatchways. The breeze, blowing as it was into her starboard side, would have taken it back into the gunners' faces. Which, thought Gurney as he looked at the widely-scattered splotches of foam that marked the fall of the shot, would not help their aim. And their aim in the first place was none too good. A big gun was a hard thing to train and lay in any event, and rumour had it that your Egyptian wished to have nothing to do with so laborious a process. So when the weather guns fired, the shot went miles high; and when the lee broadside came into play, the shot merely plunged into the sea.

A shout caught his attention. The gig, oars going at a rate that must have been close to fifty to the minute, was shooting towards him, zigging and zagging wildly through the shots that churned the water to foam round her. Never mind that those same shots were intended for Gurney; high as they were, the gig was in some danger. He tried to yell at them to stay back, but a gobbet of spray caught him in the mouth and choked him. By the time he had recovered his breath, the gig was a mere twenty yards away. Another shockwave buffeted him, jolting his kidneys painfully, and the gig leaped up and sideways, falling into the sea almost on her beam ends. But when she fell she still floated, and Gurney could hear the sound of deep and serious cursing coming from her stern. It would not, under ordinary circumstances, have appealed

much to Gurney as a subject for listening; now, however, it had angel choirs beaten by several lengths.
The gig came alongside him so smartly that she appeared to skid. The Turk's broadside was silent; re-
loading, Gurney guessed. Even a top-notch gun crew
took a good two minutes to sponge, load, wad, prime
and fire; and it looked as if the Egyptians were a good
deal less than top-notch. Even so, there was something
about the silence that spoke of thunder to come.
Suddenly the water seemed cold, and Gurney's teeth
began to chatter. When two men caught him, one
under each arm, and heaved him into the gig like
a sack of potatoes, he stayed a moment on the grat-
ings, limp with relief. Then he rose and looked about
him.

Mather, feet widely braced against the gig's twisting
as he wove it across the waves, was roaring the time
to the oarsmen. As Gurney watched, the American
turned a minute-glass.

"What's your rate?"

"Forty, Captain. It's not the real thing, of course,
but it's not bad practice."

War as practice for a gig-race. Gurney, conscious
of a slight feeling of unreality, shook his head. Smoke
bloomed suddenly from the Egyptian's gunports, and
the air was full of whirring iron. Most of it went high;
one shot, however, did not. It came up almost parallel
with the gig's starboard side, passed three feet from
where Gurney stood, then ripped the head from the
shoulders of the bow oarsman, tore away the top foot
of the stem, and skidded crazily away across the blue
surface of the sea.

Gurney vaulted over the three rows of men, shoved
the headless corpse into the bottom-boards, and set to
with the oar. Mather, still at the tiller, was beside himself. "O, you Godless wog bastards!" he yelled, "not
only are you buggering up my lovely boat, but you
have knocked the jolly nob off the only man in my
crew who can row bow oar. O, you bastards"—all

the time stirring the tiller so the gig dodged like a rabbit under fire, drawing always closer to *Vandal*. And *Vandal* herself was swooping down on them now, the gig and the schooner closing at a combined speed of close to fifteen knots, moving towards the extremity of the range of the Egyptians' cannon. But the Egyptian was moving too, though ponderously. The flagship's nose was coming up towards the wind, and then a little speck of white water appeared at her bow. And her guns were speaking—not the heavy crash of a full broadside, but raggedly-spaced single shots. Not badly aimed, either, thought Gurney as a waterspout kicked at the gig's starboard, gunwale.

Then *Vandal* bore down. Gurney flung the gig's painter to a man at the rail, then made ready with a fender as the rope tautened. As he went up the side the slings were already on the gig, and two minutes later she was swung onto the deck.

Gurney ran aft. "McIver," he yelled. "Put her hard on the wind and we'll be away." *Vandal* came up, heeling steeply to starboard. He turned his glass on the Egyptian. The great ship was coming up on the starboard tack, her royals and skysails shivering at the luff as the helmsman squeezed every last inch to windward. A string of bunting burst from her signal halliards, and the sails of the fleet began to fill one by one. But *Vandal* was unmatchable in light airs, and she sailed a good five degrees closer up than the ponderous ship of the line. The only other ships in the armada that might have matched *Vandal* were far on the flanks, and they would never catch her now.

McIver came aft, still in his Naval uniform. "We're away, it would seem, Captain. Why I don't know. With all due respect, Captain, that was one of the stupidest damn things I have ever seen."

Gurney could not find it in himself to disagree. Basreddin was standing at his side, too. "One day," said the Sufi, "you will throw yourself into the water from a great height and you will not come up. You are like a stone that skips across the surface of the sea, kept in the air by its momentum; one day you may move too slow and you will sink." A grin split his beard with a crescent of white teeth. "But it is good to see you back."

Gurney watched in silence as the towering canvas of the Egyptian dwindled and fell below the horizon. In his mind the events of the day tumbled one over the other, returning always to the white spraddle of Kapraj Bey's body, nailed by his sword to the rich carpets of the Pasha's quarterdeck.

Then he turned and walked aft, stopping as Arabella got up from the hatchcover where she had been sitting and took off her cocked hat, shaking her head so the long, golden hair fell to her shoulders, rippling and shining in the sunlight. Forward, *Vandal*'s men saw the helm go over, and Mather's deep voice began.

Rolling 'ome
Rolling 'ome
Rolling 'ome across the sea
Rolling 'ome to Merry England
Where kind friends do await for me.

* * *

At the maintruck of Ibrahim Pasha's flagship, the lookout trained his glass on the schooner, now far to windward. He was amazed to see the two uniformed figures, the one with short hair and the other with gold hair to the shoulders, embrace passionately. Then a knot of people, among them two women, came on deck: and the schooner put down her helm and set her bowsprit to the westward.

ABOUT THE AUTHOR

Born in 1948 in Scilly Isles, SAM LLEWELLYN was educated at Eton and Oxford. In the course of his extensive traveling he took part in such diverse activities as running a Spanish nightclub, baiting shark hooks professionally, living off the land in Norfolk, working at Sotheby's in London by day and with a rock group by night, and finally editing at Pan books. Now married, he lives in Canada and divides his time between Toronto and a desolate cabin on Georgian Bay where he pursues his hobbies of sailing, fishing and bird-watching on cross-country skis. Mr. Llewellyn's first novel was *Sea Devil*.

THE LATEST BOOKS
IN THE BANTAM
BESTSELLING TRADITION

Meet swashbuckling
George Gurney in this
special preview
of the opening pages
from his perilous
first adventure.

SEA DEVIL

---

by Sam Llewellyn

Mathias Otway, owner of the coach, horses, and servants, stamped his dress pumps in the paneled hallway and cast a complacent eye over his reflection in the gilt pier glass as the porter took his greatcoat. He never failed to be impressed by what he saw. A stout, sallow man of two-and-fifty years, puffy jowls confined by a high wing collar with a white cravat, thinning hair brushed, curled, and cropped à la Brutus, he could pass, he told himself, for a youngish forty. His close-fitting three-quarter-length coat of black broadcloth with silver buttons and his buff knee breeches and hose gave him an air of the no-nonsense countryman with a hint of the fashionable cleric. A combination, he assured himself, calculated to inspire confidence. A confidence which was no more than the due of a merchant as successful as himself. For Mathias Otway, despite his recent acceptance by the noble and influential members of the *ton*, made no secret of his mercantile past. Though there were, admittedly, men of ill will who whispered that his recent marriage to the impoverished widow of Lord Mountolivet, herself now unhappily deceased, had been contracted in pursuit of ends less spiritual than self-interested. And those same ill-wishers would from time to time intimate that in earlier years he had been over-closely concerned with such dubious activities as the stuffing of companies and the short selling of stocks not his to sell. Still, the stones of the debtors' cells in the Fleet told no tales. Besides, it was now obvious to the most censorious eye that the excesses of his youth were well behind him. With a final ingratiating smirk at his reflection, he turned and waddled into the assembly room, bowing to right and left as he drew his white gloves onto his pudgy hands.

The soirée was well advanced. The brilliantly lit room was almost filled with a throng of ladies and gentlemen; at the far end a small orchestra was sawing its way through a piece by the newly fashionable Italian composer Rossini. Otway remembered his dancing master playing it to him a short while ago. He smiled inwardly. He was beginning to feel quite at ease with these glittering lords and ladies, empty-headed idiots for the most part, with their foolish prattle of the play, the concert, and the rout; yet it had taken a long and concentrated effort to learn the manners and codes that constituted the key to their select and immeasurably powerful circle. But then Otway had been fascinated by the machinery of power for as long as he could remember—since the day he had turned his back on his parent's few poor and windswept acres on Cranbourne Chase and set out, his father's small savings in his satchel, for the navy yards at Portsmouth. It had taken thirty-five years—years of bullying, wheedling, conniving, bribery, and unscrupulous manipulation; but now there remained but one small gambit between himself and the happy outcome of his schemings.

Otway took a sip from his glass and let his eye rove over the crowd. There was old Lady Montague-Stanley, one eye fixed adoringly on a dancing-masterish foreigner and the other keeping a close watch on her brandy-nosed husband lest he slip away to his opera girls. It seemed likely that the foreigner, whose flashing teeth were doing journeyman service, was more interested in the famous Stanley diamonds, which crusted most of the visible portions of his admirer's wrinkled anatomy, than in her conversation, limited as it was by her complete deafness and incipient senility.

And in the corner farthest from the orchestra a circle of young bloods bayed around Fenella Markham, belle of last year's season, whose incorrigible flirtatiousness had become the despair, Otway had heard it whispered, of her noble but penurious father. My lord Markham, already broken by his enormous gambling debts, had pledged what remained of his estates to the moneylenders in an attempt to find a suitable match for his daughter; but the light-minded hussy found it more diverting to spread her favors widely among the romantically inclined throngs of young officers on half-pay like the pup Gurney, unemployed since the cessation of hostilities with France and America, who now haunted the salons of the capital.

George Gurney, unaware of Mathias Otway's unflattering cogitations on him and his ilk and locked in an extremely shallow conversation with the undoubtedly beautiful but even more certainly bird-witted Fenella Markham, stiffened as he saw the merchant's heavy figure framed in the doorway, the cold eyes sweeping the crowd. "Mr. Gurney!" Miss Markham was looking at him strangely. "I declare for a moment I thought you were in a taking! What a fierce, cruel look you sometimes have!" She fluttered—engagingly, her mother told her.

George forced a smile. "No doubt 'twas at the thought of having to leave you so soon, Miss Markham. For there is Bruiser Carstairs, and I am sure you have much to say to him." And with a smile that lit up his pale blue eyes he turned and made his way swiftly through the crowd.

A tall, well-made young man of some two-and-twenty years, this Gurney. As he walked across the room, he drew many eyes, admiring and disapproving. His admirers said, to themselves or whoever was near at hand, that he was such a charming boy—so brave, they heard—quite a fire-eater—poor fellow was wounded off Cuba, you know, which accounts for his limp—charming, frank, open face —eyes a bit mad, of course, but you can't have everything. His detractors muttered similarly, though they tended to stress other facets. Impertinent young devil—natural result of being too lucky too young—gambles like a crazy Chinee— bound to come a nasty tumble soon—shan't be sorry—disturbing influence—off to the tables again, no doubt. But Gurney paid no heed to the emotions he aroused in the breasts of those around him, even if he recognized them, which was doubtful. He was deep in talk with Ivo Dauncey, whom he wished to consult about the undoing of Mathias Otway. Dauncey, a tall, dark youth wearing the same sort of semi-naval uniform—blue coat, brass buttons, white breeches—as Gurney, waved a dismissive hand. "Sorry, old boy, urgent business. Game o' whist and a good 'un, I hear. Shall I keep your name in reserve?" Gurney grinned. "Yes, please do. My creditors are becoming somewhat importunate. I'll speak with you later." ...

Otway drained his glass and picked his way across the room to a table set apart behind a small ornamental railing, where a dark Frenchman with small, shrewd eyes and an unfashionable abundance of lace at his throat sat deep in conversation with a foppish, pale-haired exquisite whose beak of a nose failed to compensate for his lack of chin. Otway addressed himself to the latter, bowing.

"My lord Fotheringham! It is indeed a pleasure to renew your acquaintance! What brings you to Vernon's on such a desolate evening?"

The youth rose to his feet, bowing awkwardly. "Mr. Otway, is it not? It is indeed a great pleasure, don't ye know, to see you again. Monsieur le Comte de Fauvenargues and I were just discussing his new venture in the Peruvian mines, which he declares are the veritable Eldorado. But you do not know each other? Allow me to present you."

As Otway rose from his bow, he caught the

Frenchman's eye. The foreigner nodded almost imperceptibly, and Otway allowed his right eyelid to droop the merest fraction.

The three men seated themselves, and Otway composed his features to a look of fascination as the callow Fotheringham stammered his enthusiasm for the schemes of the enterprising count. "I take it, then, that you're a man not averse to a little . . . speculation?" Otway smiled fatly. "Well, well, this is the stuff of the rock on which Albion stands. How fine it is, in this day and age, to meet a man with the adventurous spirit of a Drake, the imagination of a Pitt, the resolve of a very Nelson!" The Frenchman hid a smile behind his jeweled fingers; Otway threw him a warning glance. "I declare," he continued, "that it would be a vast pleasure to hazard a rubber or two with such a spirit. If Monsieur le Comte would be pleased to join us"—the Frenchman waved an acquiescent hand—"we need find but one more to make up our four." He beamed at Fotheringham, who returned a looselipped smirk. "Well, that's settled. And unless I am mistaken, that's young Ivo Dauncey. Duke of Carlisle's nephew, don't ye know. Charming young fellow, great friend." He waved a white hand. . . .

It soon became apparent that Otway and his partner were by far the better players. Though the Frenchman was obviously a veteran at the game, Fotheringham revealed himself as an abysmal duffer from the moment his fumbling fingers touched the cards. Dauncey watched in some puzzlement as Fauvenargues commiserated with his partner for a lost hand that any five-year-old in skirts could have won, then shrugged mentally. If Monsieur le Comte wished to lose his gold in partnership with this babe unweaned, that was his affair. Meanwhile, he was quite happy—nay, delighted—to continue taking their money, particularly in view of the two large aggressive gentlemen who had appeared at his digs that afternoon bearing bad tidings of his account with Isaac Rubin. He took a long sip at his glass of claret as Otway won the final trick of the hand and struggled to his feet.

"If you will excuse me, I must take my leave. But the night is still young, and we must not deprive milords de Fauvenargues and Fotheringham of their revenge. Dauncey, did I not see you earlier in the company of the brave Lieutenant Gurney? I know that he is one of Fortune's favorites, so perhaps you could prevail upon him?"

Dauncey vouchsafed him a formal bow, but his voice was loaded with irony. "Delighted, though I am naturally desolate to lose so brilliant a partner as yourself. If my lords permit?" Fotheringham, who was commencing to wilt under the incisive play of the merchant, nodded eagerly, and the Frenchman spread his hands in acquiescence. Dauncey rose and left the room with Otway, returning a few moments later leading a tall figure in a uniform similar to his own.

De Fauvenargues leaped to his feet. "But can it be? Is this the very Lieutenant Gurney of the *Vampire*? The intrepid argonaut who single-handed put a stop to the heinous maraudings of the usurper Bonaparte in the West India Station?"

The intrepid argonaut's unfashionably bronzed face broke into a grin. "I wouldn't put it as strongly as that, mylord. I merely did my duty as I saw fit."

"No, no, a thousand times no! *Parbleu*, but how can I demonstrate the depth of my feelings towards one so instrumental in the removing of the iron heel of tyranny from my beloved France?" And the excitable Gaul flung his arms around Lieutenant Gurney and kissed him loudly on each cheek. Gurney went scarlet as the room fell silent and two-score pairs of eyebrows lifted as one. Really, he thought, these Frogs, Jacobins or Bourbons, were impossible.

"I am deeply sensible of the honor you do to me, and I look forward to an evening of interesting play. Shall we set to?" ...

It seemed that Fotheringham's luck had not changed. His neighing laugh became more forced as trick after trick fell to Gurney and his partner. And de Fauvenargues's black brows knit aggressively as finesse after finesse failed. The swarthy foreigner seemed unable to concentrate; his play now seemed almost as incoherent as that of his partner, who was covertly glancing at his watch.

It was midnight when Lieutenant Gurney leaned back and ran his long fingers through his close-cropped yellow hair. "Well, milords, I must commiserate with you on your atrocious luck. Shall we play another rubber and call it a night?"

De Fauvenargues scowled. "Yes, *parbleu*. And for these last hands, perhaps you gallant rulers of the high seas would agree to playing for a somewhat increased stake? Milord Fotheringham agrees?"

The pale fop gulped and nodded. "*D'accord.* According to my calculations," the Frenchman continued, "milord and I are some fourteen hundred guineas to the bad. May I suggest that we play, *désormais*, for a hundred guineas a point and a thousand on the rubber?"

Dauncey looked at Gurney. "Pretty steep that. You game, Gurney?"

Gurney nodded. A small voice at the back of his mind kept telling him that his choler was getting the better of his common sense; but he angrily silenced it and picked up the cards. God knew that he hated this humiliating grind, playing whist with nincompoops and sharks to supplement the pittance that the peacetime navy called a lieutenant's half-pay. But it was the only way for a gentleman and a thousand times preferable to the sort of shabby-genteel living death he had seen creep up on his former shipmates, marooned in their lodgings in Deptford or Portsmouth just as surely as on any Bahamian cay.

At least he was still fighting, and the winner's laurels were enticingly close. For if Gurney's plans matured aright, Mathias Otway's days as cock of the walk were numbered. The days when a black-birder—a slave trader, not to dignify so vile a commerce with a pet name—could openly come the nabob in the salons and gaming rooms of London had passed with the coming of Fox and Wilberforce. Now, with the information Gurney had at his disposal, Otway would find his Whig friends avoiding his eye, becoming suddenly engaged in confidential conversation when he entered a room. The rotten borough to which he currently aspired would be quietly transferred to a more discreet man—not because of any deep scruples in the Whig conscience, but because of its solemn adherence to the tenets of the Eleventh Commandment, "Thou shalt not be found out." To turn a blind eye to the orders of one's superiors and act on one's own initiative might be a permissible naval tactic—Nelson had proved as much—but in politics a more searching regard for the proprieties was the rule. Otway would founder without a trace, and the fair Arabella, his stepdaughter, no longer a lucrative match for some scatterbrained lordling, would be Gurney's for the asking. As she already was, had her own preferences counted for anything in the matter of her life's partner.

Gurney grinned as he contemplated the ruin of his enemy's schemes. But as he dealt the cards, he caught the count's eye, in which lurked a hint of —was it avarice? cunning? His whole body was suddenly tense, imbued with a curious numbness, the dull oppression he used to feel before action, rocking heel to toe, toe to heel on the pocket-hand-kerchief quarterdeck of the *Vampire*. Last time, it had been the precursor of a sweat-soaked hour on the surgeon's table with the sawbones carving at his leg after a privateer's musket ball ...

Gurney took a pull at his claret glass and dealt.

The size of the stakes seemed, if anything, to have discomfited de Fauvenargues and his partner. Fotheringham was drunk, beyond reason, unable to play his cards otherwise than at random. De Fauvenargues's cards were better and his playing improved, but not enough. After two honors hands had gone to Gurney, the Frenchman began to mutter under his breath. Now it was Gurney's deal. The two lieutenants, if they won this final hand, would carry away between them as much gold as they would have got from a fair-sized prize. It was too easy. Far too easy. Gurney could understand the gaping Fotheringham, always anxious to impress, pouring good money after bad; but the Frenchman looked to be too experienced to play for such stakes against two such notoriously cool heads as Gurney and his comrade-in-arms. The short hairs at the nape of Gurney's neck prickled warningly as the count leaned towards him, his thin lips twisted into a disagreeable smile.

"It seems to be your lucky night, hein? I fear that my poor skill has deserted me completely. Such cards! And my partner"—Fotheringham was swaying glassily—"will, if I am not mistaken, soon be indisposed. I have played in many places, from Pondicherry to the Americas, but I have seldom seen one so young or so lucky as yourself. Fortunes of war, I think? Your exploits on the high seas, I have heard, often hinge on subtle *ruses de guerre*. *Tant mieux*. But when these *ruses* are applied to the card table—"

Gurney's face drained of blood. "What exactly are you trying to say, monsieur?"

"Simply that there comes to me a slight suspicion that the cards you are dealing have more to them than meets the eye. Or at any rate, the eyes of milord Fotheringham, Lieutenant Dauncey, and myself."

Gurney leaped to his feet, the Frenchman's mocking grin dancing before his eyes. Fotheringham's mouth hung open, and Dauncey was leaning wearily back in his chair, minutely examining his fingernails.

"You realize this means blood, sir? My friends will be calling on you shortly. Meanwhile, I must ask you to consider this game at an end."

"Not so fast, my fine young friend." De Fauvenargues was squinting at the back of the queen of clubs. "Gentlemen. You see that the roundel in this pattern resembles the face of a clock? If you look closely, you will see a light pen stroke in the one o'clock position. It is not easy to see in this light; but Lieutenant Gurney is famous for his excellent eyesight."

Dauncey put out a languid hand and picked up the card. "He's right, you know. But I must say that I feel it's a little early in the day to level such serious accusations. The scandal will be frightful. So, entre nous, should we not turn out our pockets? I am sure that we will thus allay all suspicion. Admiral Jessop? If you could arbitrate until we have cleared up this deeply embarrassing misunderstanding?"

The portly red-faced officer nodded and rose.

A heavy silence spread from the gaming tables to the ballroom as the four men placed the contents of their pockets on the table. Gurney dug into his waistcoat, produced watch, seals, chain, card case, and purse, and thrust his hand into his coat. Dauncey grinned as a mummified backbird's wing flecked with albino white joined the small pile on the table; then his jaw dropped as Gurney drew out his handkerchief and flung it down, scattering from its folds a pack of cards of the same pattern as those already on the table.

The admiral's eyes were cold as he turned to Gurney. "Hrrmph. In the circumstances, it seems that you have no cause to ask satisfaction of Monsieur le Comte. Perhaps you should withdraw to put your affairs in order." A rustle of whispered conversation swept through the gathering like a breeze. Gurney, white to the lips, swept up his possessions and limped from the room, the crowd parting before him like fairgoers before an itinerant leper.

From the Lady Arabella Mountolivet:

My darling George,

What, oh what have you been at, my only love? There has been the violent brouhaha here since you left; I think that the odious Mathias has quite taken leave of his senses. But wait. Let me begin at the beginning.

Three days ago that gamekeeper Zebedee Watkins came up to the house—the *house*, my dear; the gall of the man!—looking for Mathias. A rational man—and you know how my charming stepfather prides himself on his rationality—would have sent him packing forthwith (he does stink so of ferret). But Mathias took him by the elbow and steered him into his writing room. I didn't exactly listen at the door, but I couldn't help overhearing some of what they were saying. Watkins was mumbling—you know, you could cut his accent with a knife—something about "that damn' young lieutenant tumbling to the blackbirding lay," and Mathias was squealing like a pig. Then he flung out of the door and up into the attic (our attic, George; you remember? Oh, how I miss you). A few minutes later he came stumping down again with a chest of papers, the same chest you spent so much time with just before you set off for London. Then he burned the papers in the library grate and bellowed for his carriage. George, I hope that this letter reaches you before he goes, for I collect that he means you no good. I need not tell you of all people that he is a hard man to cross— my poor mama's fate bears testimony to his hypocrisy and malice. Beware!

Meanwhile, with all my heart, dearest George, I remain your adoring

Arabella

Gurney laughed mirthlessly and poured himself another half-tumbler of cognac. He felt bloody awful. The air in his room was cold and damp, and from time to time he coughed raspingly. His throat was sore, his head ached, and his eyes were red and gritty in their sockets.

Since he had arrived at his humble lodgings at the Three Tuns in Whitechapel at four a.m., he had not slept a wink. It was now nine o'clock in the morning, and a dingy light was glimmering through the cobwebby mullioned windows. The snow had turned to a raw gray drizzle, beaten by the wind over the marshes to the east, moaning listlessly in the rigging of the ships lying moored in the West India Dock.

He picked up Arabella's letter for the hundredth time. Too late, too late by one meager day. That swine of a gamekeeper, with his confidential manner and his fund of rustic lore. What a fool Gurney had been to question him so closely about Otway's comings and goings! Once he'd seen his line of inquiry, he'd strung him along until he was sure of his man and then simply reported the conversation to his master. Good and faithful servant indeed! He'd certainly cooked Gurney's goose for him.

It had been prettily done; the Frenchman must be a past master at the noble art of cardsharping. First his careful dealing of the cards to put himself and the idiot Fotheringham onto their losing streak, then the switching of the cards on the table for the marked cards in his pocket; and finally, the planting of the original pack in Gurney's pocket while he was going through that Bourbon rigmarole as they were introduced. The whole thing stank of Otway. And it was clever. Devilish clever. Impossible, now, to reveal Otway for what he was; the word of a man on whom lay the disgrace of cardsharping (Old Jervey Hutchinson had once told him, in Jamaica, "Three disgraces, George. Adultery—not good, can get you killed. Drunkenness—beastly. Cardsharping—worse than dishonor. No redress, no excuses.") would have no influence with the worthy merchants on 'change; and still less with the toadying Whig lickspittles, "radicals" in name only, in Parliament. But there were other ways . . .

Half an hour later, two voices raised in violent altercation floated up the stairwell. Gurney grinned, stuck his head around the door, and yelled, "Romeo! Romeo! wherefore art thou, Romeo?"

The small man disentangling himself from the slattern's apron, in which he had become raveled during what looked like a determined assault on her honor, turned his face upward, an expression of deep romantic passion printed large on his narrow brow. "But, soft! what light through yonder window breaks?"

He was up the stairs in two bounds, a ragged little Cockney, his twinkling eyes barely separated by a lengthy crimson toper's nose, a broad grin on his face. Gurney ushered him to a chair, and with all due ceremony offered him coffee. An expression of deep disgust swept over the mobile features.

"I am surprised, werry surprised, that a gentleman normally so goodsensical as your lieutenantship should indulge in a beverage so harmful to the spleen and generally deleterious to the internal plumbin' as the juice of the bean."

Gurney grinned and poured him a half-tumbler of gin. Romeo stuck his long nose into it, took a pull, wiped his mouth fastidiously with the frayed sleeve of his overcoat, and made an expansive theatrical gesture signifying that he was all attention. Gurney told him of Arabella's letter and the events of the previous night. The actor, head rolled back on his scrawny shoulders, pursed his lips in a soundless whistle and leaned forward in his chair.

"'Ere, try a drop of this." And he poured a generous measure of Gurney's gin into Gurney's coffee cup, topping up his own tumbler as if inspired by an afterthought. Then he fell into ruminative silence.

At length, he joined his hands fingertip to fingertip under his nose. "Werry pretty. Ho yus, a most attractive tale of skulduggery and mayhem. It occurs to me that were this to get into the wrong hands, a most scurrilous and damaging broadside could be made of it. Most unfortunate for the upright Mr. Otway, of course, but then a man of his bottom has nothing to fear from the ravings of the gutter press. Provided, that is, he can prove his case."

"Very good, Romeo. I knew I could count on you to go straight to the heart of the matter. The way I see it, Otway had so much money tied up in his slaving that when he cuts his connections—and by God he'll be bound to, with the world watching his every step—his affairs will be in a highly precarious state. Then we must watch which way he jumps and try to catch him off balance."

"We'll cover the town from Bow to Hampton Court. No peace for the wicked, oh dear me, no."

"Excellent. One more thing, though. I need you to take a letter to Dorset for me. Do you still ride as well as you used?"

Romeo's diminutive chest swelled like a turkeycock's. "Hi should say so, not half. Tomorrow noon I'll be there, you can bank on it. Ho, hum, 'partin' is such sweet sorrow,' as the Bard said. Back in an hour. Don't worry about nothing, just get your letter writ." And clapping his disreputable hat on his even less reputable head, the great actor sped down the stairs and into the street.

Gurney found himself much cheered by his interview with the resourceful Mr. Copley. The symptoms produced by the emotions and overindulgences of the previous night had withdrawn into the background of his consciousness; but still he plunged his hands into his pockets and stared gloomily from the diamond-paned window of his room over the gray, glistening cobbles and slates without. How, in God's name, to tell Arabella that he intended to separate himself from her for a period in excess of a year? He knew her too well to think that she would let him go meekly. She was not one of your accommodating doormat sort of women, thank the Lord. Even Otway had from time to time been given cause to regret that he had caught the scornful side of her whiplash tongue, and Otway's hide was notoriously impervious to such lashings. Gurney's heart ached with longing at the prospect of seeing Arabella again; but he was also conscious of a lively trepidation at the thought of breaking the news to her about his plans. He turned on his heel away from the window, sat down at the table, and began to write.

Gurney, framed as a cheat, loses his love and flees England in disgrace—swearing vengeance on Mathias Otway. George's quest for revenge takes him on a dangerous odyssey culminating in a thrilling sea chase.

Now read the complete Bantam Book, available wherever paperbacks are sold.